The Witch and the Tsar

OLESYA SALNIKOVA GILMORE

HARPER
Voyager

Harper*Voyager*
An imprint of HarperCollins*Publishers* Ltd
1 London Bridge Street
London SE1 9GF

www.harpercollins.co.uk

HarperCollins*Publishers*
Macken House, 39/40 Mayor Street Upper,
Dublin 1, D01 C9W8, Ireland

This paperback edition 2023
1

First published by HarperCollins*Publishers* Ltd 2022

Printed and bound in the UK using 100% renewable electricity at CPI Group (UK) Ltd

This book is produced from independently certified FSC™ paper to ensure
responsible forest management.

For more information visit: www.harpercollins.co.uk/green

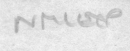

and the
Tsar

Olesya Salnikova Gilmore was born in Moscow, Russia, raised in the United States, and graduated from Pepperdine University with a BA in English and Political Science, and from Northwestern Pritzker School of Law with a JD. She practised litigation at a large law firm for several years before pursuing her dream of becoming an author. She is most happy writing historical fiction and fantasy inspired by Eastern European folklore. She lives in a wooded lakeside suburb of Chicago with her husband and daughter. *The Witch and the Tsar* is her debut novel.

For my husband, Sean, without whom this book and this extraordinary life would not have been possible

IVAN THE TERRIBLE'S RUSSIA
IN THE WORLD OF
THE WITCH AND THE TSAR

ARCTIC OCEAN

White Sea

NORWAY

SWEDEN

FINLAND

Baltic Sea

Novgorod

Pskov

LIVONIA

DENMARK

Staritsa

Rzhev

Aleksandrov
(Ivan's
Aleksandrovskaya
Sloboda)

Yaga's
Hut

Moscow

Ryazan

THE NORTH

URAL MOUNTAINS

RUSSIA

Extent of
Ivan's Russia
in 1533

Extent of
Ivan's Russia
in 1584

SIBERIAN
KHANATE
(conquered by
Ivan in 1583)

KAZAN
KHANATE
(conquered by
Ivan in 1552)

Extent of
Ivan's Russia
in 1584

ASTRAKHAN
KHANATE
(conquered by
Ivan in 1554)

LITHUANIA

POLAND

Kiev

UKRAINE

Black Sea

Caspian Sea

PART I

As for sorcerers and those who cast spells:
if you wish to call on the name of the Holy Trinity,
if you are one who makes the sign of Christ's holy cross,
you must utterly forsake such people.

◆

St. John Chrysostom, quoted in *The "Domostroi":
Rules for Russian Households in the Time of Ivan the Terrible*,
edited and translated by Carolyn Johnston Pouncy

1

LATE MAY 1560

WHEN MY OWL landed on my shoulder, I knew heartbreak was not far behind.

It was not that twilight tasted different, though on my tongue, the humid spring air had the bitterness of snowfall. It was that, even this deep in the Russian forest, dusk bled into the light with infuriating leisure. The clouds had smothered the last of the sun's rays in scarlet. Yet day clung on, delaying what mortals intended to find their way to my izbushka.

The log hut stood on chicken legs, not swaying or spinning or even pacing, as unnaturally still as me. I usually fidgeted with impatience, eager for my first client to appear, for my work to begin. Now, unease wrapped around my throat, silent as a viper.

My owl could only be here to deliver bad tidings. Like her namesake, night, Noch came in the company of darkness and shadows. It was then the mortals arrived with their fevers, skin infections, and stomach poisons; with the burns from the fires that spread too quickly in their cramped wooden villages. They did not approach me in the light of day, even if it was waning. Not unless they brought disaster.

Noch's bright yellow gaze fixed on me pointedly. She let out a screech loud enough to reanimate the skulls on the fence encircling my izbushka.

They are here, Ya. Her voice, in the language she spoke, reverberated through my mind, becoming words I could understand.

"Already?" I asked in Russian. Someone was coming. Someone desperate enough to risk being seen. "Who is it?"

What am I, your servant? You will see. A downy wing brushed against my cheek teasingly as Noch ascended into the air. But instead of hurling herself back into the sky, she flew into my hut through the open door, shedding several dove-gray feathers in her wake.

I picked up a feather, considering it. My owl never went inside of her own volition, valuing open sky and freedom above all. I strained my ears and waited for the first footfall. All I heard was the song of the crickets and the leaves, rippling in the breeze that had rushed toward me, insistent and oddly cold. Fluff drifted from the ancient cottonwood trees, settling onto the wooden steps of my hut like tufts of snow. And I had just cleaned them.

"Come down, Little Hen," I said to my izbushka, and she obeyed, folding the chicken legs beneath her so she looked almost like a regular house.

I tightened my hold on the broom and swept at the steps with renewed vigor. The hut jerked away, being unbelievably ticklish. The two shuttered windows, one on either side of the door, glowered at me. Their red and blue carvings brightened in indignation.

"Hold still, Little Hen," I said, and swept on. But I kept a close eye on the wood beyond the skulls.

My hut sat in a lush glade surrounded by towering, age-old trees. Overgrown pines and spruces jostled against starved yet stubbornly resilient birches. The oaks stood gravely, expansively, ready to pass on their energy to anyone who asked politely. The wispy grass had grown knee-high and tangled, the forest floor ripe with mushrooms, wild strawberries, and violet petals fallen from geraniums in bloom. Out of this chaos of living things a large man stepped out, all in black, face obscured by a wide-brimmed hat.

I stilled. "Who goes there?"

The man halted at the fence, no doubt trying to decide if the skulls there were human. "Is this the izbushka of Baba Yaga the Bony Leg?"

With my unease temporarily forgotten, my cheeks flushed with familiar indignation. Not many dared to say that name to my face. "It is the izbushka of Yaga."

Fool, I almost added. *Do I look like a baba?* I was not a *babushka*, lying on my stove in the throes of advanced age and infirmity. Nor was I a hag, a demon, or an illness. Nothing about me was ill or demonic or old, except the occasional thread of silver in my wild black hair. My father may have been mortal, but Mother had been a goddess since before the Christian god had come to Russia. Because of her immortality, my body had not aged past thirty after centuries on Earth. I sent a little prayer of thanks up to her.

The man stood motionless. His features were weathered and very plain, most covered in coarse black hair, as was the fashion. No outward ailment spelled disaster. His illness, though, could be of the internal or spiritual variety, even of a romantic one.

Either way, it was best to put him at ease, as was my practice with new clients. Those who came for succor found it in my hut. Healing filled the empty hours of my days, kept my hands occupied and my mind busy, gave me a sense of purpose. If I could live among mortals, healing and advising them, I would.

But the legend that clung to me—the legend of Baba Yaga, built on lies and ill will—prevented it.

Afraid now that he would flee, I reverted back to politeness. "The skulls are not human," I said softly. This part of me labored tirelessly to convince the mortals that I was not the Baba Yaga they had heard of, that I was no human-eater. "Animal bones ward off evil," I added. Near the skulls, thistle and juniper grew thickly to protect against demons.

His dark eyes narrowed as he drew closer. "Where is she, this Yaga?"

"I am Yaga." Who else could I be?

"Pah! A fine trick this is, woman!" he blustered. "I have traveled all the way from Moscow to see the vedma, and I will not be trifled with."

I had not flinched at the word *witch*. I had made my peace with it long ago. But I shuddered at the man's mention of the capital. Though I had never been there, I knew Moscow was at least a day's ride on horseback. Whoever came from there did so when their prayers had gone unanswered, when the mortal healers had thrown up their hands. They came in the depths of their despair. But this man was not despairing. Quite the opposite.

"By all accounts," he went on, "Baba Yaga is practically at death's door, she is so old. Deformed, too, with an iron nose and a bony leg, fangs for teeth, barely any hair. Yet here you stand, young enough to be my daughter, claiming to be the crone herself!"

My cheeks burned. It had not occurred to this thick-headed muzhik, this idiot of a man, that what he had heard was nothing more than a rumor. One that was viciously invented and flung out into the world to reduce any unmarried, reclusive woman to a hag or a witch.

"You go too far, sir," I said in a hard voice, forgetting the fear and any attempt at politeness. "You who are in such need that you seek me out in broad daylight only to ridicule me. Well, good riddance." I gripped the broom and spun on my heel toward my hut, about to tell her to stand and take me with her.

"Wait," said the man. Desperation had crept into his tone. "If I am indeed speaking to the one whom I seek, then I meant no offense—"

"Even so, you had best be on your way—" I couldn't help turning to look at him. Now he was despairing; his face had paled beneath his beard.

"Please—" He raised a hand as if to physically pull me back. "Do not punish my illustrious mistress for my ignorance."

My brow furrowed. "Your mistress?"

The man gave a solemn nod. He glanced toward the wood and let out a whistle that shook the very cottonwoods above us. Fluff fell in clumps onto the hut's steps.

I hardly noticed. On the well-bred white mare emerging from the trees sat a hooded figure, elegant as only a highborn woman knew how to be. My eyes caught on the rich velvet of her cream cloak; the fur trim, odd given the warm weather; the little bejeweled fingers gripping the reins. A pull on the hood revealed a headdress encrusted in bloodred rubies, then the face beneath, thin and drawn, cold as marble.

Though it had been years since we had last seen each other, I would have recognized her anywhere. It was Anastasia Romanovna Zakharyina-Yurieva—the tsaritsa and wife of Tsar Ivan IV of Russia. But what was Anastasia doing here? Nothing short of disaster could have compelled the tsaritsa to risk her reputation by seeking out a reclusive witch.

Indeed, she was a shadow of the rosy-cheeked maiden who had come to my izbushka more than a decade ago, on the cusp of greatness, days away from the bridal show that would catapult her into royalty. The viper of unease tightened around my throat. That girl was gone. Here was a wraith at death's door. This day *had* brought heartbreak. I could see the tsaritsa's situation was not just disastrous; it threatened her very life.

2

LEAVING THE GUARD to keep watch outside, I ushered the tsaritsa into the darkened innards of my hut. Little Hen was used to clients coming and going and usually behaved herself enough by staying low to the ground so as not to frighten anyone. I hastily lit a few stubby beeswax candles. The scent of burning honey filled the air as I turned back to my royal visitor, swallowing hard.

Her tears had dried, her dull brown eyes taking on a chillingly distant look. Where were the flecks of gold, the quick wit, the uncharacteristic warmth of someone of her social standing? Her vibrancy was gone. Her skirts rustled like dried-up leaves as she sank onto the stool I offered her with the tired, defeated air of one who wishes never to rise again.

A few wandering chickens clucked at my feet. Noch hooted from a shadowy corner. The tsaritsa probably found this—me—uncivilized, disgustingly rustic, even.

But she only said, "It has been months. The doctors do not know what it is. I do." She struggled out of her cloak. "I am dying."

The bell-sleeved, flower-patterned letnik gown dragged her down as if bloated with seawater. A little shiver darted up my spine, almost prompting me to ask the tsaritsa how many dresses she wore. For wealthy women, it was customarily a minimum of three. But it was clear it was not the dresses plaguing her.

There was sweat on her brow, a redness at her mouth and eyes, though her skin was missing the telltale blotches and swellings of pestilence. An internal imbalance was possible, but those were the hardest to heal. An illness of the mind or spirit? Stooping under the dry herbs and flowers hanging from the slanted ceiling, I crossed the room to an iron cauldron bubbling over a fire that never went out. Iron possessed mystical and protective powers.

"It has been some time since you visited me," I said slowly, brushing aside a purple lavender blossom. "Thirteen years?"

"With the wedding, I . . ."

"I have heard weddings eat into time like moths. What about after? I tended to your family for years. To be forgotten so quickly by you and your mother was quite the revelation." I bent over the cauldron and ladled out hot water into a bowl fashioned from bone. Steam billowed into my face as I flushed with resentment. Or maybe disappointment.

How would the great Earth Goddess Mokosh feel about such neglect? I thought about my beloved mother, the protector of women—of their work and destiny, the birth of their children. I glanced up at her symbol, the wooden horse's head hanging above the cauldron.

We provide succor regardless of wounded pride, she had once told me. *Pride is an illusion and the path to conceit. Gods may be guilty of it, Yaga, but not you.*

But our gods, the ancient ones born of the Universe, had been worshipped then. While Mokosh had not spoken of it, tales say she helped to create the Earth with Perun, the Supreme God and Lord of the Heavens, and many other gods besides. Perun forged the sky with his thunderbolts; Mokosh gave birth to the land. Her spindle spun the cloth of humanity, thread by thread, woman by woman, life to death, generation after generation. She was Moist Earth, mother of all living things and my actual mother.

Eventually, mortals began to worship the Christian god. While some believed in the old gods as well as him, I doubted the tsaritsa was of their number, living as she did in the center of the Orthodox Christian faith in

Russia. Yet before her ascent to the court, she had gladly partaken of what infuriatingly limited talents I had inherited from Mokosh.

"*I* made you a tsaritsa," I said. "*I* provided your mother with the herbs and charms that got the court to take notice of a dead aristocrat's daughter. Or have you forgotten?"

The tsaritsa stared into my too-light blue eyes, at my unbraided hair and exposed browned arms. They were covered in pictures inked into my skin—of suns and moons and stars, of living things. Perhaps she assumed the nails and teeth studding the belt on my tunic were human.

To my surprise, she said, "Of course I remember." Then she swept off her stool and knelt at my feet. "Yagusynka, I do not fear death. I fear what would happen to the tsar and to my sons, especially to our heir, Tsarevich Ivanushka, if I were to die. I am desperate for your counsel." Her voice was soft, charged with emotion.

The heat left my face. It was so like her to fear not for herself but for others. Rumor had it that marriage had tamed the tsar's naturally violent ways, that his tsaritsa restrained his worst impulses. Her intelligence and faith guided him. If something *were* to happen to her, it would not just be her sons who suffered. It would be Russia and her people.

"I am providing you counsel, am I not?" This was said tartly but with a twinkle of good humor. I did not hold on to anger for very long. And I was remembering not Anastasia's neglect but *her*. Mother had been right. This was not about my pride, wounded though it may have been. This was about Russia's tsaritsa, about Anastasia herself, the girl I had known.

In the hut's only room, an oak table was wedged against the window adjacent to the brick, flat-topped pech oven where I prepared my potions and salves, performed my rituals, cooked my meals, even slept.

I beckoned the tsaritsa over to the table and bade her to hold a wire dowsing rod over a bowl of water. But when she did, it did not stir. This meant there was no illness of mind or spirit.

My eyes shifted to the shelves lining the back of the hut. They drooped with animal skulls, pelts, and feathers; homemade rubs and balms; vials of hair, fangs, and claws. Suddenly, there was a rattling on one of the shelves—the unicorn horn, actually melded from mammoth remains, had slid forward. Why, that was it! Little Hen knew my possessions far better than me. I whispered a word of thanks to her and had the tsaritsa bring the horn to her chest.

She did so with a childlike trepidation, becoming the young maiden from years past again, lowering a wreath of daisies onto my hair, the feeling of belonging warming me along with her smile. She was not yet thirty and too young to talk of dying.

In a rare show of tenderness, I grasped her fingers and murmured some words of encouragement. Then, I placed a wafer of beeswax into the bowl and, beside it, a white egg and a crooked dagger.

Beads of moisture began to slide down the horn. The ivory had darkened to onyx.

It was as I had feared. "Poison," I was barely able to whisper.

The tsaritsa dropped the horn with a little yelp. It clattered onto the table, belching wisps of smoke. "Who would want to poison me?"

"That I cannot say," I said. "But we must perform a ritual to draw the poison out—"

"A-a ritual? Lord help me!" The tsaritsa gripped the cross at her neck and muttered some words. She proceeded to cross herself. Again, and again.

This did not shock me. My clients had mentioned the royal court's devoutness—specifically, the tsaritsa's devoutness. "The ritual will draw the poison out of your body," I explained, "without any curses or jinxes, invocations to the Devil or his worship, or any such evils. It will leave you not a little tired but hopefully purified."

"Oh." Her hand stopped in midair. "All . . . right."

A deft flick of my blade, and her blood trickled into the bowl. I asked her to lie on the wooden floorboards, where I covered her with a white sheet for protection. Into the bowl I added the yolk and a shaving of the unicorn horn. Beeswax captured illness, egg renewed life, bone enabled the ritual to work. It was all done quickly and efficiently, poisoning being a familiar affliction, brought on by rotten foods or else envious neighbors.

Noch snuffed out the candles, leaving only a sliver of blue light in the hut, the moon having risen outside while we talked.

Circling the tsaritsa with the bowl three times, I started to chant some words, all in Russian, most nonsensical. It was not the words that mattered but the intention behind them. I kept my focus on that, on seeing her better, on her being whole. The beeswax in the bowl pulled me toward the tsaritsa, yet I dug my heels into the floor and refused to move. I felt the answering pull from her illness as, little by little, the beeswax pried the poison out of her body. A stream of black particles rose from beneath the white sheet.

My focus stayed on the tsaritsa, my chant heightening in pitch and ferocity, as the black particles whirled through the hut. I felt Little Hen clench as she dug her chicken legs into the ground, bracing herself.

A window shutter came loose, and wind gusted in with a mournful howl. My treasures rattled, the cauldron creaked, the chickens flapped their wings in terror.

But my gaze was trained on Anastasia, hoping, praying the ritual worked.

The wind had died down to a whisper, brushing against my bare skin like the bloodcurdling touch of someone unseen. The air carried the faint smell of unshed snow. Little Hen had quieted and settled along with the chickens.

Well? Noch's eyes found me in the darkness. She swung her beak toward the bowl resting above the unmoving tsaritsa. *Aren't you going to look?*

I shook my head. "Let us give it a little more time."

If the mass inside the bowl absorbed the black particles, the poison had been expelled from the tsaritsa. If not, we would need to perform the ritual again. Sometimes, the poison accumulated in the weakened body to such an extent that the beeswax was not able to pull it out all at once, or at all. *Peace, Yaga.* Absorbtion took time.

Noch flapped her wings. *Where you get your patience, only the gods know.*

"Good thing I am the one performing the ritual, no?" I winked.

While Noch rekindled the candles with a dry tut, I roused the tsaritsa.

I ushered her back to the table with a reassuring smile and a cup of cranberry and honey kissel to restore energy lost during the ritual. The pech was warm at my back as I sat on the bench opposite her with my own cup. Standard rituals like this took little of my own energy, yet it was still nice to sit and drink something hot and sweet.

But who was her poisoner? While I could determine a spell's owner, I needed a trace of magic for the counter spell to do that. This is why poisonings were complicated; poison wasn't magic itself, which made the poisoner difficult to identify with magic. Reason had to be resorted to. Facts gathered, life at court dissected.

"Your Majesty—"

The tsaritsa covered my hands with hers. "There is no need for formality, Yaga. Not with me."

Even when ill, she tended to my ease and comfort. But my head was too full of her unknown poisoner, that would-be killer. "How is the tsar, Anastasia Romanovna?"

Despite her paleness, her cheeks glowed, and she smiled. "Oh, Yaga, my lord husband continues to dote on me. Ours is a love that is true."

What *was* true love? Some said it was to need another as much as air, to ask nothing of each other beyond affection. Maybe it was just chance, married to the will of the gods. When I had felt the ache of it in my own heart, I had understood that true or not, chance or not, love did not last. It fizzled like candlelight, burning low and weak, then went out. But not without exacting a price. I trusted it not, especially in a tsar. Rulers had been known to get rid of their wives, if only for the sake of variety.

"He is not angry with you?" I probed after a drink of kissel.

"Why would he be? I have given him two healthy sons, pray for him daily—no, hourly—accompany him on pilgrimages across Russia on foot, care for his people as I care for my children—"

"Fine." I pushed aside the foreboding that pricked me at the thought of Ivan, though I had never met him.

"Do you not want a husband, Yaga? A family?" The tsaritsa glanced around my hut with a look of pity, and I felt Little Hen give a tiny tremble. "There is nothing better in this life than to love another."

Instead of romantic love, I thought of my beloved mother.

It had been hundreds of years since I had last glimpsed her, long before the dawning of the new millennium, as a girl of fifteen. We had stood on the porch of an izba hut, not ours, the awning of icicles drizzling my face with dirty droplets as the March landscape melted all around us.

Mother's hazel eyes were shaded black in the moonlight. "Stay and finish your work, Yaga. The ill babes need you." She brought a hand to my cheek. A tendril of hair escaped from her long, thick braid, the color of burnt wheat. "I shall meet you back home tonight." She pressed her lips to my forehead, and then all I could see was her trailing cloak, as scarlet as spilled blood.

Had she known this would be the last time we would see each other? On the following morning, when I returned later than expected to the mortal village where we had lived together from my birth, I found our village and our izba burned with enough evidence to convince me Mother had been inside. Immortal did not mean invincible. The fire had destroyed not only the one permanent home I had ever known, but any security, family, and happiness along with it.

Back in my hut, my heart throbbed with suffocating emptiness. I pressed it down with a firm shake of my head. The tsaritsa spoke of a different love. "As a woman, to love a man is the same as to belong to him, to be owned by him," I said. "Marriage is not a rite I am familiar with, but if husbands are like other men, they only smother."

The tsaritsa took a tiny sip of kissel. "Not if you find the right man."

"My independence is too dear," I said sharply, and drained the rest of my own kissel.

But what *was* independence? Being on my own? Except for the obvious complication that I would outlive any mortal husband, it was actually the freedom to see clearly, to truly belong to myself. Better to be resigned to this life, *my* life, than to aspire to one that was out of reach for an immortal and freethinking woman like me. And I wasn't alone. I had Little Hen and Noch, as well as my wolf, Dyen, and the chickens.

I gave a nod, closing the matter, and rose to check on the mass in the bowl.

My fingers shook as I peered in. But the beeswax and yolk were coal black; this meant the lethal dose of poison had been expelled, the tsaritsa's body purified for now. With a glance at the horse's head, I said a quiet prayer of thanks to Mother—though she was dead and gone, I still prayed to her. Then I threw the mass into the pech along with the white sheet. Their ash would later be used for a temporary anti-poison charm, to protect the tsaritsa from further contamination after she left my hut.

I sat back down. "Who is new at court?"

"Many boyars," the tsaritsa said vaguely, referring to the ruling elite descended from old aristocratic families, ranking only below princes. "They come, and they go."

"Is there anyone newly close to the tsar?"

"Yes." The tsaritsa pursed her lips. "A boyar called Konstantin Buy-anovich."

At first, the name she said was just a word. Then it grasped me by the throat, almost choking me. "Buyanovich? As in Buyan? No family name?"

"If he has one, I have never heard it."

I reclined back, the warmth from the pech suddenly furiously hot.

Buyanovich, or *son of Buyan*, was a clever name, as far as made-up names went. And it *was* made-up. Not many knew of the place, though one enlightened poet had written a ballad about an elusive island in an unknown ocean appearing and disappearing with the tides. This island belonged to Koshey Bessmertny—a being who had separated his heart and his soul from his body and hidden it inside a needle that was hidden inside an egg. A duck had eaten the egg, a hare had eaten the duck. The hare was buried in an iron chest in a land not of this world. As long as his soul was safe, Koshey could not die.

For *Bessmertny* meant *deathless*.

Of course Koshey hid behind the name Konstantin Buyanovich. I imagined him now, his shoulder-length black hair, his dark eyes flashing with passion, those flatteringly high cheekbones . . . Would he look the same? Did it matter? He was at court, despite his promises to be as far from it as possible.

We had known each other long ago—as competitors and sometime friends, even lovers once, just once, may the gods forgive me—and we had both made promises to cease meddling in human affairs.

"Do you know him, Yaga?" The tsaritsa was watching me. "I . . . his frown lines are so distinct, so deep, I am convinced they hint at evil deeds."

I could envision the little half smile that had etched them. When he boasted about wooing a betrothed woman, "all to win our bet, milaya moya, my honey, my darling." When, "for our challenge, my kotik, my pussycat," he pitted two princely cousins against each other, making them both desire the crown more than life itself. If not evil, those deeds had led to sorrow. And if Konstantin Buyanovich was at court, there was mischief afoot.

From the pech, I scooped up a handful of ritual ash, explaining to the tsaritsa that marking her with it would temporarily protect her from her poisoner, though the charm would eventually wear off. I smeared the ash across her forehead, above her breast, on her stomach. "I am sorry to have ruined your lovely dress, Anastasia Romanovna," I said with genuine regret. "But morning is wiser than evening. You must go now."

She did not stir. "Should I be concerned about Konstantin Buyanovich?"

Should she? He had never before killed an innocent. Still, he had broken our agreement by reinserting himself into not only human affairs but royal ones.

"Be wary of him," I said, choosing my words carefully.

"You could come with me . . ." The blush wilted as it sprang into her cheek.

"To Moscow?" My laugh came out high-pitched and charged with hope. "Oh, my dear Anastasia Romanovna, my place is in the woods. Besides, how would you even explain me to the tsar?" Yet my heart leapt. Company. Conversation. To be truly needed.

"You are a dear friend of the family, Yaga. Let me worry about my husband."

My heartbeat slowed as her idea became more real. At the start of the millennium, when I had been out in the world, there had been no cities, barely any royal courts, no Russia to speak of, only her ancient predecessor, Rus', a prince called Vladimir, and a new belief with a new god resisted in the villages. If I left my forest, I would be akin to a mortal elder, adrift and sick at heart, longing for a vanished time. When I was a daughter of Mokosh, not a witch; when men worshipped me instead of calling me the Baba Yaga hag.

But the tsaritsa's poisoner would make another attempt on her life if I were not there to stop it. What would happen to her then? What would happen to Russia and her people?

"I will consider it," I said at last.

I did not remember when I first met Anastasia. In those days, she would often accompany her mother, Uliana Ivanovna, when the boyar's wife had need of my charms or rituals. Unlike most of my clients, Uliana Ivanovna would come in the soft quiet of day, when her husband was preoccupied and she was able to escape her women.

I did remember when I first realized Anastasia was destined for greatness.

It was a snowy day in January 1547, crisp and brilliantly cold, the sky tinged with lavender and rose, a sign of swift-footed twilight. Uliana Ivanovna had brought Anastasia with her. The mother's dark eyes were wild with excitement. "Grand Prince Ivan has crowned himself tsar! He is tsar of all Russia!" she said in lieu of a greeting.

I shivered. *Tsar* carried a new level of absolute power, one not used before.

"Everyone is wondering who the new tsaritsa will be, for our tsar is to marry." Leaving her daughter out in the cold, Uliana Ivanovna pushed us into my hut.

As Uliana Ivanovna talked and talked, I looked out the window at Anastasia. Her uncovered hair shone golden as she tilted her head up to the pale sun. Suddenly, a man, a client of mine, appeared on the edge of the clearing in a dublenka and valenki boots.

My legs made ready to spring out the door. It would not do for one of Russia's oldest families to be seen with a witch. And, being a well-bred noblewoman, Anastasia had no exposure to the outside world, or men. But the girl spoke to the man easily, though I could not hear what she said. He smiled, visibly enraptured, and bowed to her deeply. Then a woman in a shawl appeared, another client, then another and another, until a group of them congregated around the maiden. All wore tattered clothing, all had lines of suffering etched into their faces, all were ordinary folk. Yet despite the pain they had brought to my door, they smiled and even laughed, at ease and comfortable with Anastasia, though they were her inferiors in birth, rank, and wealth.

My wonder turned into incredulity when she took off her rich, fur-lined shuba. She gave it and the matching fur muff to the first man before unclasping her collar and cuffs, both swathed in pearls, and handing them to a woman at her elbow. The gold necklace and earrings came off next, followed by the silver bracelets, until the girl stood in only her ivory sarafan dress. The peasants knelt at her feet as if she were their mother and they her children as she placed a gentle hand on each of their heads.

In that moment, she was not a girl but a woman. In that moment, not only did I like her, I respected her.

I had known then that Anastasia was no ordinary maiden, that her destiny marked her for something greater. To rule and to care for people. To be the tsaritsa of Russia.

It had been thirteen years, and yet Anastasia's character was unchanged. I looked on as she chatted with her guard in the same easy manner, and I wanted to help her despite all the reasons not to, all the reasons to stay and not venture into the world.

As they started toward the wood, gray-green and wrapped in a fog that hovered eerily over the trees, I heard a shriek. A black raven swooped down from the sky. It folded its great wings and settled onto a skull, a glaring raven's head.

"Shoo!" I gestured for the raven to move on.

But it stayed motionless. Not surprising. With the exception of owls and eagles and a few others, birds rarely listened to me. Seeing a raven was thought to be an unfavorable omen; it often foretold death. I was about to retrieve my broom when, near the tsaritsa and her guard, a second raven landed on a broken tree.

"Do not consider too long, Yagusya," she called out, mounting her mare. "I will be waiting for you!" And before she was swallowed by the wood: "Goodbye!"

Do svidaniya was on my lips when the raven perching on the tree spread its wings and, with another wild shriek, took off after the tsaritsa.

The other raven peered at me, head tilted, charcoal eyes keen.

I had no doubt it was here at someone's behest, perhaps that of the tsaritsa's poisoner or someone else at court who sought to watch her. Ravens reminded me of freshly dug graves, of empty trees in November, of oily black rats scurrying down claustrophobic corridors.

I felt its persistent presence long after I had turned my back to it. Clearly, Anastasia was not the only one being watched. It made me want to shut myself up in my hut, to tell her, *Little Hen, rise up, let us go away, far away, where no ravens and no people can find us*, instead of considering venturing into a world no longer known or even familiar to me.

3

I HAD ONCE KNOWN the world beyond my doorstep well. After my mother's death, I had continued to live among mortals.

I never stayed in one place long. Instead, I traveled from village to village, healing the ill and injured, comforting the dying, and—my strongest affinity—helping women. Leading their babes into the world, assisting sleepless mothers with their newborns, guiding maidens in their spinning and weaving, counseling young wives praying for babes or else marital harmony, helping ladies to kindle the passion of new and old lovers alike. I did what I could for whom I could, always welcome among those I visited. But then, my relatively quiet, productive existence changed overnight.

I thought back to that day. The snows had started after darkness fell. I was shivering on my pech in my then izba when there came a knock.

A woman stood on the porch. I instantly knew her fine features and violet eyes—my former client, Princess Milovzora. She whirled into my hut in a cloud of wintry air, perfumed in rosewater and oil, her gold-threaded skirts swishing violently. The cloak she wore was covered in snow.

"What is it, Zora?" I asked, panicked. She must have ridden for days.

I took her wet cloak and hung it on an iron hook jutting out of the door. "What has happened?"

"Bulat has done it—he has done it at last, dear one!"

I relaxed a bit. I loved Zora, had treated her for debilitating aches in her head when I had lived in the village belonging to her family. We had grown close, talking for hours, attending village festivals and celebrations. But she had a tumultuous relationship with her brother, especially after their parents had died. Bulat saw his sister as a threat, being blessed (or cursed) with an independent streak that led her to deny every suitor, preferring instead to wait until he died in battle and left their ancestral home to her.

"He sold me, the bastard, the lowly vermin!" She threw herself onto my pech face-first. "Sold! Enslaved! Utterly and completely betrayed!"

I hesitated. "Are you to marry, Zora?"

"Do you know of any slavery more miserable to women?"

I did but didn't say so. Her eyes were so indignantly large they took half her face.

"I have been betrothed to Spiridon the Warrior, now so old he can barely see!"

I put Zora to bed with a pin in her hair to make for a smooth fall into sleep, but not before giving her a potion with valerian and lemon extract, charmed to calm her nerves, along with a little otvorotnye koreshki, herbs meant to repel this Spiridon's love, if he had any.

Bulat arrived with morning.

"Where is she?" he demanded in the way of all irritable, entitled men. His hair, as black as his sister's, fell in dirty, wet streaks across his too-prominent forehead.

"Asleep." I took a step back, having encountered a heavy whiff of garlic from Bulat.

"Hand her over—now."

I took a calming breath. Bulat had never been able to listen well, or at all. "I cannot do that. Your sister has asked for my protection, and I intend to give it." She was not the first to flee from a betrothal, nor would

brother's schemes as if I were a stranger. How easy it had been for her, even easier for the villagers to threaten me with their blades and pitchforks, a princess from a faraway village providing the perfect excuse to attack me. I had no husband and knew too much, my independence a thorn in their sides. Once their faith in the old gods had gone, their acceptance had quickly slid into suspicion, into mistrust and alienation, into threats.

"Go," Yersh had said. "And do not return unless you want your throat slit."

I was no longer the daughter of the Earth Mother, put on a pedestal, venerated, lifted to the very stars. I was an aberration, an impurity, someone other. In short, a freak.

I never saw Bulat or Zora again, though I had heard my former friend had indeed married Spiridon, who had died shortly after, along with her brother. I was glad that, for her sake, she was able to live as she had wanted to.

I moved to another village, and another and another, but those ended in the same way, with the same words. That was when I settled in my glade with my animals, and Little Hen found me. I liked to think she had been a gift from Mother, who still watched over me from somewhere, though I knew precious little about a god's death.

The woods became my sanctuary, a safe haven, where my heart didn't ache with sadness at human changeability, where they could no longer hurt me. They would have to seek me out, to brave the darkness and snows for my advice and succor. Though lonely, this life suited me. If not for the tsaritsa, I would never even have thought of leaving it.

I had settled in this particular glade as it was one of the few in Russia with a passageway to Nav, the Land of the Dead. To travel there, a very powerful, very old earth magic was used. Mother had taught it to me, as she had in ancient times to koldun and koldunyas, mortal folk healers and sorcerers who were descendants of volkhvy priests and who worshipped the old gods. Nav was the only land through which the Water of Life flowed, and Mother and I had occasionally fetched the elixir for our healing.

Rumor had it the elixir could bring mortals back from the dead and give them immortality. But this was an overstatement. It simply healed when my charms and rituals proved ineffective. If the mortal was on the border between the Lands of the Living and the Dead, the elixir could give their spirit a gentle push back to the living.

I relied on the Water of Life as a last resort in my healing. Of course, my stores had turned up empty when I had looked for it the night before. I wanted to replenish them before my clients came that evening and to have with me if I set out for Moscow. But the memories of Zora and Bulat and that village came back to me now as I considered entering the world again, not inspiring confidence.

It was morning, and I opened the hut door with my usual, "I hope you slept well, Little Hen. Might you let me down?" At eye level, all I could see was thick trees. A piece of blue expanse glimmered between the heavy boughs—the river, some distance away.

Little Hen shimmied beneath me, performing her routine morning stretches. When she was ready, I gripped the door frame as the chicken legs folded beneath us, and we swooped to the ground at a dizzying speed.

My fingers tightened on the iron pot in my hand, the air nipping at my skin like a frost come too early. The raven was still keeping its demonic vigil on one of the skulls surrounding Little Hen. I waved at the filthy bird, shouted for it to go away.

But the raven did not lift a feather. It did not so much as caw in the deep hush.

Noch, who generally left when morning came, whirled out of the hut and into the sky with a very dramatic *Finally!*

The sun was skirting the top of the wood, its rays white and pure. Day had come, and with it my abnormally large and tawny wolf, watchful as ever, his amber eyes assessing me from the dense foliage of the underbrush. Dyen, meaning *day*, silently followed me as I turned the corner of my hut and hens scattered before us in alarm.

Behind the izbushka, on the border between the Lands of the Living and the Dead, I knelt to kindle a fire. The grass there was long worn thin with footsteps.

When Mother and I had fetched the elixir, there was no shortage of talk and laughter between us as we strode to this very glade arm in arm. It took us some hours to get here from our village, and it became our time to catch up on the latest tidings without the mortals seeking us out, our animals needing care, or the myriad other tasks that consumed our daily existence. Did I now hear our words, her shriek of a laugh?

No, just the wail of the wind. Mother was gone. Luckily, she had left behind Dyen and Noch, both immortals like me.

My wolf stuck out his tongue and growled. *The air smells different today.* Unlike Noch, who had a flair for the dramatic, Dyen was nothing but straightforward.

The sun was playing hide-and-seek, the sky turned fiercely purple, a swelling on very pale skin. I sniffed at the air. Dyen was right. Beneath the acrid smell of the flames, there was a wintry sharpness. The ground under my knees was cold and damp. For a minute, I found myself not in the glade of tangled green leaves but in one of snow drifts and white-robed trees. I felt the wind on my face, and the image vanished.

Dyen growled again. *Where did you go?*

"I am not sure," I said, bewildered, not used to visions. "I thought I saw . . . snow, winter. But it cannot be." I cleared my throat. "I smell it, too, the cold in the air. Something in the land is off. Maybe in all the lands."

Which is why you should not go to the Land of the Dead.

"But what if a client needs the Water of Life? No, I must go and fetch it, or I will be uneasy." And I would need the elixir if I were to go to Moscow, to Anastasia . . . But the capital and the tsaritsa were far away. Surely leaving the woods and my clients was not the right course.

All right, said my wolf, sounding not at all convinced. *I wish I could go with you.*

Only those blessed with knowledge of earth magic could travel to other lands—the Land of the Dead, the Heavens, possibly more that existed—yet not all of them. I could access just the Land of the Dead, as Mother had taught me no further. Birds, too, could travel to what land they had knowledge of.

I shall watch over you, said Dyen, installing himself near the border. *Be careful.*

I tossed a handful of curling brown mushrooms into the fire. Then a shaving of bark from the Land of the Dead and a pinch of its sooty soil. The smoke swelled before drifting to and distorting the fence with its long-fossilized heads of once-living bears, coyotes, and foxes. Closing my eyes, I felt the power of the border, the ground beneath it, and I reached for it. The glade and smoke vanished; my mind opened to the Land of the Dead as I tasted each word of my chant. A flick of the dagger, and a few drops of blood fell from my fingertips. The heat from the fire intensified, searing my cheeks and nose.

I blinked my eyes open. Slashed at the smoke with my blade. My skin stung from the cut, though nonfatal wounds tended to heal quickly. The glade came apart like torn canvas to reveal a slit of darkness—the passageway to Nav, the Land of the Dead.

But something was wrong. Along the edges of the tear, patches of ice shone like glass.

I ran my fingers over the frost, its cold biting into me, as clumps of snowdrops sprang up from a ground covered in snow. Impossible! Morozko, the Lord of Winter, was supposed to be dead in the summer, the ice and frost with him. My hand shook as I bent to touch the drooping flowers, now spreading as if enchanted. If I didn't move quickly, they would bar my way. Disoriented and confused, and with one last look at my wolf, I forced myself through the passageway.

The smell always hit me first—dusty, stale, with a hint of rot. I walked past the rough stones on either side, swaying a little, leaning against the stones when I could, weakness being the usual side effect from earth magic and from traveling between lands. I hummed softly. The quiet always hit me next, especially with the white blossoms decorating the passageway in funereal boughs. For snowdrops were death's flower and a sign of misfortune. As if I needed any more of that.

I made out the gnarled roots of the World Tree, the great oak connecting Nav to Earth and Earth to the Heavens. The Tree's highest branches were said to reach across the very Heavens, with heart-shaped leaves of the deepest emerald hues and magical red apples that gleamed like rubies. Above, the moon and stars twinkled at the sun's side. Firebirds soared between branches balancing entire palaces belonging to the gods. The Tree was supposed to be its own passageway, where gods traveled freely between lands.

Because of the mortal blood in my veins, such otherworldly curiosities were hidden from me. I squinted anyway, hoping to catch a glimpse of a celestial face or hand, a little piece of the divine. All I saw were the souls of the dead mortals. They slid down the Tree's shadowy trunk in glowing droplets before disappearing into the bluish mist on the other side of the river, the one carrying the Water of Life.

I couldn't cross the river. Past the mists, Volos, the Lord of the Dead, guided newly arrived souls. He did so grudgingly, since he could not travel up the Tree.

"I should rule the Land of the Living instead of that old thunderer, Perun," Volos had frequently told Mokosh and me. "Not this darkness, this death. After all, I am also Lord of the Living. God of the beasts! Patron of shepherds and knowledge and art! Protector of crops and fields and harvests! Of trickery and magic, too."

Volos would fly over the river in his cattle-drawn sled to meet us.

I could still see his face, one half young and strong, the other old and withered; his beard, one half white, the other rich and earthy; his expression like Nav's stones, cold, detached. Likely planning what he would steal from his nemesis next. His flocks? His followers? His lovers? Each theft instigated another battle for the sky. Each battle drew out the gods, forcing them against one another in the eternal war between lightness and darkness; for all gods were descended from either Belobog or Chernobog—

ancient, dual deities of light and dark. Each battle ended in a victory for Perun and a loss for Volos, imprisoning him anew in the Land of the Dead.

Yet Volos persisted. "I will take the sky next time, the final time. Are you with me, Lady Mokosh?" he would ask Mother eagerly, his cheeks glowing like sun-drenched pebbles, the horns on his head sharpened. "You could be my queen, my love."

Mokosh did not approve of gods' battles, in love or war. "The mortals need us to alleviate their suffering, their sicknesses, their heartaches, not squabble with bored immortals who have nothing better to do." Her parting glance at Volos would be hard, accusing, and he would be off, whipping his poor cattle so mercilessly the beasts cried out in pain, the sled leaving deep grooves in the soil as it jerked into the air.

Volos and Perun had not shown themselves to me since Mother's death. Even then, I had only seen Perun a few times, in the Land of the Living, in the instant before a sunrise or a storm. And Volos had not started a battle for the sky since before I was born, when he had stolen Perun's wife, the Lady of the Rain, Dodola. It was said many gods perished in that battle, but the land forged was Rus' herself. The gods walked among mortals at first. But when people stopped worshipping them, most had withdrawn from human affairs.

Now I crept along the plateau. The black soil was grainy under my boots, the air muggy. But as I approached the river, I drew back with a little gasp.

The entire shore was covered in snowdrops. They glistened in the dimness like waxy lilies left on a fresh grave. Beyond them, the water was not its usual ebony color. And it didn't ripple as water should. It was frozen under a thick layer of ice.

Not even in my coldest winter on Earth had I seen the River of Nav anything but rushing, gurgling, alive. After all, only the Lord of Winter could freeze it. And he was dead in the summer, only resurrecting with winter.

On the other side of the river, souls flickered through the mist. One suddenly became more substantive than the rest. It was a figure—a woman?—with floating gray hair and a shrunken body. Darkness unspooled from her rags not unlike snakeskin. She pointed one bony finger at me. Her deformed mouth opened in a scream that pierced me with its agony, that of a prisoner, alone, desperate. Then the figure was gone.

Another vision? No, it was my imagination. Only my imagination. I forced myself to return to the problem of the frozen river, of leaving without the elixir.

You do not give up easily, Yaga, I said to myself, having recovered a little.

I clutched the iron pot in my hands and, summoning all my strength, swung it against the ice. Flecks of ice pelted my arms and neck like tiny blades. A dull echo reverberated through the air, then nothing. Jaw set, mouth twisted in the effort, I brought the pot down again and again. But I soon grew breathless, my weakness returning, and my arms became heavy. My skin, pimpled with gooseflesh, had turned raw and red.

"Chyort voz'mi," I swore. *The demon take it.* The ice remained indestructible.

Why had winter returned, preventing me from taking the Water of Life? I broke off a snowdrop and thrust it into my pocket, hurrying toward the passageway before the ice grew over it and trapped me in the Land of the Dead.

I stumbled out of the passageway, head spinning and body depleted—to a howling Dyen.

Thank the gods you are back. Look—

My heart sank. The ice along the tear was hardening, the snowdrop blossoms crystallizing into stillness as if forced under a looking glass.

Instead of sealing closed, the tear froze, becoming too narrow for me.

Rain started to fall. The wind blasted at our backs as Dyen and I darted to my hut just in time—we had barely tumbled inside, dripping and gasping, when Little Hen stood abruptly. I held on to the walls as she shook off the increasingly heavy rain and ambled through the woods, seeking shelter. Past the window, I glimpsed the raven flying after us. I pulled on the frilly white curtains in irritation, closing them.

I sat on the bench and felt for the strange, enchanted snowdrop in my pocket. I would use it to see which immortal had enchanted the flower, and unlike in the poison, it was possible their touch, and their magic, still lingered. I assembled the ingredients I would need for the identification spell my mother had taught me long ago.

Dried serpent's flesh for understanding, a chicken leg for divining. I fetched my mortar and pestle. Contrary to Bulat's rumor, my mortar was too small to take to the skies in, and I had no means to charm it into flying. I ground razryv-trava, to find whom I sought, with blue and red erek blossoms, to hide my deeds from prying eyes.

The ingredients went into the ever-ready, bubbling cauldron, over which I said some words to encourage the spell to work. The water hissed and spat, releasing wisps of smoke that burst into an array of colors: The deep blue of ice in shadow. The bright red of falling maple leaves. The fiery green of poisoned apples. I let out an excited little trill.

I had just thrown the wilting flower into the cauldron when I glimpsed white flecks of dust on its lip. Something landed on my nose—a flurry. Another and another until snow started to fall, as if the ceiling had been torn open on a snowy winter's day. The dangling herbs became shrouded in white. I blinked, realizing the dust on the cauldron was really ice. It slid along its sides to the floorboards, to my very feet.

Barely breathing, I backed away. My boot snagged something on the floor, and I stumbled. A noise between a moan and a scream escaped me.

Half-buried in a mound of snow on my floor was a yellowing face. Empty sockets. A hole for a mouth. Disintegrating wisps of hair. One rigid shoulder wrapped in a colorless rag. And a drop of blood, trickling out of the would-be mouth. I crumpled into the snow in horror, even as I struggled to push myself away from the dead thing. Almost immediately, my limbs went slack, and my eyes widened.

A black mist was rising from the cauldron like a tendril of smoke—or, I realized, like the tsaritsa's poison. It drifted into the air, gathered into a dark cloud, and rushed at me.

When it came, my mouth filled with ash and rot. I tasted loneliness, despair, achingly familiar, my own. I saw the figure from Nav, its rags shedding like scales, its blackness surrounding me, pushing into me. My scream was ragged, blending in with that mournful howl, that cry of pain, deep-set, old, incredibly intimate. It chilled my blood. Cowering on the floor, I pressed my hands over my ears, willing for it to end.

The next moment, Dyen was licking my cheek. I lowered my arms.

The snow, corpse, and mist were gone. My hut was as empty and cheery as ever.

What is wrong? Dyen was gazing at me.

"You didn't see that?"

See what?

I shook my head. "Another vision."

Does it have to do with the immortal who enchanted the snowdrops?

I thought of the snow whirling through my hut just seconds earlier. I strode over to the cauldron and looked inside. On the surface of the potion, I saw a large, cloaked man with a long white beard and what looked like a scythe in his mittened hand. Though I had never met him before, I knew him to be the Lord of Winter. It was as I had feared—Morozko had somehow come alive in the summer and was bringing winter with him, enchanting snowdrops, maybe even freezing Nav's passageway and river. But who was the woman imprisoned in Nav? And why had she appeared with my spell?

My head spun. Little Hen had stopped moving, and I rushed to the door, pulling it open and gulping the rain-soaked air as if it were the elixir itself.

The raven watched me from its perch on a pine branch just outside the door.

Clearly, ravens were spying for an unknown master, not only on me but on the poisoned tsaritsa. And there was something very wrong in the land—winter in summer, a vision of darkness and death, Morozko returned. And Koshey, too. I didn't believe in coincidences. The fact that the tsaritsa of Russia was being poisoned at the same time that the land was being threatened by these strange forces made me very afraid.

What if the vision prophesied her death? And with her the death of an entire country?

My heart quickened. Regardless of my reluctance to involve myself with men and their world, I had to determine who wished Anastasia harm, had to protect and save her—for her sake as well as the country's. And to do that, I had no choice but to go to Moscow.

Interlude

DEEP IN THE forest, behind an izbushka that stands on chicken legs, there is a patch of ground that has been worn by many foot-steps and many fires. Ice creeps insistently along the cracks in the earth, dusting the grass on its way to the hut, which is still and sleeping now that its owner is gone. A web of frost forms on the chicken legs, the wooden steps and the iron lock, the dusty path that leads to the skull fence, then beyond it, into the woods, where the trees are veiled in ghostly white.

Frost settles on the road into the village, too. It is a small village; no one can ever remember its name.

Natalya Antonovna notices ice on her bedchamber's window and promptly closes the shutters, plunging the room into darkness. Vera Mitrofanovna finds no eggs under her hens—alas, it is to be kasha again for breakfast. And Rodion Mikhailovich's prized cucumbers are frozen; the poor man will have to go without dill pickles this winter. There is a chill in the izbas. The villagers pull shawls and furs from their trunks.

By the izba of Afanasi Sergeyevich, famous for his homemade beers, meads, and wines, an old bench stands. Many villagers stop by there for a drink or two, especially on warm summer nights. At least one of them usually falls asleep there, too drunk or too happy to go home and deal with his wife.

On this bench, on this particular morning, sits a stranger. Ice covers the black leather of his boots, the rich brocade of his long garment, the precious stones on his collar. There are crystals in his coppery-brown beard. His skin and lips are tinged blue.

A little girl in a bright red sarafan screams.

"Merciful Lord!" A peasant woman nearly drops the milk jug pressed to her generous waistline. "Something is wrong with that man!" She points. "He needs help!"

Several villagers hurry over, recognizing the man they had drank with the night before. An aristocrat, from the old Adashev family, on his way back to a royal court he will never reach. For when the villagers approach the bench, they see the man is dead.

4

EARLY JUNE 1560

"ICONS!" SHOUTED A merchant in a pigment-stained apron. "Beautiful icons! Of the Mother of God, of Saint Nicholas, of Saint George! Of any saint—" His eyes grew large at my hair, come out of its braid in dirty wisps after days on the road; the muddy hem of my skirts; the stick of elder and the massive wolf at my side, both taken for protection.

That was the general reaction of the Muscovites, though I had put on a long-sleeved gown to hide the ink on my skin, tried to calm my unruly hair, and done my best to conform. To be the devout wise woman, not the wild witch Baba Yaga. Well, so much for that. I suddenly missed my woods desperately, especially Little Hen, to whom I had said goodbye just that morning. I promised I would return to the glen when I could. In my absence, as she had before I had found her, Little Hen would rest and hibernate. Meanwhile, Noch would meet me in Moscow in her style— when she felt like it.

I had known of commercial posady, or *marketplaces*, but I had never imagined their bustling activity or breadth. This one, taking up street after Moscow street, seethed under the hot sun and sharp blue sky. So many merchants converged in one place, selling so many wares, displayed in so many brightly painted stalls and shops. Crafts—iron stirrups and leather saddles, wooden vats and wooden sleighs, candlesticks and silver. Jewels, shoes, and fabrics—silks, damasks, even lace and furs. Foods—preserves and honey, salt and spices, meats and fish, red and black caviar, baked bread and colorful cakes.

I breathed in the rich aromas, almost tasting the salt in the sturgeon and salmon, the smoky flavor of the roast chicken, the yeast in the pastries. And the human sweat, mingling with the smoke blooming gray above the city and its numerous fires. Nausea clutched at me, though I rarely got ill. What a contrast it was to the fresh forest air!

The press of bodies was unbearable. And the noise! Merchants shouted their wares, laughing and cackling as they haggled with buyers in spirited tones. Women shrieked, children bawled. Dogs barked, horses neighed. Carts thundered by. And the incessant creaking of the wheels, the cracking of the whips! I had grown so used to my izbushka's silence that I squeezed my hands over my ears, or surely I would go deaf.

"To your health, boyarin!" A man with oily hair, standing close, brought a cup to his lips as his burly companion raised his. "And to yours, boyarin!" Of course, the men could not be boyars; by the looks of it, they were engaged in a bit of playacting before beginning to sing, off pitch and quite merrily.

Out of this crush of humanity, a naked man appeared with a tangled beard that reached his feet. "People of the Orthodox faith, repent of your sins!" the holy fool said with his gaze on the sky. "Do not drink, whore, or pass your days in debauchery! Walk in the path of righteousness—the path of God!"

Several women whirled by, their velvet sarafans a rainbow of dazzling colors, their scarlet kokoshnik headdresses piled high on their heads like layers on a cake.

The uproar dissolved when I came to a square with a church. Its onion-shaped domes and towers swirled green, red, and white above a ribbed roof; its golden crosses pierced the very sky. The Cathedral of the Intercession of the Holy Virgin, better known as Saint Basil's, blossomed into the chaos around it like a flower.

A carmine-red wall, so long it was difficult to tell where it ended, rose behind the cathedral. In contrast to the wooden city, the wall was constructed of brick. While many Russian cities and towns had similar citadels, the Moscow Kremlin was home to the tsar, his family, and his most trusted nobles. Within, towers encased a cluster of palaces and more cathedrals. As the sun's rays touched their cupolas, they burst into a flame of white light. My breath stopped in my throat; never had I seen such beauty built by man.

Beyond the gilt city, rows of wooden izbas, stone palaces with courtyards and gardens, and small domed churches spread across emerald fields and meadows, the Moskva and Neglinnaya Rivers cutting through the land in bands of azure blue.

No one could have anticipated that rustic Moscow, with its previously wooden fortress and agricultural way of life, would be the successor to the opulent Kiev or the mighty Vladimir, those long-dead capitals of old Rus'. Moscow was glorious without being opulent and without being mighty. It was glorious, though it was too broad, too dirty, and too busy. It was honest. It was entirely itself. I liked it immediately.

By the time Dyen and I reached the Kremlin gates, my feet ached and my mouth filled with dust. A knot of guards in bloodred woolen greatcoats and orange boots loitered near the wall, talking boisterously. Congregating men seldom led to a favorable outcome, and the vile raven was circling overhead, cawing and jeering.

I recalled that horde at my door with their torches and blades, Zora and Bulat, the betrayal and lies. I met Dyen's gaze, and he let out a deep-throated growl.

A guard strode over to me. His scar twisted fiendishly from his forehead to his chin. "What have we here?" he said, peering at us. The blade at the end of his pikelike spear sparked in a sun that had gone from hot to scalding.

My throat turned to gooseflesh. A deep enough swipe across it and darkness! Death! I hated the mortality in my blood. It made me weak.

And I would not be weak. I had survived for centuries. I had a god's blood in my veins. I was a witch. What were a few men to me? I tightened my grip on the stick of elder, about to tell the mortal to go to his version of Nav, when a small, thin woman in black robes emerged from the knot of guards.

With such mournful, conservative clothing, I expected an old woman. But she was likely in her midthirties. And despite a small head and a pointed nose, she had a pretty face, with blue eyes and hair the color of straw, wisping from her wide kokoshnik.

"Is this how you treat a guest of the tsaritsa?" she asked the guard, her voice surprisingly shrill and inconsistent with her fine features.

How had the palace learned of my arrival so quickly? I glanced up at the sky, at the raven that only seconds ago had been screeching and flapping its wings above me. Now it was gone.

Dyen growled, throwing the woman a skeptical look. *I do not like her.*

"You do not have to like her," I whispered to him. "Now stop making me look mad for talking to a wolf."

He snorted. *Mortals already believe you mad.*

Before I could respond, I felt the woman's long-nailed fingers on my elbow as she pulled me forward, past the gate and into a spotless courtyard.

There, white-walled palaces competed with equally white-walled cathedrals, their golden domes and cupolas reflecting the envious, hot glare of the sun. An emblem of a double-headed eagle rose above the pointed towers and tiled roofs. Christian crosses reached into the sky, as if to prove their divinity, their claim to the Heavens.

"So, you did come after all," said the woman. "Welcome to the royal court of our pious, heroic, and handsome Majesty, Grand Prince and Tsar Ivan Vasilyevich. I am Kira Armikovna, the Great Mistress of the Court and head of Her Majesty's household." She eyed me narrowly. "You must be Yaga. Pray, what is your father's name?"

Mother had never spoken Father's name. She had raised me alone, a mother and a father both. "Mokosh," I replied.

Had a shadow crossed Kira Armikovna's face? No, I must have imagined it.

She was now pontificating about the splendor of the Kremlin, which consisted of numerous palaces adjoined by numerous passageways and stairs, treasuries and armories, storerooms and cellars and icehouses, bathhouses and stables and prisons.

The three buildings that apparently mattered most faced the courtyard. The Granovitaya Palata was the principal palace and so the most prominent. Off to the side was the Terem Palace, reserved for the tsaritsa and her women. And between the Granovitaya Palata and a cathedral stood the Golden Hall, where foreign ambassadors were received. Other palaces, halls, and churches hid behind them, though it was in these three buildings, in rooms aptly dubbed parade chambers, that official engagements were held, feasts celebrated, and social life in the Kremlin flourished.

Kira Armikovna paused for breath, and I hurried to ask, "Is the tsaritsa well?"

"His Majesty the tsar has forbidden any talk of his tsaritsa's well-being. The evil eye is everywhere." Kira Armikovna crossed herself not once but three times.

I had no time for this. "If you could please take me to the tsaritsa—"

"You are to see the tsar first." Kira Armikovna picked up on my distress too easily. "Our knowing Majesty sees all, your arrival included," she added with a sudden flash of spite. "He requests your presence in the throne room of the Granovitaya Palata."

Were the ravens the tsar's? But it couldn't be. While the tsar was powerful, there was no way that he, a mere mortal, had the means to command birds. Still, the raven must have reported my whereabouts to someone. Perhaps even the immortal Koshey. I would need to think on it.

I tried to tell Kira Armikovna that I had no wish to offend the tsar with my unkempt appearance, really wanting to see Anastasia, but the woman dismissed me with a cheerful flick of her wrist. Not desiring to create a scene on my very first day at the Kremlin, I nodded in acquiescence. She tried to prevent Dyen from accompanying me, but a growl from him put paid to that notion. He did not have my scruples.

We approached a palace by an awning-covered stairway, its walls like the skin of a pomegranate, intricately carved out of marble. The journey from the ground floor to the first floor proved too quick. Before I knew it, we had walked through an anteroom and into a throne room with dark bronze chandeliers, the boyars and their wives glittering and staring and whispering, and Tsar Ivan Vasilyevich, regal and imposing on his throne.

Behind the tsar, hundreds of candles lit a tapestry of powerful black horses and men in armor on the cusp of battle. My own battle was about to commence. In a swoop, the courtiers had backed away, and there was nothing but empty space before me.

"In this court, our women curtsy to the tsar." The voice of Ivan Vasilyevich was deep and rumbling, reminiscent of thunder promising the blackest of tempests.

What little knowledge I had of royal etiquette fled from me. The hall was so stifling, the courtiers so numerous, so silent. Not even the presence of a wolf rattled them. They stared at us as if we were an exotic curiosity meant for their entertainment.

"Lower down," whispered Kira Armikovna.

Slowly, I got to my knees. I pressed my palms against the cold floor, a shiver rippling over my skin, and bowed my head.

I saw a pair of red boots and felt a strong, warm grip as the tsar pulled me up.

Ivan was a giant, with broad shoulders and a muscular chest. But it was his features that tore the breath from my body. His penetrating dark gaze, his long nose and high forehead. I cringed as he raised his arm. But he only made the sign of the cross, his handsome face lifted to the ceiling. He seized the cross that hung from his neck and kissed it reverently. Its jewels caught the candlelight, momentarily blinding me.

The tsar held a hand to his chest. "You may call me Ivan Vasilyevich, for I owe you a debt of gratitude. My wife talks of no one else."

A rustle went through his courtiers. Now they were rattled. Doubtless, it was by the fact that a stranger could win the tsar's intimacy so quickly.

"Your wife is wise." I paused, adding, "Ivan Vasilyevich."

"She is sweet." He tilted his head. "She often overlooks the faults of others."

"Yes, I can see that." The words had come out unbidden. Stupid!

There was a moment of frozen silence. Then, gripping his golden belt, the tsar began to laugh, his dark red beard rippling. The laughter spread to his courtiers until the room echoed with it. "Fools!" The tsar looked about. "What are you laughing at, hmm?"

His courtiers bent low in a rustle of silk skirts and squeaking boots.

The tsar dropped to one knee. Despite my protests, he grasped Dyen's snout and appraised him. "I have a particular affinity for beasts—we recognize each other." He gave a surprisingly still Dyen one last caress and bounded up. "So, you are the savior of my wife, God willing." He crossed himself and kissed his cross. Then, he took off in the direction of his throne, where he spat three times over his left shoulder and brushed his knuckles against the seat. "We do not want to put the evil eye on your fine work!" Oh, gods. The evil eye again. But the tsar was already beckoning me to come closer.

I silently begged Dyen to stay before starting toward the throne.

My mouth opened in wonder as I passed the colorful murals on the curved walls, of altars and thrones, of prophets and princes. Then the central pillar with its lifelike reliefs of snakes, dolphins, and pelicans; its shelves of gold and silver plates and goblets. Next to icons, tableware was second in importance in any Russian dwelling. The tsar's was no exception.

The throne itself was smaller than it had seemed from across the room. More spartan, too, being a relatively simple, straight-backed chair with ivory panels. Next to the throne, a man stood. Tall, trim, with black shoulder-length hair, a short beard, and dramatically high cheekbones that many a maiden had lost her mind and heart over. His arm rested casually on the throne, as if he meant everyone to know it was in his keeping. The familiar burnt orange light flared in his black eyes. Recognition.

The lying, duplicitous knave! If I had not left my stick of elder outside, I would have flung it at him. For it was indeed Koshey Bessmertny, known here as Konstantin Buyanovich. I took small breaths of the hot, stale air. It smelled of terribly old things.

Ivan Vasilyevich placed a jeweled crown in his hair and sat down, one leg hitched over the arm of his throne. His clothing was the plainest of all his courtiers, in their gold, silver, and pearl-embroidered brocades and taffetas, their silks and velvets, their feathers and ribbons. Aside from the gold belt, he wore a sepia-colored, knee-length rubakha with a pair of trousers. That was all.

"This is my advisor, Boyar Konstantin Buyanovich." The tsar gestured to Koshey, who bent low, joining everyone in the room, who were all either bowing or curtsying. The tsar had not told his courtiers to stand.

"Rise, everyone, rise," he laughed.

Then he turned back to me with those too-keen eyes, taking the measure of me, calculating how far they could push. He proceeded to ask his questions. *Where did I hail from? What city, what part of our great and powerful country?* I had no doubt he already knew everything about me, though why he would let the Baba Yaga witch come to his court was unfathomable to me. Yet my nerves quieted. The tsar was putting on a show.

"You live *in* the forest? By yourself?" he asked, as if he hadn't quite heard me. "With no husband to protect you?"

"Yes, Ivan Vasilyevich," I replied carefully. Husbands and crosses were the obsession of his court. Any trace of cavalier, freethinking attitude, and I would be whisked from this place as fast as a heart was sometimes known to fail. "Unfortunately, I never married." I bit my cheek to keep from smiling, tasted blood.

The courtiers had started to whisper, their talk whirling through the hall like a bone-chilling gale. Yet the tsar continued to pelt me with questions. I answered them dutifully, solemnly. What choice did I have? *Yes, I pray, daily, hourly. No, I do not go to church. I am just a woman, only a woman. I fear to go into a village I do not know with men I do not know.* I kept my gaze down as a woman should, silently adding, *Oh, yes, Christian tsar, I worship and pray, to the same gods you consider pagan nonsense.*

"It is that vedma, that Baba Yaga said to be living in the woods!" came a muffled whisper. Then, something about chicken or goat legs, an iron nose—or was it iron teeth?—a fence with skulls of the poor boys and girls I had forced into my pech.

My heart gave a sad little flutter; my legs felt like holodets jelly.

The words of the elder in that village where I had been betrayed so horribly came back to me. *Go. And do not return unless you want your throat slit.*

"Do you own a cross, Yaga Mokoshevna?" asked the tsar.

Of course, of course. No matter that it had been at the bottom of an iron chest, rusting and rotting away. I showed it to him, my fingers trembling only a tiny bit.

"Who called this God-fearing woman a vedma?" The tsar's eyes roved the rows of his courtiers with an alacrity bordering on frenzy. "Show yourselves!" he barked.

"It was I, Lord Tsar." A man bowed low. His cape, meant for princes and generals, fell from his shoulders in richly embroidered layers.

The tsar looked at him coldly and gestured to someone. From the shadows, several guards stepped out. "Take this man away," said the tsar. "He has offended my guest, and therefore, he has offended me."

"No, my lord! Tsar!" The man struggled vainly against the guards, who escorted him out of the room that much faster.

"From the woods to a royal court," the tsar murmured as if nothing had happened. "Extraordinary." His quick eyes bored into me. "My wife has known you for years. Yet this is the first I've heard of you. Why are you here, Yaga Mokoshevna?"

"To—" Though the tsar talked openly of my saving his wife, it was best to tread lightly, since healing was under the purview of the church. "To keep Her Majesty company during her illness," I finished with some effort.

At first, the tsar was silent. "As you can all see," he spoke finally, "this is a woman of God. If anyone else dares to call her a vedma, you shall answer to me."

A rustle and a squeak, and the courtiers once more prostrated themselves. Thank the gods. Maybe in time they would see I was not the rumored Baba Yaga, curse that ill-begotten legend, that death of my reputation and good name. Maybe they would even stop their gossip long enough to allow me a modicum of respect. I, too, had feelings.

"After all, if she is a guest of myself and my tsaritsa, she cannot possibly be a vedma," continued the tsar. "No, she is a woman of great knowledge and is, accordingly, to be treated with the utmost respect." The tsar's expression was bright as he gazed at me. "You are welcome at court, Yaga Mokoshevna. Perhaps while you are here, we can find you a proper cross and, God willing, a husband also."

5

THE PRIVATE CHAMBERS of the tsar, prominent boyars and nobles, and hapless guests such as I were ensconced in multitiered wooden houses behind the palaces in Prince's Yard. It took what seemed like years to reach them. My insistence on seeing the tsaritsa fell on deaf ears as Kira Armikovna forced me into a tour of the Kremlin, with three lectures on court protocol. She deposited me in front of the heavy door that she said led to my chamber and left me with a specific appointment time to visit Anastasia later.

As I went to push the door open, I suddenly sensed that the chamber on the other side was not empty, that the person inside was familiar. And I did not even have Dyen with me. Wise as ever, he had run off the minute we had left the throne room.

I had to deal with Koshey alone. For I knew it was him in my chamber.

Koshey and I had met back in the thirteenth century, when Moscow had been a mere settlement and a Mongol khanate, the Golden Horde, had ruled old Rus'. Many battles broke out between the Russians and the Mongols. I would frequently travel in Little Hen to tend to dying soldiers across the land, where they lay in lonely fields and meadows. To them, I was not the Baba Yaga witch, but a savior, bringing salvation the moment hope was lost. I healed what men I could; I gave the rest swift, painless death.

On the day I met Koshey, the battle had been over too quickly, both sides butchering each other as if in a trance. By the time I ran out onto the field, except for the cries of the dying, it had quieted. Overhead, the dust was just settling. The summer sky was alarmingly colorless against a land vibrant with blood. The white linen of my shift turned a bright, ruthless red as I knelt beside a dying Mongol soldier, his face tearstained beneath the grime of warfare. A wound the size of my fist festered and bled in his abdomen.

I had just sprinkled the Water of Life upon it and was in the midst of stanching the blood with my hand when I saw a man walking among the bodies nearby. It was Koshey, though I did not know it then. His appearance had largely been the same, except for his eyes, which were somehow more human, without the hard glint they took on later.

"A healer," he had said to me once he approached. "An interesting sight on a battlefield as deadly as this one." He peered at my patient, whose moans had softened, wilting like his life before the elixir did its work, *if* it did its work. "You shouldn't waste your time on this one," he said quietly.

"Why not?" I didn't glance up at Koshey, being too busy with the wound. The man's blood was all over me, sticky, clinging, its sickly-sweet smell rising with the heat.

"He is as good as dead already."

"You are entitled to your opinion."

I caught the arch of one heavy black brow, the sharpening of his eyes. Did I see an orange light kindle there? "I bet he will die."

"And I bet he will live," I shot back, though the Water of Life didn't always work.

"Let us see," Koshey said with a glimmer of a smile.

We waited, and we watched as the man stopped moaning, as blood stopped flowing from his wound, as his color slowly returned to his skin.

I removed my hand from the wound. I hid my smile as Koshey leaned down and examined my patient while shooting incredulous glances at me. The man blinked up at us, speechless, just as incredulous.

"How did you do it?" Koshey asked, his voice uneven, clearly awed. "He was dying. I saw him bleeding out. No one comes back from that."

This time, I couldn't hide my smile. "With me they do."

His lips parted. He tilted his head. "Who are you?"

"Just a woman—a healer."

Koshey opened his mouth, then closed it. He fingered the fabric of the man's dusty blue coat. "You saved a Mongol today only for him to kill a Russian tomorrow."

"Or perhaps he will return to his land, maybe to a family."

"Perhaps." Koshey placed his broadsword on the ground.

I didn't take my eyes off the sword. "He is human and deserves a chance at life," I said, hoping my voice didn't beg. Koshey was clearly Russian—part of me expected him to kill his enemy. Whether he was immortal or not, I couldn't tell.

Instead, he extended his hand to the man, who, after hesitating for a brief moment, took it and stood, dazed and slow, but alive. "Tell this woman spasibo for your life."

The man squinted at us, clearly not understanding our words, stuttered out something in his own language, and took off at a run.

Koshey picked up the man's sword, forgotten in haste. "Might be useful," he said, putting the sword in a large bag I had not seen until now. When he noticed me watching him, he laughed. "I am a self-professed hoarder."

I didn't smile. "I won our bet. What do I get for it?"

"You tell me," he said, amused, still smiling.

"Answer me this question: Why did you let that man live?"

Koshey turned his gaze on the field around us, at the dying soldiers, at the hollow expanse of a suffering land. "Maybe even my enemy deserves to live. Or maybe there has been enough bloodshed today."

For a soldier to let his enemy live despite the entrenched inclination to kill touched my heart with a flame. And as he looked out onto our land, on the people dying and bleeding on it, no matter if they were Russian or Mongol, I saw pain, deep and endless and raw, open inside him like a ravine about to swallow us. There was light there, light that left me hopeful. Perhaps life, possibly even goodness, did exist, even in a soldier, and it prevailed in the world after all.

Only after he had gone did I realize Koshey wore no armor and held no shield. I had heard talk of such a man, more immortal than mortal, who fought for Rus' without armor or fear or, indeed, without any scruples, with a fervor for the motherland that put even our most famous heroes to shame. Once we were better acquainted, and he had found out who I was, he told me that Mother Russia kept the last vestige of his humanity intact, that battling for her was the obsession of his existence.

That was why I had needed to save Koshey Bessmertny. To free the light I had seen in his eyes, however brief and fleeting.

We would bet on small things, at first. *You cannot obtain those seashells, the ones with snatches of rusalka sprite song,* he would say, and I would bet I could, then keep the seashells. *You cannot find a ring engraved with that age-old charm to ward off danger,* I would challenge him, and he would find it, pocketing the trinket, hoarding valuables like a dragon would his gold coin. Those bets soon grew into whether wild strawberries could be found in winter, whether a fiery orange feather could fall from a firebird. Once the objects had turned into deeds—if a bride could be stolen from her bridegroom or a lost bridegroom found or a princess sold into marriage—the price of the bets turned into favors, promises, and, finally, kisses stolen under the cover of dark.

Everything changed when the Prince of Moscow, the charming, dark-eyed Yuri Danilovich, unluckily and most tragically became entangled in our betting game.

One midnight, the prince came to my izbushka, begging me for a fast horse to reach the Golden Horde before his cousin Dmitri did. The treacherous Dmitri was on his way to the Khan to plot against Yuri and dethrone him. I led Prince Yuri behind my izbushka, where the herd of snow-white mares I kept in those days grazed in the silent, silky moon-light, as blue as the light reflected off the deepest of waters. I gave him my most prized mare, Shustraya. Unfortunately, and to my eternal re-gret, Koshey found out.

"I bet my horse, carrying Prince Dmitri to the Horde, will outrun your horse *and* your prince," Koshey said, walking over to me and my mares.

I shook my head. I took a speckled red apple from my wicker basket and fed it to Lastochka, my second favorite mare. "Yuri will beat him—he has to."

"Why?" Koshey peered at me through the misty twilight.

"Yuri holds the most promise. The gods are with him."

"What gods? Where are they? Both princes are a disaster for Rus'. They are weak. And they make the country weak. They divide her, overrun as she is by those invaders, the yoke that saps her of wealth and power and life—"

I stared at Koshey. His obsession with Rus', his love for her, bewil-dered me. It defied all logic. Here was a man without a heart, yet he loved. Here was an immortal, yet he was achingly human. Here was someone who wasn't worth loving, worth saving, and yet he was. When Koshey told me the price of our bet, I did not hesitate.

"When I win, I will have you—all of you."

His words set me aflame. I hated that I wanted him to win, to have him, too. But I said, "And when *I* win, I will have your horse, Sivka-Burka."

In the end, though my mare was fast, she could not outrun the im-mortal Sivka-Burka—the largest and swiftest horse I had ever seen or heard about.

Dmitri raced ahead of Yuri to the Golden Horde, telling the Khan the lie that his cousin had stolen the tribute owed to the Mongols. The night of Yuri's arrival, Dmitri hid in the prairie grass near the highway. Under the stars, men let go of their defenses, left themselves bare and open. When the starlight was strongest, and while my mare Shustraya was at the river's edge, Dmitri hacked poor Yuri to bits. Shustraya later recounted how Dmitri had left his cousin's remains forgotten on the road as she had barely been able to flee from the bloodthirsty prince.

Dmitri paid with his life; the Khan executed him for murder. I paid with my body, on one cold, wet night, when Koshey came to my hut to collect on our bet.

As soon as Little Hen had descended, with great unwillingness, to let Koshey in, he swept toward me without a word and crushed his mouth onto mine, hot, demanding, impossible to resist, having been dancing around it for years. My body burned when he hitched up my skirts, stripped me of my heavy pelts and furs. How I hated that instead of fighting him, screaming at him, begging him to stop, my legs wrapped around his waist eagerly. I may have lost the wager and my prince, but it did not feel like it.

That was wrong, but what finally shook me out of Koshey's spell was what followed. When we were done and lying in each other's arms, he admitted why he had really come. That there were men after him, men who had been loyal to the princes—and to the gods they secretly worshipped—all livid with Koshey, whom they thought to be entirely behind the princes' deaths. And I happened to know the gods, who were Dazhbog and Svarovitch, the sons of the Lord of the Sky, Svarog. They had been friends of Mother when I was a child, the few gods whom she had let near us. If the gods could be persuaded to stop, or at least delay, their pursuit of Koshey, then . . .

I did not understand. "Delay them?"

"So I can escape." He was already pulling on his cloak.

I blinked. Our bed was still warm, and he was talking of leaving. Our night had left me wanting more of him, imagining him staying with me, hoping he would confess his feelings for me. But Koshey never showed up without a bet, without a game, and here, the game had been won, me conquered. I forced myself to harden toward him. "I will not do anything, not until you tell me how you are behind the princes' deaths."

"I . . ." He hesitated. "I may have known the princes more than I had let on."

"How much more?"

As it turned out, Koshey had known the princes very well indeed, since he had been lurking at both of their courts, in the shadows, dripping poison into their ears until the cousins had become enemies—"All for Mother Russia," he insisted. "To make way for a stronger ruler, one who will stand up to the invaders once and for all!"

I felt the heat of rage. "Get out," was all I could say as tears stung my eyes, on the verge of spilling. I refused to let him see me weep.

"I will not leave!" said Koshey, incredulous. "Not until—"

But it wasn't up to Koshey. Little Hen shook him out the door head-first, his cloak tumbling over his head in a pool of blackness, and then she—with me inside—crashed through the wood away from him, farther and farther, until he was left quite behind.

I saw Koshey once more, when he returned to me on his knees, with apologies and contrition on his lips, again begging me to intercede with the gods on his behalf. I had had a chance to cool, had decided I would help Koshey this first and last time because of the love I had felt for him, my first true love. Then I would forget him. I received the scoundrel civilly though coldly.

"I will help you," I told Koshey, after I had let him beg me to my heart's content. "In exchange for your agreement that you will not meddle in the affairs of men again."

"Of course, of course," he was quick to say.

But I wasn't a fool. "If you do, I will reveal to everyone—whether mortal or immortal—Buyan's location."

Koshey stilled, no doubt realizing that during one of his most vulnerable, confiding moments, he had told me the whereabouts of his island, his fortress, the only place he called home. After a second, he said, "All right." He stood from the bench and made a motion toward me. His hand brushed against my arm, his eyes heavy-lidded, primed for seduction, whether to ask for another favor or for comfort, who knew.

I pushed his hand away. "You are as dead to me as our princes. Go, and never show yourself to me again."

Whatever light lived in Koshey was a slave to darkness. After all, he had Chernobog's dark blood in his veins. He was a poison that ate into me until nothing else mattered, descended as I was from the Lord of Light, Belobog. This was the price for the loss of any given game, his darkness cloaked in furtive kisses and empty promises.

After the princes' deaths, I had made my own promise to myself—to never again become involved in mortal affairs. Or to fall in love. For it had been false. A glimmer of evaporating light, nothing more. I might have broken one promise by coming to Moscow, but the second was one I did not intend to break.

I pushed the door to my chamber open and entered.

Koshey stepped out from behind the silken, green hangings. They rippled, seaweed-like, around the canopied bed.

"What are you doing here, Koshey?"

"How often do I have to ask you to call me Kostya?"

"Just once more." I refused to say his nickname, to admit to the long-buried intimacy. "Well?" I tapped my foot without the satisfying *pat, pat, pat*. The carpet was too thick.

"I am here to welcome you to Moscow." He made his way toward me lazily.

"After our last entanglement in mortal politics you vowed to stop your meddling. Or has your memory clouded over?" I brushed past him, inadvertently taking in a whiff of his scent, of black cherries, of mysterious islands. It was infuriating, far too familiar.

An ornately carved oak table stood under a tiny, stained glass window, in a corner with shelves bearing the Orthodox saints in their gold-encrusted icons. The faces painted on the wooden panels were watchful, even gloomy, at the prospect of sharing the room with a heretic, a pagan, a witch. I took up a long-necked jug, waiting and gleaming on a tray of silverware, and filled a cup with its contents. I brought the cup to my mouth, tasting kvass, a fermented drink from rye bread that I wished had more alcohol. The bedchamber was humid, tight and heavy with a past forced into the present.

"How callous you are," said Koshey. "Is this how you greet an old friend?"

"Well, if said friend had not broken his promise, then maybe he would be greeted differently." I paused. "I still remember Buyan's location, you know. I can—"

He was smiling faintly. The new lines at his mouth, the same ones Anastasia had spoken of, stirred, as deep as if they had been carved there by a blade. I had not seen him since the fourteenth century, yet the lines surprised me, given his immortality.

"Come, Yaga," Koshey finally said with laughter in his voice. "You know perfectly well that Buyan is now nothing but myth to humans and gods alike. And locations of floating islands can change . . ." He joined me at the table and poured himself a cup of kvass.

"You swore." My chest tightened. After having gone through all the trouble of helping him to escape, of convincing the Lords Dazhbog and Svarovitch not to pursue him, I had lost their friendship and favor. I set the cup of kvass down a little too loudly.

"We both have our weaknesses," said Koshey. "You with your potions and me—" He looked away with a helpless sigh, took a drink of kvass, and immediately put the cup down. "I had no intention of breaking my promise. But those boyars with their stupid rivalries! It was almost the end of Mother Russia just as she had rid herself of the Mongols. I could not bear to watch the backstabbing, feuding boyar clans, competing over the regency when the tsar was a boy. Seizing power, then murdering to keep it, in an endless khorovod dance. The tsar's own mother, poisoned! It was total anarchy—"

"When the tsar was a boy?" I repeated, incredulous. Ivan was now thirty, having taken the throne some thirteen years ago, which meant Koshey had been at court for a long time.

"The country was being torn apart!"

Were Koshey's eyes wet? Did a light gleam there, the one I had tried and failed to capture for years? Was this the man I had known, the one I had tried to save, to love? *Stop it*, I commanded myself. Who did he think he was? A god? "It is not your responsibility to fix it," I said quietly.

"Even so, I made myself indispensable to the tsar, working discreetly behind the scenes until . . . well, until an unexpected vacancy opened."

"An unexpected vacancy," I echoed, thinking of the tsar's former advisors, the men my clients had assured me were untouchable at court—a boyar's son, Aleksey Fyodorovich Adashev; the leader of the Russian Orthodox Church, Metropolitan Makarii; and the priest Sylvester. I had seen no trace of them in the throne room. "You expect me to believe you had nothing to do with this so-called vacancy?" *Miserable liar!*

"Nothing whatsoever." Koshey's lips quirked into his little half smile. Any seriousness bled away from him. He spread his hands, rubies and diamonds sparkling on his fingers.

A hoarder of finery! "Why can you never resist the lure of power and riches?" I motioned to his kaftan, the decadently long sleeves, the sash woven with wine-red cordonnet thread, the gold stripes on black velvet. His hat glistened with precious stones. Such a costume could only be purchased by the wealthiest—indeed, by royalty.

"Power is everything in this country." Koshey tilted his head. "Being first among princes as grand prince, and the first tsar, Ivan is as exalted as a Roman caesar. With the blood of the ancient Rurik Dynasty in his veins, he is as influential as a Byzantine emperor, as strong a warrior as a Tatar khan. Having conquered vast territories, he has unified Russia and ushered in her golden age, a new stability. I am making sure Ivan remains on the throne. Russia needs a strong ruler, a tsar, or she will descend into anarchy."

Was Koshey really doing all this for his love of Russia? I doubted it. Too far, even for him. "And Anastasia Romanovna? She is being poisoned—"

He held up a hand. "I know."

I stared at him in shock. "Well, who is behind it?"

"That I do not know." Koshey gave a small, regretful shake of the head, seeming genuine, though with him I could never be certain. "The tsar has many enemies, at home and abroad. In Kazan, though it may be ours, in Astrakhan, and in Crimea. The Golden Horde may be no more, but the Tatars in the khanates are making trouble. And the war over Livonia is here to stay."

"Why?" There was a war? I blinked. This is what Koshey did; he used his pretty words, his sharp mind, his unbridled passion for our country to draw me in.

"Livonia is strategic, being on the shores of the Baltic Sea. Their civil war may have allowed us in, but mark my words, our time there will be short. Denmark and Norway, the Kingdom of Sweden, the Grand Duchy of Lithuania, and the Kingdom of Poland will all prove to be formidable competitors for the Livonian lands."

But why did we have to compete for lands that weren't ours? For a country that was in pain? I had always deplored the way tsars and kings took what wasn't theirs at the expense of ordinary people. "Are those foreigners targeting the tsar, or the tsaritsa?" I asked Koshey.

"Both, I am sure! There are traitors here, at this very court, foreign or not, mortal or not. Just the other day, Aleksey Fyodorovich Adashev's kinsman was found frozen to death on a bench in some village near Moscow."

"Is it not obvious?" I watched Koshey carefully. "Morozko is back."

"It is not obvious at all, dear Yaga," he insisted. "Morozko is dead. He cannot be brought back in the summer. Nature does not work this way. It has to be someone else. After all, Morozko is not the only being who can bring winter. What about Lord Stribog?"

"Morozko's father? You are suggesting that an ancient god not seen in almost as long as Chernobog and Belobog, said to have been sleeping practically since the beginning of time, has suddenly awoken?"

"I am simply asking you not to make assumptions until I . . . *we* know more."

My spell had identified Morozko as the creator of the unnatural frost, unless the spell had been faulty . . . Maybe Koshey was telling the truth, maybe not. As always, I had a feeling he knew more than he would tell. I would need to find out myself how these mysteries were connected, what Koshey had to do with them, and whether the poisoning of Russia's tsaritsa was related or just an unlucky coincidence. And I would not allow my past with Koshey, his charm and passions, to deceive and misguide me.

Behind Koshey, the glass of the window was webbed in ice crystals. The afternoon sun touched the frost, and it burst into a flame of color, the sparks dancing like the vibrant, severed wings of butterflies, lit from within.

Interlude

IN THE LAND of the Dead, on the other side of the river stiff with ice, there is a green swamp so decayed, so stagnant, it refuses to even ripple. In the middle of this swamp should be a shining golden throne. But the gold of the throne has long been tarnished and mottled, its arms now adorned with verdant growths, moss colonies, and brittle snakeskins. A woman sits there, her naked body insubstantial, flickering and shifting. One second, she is young and beautiful, with black hair and glowing skin; the next, she is old and withered.

A raven lands on a half-submerged log beside the throne. *Yaga is at the tsar's court*, the bird tells the woman.

The whine of mosquitoes is persistent in the silence.

"She always threatens what is mine," the woman says finally, her voice an oddly grating rustle. "Always!" Her features become more defined, her nose elongating, a wart springing up on her forehead. "Depriving me of my mortal souls with her healing, stealing the Water of Life from my river. All because of that fool, Volos. How fortunate he is no longer the custodian of the dead."

The raven fluffs its wings, as if uncomfortable, as if clearing its throat of the swamp's weedy stench. *She does not have the elixir. After the tsaritsa's visit—*

"*I* had the passageway sealed. If only I was not trapped behind that accursed river . . ." The woman leaps onto her throne, aging, shrinking. She melts onto the seat. Then her spine straightens and her hair turns black. "After hundreds of years we finally found the one with the power we need. This tsar had shown great promise, his birth heralded by sudden storms and threatening skies." The woman's features become beautiful, her breasts full. "And now? He is nothing but a sentimental sop under the spell of his pretty wife and a vedma! This cannot be the same man who tortured animals as a boy, cut out courtiers' tongues, executed his mother's lovers, even threw his regent to the dogs! Where is that violence, that anger, that passion?" Her eyes, vicious, match the putrid green of the swamp. "He is a weak man. He is not the tsar we wanted at all."

It is there, says the bird. *It has been in him since birth. He will deliver.*

"We shall see." Wrinkles appear on porcelain skin. "She is always in the way. Always! That is why Yaga must fall." The woman's features crumple, as if uttering the name is a painful, distasteful thing. As if the prospect of what she said is even worse.

How can you . . . ? The bird stops at her look of warning. *She is a mere half mortal—*

"She is dangerous." Something flits across the woman's face. Hatred or wistfulness or a mere ripple as she ages. "No, she shouldn't just fall. She must be brought low. So low that she loses everything, everyone, even herself, as I once did."

The raven wants to take flight, to leave this cursed place and never return.

"You know what is to be done." The woman, now decrepit and hunched over, leans forward, watching the bird. "And the consequences of inaction."

6

THAT AFTERNOON, I finally glimpsed the tsaritsa. She fidgeted under a heavy brocade dushegreika jacket, the abundance of pearls on the collar and cuffs of her sarafan, the gold and diamond crown. The grayish-yellow of her face reminded me of the corpse from my vision. Maybe it *was* her impending death I had seen.

Her feverish breathlessness meant she had been poisoned again, my charms having worn off in the few days since she had visited me. The back of my neck prickled with anger, with impotence. Why must she suffer?

Despite the sauna-like heat outside, the room was ablaze in firelight and packed with ladies-in-waiting in elaborate headdresses and brightly colored fabrics that revealed as much skin as was acceptable in pious, God-fearing women. They cooled their shiny cheeks with fluttering fans of lead white, glazed yellow, and deep vermilion while keeping alive a steady stream of chatter. The prickling on my neck intensified when their eyes, especially those of Kira Armikovna, lingered on me with suspicion.

I attempted to catch the tsaritsa's gaze—the poison had to be expelled with another ritual—but she was introducing me to her eldest son, Tsarevich Ivan Ivanovich, a redheaded wisp of a boy about six or seven years old. His eyes were large and dark, his face pale. He bowed to me solemnly. In the palace's golden splendor, the little tsarevich looked lost. I smiled at him. "It is an honor to make your acquaintance, Ivan Ivanovich."

He glanced at his mother uncertainly. After a nod from her, he stepped closer, his boots as red as his father's, his back as straight as a tiny soldier's. "Lady Mother told me you are a special friend of hers," he said in a thin voice. "You may call me Ivanushka."

I knelt at his feet, my chest warming. "Then surely we are friends, too, Ivanushka. I will hold your name close. Thank you for entrusting it to me."

He frowned. "A friend? No, you are too beautiful for that, Yaga. I would very much like to marry you someday." He reddened, as if regretting the admission. Then he spun on his heel and, nearly tripping over his oversized rubakha, sped toward a toddler with pumpkin-orange hair, teetering near a wooden rocking horse.

I laughed. I had long ago embraced my harsh features, my rather large nose and chin. Many, me included, thought them beautiful. And why not? Difference was a gift. "He will grow up to be a warrior," I said to the tsaritsa as Ivanushka leapt onto the horse and swung his toy sword, slashing at phantom enemies. "And that is your other son, I presume?" I gestured to the toddler, who watched Ivanushka with a reverent expression.

Where his brother showed a bright intelligence, Fyodor Ivanovich was dull-eyed and, according to the tsaritsa, sick often. Red spots bloomed into her cheeks as she mouthed the word "delicate." Fortune had indeed favored her that he had been born second.

She sat on her ornately carved chair and stared out the ornately carved but very small window. The room had panic-inducing low ceilings, murals with gloom-filled faces portending doom, walls crowded with orange blossoms tangled in vines. The candelabra threw a dark glow over the gilded doorways and the precious stones on the upholstered furniture. Beautiful but stifling. The court's rigorous order was imposed on no one more than its women, confined to sit prettily and do nothing in its opulence. Five floors of it, to be exact.

"Leave us," the tsaritsa said, with a wave at her ladies-in-waiting.

Kira Armikovna opened her mouth. But the tsaritsa held up one bejeweled hand, and the ladies-in-waiting filed out of the room, one gently picking up the youngest prince and taking the other's hand as they went, rustling and sighing and crossing themselves, as if to arm their mistress against me. Kira Armikovna paused at the doorway to shoot me a chilling look, that of a hawk swooping down and ripping its prey apart.

Now that we were finally alone, the tsaritsa leaned toward me, her iris-violet scent washing over me. "I am so glad you have come, dear friend."

"Of course." I grasped her cold hands in mine. "I would have come sooner, but they would not let me visit you until now."

She smiled faintly. "We live under the strictest of protocols here."

"So I have learned." I squeezed her fingers, the diamonds on them digging into my skin. "But we must perform another ritual as soon as possible."

She shook her head, jewels clinking. "But you drew the poison out."

"Between your visit and my arrival at court, your assailant has given you another dose."

"My Lord God, save and protect me." She crossed herself. "Let us get started, Yaga."

"We will. But first—does your husband know you are being poisoned?"

"I told him after I returned to court."

"Good." Though I still had my doubts about Ivan, as a man and as a husband, I did not mention them to the tsaritsa. "What precautions has the tsar taken?"

"He has started a discreet investigation, verifying that all the servants, ladies-in-waiting, cooks, and maids are loyal. But of course they are."

I imagined her watchful ladies-in-waiting and nearly rolled my eyes. Anastasia's nature was trusting to a fault. "Do you have a food taster?"

"Since before my illness. Recently, a znakhar' to detect the poison, also—"

A znakhar', or cunning man, meant *one who knows*, yet most were quacks.

"—but he has not been able to discern anything," the tsaritsa continued sadly. "And everyone swears they are loyal."

Someone was lying, and I would try my best to find out who. "Let us begin, Anastasia Romanovna." I turned to the satchel with my unicorn horn, my blade and bowl, a cloth with an egg and a bit of beeswax, and several other herbs and implements. I had to make do without Noch's assistance, as she had not yet arrived in Moscow, but the tsaritsa and I got through the ritual more successfully than anticipated.

Now Anastasia sat by the window, resting with a spoon of wild strawberry jam from the forest, as I circled her chambers and inspected her possessions, from her clothing and bedsheets to her hairbrushes and pins, pots of rouge and trinkets, and even her jewels and mirrors and furniture. Any of those could have been rubbed with poison. I held the unicorn horn to each and every one of those objects, yet the horn stayed ivory, indicating no poison. I stopped in the middle of the tsaritsa's presence chamber.

"Perhaps it is not poison after all?" she asked from her place by the window.

"The unicorn horn never lies. No, your poisoner is just very clever and very careful. Speaking of—" As an additional cure, I took out of my satchel a vial with my charmed infusion of valerian root and vinegar, an antidote to poison, and khvalika blossom extract, for protection at court, and gave it her. "Drink this, Anastasia Romanovna, to further heal you after the poisoning." Seeing her pale face and large eyes, I forced a smile. "Do not worry, dear one, we will find them." The words came out more confident than they felt.

She put the vial to her lips without complaint and drank. Then she took a deep breath. "What if it does not work? I . . . keep having nightmares. Of blood puddling on white stones. Of death when least expected. Of ravens—"

"Only dreams!" But a tremor of unease rippled through me; dreams always held meaning. Regardless, I had to draw her mind from it. "Why don't you tell me about the court or the tsar? It will help me greatly as I learn my way here." For all her good looks and sweet temper, I did not doubt the young maiden I had known before, the one who had spewed forth bits of history and politics when her mother's back was turned, would not be ignorant of her husband's affairs.

"Well," she said slowly, "the tsar's closest advisors, Aleksey Fyodoro-vich and Sylvester, have recently been . . . disgraced."

"That is unfortunate," I murmured as I reached into my satchel to produce a stone yellow like wax, found in the gall of great serpents. I hung it on a silk thread for Anastasia to wear, being an antidote to most animal, mineral, and vegetable poisons.

"It is unfortunate indeed," said the tsaritsa. "Those men helped the tsar to rule the country by presiding over what was called the Chosen Council, which forced Ivan to listen to his advisors and boyars. Every-thing changed in October, on the way back from our Mozhaisk palace. Ivan received news the Livonians were stirring up trouble at the border. The truce that Aleksey had arranged with Livonia had been broken. The tsar railed against Aleksey, Sylvester, anyone who had advocated for peace. Now, Sylvester has been sent to a monastery in the North, and Aleksey—"

The way she said Aleksey's name, with a gentle lilt and red color in her cheek . . .

"—is under house arrest. The tsar is more isolated than ever. Only one man is allowed near: Konstantin Buyanovich."

I went to the window, though I didn't see the lovely gardens nor the pink-infused sky. I fiddled with the silk thread now attached to the yel-low stone. When Koshey had talked of traitors, had he meant Aleksey and Sylvester? But why would Aleksey poison the tsaritsa or, for that matter, his own kinsman, if that death were somehow related? On the other hand, if Aleksey and the priest were good for Russia, Koshey could have removed them for the second loves of his life: power and ambition. Either way, I had to focus on the tsaritsa's healing and poisoner before the other mysteries that needed solving, including what Koshey was up to, and possibly Morozko, too.

As I performed the ash charm, I asked, "What is your connection to Aleksey Fyodorovich?"

The red in her cheeks deepened. "He is a friend, a very old and dear friend."

Maybe her lover, too? Though given her devoutness and commitment to her family, not to mention her good sense, I doubted the tsaritsa had acted on what I suspected were feelings for Aleksey. "Perhaps he deserves his punishment?"

"It cannot be." A sheen of sweat covered her delicate features. "Both men are exceptionally loyal. And the more isolated the tsar is from his other advisors, the more unchecked his power and that of Konstantin Buyanovich—"

The door burst open, and in ran her eldest son.

"We found you, Lady Mother!" the tsarevich said, brandishing his toy sword. He jumped in front of me with the sword raised. "Never fear, Yaga! I will protect you!"

I smiled at him, feeling a tug toward the boy and his mother I had not felt in a long time. Not only empathy, but real concern. My heart filled with belonging here in this dark, stifling room. I wanted to help Anastasia— not out of duty or a sense of purpose, but because I cared for her.

"Yaga—" Anastasia grabbed my hand suddenly, fiercely, her eyes intense. "If anything should happen to me, can you watch over my sons?"

There was a tremor in my limbs now; she had dreamed of ravens. "My dear, your husband's paranoia is touching your head," I hurried to say, placing the stone necklace in the palm of her hand. "You shall be there to protect your handsome little tsarevich and his brother." I only hoped, prayed, *wished* I was right.

Despite Kira Armikovna's protests, I spent the night with Anastasia, making sure that she was breathing, that her heart was beating, that she was healing as she should.

The following night, unbeknownst to the tsaritsa, I slipped into her Terem Palace with a fern branch clutched in my hand to cloak me from sight. I sent a prayer up to Kupalo, the Lord of Vegetation, for an additional layer of protection as I installed myself in Anastasia's bedchamber to watch over her as she slept, to ascertain that whoever came into her chambers did so for the right reason. But nothing seemed out of the ordinary.

The next night, I tasked a few mice and a cat to guard Anastasia, though, of course, not at the same time.

What are we looking for? I heard the blue-eyed cat meow in her tongue.

"Everything," I replied. Like Dyen and Noch, other animals understood me, though I spoke in Russian. It was one of the most valuable talents Mother had passed on to me. But unlike Dyen and Noch, simple explanations were best, or else my instructions could be misconstrued. "Watch new people and the same people. Watch what they do, who they do it with. Watch for anything you haven't seen before, and what you have. Report on everything, especially if outside the tsaritsa's presence."

I showed the mice several poisons from my own stores to sniff at, so they understood them to be harmful, and explained the rest with my hands.

In addition to the remedies already used, I gave the tsaritsa amulets and talismans to wear for protection against her poisoner—herbs and blossoms rolled in wax, a bear claw, a bracelet of mammoth bones. And while I could not divine the physical source or nature of the poison, as I had no evidence, I ordered all of the tsaritsa's food and drink to go through me instead of an unknown food taster. I held the unicorn horn to each dish, each cup, each tray. And I watched her ladies-in-waiting, or tasked Dyen and Noch and the other animals to watch them—where they went, what they did, who they saw.

I sent Noch to the woods for additional supplies, as well as to check on Little Hen and the River of Nav. I would be more at ease if I had the Water of Life—just in case. But the passageway and the river with its elixir remained frozen.

Thank the gods that our precautions seemed to be working. The poisoner had not made another attempt on the tsaritsa's life in the days since I had arrived.

On my fourth night at court, I rushed back to my chamber for my cloak—Anastasia had asked me to accompany her to distribute alms to the poor in the city—but upon entering my room, I ground to a halt. The sharp intake of breath had robbed me of all sensation but shock. I covered my face with my hands, unable to bear the sight.

In the dim light of the candle, I saw the cat and mice I had tasked to guard the tsaritsa—strung up and hanging from my bed frame, their bellies slashed and exposed. Blood dripped down the green hangings in black streaks, collecting at the foot of the bed in ever-expanding puddles as dark as spilled ink.

This was not an ordinary poisoner, some envious lady-in-waiting or vengeful admirer. No, this was someone entirely without empathy or remorse—and possibly deranged on top of that.

7

"TO YOUR HEALTH, our most illustrious tsar and lord, and to the health of Her Majesty, the tsaritsa, too!" Benches were pushed back, bows and curtsies executed, goblets raised. The courtiers toasted the royal couple and drank.

Servants rushed about with bowls of wine, mead, and beer brewed from barley, hops, and mint. I caught a desperate breath in that overcrowded, airless room, finally having been forced into attending a royal feast on my fifth day in Moscow and definitely not liking it. It seemed the dark would never come, nor any kind of rest with it. Daylight still stained the small windows of the dining hall, though it was already eleven o'clock.

Between the toasts, frenzied courtiers grabbed bread loaves, cheese pies, and kulebyaka pastries laid out on gold and silver platters. There was no silverware, and I averted my face in disgust every time a dagger was taken out of a boot to cut into the stuffed dead swans, the fried and featherless peacocks, even the piglets crammed with shriveled apples. With dirty fingers, the courtiers tore off pieces of sturgeon and salmon; picked off kidneys, tongues, and hearts; scooped up meat jellies and caviar; grabbed blini, fritters, and pickled vegetables. The leftovers were tossed back onto the platters, now a bloody mess of gnawed bones, shredded skins, and stiffened fat.

Every courtier was on a quest to speak, to see and be seen. To tell his rivals in the loudest tones of his recent and most prestigious appointments, his recently acquired lands and jewels, the recent marriages propelling him closer to the tsar, who was resplendent that night in a crown with jewels arranged into laurel leaves, his taffeta kaftan dripping golden tassels. The courtiers waited to eat or to receive a chalice of wine from their tsar. If lucky, a pickled plum. If blessed, a few words with the royal family sitting at the high table with Koshey.

The tsaritsa was rosier, and she smiled. It wasn't only the rituals that gave color to her cheek; the night before, we had gone on another clandestine visit to a church deep in the city, giving out coin and loaves of bread to the poor, who seemed to gain strength in their tsaritsa's presence. They reached to touch even a small part of her, a wrist, her cloak, the hem of her gown. And she reached back, making the sign of the cross over their heads, taking their hands in hers, reassuring them with a word or two. Anastasia really did treat her people as if she were their mother and they her own children, like at my izbushka all that time ago, giving them not only her charity but hope itself.

Now Koshey whispered in the ear of the tsar, who turned from his wife to embark on an evidently all-consuming conversation with his advisor. Her smile dimmed.

My pestle in hand, grinding herbs in my mortar, I ignored the toasts, my neighbors, the pungent smell of the meats and garlic.

A sudden bang startled me. I kept my eyes down, attempting to crush a cinnamon stick that refused to be crushed. Then I heard the tsar say my name. I rose self-consciously and curtsied in the shivering, rusty-orange glow of the dining hall.

"Are you so ignorant of our ways, Yaga Mokoshevna," said the tsar, "that you do not rise when the tsar is toasted? Or the tsaritsa, your *dearest* friend?"

The tsaritsa put a gentle hand on the tsar's arm, and his face lost some of its hardness. Pressing his lips to her fingers, he stepped down from the high table, at which Koshey leaned forward intently.

"Yaga Mokoshevna," the tsar continued, "can you do anything besides grinding herbs under the table?"

Here came the test. Perhaps the tsar had initially allowed me at court to please his wife, maybe to amuse himself. But the curious eagerness of his gaze now indicated that he desired to see what I was capable of, what abilities I possessed. I had heard rumor of his fascination with witchcraft and the occult despite his belief in the Christian god. I had to impress him, to keep his favor and my place at court by the tsaritsa's side.

I whispered a prayer to Perun, asking the Lord of the Heavens and Battles for courage, squared my shoulders, and walked toward the tsar.

"The truth is, Ivan Vasilyevich, I was considering your proposition for a husband, and decided I have no need of one. Men are no mystery to me. In fact"—I let my eyes drift around the hall—"I know what every man here is thinking."

Stifled gasps. A few cries of, "My God!" The women crossed themselves with shaking hands; the men waited for the tsar's reaction, necks craning, faces rapt.

The tsar promptly crossed himself and kissed his cross. "How do you know?"

"God tells me so, Ivan Vasilyevich."

"God?" The tsar smirked. "He speaks to you?"

"You should know—you insist he speaks to you, too." Too far?

A stunned pause, then a few coughs. The tsar looked about. "Well, of course He does. I am the tsar! His chosen vessel on Earth! I rule by His divine right—"

"He tells you how to rule. He tells me how to read men."

The tsar hesitated. He could have said, "The Devil speaks to you, not God!" That is what I had expected, anyway. But he did not. "All right." The tsar stopped behind a man as heavy as a piece of oak furniture and just as severe. Under the shadow of his tall hat, his face was marred by many scars. "What about Boyar Ivan Vasilyevich Sheremetev?"

I studied the man. His square jaw was clenched, his fleshy aristocratic mouth puckered in an evident spasm of pain. "The boyar is thinking about his tooth, which hurts very much," I replied, then fortuitously recalled something a client of mine had once relayed about Sheremetev and his brother. "He was also admiring your candlesticks."

The tsar squinted at his boyar. "For what reason?"

"He believes they would fetch a good price and feed a lot of poor."

"Lord Tsar, I—" Sheremetev opened his mouth pointlessly; no denial came.

The tsar signaled to the shadows, to the guards hiding there.

"My lord tsar," came Anastasia's voice, and the murmur of the courtiers quieted. "Might Boyar Sheremetev keep me company for a time?"

The tsar paused, visibly torn between pleasing his wife and punishment. He lowered his hand, his face once more losing its hardness. "As you wish, my tsaritsa."

Unlike the unfortunate man who had called me a vedma just days before, Sheremetev was saved by his tsaritsa, her mercy and grace.

"Well, well, well." The tsar was watching me. "It looks like we have a real holy fool at our court. Only, she is no fool but a woman." He waved a hand. "Who else can you read?"

I scanned the room, noticing the press of Koshey's white-edged palms against the table. His eyes blazed more orange than black, in jealousy, in shock, unused as he was to the tsar's attention being diverted from him. But I could not worry about him now.

Passing by Aleksey Fyodorovich Adashev's kinsman, I said, "Ivan Fyodorovich is always thinking about negotiations, whether with the foreigners or with his wife." I heard a few laughs; the Adashevs were famous for their consummate diplomacy skills.

I came to a man in lustrous black robes. His jeweled medallion sat heavy and awkward on his chest. "As ever, Metropolitan Makarii's mind is on holy matters," I said. "Namely, his own salvation."

Two irate dents appeared on that stern forehead.

The tsar started to clap. The sound was like the insistent, panicked flapping of a trapped bird's wings. "Well done, holy fool. You have impressed us." His hands stilled, a dying bird's flutter. "What do you ask in return for sharing our Lord God's wisdom with us?"

"That I leave as I arrived, in one piece and without a husband. I also have no need of a new cross, being averse to worldly riches."

The tsar's eyes sparked. But he smiled. "A fair request, as long as you observe our customs. This includes rising and toasting the tsar and his family."

I curtsied deeply. I had impressed him. I was safe for now. I only hoped I would not come to regret it later.

"Oh, and my wife should provide you with a kokoshnik," added the tsar. "No proper woman, even one averse to worldly riches, should walk around bareheaded."

By the time I had made it to my chamber, it was nearly midnight. Soon, the courtiers would be spilling out of the dining hall, filling the corridors and stairs with drunken talk and singing. I gathered a few necessaries into my satchel and hurried toward the Terem Palace. While the tsaritsa was at the feast, I would perform a cleanse of her chambers. She had seen my work, but some rituals were less than savory and better done without her.

Firelight flickered on the silent walls. With their masters cheerfully occupied, the servants took their time at supper, so I traversed hallways that were empty. When I came to the outside stairway, the smells and strain from the feast dissipated. But the chill that had settled onto my skin, snow-like, stayed there. Court was proving to be an adjustment, with the press and talk of its people, its masquerading and maneuvering. With a sharp pang, I imagined my fragrant woodland, my quiet Little Hen, my humble and sincere clients.

My owl swooped down to me, her talons latching on to my shoulder. I bade her a good evening, thanked her for coming to Moscow, stroked her downy feathers. She curled into the crook of my neck with a contented hoot. Too soon, the Terem Palace loomed ahead of us. I asked Noch to keep watch and went through with my fern branch.

In the tsaritsa's chambers, I took out a decanter of vodka and a pouch with the ash from our ritual. I went about, marking the floors, doorways, and windows of each chamber. Then I sprinkled vodka into each corner of each room. I was in the bedchamber when there was a crash against the window. The decanter almost slipped from my grasp.

Two feathery shapes wrangled in the violet-blue sky. With horror, I made out Noch and . . . a raven. They twirled, caught in a moment of violence, and plunged down.

I hurried through the cleanse, chanting and peppering the floors with herbs: khvalika, for protection; odolen, against poison; dandelion blossom and red clover, to detoxify the rest.

I had just placed a bat wing under the tsaritsa's pillow, only for a few minutes, enough time for the good luck charm to catch on, when the door swung open and in strode Koshey, jaw clenched, nostrils flaring, demanding answers.

"Who did you put on that show for, huh? The boyars? The tsar? Me?"

How did he find out I was here? Was that raven reporting to him? It was possible that, as an immortal, he had the power to make them do his bidding. Were they his companions, his spies? Back when we had known each other, I had never noticed he kept them. If I asked, he would lie. If I accused, he would laugh, call me suspicious.

"You may intrigue him now, Yaga, but it will pass," Koshey was saying. "Ivan is a devout man, a superstitious man. He is afraid of demons and spirits. Vedmas, too. Before long, he will be looking to blame you. Men always do, him especially."

Who did Koshey think he was, a man lording over a wife so far beneath him that advice and warnings could be dispensed with as freely as love tokens? His threats would not mislead me, nor his suddenly scattered, fearful glance. Clearly, he was jealous, threatened by the attention I had received at the feast. "Despite being a devout Christian," I said as I fluffed the tsaritsa's pillow, "the tsar is so thankful I saved his beloved, it does not matter to him how it was done. He has invited me to court, has allowed me to stay and care for his tsaritsa. All this, by the way, is none of your concern."

The glance was gone; eagerness snagged at Koshey's voice. "I bet it will not last. That he will turn against you, banish you from court—or worse."

No, no, no. The last bet had ended in death, in princely blood on our hands. His possession of me. His using me. I shook my head firmly. "No more bets."

"Come, Yaga. Are you so sure you will lose?"

In spite of myself, I was curious. "And if I agreed, what would be the price?"

Koshey raised an eyebrow. His gaze slid from my eyes to my lips, then to the bed beside us. "Once wasn't enough, dear Yaga."

I turned from him, disgusted, and removed the bat wing from under Anastasia's pillow. I picked up my satchel. "Thank you, but no. I do not desire you, nor do I desire your bets. I am here for one reason only—the tsaritsa. I care not for the tsar or his squabbles with courtiers. Or you. Though you should not be here, I can no longer stop you. If you are threatened by me, that is your own problem."

In the past, our bets would thrill me. Another opportunity to glimpse his light, another stab at a just-out-of-reach, achingly close happy ending. Now, instead of the thrill, I felt a dreadful foreboding. I took a step back from Koshey, not fast enough. His hand was on my cheek, so cold, so intrusive, so familiar, I could not suppress the shudder.

Before I knew it, my own hand had sailed across his face with a satisfying *slap!* A red line materialized on his cheek, the one I had once pressed my lips to with such earnestness. A hit replacing a kiss, hate replacing love.

Koshey's eyes were black, holding not a pinprick of light. A storm cloud snuffing out the last of faded stars. "Do you want me as your enemy, Yaga?"

"I do not," I said seriously.

"Then if you will not bet with me, tell me what you are up to."

"I already told you—the tsaritsa."

"You are lying. How else do you explain your performance at the feast? You are trying to take the tsar from me—"

I sighed. "I have to survive at this court, same as you. The tsar needed a performance; I gave him one. The rest is contrived only by your mind . . . and your nerves."

Koshey crossed his arms. "Will you promise to stay away from him?"

"Absolutely not. If the tsar seeks me out, I am not in the position to refuse."

"Then you *are* my enemy," he whispered, rubbing his cheek.

I wished to convince him otherwise, to tell him we were friends, for the sake of everything we had meant to each other in our past. But I stayed silent. If Koshey saw me as an enemy, so be it. I would not humor him, would not let him take advantage of me again. And as we walked out of the tsaritsa's chambers, together yet not speaking, not even glancing at each other, dread unspooled inside me, dark and venomous, horribly like the poison threatening to kill the tsaritsa of Russia.

8

MID-JUNE 1560

A T THE BACK of the Kremlin's Assumption Cathedral, beside a gilded wall of icons, the tsar knelt without the pomp and theater he had displayed at his feast a few days ago. Fortunately, he did not look up when I approached. My curtsy was far from elegant; the new kokoshnik slipped forward, over my eye, almost tumbling from my hair.

We were alone in a church that was as empty as it was quiet and dark. Slit-like windows dampened the daylight, the heavily bronzed chandeliers muted. The air was cool yet smoky and sweet with incense.

"I have been praying to Our Lady of Vladimir," the tsar said finally, gesturing to the icon directly in front of him, of the mother of god cheek to cheek with her child. He crossed himself and rose. "She has been with me since I was a boy. I threw myself before her during the Crimean invasion of '41. She saved Mother Russia . . . and me."

My usual reaction to icons was a stab of jealousy. This god was exalted, celebrated in resplendent wealth; my gods were forgotten, prayed to in shameful, guilt-ridden secrecy. He had triumphed while my gods had lost. But Our Lady of Vladimir was different. Though I was a stranger in this church, a heathen, the Lady seemed to speak to me, to convey such tender sorrow, such a depth of suffering, that I wanted to weep. I realized why the Lady was suddenly so dear to me; she reminded me of my mother.

"I have surrounded myself with saints all my life," the tsar went on. "After all, I am no different from them." He got to his feet, his rubakha as plain and unremarkable as a peasant's, his hair a mass of red curls, and drifted to the other side of the cathedral.

Though my head whirled at the blind arrogance of his words, I followed him through tall pillars that stood like ancient trees cut from gold leaf with painted frescoes of angels, shepherds, and martyrs. We came to an enormous picture that stole my breath away, of knights with spears and banners, moving toward a gate where the mother of god and child waited.

The knights, explained the tsar, were the princes and saints on their way to Heavenly Jerusalem. He pointed to a red-haired rider on a black charger with sumptuous vestments and a gold crown, smiling a little. "That is the Grand Prince Vladimir Monomakh, the greatest and bravest of all of Russia's princes."

"He resembles you, Ivan Vasilyevich," I observed, narrowly.

"Well, of course he does! Like him, I am a warrior who has conquered vast territories. And like him, I am an emperor, my Russia the new Orthodox Byzantium. Can't you see I am within reach of the saints, of Jerusalem itself?" His eyes were bright; he was drunk with power, with his own inflated glory. "My reign is a blessed one," he added, completely assured of himself and his absolutism.

Here was a new brand of autocrat. Not just prince and tsar, but saint. Or a man trying to be one. Where I fit in, only his god knew.

"Not many are as holy as me, Yaga Mokoshevna," began the tsar. "Still, many try. Take Sylvester, my onetime spiritual advisor, as an example. He pretended to steer me on religious matters. But God never spoke to him as He does to me . . . or to you."

"You desire for me to be your spiritual guide?" I asked.

"No, no, Yaga Mokoshevna. I simply wish for you to read me as a man."

Is this why he had made me go through that performance at the feast?

Why he allowed me to stay at court? "If you know yourself, as you appear to, what role can I play save for offending your convictions?"

"Your modesty is extraordinary—and your candor." His laugh boomed in the echoing space like a clap of thunder. "It is not my convictions that concern me. The holy part of me, my divine right, I understand. Yet my body is loath to comply. I am besieged by aches, fears, despairs. They distract me. They trouble me. I need you to read me, as you did the men at the feast, to help me understand my human part. To heal it . . . and me."

I stared at him, at our hallowed, golden surroundings. "Then why bring me here, where I am meant to see you as a reflection of the saints?"

"To show you that the human part of me is inferior to the holy part. To God's glory. To all this." The tsar spread his arms.

But he really wanted to show me his divine entitlement, his royal privilege, his power to do what he willed with me. That I had no choice now that he had singled me out, that I was his to command. I felt cold. I really had no choice but to comply. I needed to keep my place at court, near the tsaritsa. But what would helping the tsar take? What would it cost? I stepped toward him, resigned. "If you truly desire my help, come to me as a man, in a fit of despair you cannot bear, without your crown and your jewels. Only then will I be able to read you." I turned my back on the tsar of Russia, and I walked out of his cathedral chilled to the bone.

It was an unusually dark and quiet summer night, the air heavy and dense after a recent storm, when I heard the knock. As I went to the door, the burning candle cast shadows that skittered across the red brocade cloth of the walls like startled rabbits.

On the threshold was a very different tsar from the fortnight before. His cheeks were hollow, his eyes unfocused, haunted. "I saw him," he spoke at last, lips cracked and trembling. "I saw my son."

"Which one, Ivan Vasilyevich?"

He clutched at the fur trim of his rich velvet robe, his trousers wrinkled, his chest bare. "Tsarevich Dmitri."

The tsar's first son—who had died as a babe. I dutifully made the sign of the cross. "Tsarstvo nebesnoye to him." *May he rest in the Kingdom of Heaven.* I whispered a little chant to ward off poor Tsarevich Dmitri. Later, I would steal a pancake from the kitchens and eat it while thinking of him on the threshold, so that he would move on. "Let us have some kvass," I said to the tsar lightly. "I brewed a batch with herbs to soothe the nerves." I took him by a hand that was soft and unlined, and gently pulled him into the room.

He sat in a chair, his back as straight as a soldier's. "The Lord God is punishing me. He is sending the Devil in the guise of my son, whom I just saw crawling at the foot of my bed."

That is no devil, you fool, but the spirit of your lost son. Some spirits were too attached to this world. Tortured and lonely, they haunted those left behind. I sent a quick prayer down to Volos; he would know if one of his flock had strayed, or never arrived.

"What happened to Tsarevich Dmitri?" I asked. I knew, of course. All of Russia knew. But talk drew the tsar out of the spiritual realm, back into the tangible.

"Oh, Yaga . . ." It was the first time he had used my given name; it felt as if he had found a deep secret of mine. "In the summer of '53, following my conquest of Kazan, I became ill. After my deliverance, I desired to give thanks to God by journeying to the Kirillov Monastery with Anastasia and Dmitri. We were boarding a ship back to Moscow when the nurse carrying Dmitri stumbled." Ivan's eyes filled with tears. "By the time they pulled him out of the river, he was dead."

I pressed a cup of kvass into his hands. "Drink, Ivan Vasilyevich."

And, like a child, he drank. I watched this man, broken, alone, besieged not by his humanity but by tragedy. I could read him as a man, tell him the truth of him, but I did not. Sometimes, to heal was to give comfort, to ask the questions and then to listen.

After that night, Ivan began to seek me out. We met in my chambers or his. Occasionally, he sent for me from the splendor of the Granovitaya

Palata, the glittering rooms of the Golden Hall, the vast library with its priceless collection of manuscripts. Upon his summons, he expected me to drop everything, even his own tsaritsa.

How I loathed it, much preferring her company to his, wondering if Koshey had been right and the tsar would eventually turn on me. I did not fear Ivan any more than an ordinary mortal man. Nor did I fear to leave the mortals; they had turned on me before, and I had survived. But I did fear to leave the tsaritsa. And to disobey the tsar's summons was to risk my place at court. So I made my etiquette beyond reproach, my hair covered prettily with the kokoshnik, my wit sharpened and at the ready.

Yet guilt clawed at me, knowing he only distracted from my purpose at court: to protect the tsaritsa. Especially when the poisoner struck again, the new dose administered cunningly, maddeningly—how, I could not ascertain. The evening I left Anastasia, she had been healthy and in good humor; the next morning, a wraith again.

I stayed with her as long as I could without angering the tsar, healing her with my rituals and charms and potions, performing cleanse after cleanse of her chambers, examining her possessions over and over— becoming so frustrated on one occasion that I threw the unicorn horn across the room in a blind fury.

Except for a dead spider or two, nothing was out of order.

But the more absent I was, the more Anastasia succumbed to her assailant, who somehow slipped her dose after dose of poison, making her pale and drawn, the telltale red marks and sweat marring her lovely features. And my rituals used up Anastasia's energy, debilitating her. I was afraid her heart would give out, or the poison would accumulate to such an extent that the rituals would cease to work altogether.

The treacherous poisoner hid their identity and their deeds cleverly, meticulously. Since I could not always stand guard over the tsaritsa, and since what animals I had tasked to carry out this work before had been murdered, I was careful not to take a chance with their lives unless they knew the risks. But the poisoner eluded my animals, or they disappeared. And there was still no evidence to be had. I was beginning to think that perhaps Anastasia had been right and the unicorn horn truly was faulty.

I drove Kira Armikovna—who presided over the ladies-in-waiting—to distraction, checking their pockets and hands and asking them all kinds of probing questions. Her initial distrust of me grew into open disdain. She complained viciously about what she claimed was my interference with court protocol, protested loudly each time she caught sight of Dyen or Noch indoors. I assumed my friendship with the tsaritsa threatened her own place at court, but there seemed more to it. Why? I could not say. Based on what? Only instinct. After all, she controlled much of what came in and out of the palace, and I searched her rooms furtively—but there was not a shred of evidence against her.

I wished I knew more useful spells to expose the poisoner. I wished Mother would have taught me more—about everything. Her protecting me from our world was an oversight I was now paying for. And the tsaritsa, in turn, was paying for my ignorance.

In the beginning of July, as a stifling heat swept through Moscow, the tsar grew petulant. Words were met with bitter retorts, deeds with explosive tantrums. One evening, I drew Ivan a vodka bath to calm him, to cleanse his body and mind, to purify his soul.

The white nights left a melancholy, blue-tinged dimness in their wake, cloaking the lavish decor of the tsar's chambers, as if to reduce him to the mortal man he was. From a wooden stool, I leaned over the cool, vodka-infused water, adding to it a charmed concoction of rosemary, lavender, and thyme, along with a drop of koliuka blossom extract, typically given to children to fight nighttime terrors. The herbs masked the alcohol, brightened my mood.

The water hid none of the tsar's nakedness, but I had no sexual appetite for Ivan, thinking him a child, a very disturbed child. He spoke of how I reminded him of his mother, Elena, being as I was his dearest friend, his guardian angel.

The smile on his lips did not last. It festered until, features hardening and drawing into a scowl, he spat, "She was poisoned by those *dogs*."

"Ivan Vasilyevich," I soothed, "you must not grow excited."

"Enemies surround me, Yaga! My boyars plot against me; their wives plot against my tsaritsa. She is being poisoned, and yet the most powerful man in Russia is powerless to find her assailant! How can that be?"

If I, armed with magic and animals, could not find them, how could Ivan, tsar or not? Admittedly, I had once suspected Ivan of the poisoning, but after getting to know him over these last weeks, I knew this was not the case. The longer he could not find his wife's poisoner, the weaker Ivan felt, like the impotent child he had been when his own mother had been poisoned, prompting him to lash out at everyone.

"*Everyone* seeks my downfall," Ivan kept going. "It could be *anyone* in this God-forsaken court. Consider in what traumatic circumstances I grew up, Yaga. My brother and I, with what laughter, neglect, *disrespect* we were treated after our mother's death. The boyars taunted us. They abuse me now as they did then. Why, during my illness, the one after my conquest of Kazan, they refused to swear allegiance to Tsarevich Dmitri! My fever did not break, and those *dogs* backed my cousin—"

Prince Vladimir of Staritsa, I recalled the name of the tsar's closest kinsman after his infirm brother. Vladimir was Ivan's rival and so a threat.

"Tell me, how can I trust anyone?" Ivan threw up his arms. Water sloshed onto the wooden planks. "To live through treachery on your deathbed, to imagine your wife and son murdered, your throne snatched from under your ass—"

"What about your friends?" I asked, thinking of Aleksey and Sylvester, men whom the tsaritsa believed to be loyal. She still talked often of Aleksey and fretted over what would become of him.

"My friends?" repeated Ivan. "During my illness, Aleksey's father, one of my closest boyars, also refused to swear his allegiance to Tsarevich Dmitri. All he said was, 'Your son is still in his swaddling clothes, O Lord Tsar!' before publicly backing Vladimir. There I was, in a raging fever, about to meet my maker, surrounded by traitors. The horror!" Ivan was breathing heavily, water dripping, seeping into my slippers.

I ignored my numb toes. "Is this why you dismissed Aleksey and Sylvester?"

"No. I dismissed them because they stopped pleasing me," Ivan said, watching me. "Aleksey, Sylvester, the disloyal boyars, all were forgiven. Yet I shall never forget."

Here was a tsar whose crown had made him into a tragedy, a suspicious and vindictive man, volatile and unpredictable. He loved today only to hate tomorrow. In a fit of misplaced paranoia, he could turn against anyone—anyone—even me.

Interlude

THE LADY OF Death sits on her blackened throne, an unwilling queen of a dead land, a prisoner with no visible shackles. What had her name been?

Marzanna, Marena, Kyselica, she thinks, depending on the time and place.

Black snakes slither over her nakedness, slick and wet. Under them, she feels the weight of her body, the aches and pains of old joints, of sagging skin on crumbling bones.

Seeliica, the snakes seem to hiss, mauve tongues flicking. *Selica*.

The Lady of Death takes this name as she has taken everything else, embracing it fully and completely. She did not choose her darkness, or her fate. But she has chosen her destiny, to break free of the life meant for her. She took, and she took blindly, boldly, as no one would show her the way, much less do it for her.

Aside from the snakes, she is alone. Always alone. Where are they?

Selica had tasked her servants to carry out the work she cannot do. But she is tired of waiting, tired of this dark, hopeless place. She will not let Yaga take her souls, or that tsar. Selica rises and pries the snakes off her.

She wades into the slippery green swamp, still hearing her own scream the last time she had ventured beyond its waters, when she had seen *her*— Yaga. How desperate Selica had been to leap across the frozen river! To envelop her in darkness, in death! She allows the waters to engulf her, if only to rid herself of Yaga's image by the riverbank. Seaweed twines around Selica's arms and legs; mosquitoes sing and toads trill.

She gains the shore and steps onto the plain with the mortal souls.

Her body starts to flicker. It nearly goes out, like a star refusing to shine, to live, to exist at all. The dead mortals stumble past, unaware, their outlines blurred and bluish. When they brush past her, it is as though a flame has come too near. Can she smell her own flesh? No, she is not burning, not like before. Never like before.

In the distance, the shadowy trunk of the World Tree glows as a soul slides into her domain. The light is like the sun she hasn't glimpsed in years. It grazes her skin, warming her from the inside out. Selica opens her mouth, and she drinks in the flicker of light. Instantly, her body firms and straightens, her hair grows long and black.

Mortal souls replenish her strength and youth. But only if caught the moment they enter Nav down the Tree. Otherwise, the soul walks the plain for eternity, asleep and not, alive and not. She is doing the mortals a kindness by snuffing them out.

She steps closer to the Tree, eager for more light, when weakness washes over her. She falls to the ground. The wandering souls walk over her, pushing her into the earth. Selica gives up the struggle, chastised, quieted. Like a maiden on her wedding night, buried in the bridal bed.

9

13 JULY 1560

From behind the stone wall of the manor where the disgraced Aleksey Fyodorovich Adashev was kept under house arrest, I watched the guards in their scarlet greatcoats moving through the twilight. A laugh sounded, here and there, interspersed between a phrase or two, disjointed and broken. The air was sharp with spirits, with men perspiring and living in the way of bachelors, kilometers from Moscow.

Earlier that day, the tsaritsa had breathlessly pressed a sealed piece of parchment into my hand, her iris-violet scent washing over me. "I do not know who else to trust, dear Yaga," she said. "And I would not ask this of you if it was not of the utmost importance not only to me, but to Russia. Can you deliver this note to Aleksey?"

"The Aleksey Fyodorovich on house arrest in middle-of-nowhere Russia?" I shook my head. "No, Anastasia Romanovna, it is too dangerous—"

"*Please*, Yaga. There have been rumors Aleksey is . . . well, unstable." The color in her cheeks deepened to the fiery red of her gown. "And"— she glanced about furtively—"Ivan is bringing back the Chosen Council. Sylvester has been sent for. And a delegation has been to see Aleksey. I believe he will be sent for next. The tsar intends to forgive him and ask him back to court. I need Aleksey to know this, so he has hope the negotiations for his release are not all in vain. It is all here, in this message to him."

The Chosen Council and the tsar's former advisors, brought back? It seemed too good to be true. How could Koshey possibly allow it to happen? But if a delegation had already been to see Aleksey and steps taken toward his release . . . Yet fear pulsed through me at the prospect of what she was asking of me. I could not leave her now, not after she had barely recovered from her last bout of poison. And if I were caught, I would face exile, from which I would certainly not be able to protect her. "Do not make me do this, Anastasia Romanovna," I begged her. "If I leave your side, I may not—"

"My dear—" She placed a hand on my arm. "This is about Russia's stability, her future, and is much larger than me."

Her eyes shone with such conviction, such earnestness, that though what she was saying sounded too good to be true and my going to see Aleksey was a dangerous, foolish idea, I took the note anyway, and I gave Anastasia a solemn nod. While Koshey was the tsar's closest advisor now, the tsar proved himself capable of displacing anyone he wanted, whenever he wanted it. The same went for bringing them back. I would go see Aleksey, do everything in my power not to get caught, even ask Dyen to ride with me despite his usual absence at night. Yet all I felt was a sinking of my insides, a dreadful forboding.

Back at Aleksey's house, a drifting shred of cloud obscured the surging moonlight, plunging the world into shadow. The last guard turned his back, and gripping my fern branch, I whispered, "Go." Before I knew it, Dyen was leaping over the wall, front paws out, fangs bared, and Noch was whirling after the barreling wolf. Then shouts and curses and a scrape of the gate as the latch sprung free, and I was hurrying into the yard.

In the heavy heat, the guards moved slowly, as if caught underwater, weighed down, drowning. Too fast, Dyen dived for their muskets, half-buried in a mound of pine needles and fallen leaves. Then he sprinted toward the black outline of the woods with the weapons clamped between his teeth. Fists thrust into the air; mud went flying. There was a deafening roar, and the guards set out as one after the fleeing wolf, no doubt excited at the unexpected challenge in this sleepy, remote post in the countryside.

Left alone, I considered the great house looming before me. It was mainly constructed of wood; the rest was of white stone, stained the dusty gray of moth wings. The windows were barred, prisonlike, the distance from civilization mournfully far. I climbed the outside staircase to a door studded with nails—fortunately, unlocked.

I let go of the fern, its cloak of invisibility, and I went through.

The foyer inside was not empty. Unlike the Kremlin's well-dressed courtiers, the people who leaned against the walls here wore rags, their faces dirty and marked by suffering, their skin covered in sores and welts. An odd contrast to the elaborately carved furniture, the sumptuous brocades and velvets, the colorfully upholstered walls.

I walked into a large, low-ceilinged room. Not even the moonlight penetrated the closed shutters of the only window. But it was not dark. Apart from the red glow of the icon corner, tallow candles flared on a heavy oak table. They gave off a waxy, fatty smell and thick smoke that congealed in the air like burnt milk. Poor Aleksey must have run out of beeswax. People lay on the padded benches along the walls, prayed to their god at their shrine, held hushed conversations on the carpeted floors.

"Aleksey Fyodorovich?" I whispered, hoping not to draw attention. The smoke traveled into my mouth, down my throat, and I coughed.

A few people turned in my direction before a man said, "Who is asking for him?"

I cleared my throat. "Your tsaritsa's faithful servant and friend."

The man who had spoken knelt beside a shrunken woman, holding a rag to one of her swollen cheeks. He lowered the rag to the rim of a basin and got to his feet. "I am Aleksey Fyodorovich."

I curtsied low, curious about this unorthodox courtier, more like my tsaritsa than anyone else at court. "It is an honor to meet you, my lord."

Aleksey looked at me intently. His eyes intensified from a rough pebble gray to a golden-yellow in the center, those of a lion; his unfashionably overgrown hair, bronze with flecks of orange, the mane of one. "I find it difficult to believe that you, a friend of the tsaritsa, would make it past the guards outside, let alone come here," he said in a very different voice. It had deepened, become self-assured. That of a boyar's son.

A slight smile. "The guards were easily distracted."

Aleksey folded his arms, his rubakha off-white, his trousers rife with holes. He wore no shoes. "How are you here—?"

"Yaga," I finished for him. "I prefer to speak without all of Russia listening."

"The peasants? Pah!" He gave a little, dismissive wave. "Most of them are deaf. And the others? Why, their minds have fled!"

Given the rumors, for a minute, I thought his had, too. But his gaze was quick and probing, betraying a singularly sharp intelligence. This was no madman but the calculating, wily politician I had heard of. "Even so," I said. "It concerns the tsaritsa."

Aleksey spread his hands. "As you see, Yaga, this is a sick house. There are people in all the rooms, including the unfurnished ones."

I looked around, awestruck, humbled. "How do they let you run this place?"

"They do not care what I do, only that I am miserable and alone, separated from my family as I am. Oh, and that I do not run away. Are you . . . here to free me?"

"If I were, where would you go?"

He smiled a little, his beard curling thickly around his lips, his eyes shining with a hatred that cast a strangely repulsive light over his fine features. "To the Kremlin, to kill Konstantin Buyanovich, even if it would mean my eternal death and damnation."

At the name, the breath stilled in my throat. I imagined if this man could kill the immortal Koshey Bessmertny. Surely, I would be glad my rival would rise no more. But I couldn't deny that I would grieve, too. I had, after all, loved a part of Koshey once.

I drifted from the old woman at our feet into a corner blissfully unoccupied. "Why do you want to kill Konstantin Buyanovich?"

But Aleksey only sighed. "What does the tsaritsa want?"

I handed him the scented piece of parchment.

He opened the missive and read. His face twisted grotesquely, as if a mask had been slipped over it. "Have you seen the contents of this letter?"

"Her Majesty has told me what it says, yes."

He pierced me with a shrewd, accusing gaze. "And you believe it?"

"I . . . well, if a delegation has been to see you, your release must be imminent—"

"No one has been to see me, unless you count the dogs outside." Aleksey's laugh was sharp. "I have not heard from the tsar in months, about a release or otherwise."

It was all a lie? I let out a slow, very pained breath and met Aleksey's gaze, suddenly recalling Ivan's words: *All were forgiven. Yet I shall never forget.*

As if hearing those words, Aleksey said, "The man does not know the meaning of forgiveness. Anastasia Romanovna has been misinformed."

I knew the tsaritsa's nature was trusting, that she tended to believe others too easily, but she was not a foolish woman. Either the tsar was playing games with her—or me, finally in search of a reason to get rid of the witch—or she was lied to and given false hope by someone who knew she cared for Aleksey, would do anything to help him, would *want* to believe a reconciliation between him and her husband were possible. It was dangerous for her, yes, but it was more dangerous for me. Was this a trap meant for me? If I were caught, it would put my place at court in jeopardy.

"How is Anastasia Romanovna?" Aleksey asked suddenly. His expression had softened, his eyes turning liquid gold, the wrinkles near his mouth vanishing—a brief glimpse into the young man he had been, not yet soured by life, not yet beaten.

"Her Majesty has been ill."

"All this time?" His cheeks blanched. "The tsar must blame me. He has always blamed me for everything that has gone wrong."

Despite the heat in the room, a shiver danced across the back of my neck.

"There is a monstrous appetite in him for blame and hatred, for violence and murder. Mark me, he will destroy all of Mother Russia to gratify it. And Konstantin Buyanovich will encourage it. Nay, he will carry it out. That is why I would kill him. The man may not have put me in here—the tsar took care of that on his own—but he is poison. He has poisoned the tsar. Next, he will poison Russia herself—"

Why would Koshey poison Russia? He loved her, did he not? This was either the mad ravings of a man who had lost everything, or some prophetic truth I understood not.

"How sad it is, the future that can never be with my—" Aleksey broke off, eyelids fluttering. Had he whispered *Nastenka*? The tsaritsa? "She is lost to me. My family as well. My wife, my Vasily, my Marinochka. God keep them and save them. I now live solely to alleviate the anguish of these people . . . and to kill Konstantin Buyanovich."

I took my leave of that suffering man, trapped in that suffering house, and wondered why fate was so cruel as to deny him the one thing that kept him living. But I knew—and Aleksey knew, too—that he would not leave his prison. He had not even asked to come with me. As I stole out of his house, its smoky scent clinging to my skin, my thoughts were with his Vasily and Marinochka, who I could only assume were his poor, soon-to-be-fatherless children. A tsar never kept a disgraced servant alive for long.

The Kremlin was quiet when I returned, in the deep purple of a summer night doused in starlight, when the courtiers and their palaces slept. Immediately, I went to the Terem Palace, my fern clutched in my hand for easier access. I wanted to ask Anastasia who had given her the misleading information about Aleksey's release. But I found more guards at the door of her chambers, so many that I could not slip inside as usual. Letting go of the fern, I appeared to them upon turning the corner and asked to be let in.

"No one enters without the tsar's express permission," a severe guard with silver hair informed me.

I stepped back with a twinge of unease. "The tsaritsa asked to see me, and surely, the tsar would not mind if his dear friend, Yaga Mokoshevna, tended to his wife."

"On the contrary. You are not on the list of approved persons to see Her Majesty."

He had not yet finished speaking, and already I knew my fears to be confirmed—I was caught. Clearly, someone had reported on my visit to the disgraced courtier even before I had returned to Moscow. It *had* been a trap—they had known I would go to Aleksey's house because they had pushed the tsaritsa to send me there.

Was it the tsar? Or was it Koshey? As the only other person close to Ivan, he certainly stood to benefit. And if he knew how vengeful Aleksey was, that his sole purpose in life was revenge, then he had managed to entrap us both. Would Koshey really betray me like this? I thought back to his words after the feast. *You are my enemy.*

I did not know if he was my only one. As far as I knew, it could be anyone at court unhappy with my proximity to the royal couple. I was not yet arrested or imprisoned, but the tsar now believed me to be up to something. I had lost not only his favor, but his trust—and very probably my place at the tsaritsa's side.

10

～⁂～

17 JULY 1560

A FEW SLEEPLESS NIGHTS later, I dreamed of the village where I had been born, the way I remembered it now—after the fire that had destroyed my home and killed Mother.

Smoke surges into the pink of the March dawn sky, flames spurting out of the wreckage, as I run down a scorched road, coughing and gasping for air. Mud catches at my too-long skirts. I shove aside the thought of a warm pech at my back after the endless weeks of travel, the promise of food, Mother's butter and jam blini, salmon casserole, and painted eggs for the Maslenitsa festival in honor of the sun.

On either side, instead of the log izbas, their brightly decorated window frames and doors, their intricately carved porches and fences, there is charred and disintegrating wood, warped and shapeless. Instead of roosters crowing, doors slamming, the exchange of morning greetings, I hear the unmistakable, heartbreaking sound of loss, of wails and weeping. I can only think of Mother.

Stay and finish your work, Yaga, *she had said before leaving me.* I shall meet you back home tonight.

Had she returned? I fight the mud and melted snow to our izba, but it is gone, turned to ash.

Dyen appears. She is gone, Yaga, *he says in a plaintive, broken voice.* I tried to get her out—

I do not hear the rest, not believing a goddess as powerful as Mother could just die, and in an ordinary fire, no less. But as I rush to what used to be our izba, start to dig and claw my way through the rubble, I glimpse her silver medallion—the one with the World Tree that she never took off—on a chain of now-blackened gold rings.

Everything blurs, becomes a screaming mass of white and orange and black. I can barely feel the cold ground beneath my knees as I collapse in the midst of the wreckage and lose myself completely. Mother is gone. She is dead. If only I had returned the night before . . .

I wander nearly blinded by tears through the village I have known all my life. A snowflake lands on my nose. I blink in surprise. The snow thickens, falling fat and heavy and wet. Then I see her. She is motionless, flanked by two horses with masked riders. One horse is the bluish-black color of night, the other a blur of reddish-orange. The wreath crowning Mother is of wheat and tiny blue blossoms, the sarafan hedge-green with embroidery glinting like the sun. Yet no sun shows in the still-black, smoky sky.

My heart sinks when I notice the ravens in Mother's upturned palms.

Do not despair, Yaga, *says Mokosh in a voice that carries like the wind.* It is not my death you should be worried about.

"Where are you?" I run up to her. "Whose death?"

She says nothing. Frost crystals form on her wreath. A dusting of white covers her sarafan and golden braid. Her brown face freezes; the hazel eyes stop blinking. Mother stares at me, a drowned woman pulled out of the water too late.

I cannot tell if the horses and their masked riders have also been frozen.

The ravens have not. They fly toward me in a flurry of oily wings and deafening screeches, pecking at me, clawing at my clothes, exposing my skin to the ice until I feel quite numb and dead.

Interlude

I T IS AS if Selica is dead. Her body, half-submerged in Nav's plain, is numb, perfectly still. And as she lies there, she remembers.

She had been born not of love, but of duty and obligation between two gods.

There is almost nothing to remember about the Heavens, her isolated childhood. The pale green quartz of the palace, impenetrable, confining; the ivy at the windows, meant to keep her in, the outside world out. She can still hear her echoing footsteps and her heart, throbbing at the smallest noise, hoping it was Mother or Father. They had been too preoccupied, always absent, always in the Land of the Living.

When Selica had turned seven, a chariot had come for her. Her feet were icy by the time she leapt into the dewy, star-strewn dawn. "Mama?" But hope was useless; her mother was not there. Selica knew she had to climb into the chariot, and she did.

It was silent as the chariot started its descent, the gods and goddesses sleeping like the sun. They went through clouds that enveloped them in cool mist, into the azure sea of the sky, past screaming blue jays toward the land. She yearned to see the mortals she had heard about, yet she could not. Only a fragrant expanse of green, mountains tumbling, sharp-edged cliffs plummeting, a valley flung out in all directions.

The chariot hit the earth with a teeth-shattering, earsplitting crash before plunging into the ground. Selica slipped to the floor in horror. The earth clawed at the chariot as if she wanted to devour it and Selica whole, pulling them in, burying them alive. She screamed, a tiny, sad sound, as worm-infested dirt poured in.

She continued to cower in her corner long after they had stopped, spitting dirt, seeing nothing but quiet darkness. The beating of wings emerged suddenly. Not those of a butterfly or a bird, but of something far too heavy for flight.

"Do you intend to sit there for all eternity, little goddess?"

Selica blinked up in bewilderment.

Over the chariot hovered a furry black dog with scarlet wings. His eyes glinted red like polished jasper stones. She knew him—his fame had reached even her.

"Simargl," she breathed, transfixed by his wings. They glimmered, slick as fresh blood, gossamer as the most delicate of spiderwebs. "Are you to guard me, then?"

She had heard he was the divine guardian of seed and new shoots. Wayward young goddesses, too. But having been imprisoned all her life, she had not learned waywardness. In the weak, watery light, she saw mountains buried deep in the earth, caves with yawning insides, the ground for a sky. "No one told me," she whispered.

"No one had to." His voice was a wet bark. "You were born thus. The Universe willed it. Better to reconcile yourself to your fate, little goddess, or eternity will be long."

A pitiful ache in her heart. "Am I to rot here for all eternity?"

"Until the Universe and the gods will otherwise." Simargl flapped his wings, once, and red welts formed on each of Selica's wrists. "You are free to roam the caves, but not beyond them, or pain will greet you."

Another prison, a sentence handed down by some invisible, biased judge. Selica looked down at her small and trembling body. "Am I truly that dangerous?"

"You will be. You are of Chernobog, of darkness, and you are the Lady of Rebirth. You can be reborn."

Her skin, still filthy, prickled. "As what?"

"A monster. But it is not time, ergo the chains when you bathe. You must not drown. Not yet. You will be most dangerous when you drown."

No monsters lurked in her, though. "I do not understand."

"You will."

She did, eventually, years later. She grew into a woman in that cold, dark cave, with only the winged dog for company and, occasionally, a school of rusalkas traveling through the river where she was allowed to bathe, in iron shackles, once per month.

In those days, Selica dreamed of a man who would rescue her, with blue-gray eyes like the sea and golden hair that burned fiery in the starlight. He would be a warrior, honorable and brave. And he would be human; gods were too ancient, too tired, too still. They were too hardhearted. But this man, this rescuer of hers, had never come.

Just as no one saved her then, no one saves her now. A snarl rips through her throat, and Selica rears up from the ground, hot and vengeful. She will do it all. As she has all her life, Selica will save herself.

11

I AWOKE FROM MY dream of Mother with a gasp.

Mokosh had not been at the end of that road the day I had returned to find our village all but burned down, yet I had just dreamed her as never before. She had been so real. The dream had touched my heart and soul with such detail and meaning that it felt almost like a visitation from a living god. *Do not despair, Yaga*, she had said. Was Mother not as dead as I had previously believed, trapped in some place not of this world?

I wished I still had her medallion. But it had vanished long ago. I searched for it in the chest where I had hidden it for safety within Little Hen, but I could not find it.

The seaweed-green hangings were sealed shut around the bed, along with a heavy curtain of velvet. Shadows stirred, of wings and beaks and talons. I pulled the linen to my chin, feeling the beginning of a smile on my lips as I stared up at the smooth, dark wood of the bed's canopied ceiling, imagining finding Mother and saving her.

I became aware of a ringing in my ears, the bells in the Ivan the Great Tower, and the howls and yelps of royal hounds sounding. I pushed aside the bed's curtains. An acrid smell burned into me instantly. I gasped for air, but found only smoke beyond the window. And there was ice on the shutters, reflecting flames. I imagined the snowdrops, growing like a pestilence at Nav's passageway, and the smell of snow.

The rest of Mother's words came back to me. *It is not my death you should be worried about.*

Ravens spying, even in dreams, did not bode well. Was the dream a warning from Mokosh?

I threw a shawl over my shoulders, and I rushed out the door without any further delay.

The immaculate Prince's Yard had descended into chaos. The stiflingly, proper aristocratic ladies were in their underthings, screaming and gesturing at harried, half-dressed servants dragging heavy chests in their wake. The ladies' bare-chested husbands were rushing about with buckets of water. Guards shed their coats, hats, and muskets as they ran. My eyes followed them, pulse barely there, to the plumes of smoke surging into the air—from the Terem Palace.

It was on fire.

I stared at the blinding flames as they consumed every wooden plank, every decorated shutter, every building block of luxury. Like the flames that had consumed my village, that had killed Mother and so many of our friends and neighbors.

If Anastasia was inside, if Ivanushka or his brother . . .

I let go of my shawl and started to run, not caring about my sleeveless rubakha. I peered at the ladies, hoping to see the tsaritsa as I had once hoped to see Mother. They had kept Anastasia from me since my return, but I had to get to her now.

"Where is Her Majesty?" I asked a man hurrying past with two pails of water.

He spared me no glance as he sprinted toward the palace. An alarmingly large hole gaped above the floor with the royal looms. She could not be in that chamber of gold cloth and priceless silk, could she? No, she was alive. She had to be alive.

The tsar was at the head of the firefighters. He thrust his arm into the air, his hair flaring the brilliant orange of the fire behind him. As if he felt me watching him, he turned a soot-stained face in my direction. At the hatred in his gaze, my body stilled in wait. But he was already charging into the flames, the moment gone.

Suddenly, a pair of hands grasped my waist, and a man's arms came around me. He pulled me tightly to his bare chest. I let out a piercing scream. My shoeless feet rose into the air, my rubakha billowing not at all prettily, as I kicked against him desperately. But it was useless. Between the shouts of the firefighters, the wails of the women and children, the hiss and crackle of the flames, no one would hear me.

The man stopped in the long shadow of a church. Where I should have felt his heart, beating at my back, there was nothing.

"Is she safe?" I asked. "Are the princes?"

Koshey's arms loosened, slid to my waist, stayed there. "Yes," he said.

"What happened?" I stepped away and turned to a Koshey who was thinner, with soot and grime coating his cheeks.

"No one knows. The fire started at dawn, about eight hundred meters west of the Kremlin walls, on Arbat Street. It has since been burning through Moscow."

"Curious how the rest of the Kremlin is not on fire . . ."

It was impossible for a fire to have originated on Arbat Street without disturbing the other palaces. Some villain was using it to cover up his own fire. Could this villain be the same who was poisoning the tsaritsa? Had the poison proved too slow?

Koshey did not meet my gaze, neither confirming nor denying my suspicions. What did he know? Could he be Anastasia's poisoner?

"The entire city should be rebuilt from stone," he was saying. "Each summer we deal with the nightmarish cycle of heat wave upon heat wave, followed by fire—"

"Where is Anastasia?" I interrupted.

When I had not been trying to see her or send messages and animals to her, I had spent the past three days pacing my chamber or in a dazed half sleep, imagining her poisoner near and fearing the arrest that would take me from her side. Now she seemed farther than ever and had probably been moved to different quarters.

Koshey took a deep breath. "She was taken . . . elsewhere."

"Is she alone?"

"The widow Katrina has arrived from Dorpat to keep her company. Her Majesty has suffered a relapse, and Katrina is known for curing— ah, chyort voz'mi!" Koshey swore, then flung his arms around my neck. "I beg you, leave court, Yaga. Save yourself before it is too late."

I smelled the flames on his skin, the smoke in his beard. I felt his body against mine. "Save myself? From what?" I demanded, freeing myself from him.

"I cannot tell you—" Koshey grasped my shoulders, the cold from his fingers shooting into the ink on my skin, of a horse's mane, whipping in the wind. "But all this is larger than you and me. Avoid it—"

I twisted from under his hands, pushed him away so he stumbled back against the church. "What is larger than us?"

Koshey's eyes were very wide. Were they lighter than usual, the way they were when he spoke of Russia, when he reverted to his humanity, a man with a heart? He waved a hand at the rushing humans. "We are immortals; we will go on when they will not." His voice dropped to a whisper, losing none of its intensity. "And we care for one another. At least, *I* care for you. Trust me when I say you need to leave."

He was real in this moment, stripped of his sport, his vanity. The man I had wanted him to be with the words I had wanted to hear. But it was too little too late. It was more than possible my losing the tsar's favor was Koshey's doing. The more I thought about it, the more it became clear that Koshey stood to gain more than anyone else. And even if it wasn't him, he was obviously keeping things from me. *He is poison*, Aleksey had said of Koshey. He was, and I had known it. I hardened toward him. I couldn't believe the glimmer of light. I wouldn't.

"You are trying to make me abandon a dying woman." I swallowed hard, tasting ash. "No, all you care about are bets and princes, to hoard your power and riches—"

"Is that truly what you think of me?" he said thinly, his face a mask of soot, skin, and bones. "That I am only after ambition and coin?"

"I think you or someone under your influence tricked the tsaritsa into believing Aleksey was forgiven, then sent me into a trap, all to get rid of me so you could have the tsar to yourself, and for me to lose the only mortal who has ever truly mattered to me, the only reason I came to this gods-forsaken city." I felt the sting of tears, in horror that it had all been for nothing, and that Koshey's betrayal reached this far.

"Fine," he said, resigned. He wasted no effort in denying my charge. "You have made your feelings for me perfectly clear. Just know I have tried to warn you." After a minute, he added, "I will tell you where she is if you wish it."

"I do wish it," I said coldly, and meant it. I was done with this court, the tsar, Koshey and his warnings. What remained was to find Anastasia, to save her—if I could.

"ANASTASIA!" I RUSHED into the tightly shuttered chamber of her new quarters at the Kremlin, some distance from the fire consuming the Terem Palace. Incense smothered any traces of the smoke from outside. Icons crowded the painted walls like merchants at the posad, the saints selling not caviar and cakes but the promise of everlasting life.

As if mortals would be eager for it if they knew what it truly entailed.

"Yaga?" A small, kokoshnik-laden head appeared from behind the sumptuous curtains of ruby-red tartarine enclosing the four-poster bed. Sallow skin, sores at the mouth, pink rimming the eyes. Despite the heat, the tsaritsa wore multiple gowns under a scarlet fur-lined dushegreika that ended at her waist in a burst of ruffles.

"My dear Anastasia Romanovna, you must take off some of this heavy clothing. Come, I will help you." I reached for her jacket, but she laid a clammy hand on mine.

"It is too late, my dear." Her breathing was labored. "One of my feet is already in the other world . . ." She trailed off and stared into the space between us. "I cannot feel it."

"Anastasia?" I fumbled with her clothes, loosening the laces of her jacket and prying the velvet open, then unclasping the gold collar at her throat and undoing the pearl buttons of her outer gown.

Anastasia coughed as though a weight had been lifted.

If only I had the Water of Life! If only that spoiled, selfish tsar had let me tend to her, and she had not sent me to Aleksey. If only I had kept my promise of protecting her and finding the person who was hurting her. If only, if only. *Enough, Yaga.*

I tore off her kokoshnik and veil, pulling out a lock of her hair. "We need—"

"No, Yaga. Katrina or Kira will be back soon. It is a miracle you are even here." The tsaritsa made a motion to rise. But the linen sheets, woolen blankets, and decorative coverlets proved too heavy. She sank back down. "I want you to promise me—" The breath caught in her throat; her lips went the pure white of swans' wings.

Swans differed from other birds, their language one of stillness and peace. Some even said they were fallen angels. As dear Anastasia fought to breathe, I hoped an angel—if angels existed—would watch over her.

"Promise me you will care for my sons, especially Russia's heir and future, Ivanushka," she whispered at last. "Protect and keep him. Help him as he grows into a man. Give him wisdom and knowledge. Teach him to be pious and kind, to care for people and to be a good prince, to love this land as he loves his mother. Protect him from—" Her words were a prayer. She stared past me to somebody else. Her god, maybe.

"You shall do all that yourself, my dear Anastasia Romanovna." I took her face in my hands. "Now, you *can* be saved," I said with more confidence than I felt; the poison had accumulated in her to such an extent, and the rituals had taken so much of her energy . . . "It is worth trying," I added anyway.

"Do you really think—?" Her lower lip trembled. "Then help me! Help me!"

"I will, but I must retrieve my implements first." I kissed her burning forehead, something catching my eye—a tiny green spot on the neckline of her gown.

It was very, very subtle, a drop or two, no more. I ran a finger over the spot, but it was crusted over. I sniffed at it, but it didn't smell of anything. I glanced around Anastasia's chamber. Except for a few dead spiders, nothing out of the ordinary.

Hesitating, I went to the door. "If anyone enters, pretend to sleep," I instructed Anastasia, still glancing about.

Just then, I glimpsed a mark on the floor next to her bed. I walked over and examined it. A footprint, dried dark green, as if someone had been walking in the woods, in the mud and moss, before stepping into this chamber. Or perhaps it was only dirt. Gods knew there was a lot of it with the fires this summer.

"What is it?" Anastasia leaned over the bed, craning her neck.

"Do not worry yourself, Anastasia Romanovna," I said soothingly. "I shall return as soon as possible."

I sped through silent passageways, down an equally silent staircase. I had never seen a palace so eerie, so unnaturally empty. Every man had been summoned to help quench the fire. Every woman was preoccupied with her household. No guards stood irritatingly keen and alert in the doorways. No courtiers kissed lustfully in the twisting corridors. No servants rushed by with kvass or fruit juices. It was as if I found myself in an abandoned tomb. All I could do was pray to Mother to keep Anastasia safe.

My mind was still in that room, thick with incense and death, and on the green footprint beside the tsaritsa's bed. I did not notice the guards in front of my chamber until it was too late. I ran straight into their outstretched arms, only realizing something was wrong when I felt the dizzying number of hands on my body, the cold, hard muzzle of a musket digging into my back.

"Yaga Mokoshevna, you are hereby under arrest by order of our most illustrious lord and master, Grand Prince Ivan Vasilyevich of Vladimir, Moscow, Novgorod, Pskov, Tver, Smolensk, Yugorsk, Perm, the land of the Bolgars, and many other lands, tsar and sovereign of all Russia!"

It was Koshey, all powdered and oil-haired, his indigo-blue kaftan dripping violet gemstones, his cap lined with white fur, his leather boots polished and pointed at the toes.

"What are you doing?" I demanded, struggling against the hands that held me.

"You are accused of various acts of treason, including—"

"Chyort voz'mi, Koshey, Anastasia is dying!"

"Koshey? There is no one here by that name." He looked up from the yellow-edged scroll from which he had been reading. His eyes were devoid of light, a placid sea of black, like the River of Nav before it was frozen. "I am Konstantin Buyanovich, and it is my duty to root out traitors of Russia, the tsarship, and the royal family."

"This goes beyond us, Koshey!" My voice had risen to a scream, echoing in the empty corridor, against the quiet walls, into the silence of the palace. "I need to save her. Please let me save her, then you can take me! Don't let an innocent woman die—"

"The crimes you have been accused of are—" Koshey was intent on the scroll, as if he would blot me out. "Firstly, of plotting against and seeking to depose our most illustrious lord and master, Grand Prince Ivan Vasilyevich of Vladimir, Moscow, Novgorod, Pskov, Tver, Smolensk, Yugorsk, Perm, the land of the Bolgars, and many other lands, tsar and sovereign of all Russia, by means of volshebstvo—"

I froze at the hateful word, *magic*. The vile, deceitful, heartless bastard!

"—and by conspiring with our lord tsar's enemies, Aleksey Fyodorovich Adashev and Sylvester, to that end."

My heart throbbed. It was as I had feared. No, it was immeasurably worse. I had been ready to leave court, to take Anastasia with me, if it came down to it. But this?

"Secondly, of plotting to overthrow the Orthodox faith and replace it with paganism by undermining our Church's laws." The cross on Koshey's chest glittered. Its rubies seemed to wink at me condescendingly, as if saying, *Fool! Fool! Fool!* "Thirdly, of plotting against the grand princess and tsaritsa of Russia, Anastasia Romanovna Zakharyina-Yurieva, by means of spell-casting, magic charms, demonic potions—"

"I am trying to save her," I said through gritted teeth, "as you well know."

"You visited her chambers, did you not?" Koshey's voice held no familiarity. "Do not seek to deny it. We have numerous witnesses attesting you were there for—" He turned to a small white-haired man in a hat almost as tall as him, like a lesovichok wood sprite with a mushroom balanced on his head. "How long was it?"

"Ten minutes, your lordship," the man said in a high-pitched squeak.

"Ten minutes!" Koshey's gaze did not leave mine. "Surely enough time to slip a tainted potion through the poor tsaritsa's lips. And who are the witnesses?"

"The Great Mistress Kira Armikovna—"

The flush was hot on my cheeks; I did not listen to the rest.

"By these acts," said Koshey, "you have committed treason against Russia, the tsarship, and the royal family. You are to be imprisoned indefinitely at the pleasure of our most illustrious lord and master, Grand Prince Ivan Vasilyevich—"

"I am well aware of his *illustrious* titles." I felt the influx of blood to my skin, the rage building within. If Koshey refused to let me save Anastasia, if he blamed and imprisoned me, he might as well be the tsaritsa's murderer. Before, we had bet and competed, yet we had never betrayed. And I would never forgive him this betrayal. No, he wasn't just darkness and poison. He was devoid of any humanity. He was a monster. "Is this how you care? Ha! A man with no heart cannot care for anything. He is not capable of it." The words were a vicious snarl. I had not realized I had spat at him.

Koshey blinked. The spittle slid down a cheek that had lost its color. He took out a handkerchief the red of a deep blush and brought it to his face. For a second, it looked like blood was spilling down his kaftan. He leaned toward me, his breath cool in my ear. "If heartless is all you believe me to be, then let it be so," Koshey said in a low, perfectly steady voice. "Remember this moment later, when you wonder how we became not friends, but enemies." He stepped back, his gaze drifting over me coldly. Then he signaled to the guards. "Take the witch out of my sight."

As they forced me into the corridor, the satin of Koshey's kaftan grazed the bare skin of my arm. I saw that his face had crumpled, his body hunched, as if he were a man who had lost everything. What would happen to Anastasia? And to Russia and her people, if her tsaritsa were to die? In horror, I started to shout, to kick, to struggle against the guards, who only held me tighter. My mother, frozen and dead, flitted across my mind. And the ravens, pecking at me, thrusting their wings into my eyes, into my mouth, until I was being blinded, choking on feathers. Blackness swept over me, and I felt and saw no more.

13

23 JULY 1560

HEAT HOVERED OVER Moscow like an unpleasant thought. The heavy wooden door of my cell was hard at my back as I lay there, stiff and hopeless, in the rubakha I had been arrested in nearly a week ago. The rushes on the earthen floor shifted under me, emitting the foul stench of piss and droppings left by a surprising variety of rodents.

I wanted to find myself in my woods with Little Hen and never leave them again.

Mother had once told me the safest way of life for a half god like me was to live among mortals. "We need them as much as they need us," Mokosh responded when I asked her why she had settled in the village of my birth.

"Was my father from here?" I persisted. She was not telling all.

A shadow had drifted across her brown features. She did not speak of my father, whoever he had been. She only said, in her unflinching, goddess way, "You must learn to coexist with humanity, Yaga. The mortal blood in your veins demands it."

As the sun's rays spilled into my cramped cell, dust flitting in the light like snow, I truly doubted Mother. When I became involved in mortal affairs that were more than healing, it ended in heartbreak. I was not fool enough to believe I had no need of mortals, but when I had tried to coexist with them, they had turned on me. To them, I would always be a witch, the cursed Baba Yaga hag. I shifted so I wouldn't see the horse, Mother's symbol, inked into my shoulder.

The bells had quieted, yet the fire still burned through the city. Its acrid smell lodged in my nose. I closed my eyes and saw the blackened remains of my childhood, the tarnished medallion, all that was left of Mother. I recalled the days after the fire, finding survivors, pulling victims from the rubble, healing their burns and injuries, comforting those near death. Afterward, unable to bear a life without Mother in that village, I had left, traveling all around, in search of acceptance, of home, indeed, of love.

I would find it among people, with friends like Zora, only to lose it when they inevitably branded me a witch and chased me off. There had been nothing left but to settle in my woods. Though I had Little Hen, my animal companions, and clients, it had been a lonely existence. Anastasia had reminded me that I was alive and breathing, worthy of belonging among people, even of love and friendship. And unlike Zora, she had never betrayed me.

During my imprisonment, I listened feverishly for news of her.

Instead of the prisons of the Annunciation or Moskva River Towers, Koshey had me confined in a cellar in Prince's Yard. My punishment was to be close enough to the life of the Kremlin that I could hear, smell, taste it, yet far enough that I couldn't see it.

Most courtiers had left Moscow for the safety of their smoke-free country estates. The few who remained rushed by my window in a whirl of muddied skirts and ash-covered boots, holding hectic, whispered conversations I heard in snatches. "He is beside himself." "He sent her to . . ." "Poor woman. No one should suffer thus."

Clearly, the tsaritsa was no longer at the Kremlin. I had sent a few tabbies, two stray shepherds, and a beady-eyed rat to find out more. Aside from one kitty's unfavorable report that Anastasia's scent had vanished, I heard nothing, not even from Dyen and Noch. Had they been captured? I sifted through my options for escape. But the animals barely answered my calls, the guards were armed and numerous, and the cell was infuriatingly secure.

I thought about that footprint, if it were possible an immortal was hurting the tsaritsa. Whose could it be? And why had I never seen one like it before? If the poisoner thought I was unable to reach the tsaritsa, their work complete, was there no more need to hide? Had they not cared to cover their tracks, or had they been too rushed?

The footprint reminded me of grass and trees, the green of the forest. It could point to Vodyanoy, the old Water Lord out in the rivers who dragged people underwater and enslaved rusalkas. There were the rusalkas themselves, drowned maidens turned sirens unable to let go of the Land of the Living. There were other sprites, nymphs, and spirits—the poleviks and poludnitsas of the fields and meadows, the treelike leshy, mushroom-topped lesovichoks, Wild Ones, and vily fairies of the forests. But like the gods, these spirits had not been seen in a very long time and never by me.

Back in my cell, the smell of tobacco wafted over to me, and I limped to the tiny window. Two pairs of marmalade-dyed boots were visible behind the iron grille above my head. I pressed my ear to the wall. There was no smoke without a pinch of gossip.

"What is the news?" A man's voice, a guard, young. "I am about to gouge my eyes out from boredom. When did the Kremlin become so tedious?"

A snort. "When the tsar took his tsaritsa and all her ladies to Kolomenskoye."

That meant Anastasia was at a royal estate more than eleven kilometers from Moscow!

"Did the widow ever heal her?" asked the first man. "Our tsar paid a pretty penny for her. Heard he promised her the entire city of Dorpat for the tsaritsa's life."

"I wish my life was worth that much," the other remarked wistfully. "Or maybe it matters not. Our saintly Anastasia is on her deathbed, after all."

I clutched at my chest, the breath knocked out of me. Deathbed?

"Could be a rumor," said the first man. "They multiply like roaches around here."

His friend grunted. "Here we are, firefighting, drinking ourselves blind, fucking every woman in sight, and our holy tsaritsa is dying from the fine air of Kolomenskoye."

"Ah, but see, that is the poetry of existence! One man will live a safe life and still die at thirty. The other will live like me and not die at all."

"You are immortal now?"

"Maybe if I fuck our prisoner. She *is* a vedma, the famous Baba Yaga—"

I turned from the wall with a bitter taste in my mouth. Our tsaritsa dying did not remotely faze these men. I scratched at my arms, leaving bloody red lines on my skin.

This blood, my mortality, was what made me so weak, so at the mercy of these mortals who only wanted to vilify me, to create a Baba Yaga out of me. Mother had urged me to try to coexist with mortals, yet she had never taught me to truly protect myself from them, and from the other forces unknown to me, the gods, the spirits, the creatures of our world, whoever was trying to kill Anastasia. The gods, too, had turned their backs on me ever since Mother's death severed my connection to them.

I paced my cell, imagining blood seeping into alabaster stones, a corpse in snow, and darkness, descending moonless and mournful over the frosted streets of Moscow.

Interlude

UNDER A NIGHT sky buried in black clouds, heat rises off the country road in a mist more appropriate to a long-abandoned grave site. A large man walks there, his cloak the color of ice in shadow, his cheeks glowing with divinity, his beard spilling out in waves of alabaster white. In his wake, frost appears, stirring up winter when she least expects it.

The wrought iron gate in front of Morozko opens easily, willed to do so.

"Advance no farther, old man." A solitary guard with nervous eyes raises his musket, props it on one tense shoulder. He smells snow.

The night, though edged with summer light, is shadowy. The other guards sleep, hot and lazy with drink. Even if they rise up like the dead, Morozko will still carry out his task. He wishes to converse with the guard, to peer into him as only a god can. But a command is a command. He pushes aside his loneliness and lifts his silver scythe.

The guard stills horribly. His nervous eyes bulge as ice spreads from his feet to his head until his body is as frozen as a statue. Morozko glides past the corpse to the manor-turned-prison of the disgraced courtier, Aleksey Fyodorovich Adashev.

The god lifts his scythe, and frost stitches over the window shutters, the bronzed doors, the stone and wood of the house. Near its foundation, snowdrops burst through the cracked soil. The manor glistens, dreamlike and silvery, sprinkled with winter.

A motion of Morozko's hand, and the light pouring between the shutters goes out. Aleksey Fyodorovich will share his kinsman's fate to be frozen in his prime far from court, a death sentence handed down by fickle gods. Death is unsavory. But that is why the Lord of Winter is here. To live, not die; to enjoy summer, not sleep through her.

On another country estate, the tsaritsa of Russia awakens in her bed, this time of walnut wood and wine-red damask. She does not know she is at her husband's palace in Kolomenskoye. It is dark, so dark, the same as the blackness she has surfaced from, but her throat feels tight, as if fingers pressed there as she slept.

"Your Majesty!" A face comes into focus, small and cruel, almost birdlike.

"Kira Armikovna," Anastasia forces out. Her mouth is dry, so dry. Before she knows it, there is a drop of something foul on her lips, green and grasslike.

Then blackness, heavy and suffocating.

Kira Armikovna hastily pulls at her skin until the wound stops secreting the sap, her lifeblood, poisonous to anyone but her. It drains, strangles, brings nightmares. There is a smear of green on her sleeve. A spider crawls along the cuff. Kira Armikovna pulls the sleeve up, takes the spider by its legs, and pops it into her mouth. She is hungry.

The emerald-green satin walls glimmer in the candlelight not unlike the swamp's surface when the sun tears through the clouds. All of a sudden, Kira Armikovna is homesick. She leans over her patient; the tsaritsa's breathing is labored, her skin the white of snowdrops. A few minutes away will not change anything.

Kira Armikovna stands, seeing her wet footprints on the floor, the usual effect of using even a little of her sap. She had no choice but to be vigilant with Baba Yaga at the Kremlin, but thanks to her foresight in burning down the Terem Palace, the witch is imprisoned and quite cowed, Kira Armikovna safe and slightly less vigilant, though she must still watch herself. She has been told Koshey Bessmertny cannot know.

She takes a candle and goes to the tapestry behind the bed, to the door hidden there, her own secret chamber conveniently close; her chamber at the Kremlin was too far. And spied on constantly by Baba Yaga and her minions, whom she had taken care of.

In her chamber, Kira Armikovna sets the candle down beside a massive bathtub. She peels the clothing from her skin and bones and gets into the tub. The cool water is fragrant with moss. It dispels her disguise. A green tinge creeps up her graying hair, which grows disheveled, her skin wrinkling and her back hunching.

Moths appear, then a reddish-orange roach pokes its whiskered head over the tub's rim. Not as nutritious as a black beetle, or even a spider, but it will do. Kira Armikovna snatches up the creature and shoves it into her mouth, leaning back with pleasure. She has missed her baths, unable to take them while Baba Yaga was at court. Except Kira Armikovna's body had become as parched as a desert, then nearly overflowed with sap. If not for the fire, she would have died. She needs the swamp, a piece of it, to survive on land. She needs the chaos of nature, sprouting, living, killing.

But Kira Armikovna will return to the swamp soon, the largest in all the lands, her reward for poisoning the tsaritsa of Russia.

In another palace, in the darkened Granovitaya Palata, the tsar sits on his throne with only his advisor for company. His clothes smell of flames, of filth, of neglect. The tsar doesn't wash or change, doesn't stop fighting the fires burning through Moscow. He cannot stop. For if he does, his fear of tomorrow will swallow him whole.

"The plans for the new palace for the tsarevich and his brother are coming along nicely, Your Majesty," Koshey says as Konstantin Buyanovich, showing the tsar the parchment with the pictures and diagrams, the lines leading to nowhere.

But the tsar says, "Once I vanquish this conflagration sent by the Devil, I shall hold a bonfire in Prince's Yard, to show Him that his flames cannot injure us. There, we shall execute one of his number, an adherent of his wicked practices, a treasonous witch who has outstayed her welcome at my court." A hatred lights the tsar's worn features. Hatred is all he has now; it saves him from the heart-wrenching sorrow.

The parchment slips from Koshey's fingers; he catches it just in time. A fire? What would it do to her? *Would* it kill her? It has been a long time since Yaga was in his life, yet he cannot imagine himself without her. "Do you really . . . that is to say, do you, my lord tsar, believe the witch poisoned the tsaritsa, given that she healed—?"

"Of course she did!"

"But my lord tsar, she arrived *after* Her Majesty fell ill—"

"And what of it?" the tsar rounds on his servant. "There could be multiple poisoners! The witch is in league with Aleksey, maybe even Sylvester, and God knows who else! My cousin? Anyone! Perhaps they have all been poisoning Her Majesty!"

Koshey bows his head. But he cannot give up. "A trial will be expected—"

"No trial." The tsar's voice is a whisper. "Heathens don't deserve one. My wife's poisoners don't deserve one. They will pay—they will *all* pay—for what they've done."

"Who, my lord tsar?"

"Everyone."

"My lord tsar, permit me to—"

But there is a glint in the tsar's eyes, unfocused, wild, like that of a beast breaking all restraints, breaking free. "Execution. We will have an execution."

"It is late, my lord tsar. And the last days have been trying—"

"You mean the conflagration, or my beloved wife forced to the brink of death? No, I have no need of daylight to make up my mind. It is made. She shall die—"

"What if . . . she shall not?" Koshey hesitates. "There are some that avail themselves of the belief that witches do not burn easily."

"Then I shall kill her with my bare hands," says the tsar of Russia, turning from his advisor. He will destroy everyone in his way. The vedma, his former advisors, any boyar or noble who dares to speak against him. His darling will live, and he will be the greatest ruler that Russia has ever seen. Or he will tear her apart.

14

※

6 AUGUST 1560

I AWOKE ONE AUGUST morning, coughing and wheezing, a sharp pain dazing me. In my sleep, I had been climbing a mountain of glass when I stumbled. All was translucent below, the land iron gray and hazy with clouds. There was a burst of red as my knees crashed into the glass. Fragments of it had flown at my throat, cutting into me, bloodying me.

Brushing aside the rushes, I peered at my knees to be sure it had been a dream. Sure enough, there was no blood, no gashes. But when I took a breath, the same pain stabbed my throat like tiny shards of glass. A cloud of smoke hovered in the air, thicker than it had been since the Terem Palace caught fire nearly three weeks earlier.

The door to my cell opened with a sudden, jarring scrape. A large hairy hand reached in, depositing a pewter bowl with my daily breakfast of burnt kasha.

"Has another fire broken out?" I tasted the acrid smell of flames and leapt to the door.

The hand withdrew hastily. "Hmph!" the guard grunted in answer. He shut the door with more than the usual bang.

The smoke deepened to the iron-gray shade of the land in my dream.

I tore off the hem of my rubakha and tied the dirty but smoke-free scrap of linen around my mouth. I paced, trying and failing to keep my thoughts from the dream.

Some called Nav the Thrice-Tenth Kingdom. It was said a mortal could reach it by climbing a mountain of glass and jumping down. Since I could not venture past the River of Nav, I could not attest to the veracity of this. I wondered if the dream meant that Earth was becoming its own version of Nav, the ground beneath me as uncertain as glass.

I had no awareness of time until a few pearly bellied mice scuttled across my cell. I rushed at them with inquiries. But they hopped up to the windowsill and disappeared through the grille. By the time a swarm of black roaches trickled past me and out of the building, uneasiness had settled into me. I scratched at my arms, the wounds there reopening.

Rapid footsteps started to echo outside my cell, followed by the crash and groan of heavy objects. Buckets? Chests? The smoke coiled black. It burned my nose and throat, seared my lungs, filled my mouth with ash. I doubled over in fits of coughing that left me breathless from gagging, the heat scorching my skin and stinging my eyes.

Bells were tolling. The Ivan the Great Tower had the only belfry at the Kremlin; no church in the city was allowed to toll ahead of it. Not that I would be able to hear it, even if it did. All I could hear was the roaring of the flames, now outside my window. The fire had come to the izba with the cellar, with me locked inside.

The wooden logs caught fire too quickly. Before I knew it, the wall I had leaned against to listen to the guards' talk was dissolving. Twisting, crackling, snapping flames fought to claim every last plank. Frenzied bits of conversation filled my ears. Footsteps pounded the floors above and outside my door.

"Save yourself while you can!" shouted a man.

"What about the prisoner?" shouted another.

"To hell with her—"

Then the voices and footsteps ceased, and I was alone. "Bastards," I whispered, if only to say something, to convince myself that alone was not so bad.

I had no idea if I could die in a fire, especially since my dream might mean Mother wasn't as dead as I had believed her to be. Perhaps I would emerge from the embers as a firebird, all aglow and shedding ash like scales. Or perhaps my mortal half meant I would succumb to the flames. Though immortal life could feel empty and long, now that it was threatened, I did fear death. I wanted to live.

The building was crumbling, coming down in a shower of white-hot sparks and splintering wood. I inhaled one shaky, smoke-filled breath and sprinted toward the blackened skeleton that had been the wall. I was about to leap into the flames when something soared through the remaining structure. Powerful front legs, a coat of tawny fur, a massive head with amber eyes. Miraculously, inconceivably, it was Dyen.

My wolf rolled onto the spot of ground not strewn with rushes and put out the flames before bounding to me. *Do you intend to stand there as the building crashes down on you?* Dyen asked with a shake of his head.

The tension of the last weeks drained out. I put my arms around his neck and, burying my face in his fur, wept in relief.

Come, Yaga. We do not have time. Get on.

I jumped onto his back, my heart weak with fright. But we were already moving fast, toward the heat, into the fire.

It was so intense, the hair on my skin burned, and smoke pushed into my mouth so deeply that immortality seemed a cruel joke. I could feel Dyen leaping beneath me. Then I heard bells and shouts. I could breathe more freely, though the smoky air still stung.

My arms loosened. We were sprinting through the Kremlin, its golden domes smothered in gray, its courtyards choked with men battling a fire bent on consuming entire royal palaces and cathedrals. Courtiers pointed at us with gaping mouths. Guards dived for their weapons, the blades flashing a blinding silver in the violent light.

The crowd at the gates thickened—a row of guards. Their red greatcoats and orange boots reminded me of a bloody sunset. Their faces were set, unforgiving, bathed in hatred for the woman, the witch, who dared to defy them.

The muzzles of their muskets were against my forehead, grazing my skin, when Dyen launched into the air. The jump was high, higher than I had thought him capable. My stomach plunged as we soared over the guards. I clung to Dyen, this time letting out a whoop of exhilaration, hoping the guards heard it and saw what must have been a wild, incredibly wide smile on my face. My cheeks hurt from it.

Two shots were fired in rapid succession. *Boom! Boom!* Then, "Shut the gates!"

We dashed through the narrowing gap just as the gates closed behind us with a clang. The guards' swearing receded the farther we sprinted into the square.

My smile of triumph fell away as I glimpsed the posad's empty stalls and shops. People must have fled when the fire had started. Broken wood littered the ground where the tables had been. Carts stood abandoned. No one haggled or laughed. No holy fool came to warn people of their sinfulness. The fire was proof of it.

Behind the plumes of smoke, a white sun blazed. The sky was too bright, too sick to look at. A flapping of wings against heavy air, and Noch was hastening forward with my satchel in her talons. Dyen showed no signs of slowing, either, though he rarely appeared once day waned. My chest swelled with warm gratitude for them both.

We turned southeast, speeding past rows of izbas and churches, then beyond the city where the previously emerald fields spread in a sea of burnt yellow, reminding me of corn left too long over the fire. Rusted over and drained of moisture.

The bells chimed violently through Moscow, faint now with the intervening distance. To Nav with Ivan for taking Anastasia from the Kremlin, for banishing me to a cell I couldn't break out of. And to Nav with Koshey for the part he had played in it all.

The sun melted into the horizon. A reddish-orange light stained the sky in its wake. Eventually, the last bit of color seeped away, leaving a blue expanse that was as deep as it was dark. August was shortening the days, darkening the nights.

I turned my face to the east. "Moist Mother Earth, subdue every evil and unclean being so he may not cast a spell on us nor do us any harm,"

I whispered to Mother, the prayer coming out stiff and lifeless. True, it was not said at dawn, neither was it offered with the requisite jar of hemp oil. But the lack of those trappings was not the problem.

My intention, my unwavering faith, had gone. Never had I felt so truly alone. For the world was a desolate place without faith. And for the first time in my life, I did not believe in mortals, in gods, in Mother, not even in myself. My chest constricted with a new kind of emptiness as darkness fell, the road to Anastasia stretching endlessly into the gloom.

15

⁓

7 AUGUST 1560

BLACK-RIMMED CLOUDS SWELLED into the dawn sky, dampening the light and blotting out what faint stars still hung suspended from the Heavens.

Dyen had sprinted with me on his back the entire night. We were close to Kolomenskoye now.

In the distance, a stone wall the color of faded ivory became visible, then the arched entrance with the strangely unguarded iron gate. We sped through it and down a walled lane that cut through ancient trees. Ahead of us loomed a sullen wooden palace with church-like onion domes. My throat tightened at the emptiness of such a large estate, usually crowded with courtiers and servants. The palace's weathercocks stirred in the wind as we went by, scraping on their hinges and emitting a creak that chilled me.

Another set of gates were thrown open with the same abandon as the first. Behind it, a white tower burst into view, followed by the rest of the tent-roofed Church of the Ascension. Its kokoshnik-shaped tiers reminded me of a sleek wedding cake. For a minute, it looked like a wedding really was taking place. Bells rang in the belfry; despite the hour, people milled by the church and on the banks of the Moskva River.

Then I heard the wails, saw the solemn black garb, the lines of grief etched into the tearstained faces, the hands sketching the sign of the cross. The men had their hats crushed under their arms, their canes trampled and forgotten at their feet, and the women were prostrating themselves on the pale and starved grass, skirts and all.

It was not until I caught Anastasia's name, whispered fervently over and over, along with prayers for her soul, that I understood. And suddenly her god was everywhere—in her people, in the sky and grass, even in my old and rusty cross. I grasped the cross with shaking fingers, starting to sob. My vision blurred, the tower seeming to tilt, its layers to melt, the grieving people distorting and becoming misshapen. Yet they could still turn against me. I should have been afraid. After all, I was a witch, an escaped prisoner and wanted woman. But even if they glimpsed my face in the folds of black cloak, I would not care. My knees had buckled, as though I were back on that mountain of glass, and I sprawled on the earth. My gasps tasted of salt and sorrow as I gave full vent to my grief.

When I prayed, it was not to the old gods, not even to Mother. In earnest, with tears falling fast and hot down my cheeks, I repeated the prayers I heard all around me to the Christian god. For my dear friend deserved nothing less than eternal life and paradise in her Kingdom of Heaven.

I was not certain how much time had gone by. It could have been hours, maybe a whole day, that I waited by the Kolomenskoye palace to see Anastasia for myself, to verify that she *had* died, part of me praying that I would not see her coffin, that she would send for me, saying it had all been a misunderstanding, and we would laugh and cry about it, sit in her chambers as we used to and talk or play with her boys.

But the grieving people pressing and jostling against me indicated otherwise. I could hardly breathe, as much from the idea of what was to come, of what I was about to see, as from the odors of incense and humanity mingling in the unbearable heat, and the dust speckling the air like snow.

The light was beginning to leave the sky when the tsaritsa's slim coffin appeared, followed by an entire procession of courtiers. The coffin made its way out of the palace entrance before starting down the alley to Moscow, to Anastasia's final resting place in the Kremlin's Voznesensky Monastery, the repository for Russia's dead princesses.

I clutched at my aching chest, tendrils of pain spiraling up and down my left arm. My heart was splintering, coming apart, breaking.

"Our poor Tsaritsa Anastasia—" A woman nearby wept, her wooden cross imprinting on her forehead. "What a rare jewel she was."

Her friend pressed a brilliantly embroidered handkerchief to her trembling cheeks. "Her beauty, her devotion, her mercy . . ."

"We shall not see the likes of Her Majesty again!"

"We shall not, we shall not."

It was rare for a royal princess to be so loved. Yet that was what I saw as I looked out at the people who had come to pay their last respects to Anastasia Romanovna. There were hundreds of them now streaming after the coffin, filling the lane with their blackest garb, their tallest hats, their most elaborate kokoshniki. Tears ran down their cheeks freely. It was extraordinary that, in spite of a deep faith in their god, these Christians wept unrestrainedly at the sight of death. Instead of hope, they surrendered to their grief and their loss, and they wailed.

One wail rose above the others—that of the tsar.

I tugged on my hood, glancing about me furtively. I had to move. Dyen had already left, as we would be too identifiable together, but not before urging me to follow suit. Yet like in nightmares, my legs refused to move. And, really, what was the harm? The tsar would not see me, not in this crowd, not with his grief blinding him.

Held up by several courtiers, he wept noisily as he trailed the coffin in his black ceremonial feryaz, the velvet hem and sleeves gathering dust.

"What will happen to the tsar now that his tsaritsa is dead and gone?" a man with knotted hair said to no one I could see.

What *would* happen to the tsar? To Russia? Anastasia had dreamed of ravens, of blood, of death. And despite the heat, winter was encroaching on summer, Morozko at large, a very clever assassin having poisoned the tsaritsa of Russia, thereby leaving the tsar to his own impulsivity, entirely uninhibited, vengeful and wild.

The tsar did not seem to be aware of his sons or his people, also griev-ing for Anastasia. The boys were a mere afterthought at the back of the procession, subsumed under the voluminous veils fluttering from the ko-koshniki of the tsaritsa's ladies-in-waiting, though thankfully Kira Armikovna was nowhere to be seen. In the cloud of black gauze, I could barely make out Tsarevich Ivanushka's little face, pinched and red from crying.

Protect and keep him . . .

I felt a stab of guilt for not granting Anastasia's dying wish. But I was disgraced and outmaneuvered by forces stronger than me, mostly because they were unknown. I had not been able to protect Anastasia, to prevent her demise and my heartbreak. I had not even been able to find her as-sassin. If I stayed, the mortals—the tsar and Koshey included—would continue to persecute me, and I would create more trouble for Anastasia's boys. I could only hope that, since the worst had happened, they would be safer without me.

As I had feared, the vision with the corpse before Moscow had been a foretelling of the tsaritsa's death. Now, with the dream of Mother, I had another warning. Something was coming, or someone. Regardless of my doubts and my shaken faith, I had to try to reach the gods, perhaps even attempt to find my mother. To discover what was happening in Russia, what the unknown forces were and why they had targeted my Anasta-sia, what the future held—for the country, for Ivanushka, and for me. And maybe I would believe in the gods again. Maybe I would believe in myself.

I would go to the North of Russia, to the taiga, where the mortal kolduns and koldunyas lived, who practiced the earth magic Mokosh had started to teach me—to learn how to reach the spiritual realm with the gods and find the answers that had eluded me in Moscow.

By now, the tsaritsa's coffin had disappeared down the lane. I turned from the palace where Anastasia had died so senselessly, from the proces-sion of courtiers who had found their grief for her so belatedly, and I disappeared into the pressing crowds, walking away from the tsar and his court. Perhaps forever.

Interlude

16 AUGUST 1560

THE COURTIERS AT the Kremlin are trickling out of their chambers. They greet one another with a flood of confusion, with a flurry of questions. The proclamation from their tsar, out too early from seclusion and prayer, is not normal. It states that all mourning for the recently departed tsaritsa, required for forty days by the Russian Orthodox Church, must cease immediately.

"But it hasn't even been ten days since she died!" the courtiers mutter, crossing themselves as though the tsaritsa can see them. But their treacherous hearts leap. They hurry back to their chambers and open the chests concealing their colorful gowns and kaftans. They retrieve their jewels. And they hide their crosses. With grief for the tsaritsa packed away like their hastily shed black clothing, the courtiers smile, and they make merry.

Meanwhile, the dead tsaritsa's husband stands towering and swaying on his throne, flushed with drink. He raises a silver chalice, brimming with wine as red as blood. "I must choose between this world and the other," he says gravely. "Here I go! Watch me, watch me!" He teeters, then jumps. Only, he misjudges the distance. He tumbles down. Wine spills onto his maroon kaftan with the double-eagle-patterned damask.

The tsar raises himself on all fours and licks the wine off the floor.

Between the carousing men and the servants carrying spirits, there are the masked skomorokhi, the jesters that wander through Russia, putting on all kinds of wild entertainments. The skomorokhi at the Kremlin are no different, though they have wandered into the grandest of palaces. They sing lewd songs, play on gusli harps, perform acrobatic tricks. They pretend to be lions, bears, even wolves. They swirl around the tsar, kicking up their legs, a khorovod ring of bloodshot eyes and leering mouths.

Now the tsar is crawling on his knees like a child. He has lost his crown.

"I see a man who looks the part of the tsar," quips one masked skomorokh. "But he crawls, and he licks the floor, as my dogs do!"

"You must still bow to your grand prince and tsar," says another skomorokh.

The first skomorokh sketches the crawling tsar a bow. "Your Majesty!"

Laughter spreads through the men, none of whom are boyars or even nobles.

In the back of the room, despite the unrelenting heat, frost decorates the window like embroidery on a rich woman's sarafan. Morozko stands there and does not laugh. He is thinking of the priest Sylvester, alone in his cell when he had stopped his heart. And the handsome boyar's son, Aleksey, too, frozen just like the priest.

Morozko glides toward the doors, ice creeping after him in silvery footprints.

He wants to stay and engage in frivolity with these mortal men. But he will not waste a minute of his precious time in Moscow on idleness. Not if he wants to return for a second summer. By the doors, Morozko pauses, cannot resist. He presses a palm to the floor, as if to feel its heartbeat, and frost spreads from his hand. He watches the men, the skomorokhi, even the tsar—and they are all dancing on ice.

PART II

Already from the sea there have begun blowing strong
winds into the mouth of the rivers Don and Dnieper. And
they have wafted great clouds over the Russian land, and
these clouds made the sunsets as scarlet as blood . . .

♦

Sofony of Riazan, "Zadonshchina," from
Medieval Russia's Epics, Chronicles, and Tales,
edited by Serge A. Zenkovsky

16

AUTUMN 1560

THE TAIGA OF Northern Russia, just south of the tundra, was made of forest very different from the one I had lived in near Moscow.

It was a dense land, dark and brooding, interrupted only by glassy lakes and cold rivers, bottomless valleys and ravines, detached and never-ending mountain ranges. Everywhere I looked, there were trees. I slid from Dyen's back, my legs cramped and sore after the weeks on the road. We were standing on a pine-scented riverbank under an already darkening sky, though it was only afternoon.

Suddenly, there came a great noise, a cracking and snapping of branches, and out of the trees ambled Little Hen.

Well, Ya, here she is, Noch called out from the hut's roof with a hoot of greeting.

"Here you both are," I said, with tears in my eyes as I patted Little Hen's chicken legs. There was frost on them. "I shall rub some sparrow fat into your legs for protection against the ice," I told Little Hen, giving her one last pat as she rocked from side to side. "Oh, how I've missed you. No palace chamber can compare."

She creaked under my touch and my compliments, hopping a little.

We settled on that riverbank, a cold, lonely existence, especially as autumn took hold and the ice and snow refused to melt. Yet I had my companions and the chickens.

At first, it was hard to forget Moscow. Its feasts and warmth, the constant buzz of activity, Anastasia and her sons. I could not stop imagining that slim coffin; Ivanushka's small white face. I hoped Anastasia had found peace and repose, the tsarevich and his brother safety. I did not pray; praying had not helped them before.

I focused on making a home for me and my companions. I cleaned out my hut, discarded expired potions and salves. My stores were depleted, so I went foraging, mostly for bark, cones, roots, and nettles. Berries, mushrooms, nuts, and herbs, if I were fortunate.

We were snowed in for much of the cold months. It was hard to believe winter had been my favorite season as a child—the cauldron bubbling with a meaty stew or shchi cabbage soup, the pech flaming with cheerful heat as Mother baked fragrant bread and meat pies. Not like the six-month winter in the taiga, where the only comforts were my companions as the blizzards raged outside. Even so, Little Hen bravely withstood it all.

Yet I was growing impatient. When Mother had taught me the earth magic used to enter the Land of the Dead, she had told me mortal koldun and koldunyas could also reach the spiritual realms beyond our world. If I wanted to try contacting the gods and someday Mother herself, I had to locate such a person—so I could learn the earth magic necessary to find the spiritual realms with the gods, and to soak up a little of their wisdom.

With spring the following year, we were finally able to explore. The taiga was isolated from civilization, uninhabited by most beasts, let alone people, yet there were individual homesteads and sparse settlements on the edge of the forests. On one of our longer expeditions, about half a day's ride from our hut, we happened upon one such settlement. It was a dirt road ending in a cold lake with a scattering of wooden farmhouses. The women were out feeding the cattle, the men doing their work in the fields or forest. But none were particularly talkative.

I had Noch listen at the windows for anyone she suspected might be practicing the old ways. One name was mentioned more than most—that of a wise woman called Dusha. Fortunately, my owl also gleaned the woman's whereabouts. The next day, I went in search of her.

Hers was a homestead in a woodland that cut through trees on fire with October's yellow light. Each leaf shone gold like the sun itself. I slid off my wolf in front of what appeared to be the main house, judging by its size relative to the other wooden buildings.

It took no time at all for a wiry woman somewhere in her fifties to answer the door. She wore a sheepskin cloak and had peppery hair threading black and silver through a long braid.

"Are you Dusha?" I asked after pleasantries had been exchanged.

"That depends." Her eyes narrowed. "Who is asking?"

I wanted to lie, to make up a name and identity, to protect myself. But with koldunyas, lying could mean losing their favor even before I had gained it. "I am Yaga, daughter of the Earth Goddess Mokosh," I said simply and truthfully.

"The famous Baba Yaga?"

"You've heard of her—of me—here?"

She studied me with eyes the brown-green of earth in summer. "If you wish to avail yourself of my knowledge," she said at length, "you shall do precisely what I say, without questions or any words at all for as long as I require. If you are ready, and if you are worthy, I shall then teach you what I know."

I almost laughed. If nothing else, this woman had nerve. "You have not even told me if you are the Dusha I am looking for. And here you are, issuing instructions."

"All right," was all she said, with a pull on the door.

"Wait—" I put out a hand, stopping the door before it closed. I took a breath. "How can I tell if you possess the knowledge I seek?"

She raised a long index finger. "Already you are breaking my rules, Baba Yaga."

"Yaga," I said without thinking.

"Breaking my rules again!" She cackled, shook her head, grew suddenly serious. "Like we mortals believe in the gods, you must trust in faith—or feel free to leave."

Ultimately, it was a feeling, mere instinct, that made me agree to her terms. "I shall abide by your rules," I said, resigned. "When do we start?"

She grinned and thrust a pail at me. "First, you shall milk my cow. Then we shall see."

I started to help Dusha on her farm. When I tried to ask her when she would teach me what I wanted to know, she would only raise her index finger, smile her unfathomable smile, and shake her head. Finally, one morning, when Molochko, Dusha's prized cow, kicked me in the face as I attempted to milk her, I stormed into Dusha's house in a rage, with a face that was bloody and hot with pent-up feeling.

"I cannot take it anymore!" I blustered, blood dripping from my nose, getting on my tongue. "It has been weeks, and all I have learned is how to be a farmer!"

"No—" Dusha's sharpness suffused her face in shadow. "I have *tried* to teach you obedience and how to listen. If you become trapped in the Otherworld, or in a land even deeper and farther away, you would need to do precisely what I say, or you will not be able to return at all."

I blinked at her, taken aback. This was the first time Dusha had spoken to me of anything but farmwork. I had heard the spiritual dimension beyond the Land of the Living referred to as the Otherworld, yet I knew very little about it.

"You desire to reach the gods, do you not?" Her gaze was hard. "And you are looking for answers—why the river and passageway into Nav is frozen, why the tsaritsa of Russia is dead, why Russia herself is dying. Am I right, Yaga?"

This was the first time she had asked me a question, and the first time she did not call me Baba Yaga. It was hearing her say my true name that made me decide to fully trust and believe in Dusha. She not only wanted to teach me her mind, but to strip away my arrogance and entitlement, to bring me down to earth where I belonged.

"I am sorry," I said with genuine regret. "If you will still have me, I will do what you say without question. I will trust in you . . . as I trust in the gods." Beyond my anger and confusion, I still believed in them.

Dusha peered into me like no mortal had before. "All right," she said.

The very next morning, Little Hen ambled onto Dusha's land and settled on the edge of the wood. From then on, I did everything that Dusha told me.

I spent each night with Little Hen. And each morning, at the crack of dawn, I walked over to Dusha's homestead and worked all day on her farm. We did so without speaking. Words were excessive, especially in the spiritual dimensions, and could get one into trouble. It was a solitary existence, Dyen and Noch out hunting most days and nights. The loneliness in that dark, cold, snowy place was extreme. And it went on and on.

A few months later, all of them as cool and gray-skied as ever, in a grove of birch trees on the edge of her woodland, Dusha spoke to me. "There are places on this Earth that are sacred—hills, mountains, groves of trees like this one. They are called svetiye mesta, wells of spiritual energy where earth magic is at its strongest." She eyed me shrewdly. "If you have a question, Yaga, ask it."

"I used to," I fumbled for words, "live by the passageway into the Land of the Dead. Was that such a place?"

"Yes, it is said Perun slashed at the fabric between lands there, creating Nav and imprisoning Volos after their first battle for the sky. You see, Earth is multidimensional, from the dimensions here in the Land of the Living to the ones up in the Heavens and down in Nav. These planes, starting with the Otherworld in our dimension, are accessible through holy places. Did your mother teach you to access the natural energy around you?"

"A little, with the ritual to enter the Land of the Dead."

"This is not surprising. Gods do not have the same awareness. You must use your mortality to access nature's energy. Only then will you be able to reach the Otherworld, perhaps even the spiritual dimensions beyond it, and those of the Land of the Dead—with knowledge, time, and practice. You may also reach the beings that live in those dimensions, the spirits, maybe even the gods. But everything has its limits, and everything has a price. Because of our mortal blood, we cannot travel to the World Tree, or see the Heavens."

I sat back, disappointed. "And what is the price?"

"The farther and deeper you travel into the dimensions, the more risk there is." Dusha sat beside me and took my hand in her rough one. Shocked at the human touch, I held my breath. But her skin against mine was warm and comforting. "Natural energy is positive, while the spiritual dimensions are negative and take a toll on the body."

I recalled the weakness I experienced after my visits to the Land of the Dead . . .

"Worse," added Dusha, "you may lose yourself there or not be able to return at all."

I imagined becoming lost in some spiritual plane. Would my body stay here while my mind fled, never to return? "I still want to learn," I said eagerly despite these risks.

"Then close your eyes, Yaga, and raise your arms up to the sky." Dusha's voice was soft and reverent. "Can you feel the cyclone of energy above you in the sky?"

I raised my arms and immediately sensed a force pressing against my fingers, as if the clouds were slowly creeping toward the Earth, toward me.

"Feel your body, Yaga, hollow, waiting to be filled!" chanted Dusha. "It is only with your entire being that you can tap into this place of earth magic, this spot of spiritual power. Feel the energy from the sky and draw it into your body with your arms!"

I felt my heart pounding and my blood heating, then my body emptying. I allowed the energy from the sky to flow into me through my arms until a warm light burst into my every cell, my every organ, my very skin—natural energy, the magic of the earth, spiritual power. It crackled until my entire being vibrated with it, as if I had come in contact with a lightning bolt and swallowed it whole.

Though I had always been attuned to nature, I had never felt it to this extent or felt such power in the earth magic. I had never known how to accept nature into my own body and harness it. Indeed, how to be aware of my body at all. Dusha was right—Mother had taught me the immortal side of earth magic, of doing without awareness, without feeling. With Dusha, I learned to listen to the natural world around me, not only to the sky, the trees, the waters, the very air, but also to myself.

This took time; months, then seasons. Life in the taiga was consuming, and we had no communication with the outside world save for an occasional visit to an isolated settlement. Time sped up immeasurably, leaving me unsure of the exact date or year.

When I was ready, Dusha taught me how to enter the Otherworld. She started in the way of all rituals, with a roaring fire built in our sacred grove of trees.

I stretched my fingertips toward the burning flames and breathed in the smoke before raising my arms to the trees and to the sky, to the power gathered there. I felt the hollowness of my body, and I brought my arms down to earth, ushering in their energy, filling me up with earth magic, with spiritual power, warm and sizzling like sunshine. My energy met with that of the fire in a spark so bright my head snapped back with the impact.

I turned to the ingredients Dusha had helped me to prepare—the white-speckled, red-capped mushrooms, for magic; poppy seeds, to embrace the spiritual; koliuka blossoms, to not miss my target; a little weeper grass with a clove of garlic to ward off any hostile spirits. I released the mushrooms and herbs into the hissing flames.

As Dusha and I started to chant, I pricked my finger with the tip of my blade, and a drop of blood fell into the flames. They flared ever brighter and hotter as Dusha spoke.

"Still your mind, Yaga. Let go of your thoughts, your body, your surroundings. You are nowhere. You are no one. You are nothing."

The light from the fire flickered behind my now-closed eyelids as I let go.

"Now reach out to the Otherworld with your arms and embrace it."

I felt the press of something filmy against my fingertips. It gave like a bubble, and I opened my eyes. There was the fire, the closed-eyed Dusha, the grove of trees. Beyond them, I heard clinking and indistinct chatter. Then a silvery laugh, followed by a waft of air, as if something had flown past. I heard a weeping, too, and a deep rumble, near the frosted-over pond. Before I could venture deeper into the Otherworld, I heard Dusha's voice from very far away: *You must come back now, Yaga.*

I peered into the trees, eager to see the clinking and chatter, but obedience came first. I let go of the Otherworld, came back to my mind and body, blinked my eyes open in surprise—I had thought them already open. Blackness gathered at the edges of my vision. I could barely sit up; weakness weighed me down and made me light-headed.

Later, Dusha told me I had heard the feasting and dancing of the spirits, the leshy and Wild Ones, the lesovichoks and vily fairies. The sad crying of the rusalkas, too, frozen in the pond in winter, and Lord Vodyanoy, complaining about their poor humor.

"Will I be able to see them?" I asked Dusha, trying and failing to conceal my excitement.

She shook her head. "People believe in the spirits less than ever, Yaga, less even than they believe in the old gods. You will hear them, maybe feel them, but you will rarely see them even in the dimensions. They have withdrawn from humanity."

"What about the gods? My mother?"

"Your immortality may allow you to reach certain gods. But most have withdrawn to the Heavens. If they climb down the World Tree to the living, they do so in a dimension past the Otherworld. It is unclear how far or how deep. It would take—"

"Knowledge, practice, and time." I sighed, brushing the grass off my knees.

Dusha gave a nod. "And strength."

Weakness still pulled at me, though I had eaten some berries to revive myself.

"There are several conditions for when you attempt to reach the gods," continued Dusha. "First, a tie to the god, either a place, a plant, or a memory, to catch their attention and bring them closer. Second, a connection that works both ways, meaning, a god willing to answer you. And third, and most important, the god must be living."

I swallowed, weakness once more washing over me, and disappointment.

"Your Mother is dead, so I believe her to be in one of Lord Volos's kingdoms. Like in the Land of the Living, there are many dimensions, or kingdoms, in the Land of the Dead. But it takes great strength to reach them, for not only are they far away, they are in a land that is dead. That is why it would be easy to lose yourself there, or not return at all."

Because Mother was the hardest to reach, I practiced reaching the god with the strongest tie to the wild land of the taiga—the Lord of Vegetation, being the life force in Russia's plants and forests, the spirit of water in her seas and rivers. I hoped Kupalo would answer some of my questions and illuminate what was happening in Russia.

Autumn came, and Kupalo still had not answered me. I tried other herbs, places, and memories, including ones buried deep inside me. I recalled the summer solstice festival Mother and I had celebrated in honor of Kupalo. If I tied my ritual to this festival, if I worshipped and honored the Lord of Vegetation on this particular day, maybe I would get through to him. But we were past summer now, too close to winter, and all I could do was wait.

17

SOME TIME LATER

DUSHA AND I planned the rituals of Kupalo's summer solstice with the strictest care, exactly as Mother and I had once observed them.

The night dawned finally, clear and cold, and very, very dark. Dusha and I started a bonfire in our grove of birch trees. In the last few summers, many trees that were supposed to bloom had forgotten to. The grass had refused to grow. Winters were worsening, the cold bleeding into the few warm months left. As if nature was confused. Or the Lord of Winter wanted summer along with winter, the greedy bastard.

But our fire melted the darkness and the frost. Instead of trying the same tired ritual, Dusha and I sang and danced around the fire with abandon, gripping straw idols of Kupalo and tossing last year's herbs into the flames. The moon floated out of the cloud of smoke, and a great swath of sky became visible, the stars bright and sharp, like watchful eyes. I felt the welcome heat of the fire, a roaring blaze now, as we stripped our clothing and left our skin naked to the velvet of the night.

The summer solstice was the time for Kupalo's plants and flowers to come alive, for the earth to reveal its secrets. It was the time for magic.

"It is nearly midnight, Yaga," came Dusha's voice from the other side of the fire.

"Yes, dear Dusha." I picked up the waiting basket, and we went into the forest.

The pond with the rusalkas was unfrozen. I imagined them walking past me in the Otherworld, also naked, also with their hair wild and free. I parted the dry reeds and kneeled at the water's edge, looking for the arrow-like plant with the nine leaves, its magical properties more potent if gathered at midnight, most potent if gathered on the summer solstice— kupalchik, meaning *to bathe*, named after Kupalo himself.

Moonlight burst from the trees, and I glimpsed flickers of red and blue and green, shining in the undergrowth like scattered jewels. I gathered the blossoms into my basket. Then, in the first flush of dawn, we wove garlands from wild shrubs and bathed in the cold river with the garlands around our necks. The water purified me, washing away the filth, all the worry and regret, even the past itself. As the sky brightened with the pink and purples of taiga flowers, we let our garlands float away with the current and went back to Dusha's house, but only after making sure the fire smoldered out, as was the custom.

Inside, we shared a warm cup of milk and some oats. Over the table, Dusha said, "The kupalchik plant has more power if it is worn close to the heart and bound in a gold or silver chain." She riffled through her pocket and produced an amulet with a locket on a silver chain. "You can put the herb in here if you like."

I gave her a grateful nod. "How long until I can try reaching Lord Kupalo?"

"Three months to the day," she replied.

Then I would wait. And this time, I would perform the ritual in another holy place, a sacred one, a temple where ancients used to divine the future—the banya.

The time passed by quickly. Exactly three months later, no sooner and no later, I walked from Dusha's house to her log bathhouse.

I undressed in the outer room, leaving only the silver amulet with the kupalchik inside before passing through to the banya. It was hot and steamy. The stones in the stove smoldered burnt orange in the half darkness. I took more kupalchik out of my satchel and scattered it on the floor among the rushes. I sat down, cross-legged, in the middle of the banya and channeled its energy until my magic crackled through me. Instead of attempting the same ritual, I closed my eyes and felt my power mingle with that of the banya.

I let go of my mind and body, and I reached for the Otherworld.

I heard footsteps, a whispering, the trickle of water—likely, the bannik spirits. I reached for the next dimension, with heavier, more human footsteps and a low hum of conversation, even laughter—the ghosts trapped in the Land of the Living. Then the next, with only a rustle here and there—the older beings, the ones who had forgotten how to move and talk and laugh. The next blinded me with light and was as clear as day. I saw an oak tree there, and a face, lovely and godlike. But as soon as the blue eyes met mine, I felt a push, and I was falling, spiraling, screaming back into my body and the banya.

Weakness weighed down my head and limbs. There wasn't enough air. I pushed out of the banya into the cold night—and the pool dug out behind the bathhouse. The water was half-frozen. Shards of ice stabbed my skin as I submerged, my breaths coming out in spurts, my head whirling from the contrast between intense heat and intenser cold.

My breathing slowed at last, and I relaxed against the pool, watching the ice melt, the steam billow. Had I glimpsed Kupalo? I had never seen any spirit, much less a god, in the dimensions.

As if in answer, the water in the pool started to ripple.

It swirled faster and faster, though there was not a current of air. The sky and trees reflected on the water disappeared, brushed aside by an invisible hand. In their place, shapes and figures formed, then colors, moving pictures in a looking glass—a vision?

On the water's surface, black-clad men were riding black horses, armed with axes and spears. Brooms were stuck in their quivers, severed dogs' heads tied to their saddles. Drops of blood trickled from the dogs' heads, landing on the pristine snow like flecks of crushed ruby. Behind the men, I recognized Moscow's Kremlin wall, its square and posad. People rushed about, white-faced, panicked, clutching their possessions, the hands of their kin. One swing of a blade and they fell dead in a burst of scarlet.

I almost squeezed my eyes shut in horror.

When the image changed, the men rode on empty roads in a starved countryside. At the head of the army was an imposing man wielding a staff—the tsar. Now I could not look away even if I tried. His once flaming-red hair was faded and thinning, his once handsome features roughened, his beard threaded with a grizzled silver that aged him. Next to the tsar rode Koshey. His face, once so beloved, was now entirely foreign to me.

The image was replaced with that of the World Tree. Souls slid down its trunk so fast, in such numbers, that it glowed. Why were this many souls coming into Nav?

Then I saw a decaying swamp with a golden throne—the seat of the Lord of the Dead. But instead of Volos, on the throne sat a being, wavering like a spirit, free of flesh and blood—the ragged woman I had seen in Nav on my last visit there. A raven fluttered onto a log in front of her, transforming into a man. His face was hidden as he knelt before the throne. But the black hair sweeping across his shoulders was all too familiar.

How was Koshey in Nav as a raven? I would not be surprised if he had been the raven following me in Moscow the whole time. Or else had sent his ravens to spy on me.

The image twisted, and a bald, bearded man teetered down ice-ridden streets—the same man I had seen in my cauldron after the identifying spell. It was the Lord of Winter, Morozko. Behind him, the golden domes of Moscow's Kremlin looked rusty in the graying autumn light. He raised a scythe, and snow whirled through the air.

I had seen traces of him during my summer in Moscow. Now he was walking the streets of the capital. No doubt he had also frozen Nav's passageway and river.

A raven fluttered down to Morozko. The bird transformed into Koshey.

The ripples on the pool's surface intensified, sweeping the men away. The water became just water, reflecting the trees and sky. I plunged my hand into it, hoping the images would return, hoping I would understand them. Were they real? It was Russia but not the Russia I recognized. It was the tsar but not the tsar I had known. And Koshey and Morozko were serving the woman on Volos's throne, perhaps death itself and certainly Volos's usurper. Suddenly, the hair on my arms rose.

On the edge of the pool, barefooted and glowing with the divine, stood the same man from my ritual, the opposite to Morozko's darkness, the Lord of Vegetation.

I stared at Kupalo mutely. My tongue felt frozen, as if Morozko had touched it with his scythe. Kupalo was young and fair, yet the crown of wildflowers in his pale blond hair was wilted. His cloak, instead of a bright white, was a deep black, unfurling like the petals of an ebony tulip, threatening to envelop me. His expression was severe.

I opened my mouth, to ask him to explain the images on the water's surface, whether they were real. But he vanished before I had the chance.

I wasted no time. The very next day, I said goodbye to Dusha, made plans to meet up with Noch and Little Hen later, and rode off with Dyen through the taiga—back to civilization, and to humanity. Whether the vision in the pool was real or not, the past, present, or future, Kupalo had shown it to me, which meant the country was in trouble.

No matter what mortals thought of me, Baba Yaga or not, I would not abandon my motherland. I had had a crisis of faith in the gods, in Mother, but here was proof they had not forgotten me. Kupalo had answered. Maybe not with everything I had wanted to know, but enough to convince me it was time to go back. I knew more now, and I was stronger, even with the mortal blood in my veins. But most of all, my country needed me.

As I had surmised, gods were changing the world's natural order, whether it be the Lord of Winter with his summer mania or the missing Lord of the Dead and his mysterious usurper. And Tsar Ivan was persecuting not actual traitors but ordinary people, with Koshey goading him on, just as Aleksey had predicted. The vision with the corpse, maybe also my dream of Mother, had not been a foretelling of Anastasia's death but a warning of what was to come, of what *had* come. I just did not know what it all meant.

Perhaps by going back I would find out.

And as the daughter of the Great Earth Mother Mokosh, I had a responsibility toward mortals, toward Ivanushka and his brother, whom my dear Anastasia had wanted me to protect. Maybe I would also find out why the tsaritsa had been assassinated, and by whom. My wounded pride at being called a witch, the Baba Yaga, had to be put aside. The people and Anastasia's sons needed me. And I had to try to help them.

18

OCTOBER 1568

DYEN AND I had been on the road for days when we came upon a small fishing village on the northern coast, nestled against the sea. Boats should have been fluttering on the water, markets overflowing with goods, docks crowded with men unloading treasures captured that morning. It should have smelled of salt, mist, and windswept shores. Instead, I inhaled the stench of blood. Horror grasped my throat so tightly I couldn't breathe.

The harbor lay beneath a sky curdled with clouds. The boats drifting in the bay were destroyed, their masts bent at odd angles, their sails torn. The canvas flapped in a gale blowing coldly from the water. Dyen and I walked through what used to be the village posad, its stalls wrecked, the fish gutted and strewn on the ground. I sidestepped a stream running red with blood. I swallowed, fighting off a wave of nausea. The blood was pooling around dozens of motionless human bodies, lying mutilated and disfigured on the docks, in the posad, on the street looking out at the sea.

Except for the corpses, the village appeared deserted.

Who would do this? Dyen asked in the tiniest of voices.

I shook my head, realizing my cheeks were wet with tears.

A sudden shout, and three men in black greatcoats were hurrying toward us.

I shuddered. "They look like . . ."

The men from Kupalo's vision?

I nodded, sure now the vision had been real. I was glad Dyen was with me. My stick of elder, too, against unfriendly animals and evil men, sturdy and warm in my hand; as was the dried bat at my breast—an effective, if not a little foul, charm for good luck. As the men came closer, I breathed in sweat and spirits, a shock after the pure mountain air.

"What's your name, woman?" one of them demanded.

There was blood on their faces, probably their clothes, though I couldn't see past the black. They laughed at the fabricated name I gave them, at the strangeness of my clothes, at Dyen, who barely restrained himself, as they passed around a bottle of spirits.

"What year is it?" I asked the men.

But they just shook their heads and went on laughing. Finally, one said, "It is 1568. How can you not know?"

So, I had been away from civilization for eight years. I put a hand on Dyen's neck, to steel myself. "I have been living in the taiga," I replied finally. "Who are you?"

"Who are we?" repeated another man, incredulous, his beefy neck layered with golden collars and freshwater pearls. Likely looted from some unfortunate woman's house. "Why, we are the chosen ones! The army that protects Mother Russia from traitors and foreigners. The Oprichnina carries out God's holy work."

I recalled Kupalo's vision, the rampage of these same men through Moscow, and I gestured at the bloodstained streets, at the dead, still and silent. "Holy work? Have you no shame?" My face flamed with heat as I took them in—the gleeful smiles, the laughs, the absence of remorse. I thought fast. On my way into the village, I had seen dams holding back the water from the rivers, preventing the sea from entering the land. This far north, they were conveniently simple constructions of earth and wood.

"Break the dams, dig through them, hollow them out," I whispered to any animal who would listen, and to Dyen to help relay the message. "Let the water run free."

I had never called to so many animals at once and for such a difficult task. But Dyen wasted no time in giving a great howl into the sky. Meanwhile, I forced myself to keep talking, to keep the men focused on me. "I shall go to the tsar—"

"Our lord tsar, our beloved Ivan Grozny, is the one who sent us," the first man said, not taking his eyes off my wolf.

Grozny meant *thunderous, dreadful, terrible. Ivan the Terrible.* What had the tsar done to deserve the name? "The tsar sent you to destroy a village and kill innocents?" It was bizarre, it was madness. But I *had* seen him at the head of these men in the vision . . .

"They were traitors."

"Traitors?" I echoed, voice barely there. "What did they do?"

"Eh, a tax payment was not satisfied. It is unfortunate the tsar isn't here. Frequently, he comes with us."

"We are too far north," the man with the pearls said lazily.

Behind the men, a brown bear lumbered down the docks. My heart beat a little faster. The animals had heard me, and they were coming.

"Shall we take her? Flay her alive, or cut her throat nice and slow?"

"We could do all three!"

Next to me, Dyen snarled. A few eagles and storks, not as flighty as other birds and quite useful, flew above us. In the distance, a wild boar charged. Several dogs and a pack of gray wolves, too. I was emboldened now, my self-possession returning, and I put my hand on my wolf, keeping him back.

"Do you know what we do to the fairer sex, dorogaya?" *Dear one.* The first man stepped closer. "We fuck them, hard, then herd them into the woods to hunt."

The bitter tang of spirits, mingled with spoiled fish, wafted toward me. A rat and a mouse slipped by. A couple of gophers and a couple of moles, a family of chipmunks. "The gods shall punish you," I whispered, taking small sips of air. "Your god, too."

"Oho! A heathen." He leered. "The tsar executes the likes of you on the spot."

That is it. Dyen leapt in front of me.

The ground gave a shudder, the rush of water filling my ears, as the men lunged at us. Dyen ripped into two of them, sending shivers along my spine. The vilest one came at me with a knife, still leering through the blood on his face. I ducked, spun, avoided the singing blade. Did my best to fend him off with my stick.

As the man's blade swished too near, a wall of water appeared around the corner. It was hurtling toward us. My skin burned, as though a wasp had stung me. When I put a hand to my throat, my fingertips came away scarlet red. The blade had not just come near. It had grazed my neck. Blood oozed from the open wound, wet and sticky. My head became fuzzy, my vision blackened. Dyen caught me the minute I felt myself fall.

I heard my wolf's words of comfort, the men's frenzied speech and swears. But there was too much blood, soaking my clothes, burrowing into my skin, staining me. And the water was everywhere. In my nose and mouth and boots. It weighed down my skirts until I was sinking into the blackest depths of the sea like a drowning woman, shipwrecked and without hope.

A rocking motion forced me out of the deep.

I lay on a raft of rough-hewn planks that drifted down a flooded street with izbas on either side. The light was a sickly yellow, the sky low and looming, fading into the pewter-colored water. I breathed in the sea—not the blood—and sagged with relief.

Finally! Dyen leapt at me excitedly, licking my cheeks. *I was afraid . . .*

I shook my head and scratched his ears. "You never have to be afraid for me, my friend," I told him, burying my face in his fur. Suddenly, I looked up. "Where did the animals go? The ones who helped us?"

They built this raft for you, then left.

I leaned against Dyen, relieved the animals had escaped before the water had engulfed the village and had suffered less harm than I had. My hand felt for the wound on my throat. But it had healed, the blood washed away.

The same was true of the village. It was quiet, the mortals killed by the black-clad thugs slumbering in their watery graves, the gutted fish returned to the sea, the streets cleansed. Yet this didn't ease my dread. What had happened for the tsar to lash out at his people with such cruelty? *Ivan the Terrible.* My bones creaked with cold, with the bitterness of this new, very real Ivan and his brutish army. The chosen ones, Oprichnina. Somehow connected to wayward gods and Koshey. Kupalo had wanted me to know this, to return for this, perhaps also to help the Russian people.

To do that, I had to fulfill my promise to the best woman I had ever known, who had loved Russia and her people more than anything. I had to find Ivanushka and his brother.

Dyen and I headed south, the countryside around us more desolate than ever, the tang of blood rising up my nostrils and staying there.

The road should have been teeming with colorfully painted troikas, but it was empty, the fields left uncultivated, the landscape gravestone gray beneath a clouded-over sky. Instead of bells tinkling from the sleds and lively merchants conversing, a grim silence hovered. As if we should not be here.

A chill crept up my spine, the brush of ghostly fingertips against my back.

The part of the country we were traveling through, though more populated than the taiga, was still hundreds of kilometers from Moscow and, therefore, still considered the wild North. We passed towns and villages as empty as the road, their izbas and workshops abandoned, their posady vacant. My heart ached at seeing other villages that had been left in ruins, some even burned to the ground, a painful reminder of my birth village and its fate. That's when I truly cursed Ivan the Terrible.

Though it was just October, snow bleached the road white, and the wind that blew at us was so raw and harsh it scratched my already swollen cheeks. Even the sparrow fat I had rubbed into our bellies for protection against frost did nothing.

Do you feel that? Dyen's breaths were coming out in gasps.

I nodded. "Someone is here." Someone divine. I almost laughed at the years I had spent trying to reach the spiritual dimensions and the gods there. If only I had known that as soon as one god answered, the others would follow. Or maybe my work in the fishing village had caught their attention.

Suddenly, I heard my name.

The voice that had spoken was as deep as valleys, as echoing as ravines, and the decrease in temperature had to mean the Lord of Winter was gracing me with his presence.

Sure enough, the bearish man from Kupalo's vision appeared on the road, in a tunic stitched from snowflakes, his scythe of ice glittering lethal. I lifted my eyes to his, spiraling blue and white like icicles, and shivered. The rule was to never, ever show the Lord of Winter how cold one really was. But the flash of fear was too real. If he wanted to, Morozko could freeze me as effortlessly as the fields, half goddess or not.

"Tell me, Yagusya, are you warm?" he asked, just as my wolf let out a growl.

I put a restraining hand on Dyen's neck and whispered, "Let me speak to him." Then, barely keeping my teeth from chattering, I said, "Of course, Lord Morozko."

He smiled. "Is this your wolf?"

"Don't touch my wolf." Too sharp. Yet Dyen had listened and kept still.

"Ah, but I can feel his blood." Morozko spread his mittenless, paw-like hands. "Yours as well." He regarded me with his icy gaze. "There is no need for formalities, my lapochka, my sweet. Call me Roz."

"All right, Roz. The blood is in the air. That is what you smell."

"Maybe." His smile sharpened. "Last we heard you were dwelling in the taiga. You should go back there."

So, they *had* seen my work in the fishing village, and they were threatened. "Your warning is just patronizing enough to belong to Koshey Bessmertny. Very well. I have been warned. Now, tell me, do the oprichniki really answer to the tsar?"

Roz glanced around, uneasily. A string of ivory symbols came into view on his bare scalp. Who did he fear? The wind had died down, the flurries had slowed. When he finally spoke, he did so haltingly, his young features appearing worn. "Yes, they answer to the tsar," he said finally. "Their very name, oprichniki, means *separated ones*."

I clung to Dyen, to his quiet strength. "Separated from what?" *Or from whom?*

"Together with the tsar, from Russia and her boyars."

"So, they are his army?"

Again Roz looked around. "They are . . . Ivan's personal guards in a separate kingdom belonging to him within Russia called the Oprichnina." Roz no longer hesitated. "Ivan has complete autonomy there. No restrictions, not even from his boyars. Only the land and army not part of the Oprichnina, the Zemshchina, is still ruled by the tsar along with the Boyar Council. But in all the Russian lands, he can deal with any man. To confiscate his property, send him into exile, execute him. No hearings, no interference."

I felt a burst of panic at the dire situation in Russia; at the vengeful, paranoid tsar, striking out at invisible enemies. But since he was a child, Tsar Ivan had fancied himself to be the target of those powerful enough to desire the crown. He saw conspiracy even if there was none. Everyone knew this. Bewildered, I asked, "How could the boyars have agreed?"

Roz shrugged his wide, bulging shoulders. "Ivan threatened to abdicate."

"Why not let him do it?"

"I suppose they were afraid. The Rurik Dynasty has been on the throne for more than five hundred years. The people doubt Russia can survive without them. Only us immortals have seen it, lapochka, when there was no tsar, no dynasties, no Russia at all." A fire lit in those cold blue eyes. As if, tired of having seen it all, he waited for a new Russia with a new dynasty of tsars. Immortals liked nothing better than novelty.

I shook my head. "But he is murdering ordinary people . . . It makes no sense."

"He is hunting traitors across the Zemshchina lands," Roz said quietly, his face drawn, as if deploring the work of Tsar Ivan and his thugs. "Brooms symbolize his intention to sweep away treachery, dogs' heads to destroy his enemies."

"Surely, he doesn't consider his own people an enemy . . ." But I remembered Aleksey and Sylvester. Anyone could be called a traitor in Tsar Ivan's Russia. I met Roz's gaze. "Why are you telling me all this? Don't you serve the tsar?"

Roz tilted his head, and a sprinkling of ice crystals inked there slid into view. "Not only are my victims cold, Yaga. I am also. I hate death as much as they do. It is lonely, dull, utterly dismal. That is how it began. I wanted to live not just in the cold months. To be around mortals as they lived, loved, and feasted. How they used to worship me!" He averted his eyes; I felt a lick of heat. "Because of the winters I have had to summon, they have started to fear me. It makes me sad, all this death. Living has become a chore."

"So, you do serve the tsar, but you do not want to? What about Koshey?"

"I was commanded to warn you, so you return to the taiga and not interfere. But talking to you . . ." He fumbled with his scythe. "Perhaps you should not listen to me."

"But you are a god! Why keep bringing winter for some mortal tsar? Someone else must be forcing you—" Suddenly, I recalled the spirit from Nav. "Is it the woman on Volos's throne? Who is she? What does she want with you and the human souls?"

"How do you know about her?" Roz backed away. His scythe flashed, sending sparks dancing across my vision. "She is the Lady of Death—"

"No," I countered, "Volos is the Lord of the Dead. Where is he?"

Roz shook his head mutely. His cheeks were so white they bled into his beard. He brought his palms together, liquifying, the flurries and wind going with him.

"Wait." I leapt off Dyen. But Morozko had already melted into the earth.

I suppose you will not be listening to the Lord of Winter's warnings?

I turned back to Dyen. "Not even a little."

Interlude

IN NAV, THE World Tree dazzles with light. Souls slide down its trunk at such dizzying speeds, the plain on the other side of the river is growing crowded with spirits. They shove one another over the dwindling space, and they wail. Their frustration, their suffering, escapes into the air and eats away at the twisting, cancerous roots of the Tree, even at its highest branches in the Heavens.

There, the sky is an acid blue. The moon is cold, the sun unnaturally wan.

The rosy-cheeked gods and goddesses run to the Tree in their shimmering garments. They whisper to each other, horror-struck, as the leaves rupture with red-orange spots, then rust and curl, withering before their eyes and spreading the stench of rot and death. They did not consider the consequences when they left Earth for the peace of the Heavens. For if the Tree is blighted, the world will be also. Indeed, the land heaves with violence, with crime, with war. Winter and death are laying claim to it.

"We must go back," one god says as he looks down at the land. His black cloak billows behind him like a shred of escaped night. It is Kupalo.

"You have answered her, even warned her," says Perun, his golden mustache rippling. "We cannot do more. The mortals stopped worshipping us long ago."

"But there will be much suffering—"

"There will." Perun is resigned. He used to hate the humans for their disloyalty, their changeability. Now, like an afterthought, only sadness remains. He adds, in the softest of voices, "The mortals should not have forgotten their prayers and sacrifices to us. They should not have destroyed our shrines and temples, accepted another god into their hearts. They have been ungrateful. Is it not why we retired from their affairs?"

The firebird that sweeps over their heads does not screech as firebirds do. The fiery orange of its wings is strangely faded.

"What about the Lady of Rebirth?" asks Kupalo, changing tack. "Selica needs to renew herself and the land, yet she is in Nav, killing the Tree with her desperation. Meanwhile, Morozko's loneliness is disturbing the seasons. And Volos is, no doubt, planning his next attack on the sky. The balance in the Universe is being upset."

"It is," agrees Perun. "But now that it has started, we have to let it run its course."

Kupalo opens his mouth, to argue, to make Perun see, to have him understand.

"We cannot become involved," the highest of gods says pensively, his hand tightening reflexively on his iron bow. His thunderbolt arrows, in their iron quiver, flash the silver of his hair. "Not until the battle comes to us. And it will, in time. No, we hold fast. We stay in the Heavens. We let the wayward gods and their humans try to resolve this mess."

19

I HAD HEARD IVANUSHKA and his brother were alive and assumed they were back at the Moscow Kremlin. Though it had been years, I did not doubt Baba Yaga had not been forgotten in the capital, which meant the risk of my getting caught there was very real. Morozko's warnings also gave me hope I could make a difference in Russia. If I could find the oprichniki before they did more harm, perhaps I could help the suffering peasants, just a little, before taking on Moscow and whatever waited for me there.

It was in the northern forests, at nightfall, that I began to pursue Tsar Ivan's thugs.

Moonlight did not reach so deep into the wood, not through the trees with their canopies of dead branches, or the looming hills, painted over with black shades and veiled in wintry mists that hid any trails from sight. A weary traveler could lose themselves there. Or encounter trouble. Armed with a fresh stick of elder, a dried bat, and a rubbing of sparrow fat, I whispered to the animals from under the cold, starless shadows. To the packs of gray wolves with fangs that tore into flesh, to the herds of reindeer with their twisting antlers, to the ravenous bears, even to the foxes, squirrels, and rabbits.

The animals listened, and they came, disapproving of this Russia with its starved land, its rivers of blood, its maddened tsar.

We attacked the unsuspecting oprichniki as they traversed the land in their caravans, sleds, and wagons, either empty on the way to the villages or else already piled high with the spoils of their terrors—the icons, jewels, and furniture looted from the towns, as well as any churches and estates on their way. We scared off the thugs and returned the goods to the people, though I still mostly shied away from mortals.

I had worked with Dusha, had encountered mortals in the taiga settlements, but I was no longer used to living among people, preferring my woods to their villages, the events in Moscow all those years ago still fresh in my mind, a reminder not to get too close. I would help them from deep in the forest, unseen and unheard of.

Several months passed in this way. On a January night with very little snow but with a bitter frost, we waited in the trees for an incoming contingent of oprichniki. We had not had time to stop their terror of a nearby village, but we could still intercept their loot.

Suddenly, there came shouts, the resounding clash of blades, the panicked neigh of horses. Dyen and I looked at each other in alarm. This late, we were accustomed to the quiet sleepy tread of the oprichniki, the measured click of horses' hooves. Not this noise.

Do you think someone attacked them before us? asked Dyen.

"But who?" The peasants were so terrified, they offered little resistance.

A group of men, Ya. Noch, whom I had sent for soon after starting my work against the oprichniki, landed on my shoulder. *They are fighting the bastards!*

I did not waste any time. I hurled myself down the frozen path with Noch and Dyen at my heels.

We came upon a shifting mass of shadows, stomping horses and darting men with blades rising and falling, striking and parrying. It looked like a massive contingent of oprichniki—at least a dozen caravans and almost double that of men. But who were the other men, the ones fighting the tsar's soldiers?

"Rise up," I whispered to the horses still tied to the caravans.

They reared with their manes flying, breaking through their harnesses—several caravans toppling and crashing to the ground—before starting toward the wrangling men.

I only hoped the men fighting the oprichniki would not be harmed. And if they were, I would help them. Heart pounding, feet at the ready, I tightened my hold on my satchel and squinted into the tangle of horses and men. Among the black-clad oprichniki, there were flashes of red and yellow, green and blue. As if sensing my eyes on him, the man closest turned and looked directly at me. He wore a pair of red boots and a brightly painted mask of beaten metal—the same ones, I realized, worn by the skomorokhi jesters who wandered into the villages and towns of Russia, entertaining people with their rowdy songs and jokes. He turned back—*she*, for I saw a dark braid whip behind her as she went on sparring with the oprichnik as if she had never been interrupted at all.

"Be fierce, my friends, and may the gods keep you," I said to Dyen and Noch over my shoulder as I darted forward.

I spotted a few men, not in oprichnik black, lying on the ground. I grabbed the nearest one by the shoulders and dragged him toward the trees.

I had just kneeled beside him, when a scream tore through the night. Then, a "My lord!" And a muffled, smothered "Ivanush—!"

"Go," whispered the man. "I will be fine. The wound is not deep."

I was barely able to stammer out a reply. Heart pounding, chest flaming with bewilderment and hope, I staggered to my feet before blindly rushing in the direction of the scream.

A tall, masked man was leaning over another man lying on the ground.

I caught sight of blood, dark and still flowing in the abdomen. "We must get him to safety!" I shouted above the noise. At their hesitation, "I am a friend—let me help."

They relented, the tall man rushing to my side to drag the wounded man into the trees. There, I dropped to my knees and examined the wound with shaking hands. I wanted to lower my patient's mask but refrained. He wore it for a reason.

I turned to my satchel and, rummaging within, produced a clean cloth. I used it to press on the wound, eliciting a sharp intake of breath. I cleaned the wound with a little water, then placed on it three leaves of witch hazel and three stalks of horsetail, to stop the blood for good. I added a sprinkling of a fusion I had made and always kept with me, of thyme, calendula, and tea tree oil, charmed to prevent festering. Finally, a dash of my healing ointment, of snakeskin, bat extract, and a fleck of hard-boiled egg.

The wounded man—boy, for he was slight—was quiet. He had lost consciousness. And he was very, very cold. I wished I had the Water of Life. But when I had sent Noch to check on Nav's passageway, she had notified me it was still frozen.

The tall man stood over us uncertainly, but his eyes showed through his mask—gray, and unsettlingly watchful. They missed nothing. He stepped forward and lifted his mask, just enough for me to see the stubble on his chin, and his mouth. "Our camp is not far," he said in a deep, self-assured voice, "a few hours, maybe."

"A few hours?" I wished I had sent for my hut sooner. "Noch," I whispered to the night air, and my owl swooped down. "Find Little Hen and bring her to me."

Normally, I wouldn't fly that far simply at your behest. She peered at the wounded man. *But under the circumstances . . .* She unfurled her wings and shot up into the sky.

The tall man's eyes were big and round through his mask.

I whispered to the oprichniki's horses next, but they had galloped off into the woods, no doubt hoping never to be found again. The fighting had lessened, only a few isolated sword clashes reached us through the trees. I peered between the branches, seeing the unmoving bodies of the oprichniki in pools of blood, their horses gone, their caravans abandoned with the stolen goods hopefully still inside. Canvas flapped back and forth in the blustery wind, which carried with it the bitterness of winter, the stench of blood.

"Will you cease watching me and *do* something?" I asked the still-staring man.

I saw a flash of teeth below his lifted mask. "My apologies, my lady. I simply have never seen the likes of you. My horse is just past these trees."

Only after he had left did I lower my patient's mask.

The young man lying before me *was* a boy, no more than fifteen years old, with a pale face and reddish hair. It was so improbable it felt like the will of the gods. But I recognized him right away. It was the little lost tsarevich. It was Ivanushka.

Once the tall man returned with his horse, he removed his mask and gloves. He could not have been older than five and twenty, with a young, handsome face yet a mature air and bearing, likely due to his self-assurance and straight-backed, expansive presence.

He reminded me of someone.

"Finish up here, then return the goods to the villagers," he instructed another masked man over the sound of the wind. His steady gray gaze settled on me next, then on Dyen, whom I had left just beyond the trees to keep watch over the tsarevich. "That is an exceedingly large wolf . . ." The tall man contemplated me. "You must be Yaga Mokoshevna."

How did he know that name? I ignored his question. "What is the tsarevich doing here?"

"Will he live?"

I paused. "Yes."

He looked at me a little too long, a little too thoughtfully—in curiosity or in appraisal? "In that case, my lord tsarevich Ivan Ivanovich can tell you himself."

Ivanushka's name, said out loud, meant he was real, not some unreachable prince, far away in Moscow. My heart lifted at the same time that remorse flooded it. All I could think about was Anastasia, dying in that oversize bed in that stifling chamber of firelight and death, asking me to care for her sons, for Ivanushka. Begging me to seal it with a promise. The pain, the one that had dulled but never truly healed, was back, aching more fiercely than ever. I regretted not saying yes to her, merely responding that she would be able to keep them safe herself. Silently, I made the promise now, hoping that, wherever my Anastasia was, she was listening. Now that I had found him, I would protect Ivanushka and make certain her youngest son was safe. And I would help my country and her people with her heir at my side—whatever he was doing in the North, it was against the oprichniki and, therefore, for his people.

"Where is the tsarevich's brother, Fyodor Ivanovich? Is he also here?" I asked the tall man, whose gaze had not shifted from me.

He gave me a short laugh. "Why would he be here?" I must have looked alarmed, for he softened. "There is no cause for worry, Yaga Mokoshevna. Fyodor is an extremely pious young man. So he is safer than anyone in Russia. All he does is visit the tsar's favorite monasteries and pray there to no end."

My anxiety eased a little. At least Fyodor was not gallivanting all over Russia like his brother. "How do you know me?" I asked.

"We heard a band of oprichniki was killed in the far north," the man said with a gleam. "And we have been receiving reports of lost sleds and caravans from the Oprichnina. This led us to believe someone was on our side. Ivanushka, having recognized your wolf from the reports, insisted it was you. We hastened to these parts for this reason and had just made camp when we heard of the large contingent of oprichniki heading into these woods and, well, couldn't resist." He laughed a little.

I noticed the confident, bold way he tugged on his gloves. He was an aristocrat, some boyar's son; of this I was sure.

"Come, my lady," he said, "let us harness my horse and find us a caravan."

Once this was done, a few men carried a still-unconscious Ivanushka into an emptied caravan. I refused to leave his side, and Dyen agreed to meet me at the camp. Before that, he would pass along our location to Noch through his network of wolves.

The man, watching me intently, offered me his hand. "Let me help you inside."

But I stood still, peering at him. The unwavering gray gaze, the longer-than-fashionable blond-streaked hair, the intense fervor. I had seen it all before, on someone else. "What is your name?" I asked him.

"Vasily Alekseyevich Adashev," he said without pause.

I recalled Aleksey telling me his family, including his son Vasily, was lost to him. "I knew your father, once." I was afraid to ask the next question; because I rarely approached mortals, I was not caught up on the latest news. "How is he?"

Vasily's face betrayed nothing. "He has been dead these eight years."

"Eight years! Tsarstvo nebesnoye to him." I crossed myself. "How did he die? I met him very near his end."

"We do not know. He never made it out of the house they had him locked up in. One day, they discovered him and all the people he had been helping frozen to death. The official cause was fever. We never found out why they were frozen."

The frost bastard, Morozko, that was why. But I couldn't tell Vasily that. After all, men had closed their minds to the old gods long ago.

Vasily again offered me his hand. This time, he gave me a bright, unguarded smile that took me quite by surprise. I placed my hand in his. It was unexpectedly rough and calloused, a soldier's hand. He blinked at the crescent on the inside of my wrist. In one deft movement, he lifted me into the caravan, his grip warm and sure. I had not realized I was holding my breath. Then the contact between us was broken, and Vasily Alekseyevich was walking away to take his place at the front of the caravan.

But for one sudden, shocking second, his eyes cut back to mine. Then he rounded the corner and passed out of sight. A minute later, we jolted into the night.

20

JANUARY 1569

THE TSAREVICH LAY in a curtained bed at the back of his tent, not awake, but his breathing had steadied, and his wound no longer bled. Most importantly, he had survived the night.

Asking Dyen to watch over Ivanushka, I decided to venture out for some fresh air.

I had been with the tsarevich ever since we had brought him to camp the night before. Everything else was a blur, the faces peering at us worriedly as we carried Ivanushka out of the caravan and into the tent, the flat black stones I had charmed into speeding up the healing process, not to mention the endless herbs and roots I had put on his wound all night, to keep away fever, to bring a little luck.

The musky smell of men, of confinement, was muddling my head. Years of open air, and suddenly, a small, tight space.

I lifted the tent flap, sunlight cutting into my eyes. It was bright for January, and I blinked to adjust to the flood of light. Then I saw the camp, no more than a collection of tents and bedrolls around the fire, the air cold and smoky. It tasted of salt and brine; fish sizzled over the flames.

Nauseated, I started to turn back when a pair of gloved hands gripped my arms.

"Yaga Mokoshevna." Vasily smiled. "How is our prince?"

Vasily lowered his arms, and I cleared my throat. "He is well," I replied. "Let us hope his recovery continues."

Vasily did not cross himself, nor did he offer up any prayer of thanks to his god. Instead, he gestured toward the fire. "You must be hungry—"

"Oh, I—" I pressed my lips together, the smell of frying fish wafting over to me.

Vasily laughed. There was something fearless, even daring, in it, being completely unbridled. "No fish in the morning, eh?" He brought his face close and whispered, "I quite agree with you, but do not tell Yaroslav, or he will refuse to give me any more food. I can get you a bowl of kasha, if you like. In the meantime—you can meet everyone."

He motioned to the people gathered near the fire, all in mismatched, homespun coats, with quilts and blankets thrown over their shoulders. A ragged man with gray hair and a beard, likely Yaroslav, leaned over the fish. The others extended their hands toward the flames, talking and laughing. They grew solemn as we approached. There were about a dozen of them, besides the few I had seen in and around camp.

A woman approached us. "Baba Yaga—in the flesh."

"This is Yaga Mokoshevna," Vasily said, introducing us.

"Yaga, please," I said, not taking my eyes off the woman. She had a pretty face, though its angles made it more severe than it should have been, with cheeks as red as apples and a long, dark braid any woman in Russia would sell her soul for. She seemed the same age as I looked, but her eyes betrayed her; they were as dark as her hair and contained within them hundreds of years. "And you are?"

"Marya Morevna." Those sharp, quick eyes did not leave mine.

I was disoriented. I had heard of her, of course. She was a princess, a warrior, ruling over a tiny kingdom before Russia had swallowed it. She was known to have fought bravely against the Mongols and their Golden Horde, back when they had occupied the Russian territories. I had thought her to be a myth, certainly, not a real person, a real woman. But I recalled her fighting the oprichnik the night before—for it had been her—and wondered if she also possessed magic, as was the rumor, and if Ivanushka, Vasily, and the people in this camp knew who she really was.

"The hardened she-warrior—in the flesh." She *had* called me Baba Yaga.

Vasily glanced from me to Marya. "You are acquainted?"

Before I could respond, she quipped, "You are not as old and ugly as they say."

"And you exist." I kept a straight face.

So did she. But her eyes filled with mirth. She gestured to a woman by the fire, mortal by the looks of it, with golden hair gathered in a bright blue handkerchief. "This is my Varvara," Marya said in a low, tender voice once the woman had walked over to us.

"No, you are my Marya," Varvara said cheekily.

I liked her instantly. She did not seem to let people have their way with her, but had a cloudless blue gaze and a smile that was friendly and uncomplicated.

I was then introduced to the others. Most of the people at camp were exceedingly young, some were elders, wrinkled and wise. They were a mix of nobles, merchants, and well-to-do landowners, men and women and children driven from their homes by the oprichniki. There was a man in his thirties with a thick black beard and kind eyes, known simply as Sanya. He had been a landowner once, but when the oprichniki had overrun his lands, killed his mother, and threatened the rest of his family, Sanya had taken to the streets with his wife, Agniya, and their two flaxen-haired sons, Bogdan and Miroslav. There was Mitya, or Mitka, a boy just entering manhood, an orphan already. And Yaroslav and his redheaded eighteen-year-old granddaughter, Yelena, who had been driven out of their village by the oprichniki after seeing their entire family murdered. There were a few other families, the rest were single men, fiery, riotous, and wildly patriotic.

I longed to know more—how they had found Ivanushka, or how he had found them, what they were doing here, except for the obvious. But I would wait for Ivanushka to tell me. For now, I enjoyed the feel of the fire against my skin; Marya and Varvara's pleasant conversation; the warm kasha Vasily had brought me, with a wildberry preserve that he had managed to pilfer from Yaroslav. Though I had been afraid to live among mortals, the people in Ivanushka's camp welcomed me generously and shared their food and warmth with me freely, though they had little of either.

I only wished Noch and Little Hen would find me, and that dear Dusha would stay in the taiga, forever if necessary. I could never have imagined a wild land like the taiga would become the safest place in Russia. Or maybe nowhere was safe.

Later that night, I sat on a stool by the tsarevich's bed in the glow of shivering candlelight. The room was fragrant with the sage I was burning to clear the air.

"You look the same," came a small voice. "How can that be?"

I dropped the scrap of dried snakeskin I had been about to fold into his wound. "My lord tsarevich!" I swept him a deep curtsy, blinking away the sudden tears. The memories of him and his mother were rushing back with a force that left me breathless.

"Rise, my dear Yaga Mokoshevna, rise. And please"—he clasped my hands in a surprisingly cold grip—"call me Ivanushka."

"Ivanushka," I repeated softly. "Thank god"—*or, rather, the gods*—"you have awoken."

"It is only because of your devotion to me, and your care," he said. "The Lord God is good for bringing you to me when I needed you most."

"How do you feel?" I asked, checking on his wound, which was coming along nicely. I fluffed his pillow and discreetly fished out the dried bat I had placed under it.

"Completely recovered!" he boasted. "Why, I could walk out of this tent right now!"

"Not yet, Ivanushka, not yet."

"I cannot believe it is you—it is really you." His eyes shone with tears.

I squeezed his hand, barely restraining myself from asking why he was here, fighting the oprichniki. He was now recalling my summer in Moscow, the last time we had seen each other, how I had played with him and how he had made me an offer of marriage. Our talk turned to his mother, how I had been her dearest, most trusted friend.

I sat back, remembering the tsaritsa's kindness, her bright demeanor, her glance, quick and lively and intelligent. We spoke of Anastasia then, only very carefully, very softly. Then I inquired after his brother, who, as Vasily had said, spent most of his time in prayer and contemplation. With Tsar Ivan as his father, I really couldn't blame him.

"He is lucky to be so satisfied behind church walls"—Ivanushka glanced down at his scraped hands—"without wanting anything else from life, from my father and Russia."

I was about to ask what *he* wanted from his father and Russia, but I saw the pallor of his face and heard the weariness in his voice. "Rest now, Ivanushka," was all I said, putting a tender hand on his forehead.

He smiled, put his head back on the pillow, and slept.

I renewed my promise to Anastasia then and there. I had been lucky to come upon Ivanushka in time to save him, and I would help him recover and keep him safe so that what happened would never happen again, not under my watch.

A few days later, when the tsarevich was sufficiently recovered to sit up in bed, I allowed him visitors. Marya and Varvara, as well as Agniya and Sanya, among a few other men, had come and gone. Darkness had fallen, yet I still sat beside Ivanushka, refusing to leave his side. Aside from me, only Vasily remained.

"Why aren't you at the Kremlin, Ivanushka?" I whispered, unable to wait any longer. The canvas walls shook as the wind screeched outside, a wild beast in despair.

"The Kremlin?" Vasily arched an eyebrow. He was sitting in the middle of the tent, where there were rugs and furs heaped upon the carpet. As usual, he missed nothing. One corner of his mouth had lifted in a smirk. "Only the big, bad boyars live there now."

"The big, bad—?"

"He jests, my dear Yaga Mokoshevna. Pay him no mind." The tsarevich gave Vasily a dismissive wave. "Father prefers the old hunting lodge, Aleksandrovskaya Sloboda, for his residence now. Aleksandrov agrees with him better than Moscow."

"It is the capital of his Oprichnina kingdom," Vasily said, voice hard. "An armed camp, for all intents and purposes. But who is really paying attention?"

The tsarevich shot his friend a look of warning. The candles bathed the tent's walls a sick yellow, like aged parchment, the canvas curling and uncurling with each burst of wind. Not for the first time, I wondered how a tsarevich could be friends with an Adashev, and how an Adashev could be so outspoken with a tsarevich.

"Ivanushka"—I hesitated—"how are you here without the tsar?"

"Father, well, he travels a lot. And at Aleksandrovskaya Sloboda, he is . . . preoccupied. I do not see him for months. So, I slip out and come fight the oprichniki."

I looked around the tent, at the maps with the crawling seas and trailing mountain ranges pinned to the stirring walls, the oak table and benches taking up one side of the space, the chests on the other. It was a soldier's tent, and it seemed to shrink at the thought of the young tsarevich roaming through the North like a runaway peasant boy. "If he knew, he would kill you," I said bluntly, a chill sweeping up my arms.

The tsarevich did not flinch. "He would."

I gave his icy fingers a squeeze before letting go. "What happened to him?"

"I do not know. Not all of it." Ivanushka's eyes were fixed on the stubby candle beside him, guttering and spitting. "They say he went mad with grief after Lady Mother's death. My stepmother, Tsaritsa Maria, is a princess from the Caucasus, possessing none of Mother's charms or goodness. She does not even try to . . . make him better."

"I think my father also loved Tsaritsa Anastasia," said Vasily.

I turned my gaze on Aleksey's son, so similar to his father but without the bitterness. Even if he had been wronged (as an Adashev, he couldn't have escaped it), Vasily did not let it show. His humor accompanied every word, every look, every smile.

"Father has turned against everyone. The state, the boyars, his friends."

"Except for his drunk, murderous companions," Vasily put in.

"It is their fault," the tsarevich said petulantly. "The oprichniki incite the violence in Father. If not for them, he would never have been driven to kill anyone."

"Yet he executed most of my kin after my father's death. And not only the men. The wives, children, and servants also." Vasily leaned back with a ragged sigh. "I don't know how I got out alive. Why me? Why was I left to relive their deaths over and over?"

He was staring at me, as if expecting an answer. Perhaps he saw the real age in my face, or perhaps I was just in his line of vision.

"Princes, boyars, nobles. Officials, scribes, war heroes. No one is spared. And the peasants?" Vasily's eyes were suddenly those of his father: pebble gray with flecks of amber, the eyes of a lion. "Well. You have seen their lot. There is blood in the palaces, in the churches, even on the roads. It flows in a river through Mother Russia! Ivan's is a reign of tyranny and terror." Vasily's voice broke. "Tsar Ivan the Terrible indeed—"

"Vasily Alekseyevich," the tsarevich said in a measured tone, "that is enough."

It was the first time I had heard Ivanushka address his friend so formally. But I couldn't blame Vasily. To lose one's family was arguably worse than to lose one's life. I should know. The emptiness in my heart was because of Mother's death. Of the many years spent alone in a world that cared not for loss or pain or biting loneliness.

Vasily's eyes were dark gray, and they had tears in them. I was quickly learning that he was bold to the point of carelessness and just as impulsive. It was no doubt why, in addition to Vasily being older and more experienced, Ivanushka wanted him at his side. He didn't soften the truth or flatter the tsarevich. He said it as it was. He was undaunted even now.

"All the tsar cares about is violence—"

"I said enough, Vasily!" the tsarevich flared. "He is your tsar. Remember that." Under Ivanushka's veneer of calm, his father's fury showed.

He became a little more like the tsar, a little less like my Anastasia. And though Ivanushka could not publicly oppose his father, my skin went cold at his stubborn defense, in private, of a tsar who sanctioned the murder of his own people. Vasily evidently thought the same; he folded his arms at his chest and looked away, clearly unsettled. His gaze quickly caught mine.

I leaned toward the tsarevich. "But aren't you fighting your father?"

"No. Father is a man driven by grief. Everyone he ever cared for has left him."

Still, it wasn't just grief that pushed the tsar toward murder. He had a gift for blame and hatred, Aleksey had said. *He will destroy all of Mother Russia to gratify it.*

"I am here to save Father and Mother Russia from the true enemy, the Oprichnina." The tsarevich turned his gaze on me. "Will you help me, Yaga?"

The Oprichnina existed because of the tsar, with Koshey inciting him and the oprichniki to violence. If there were no tsar and no Koshey, there would be no Oprichnina and no oprichniki. But Ivanushka was young and naive, defending his father out of love, risking his own life to fight those he held responsible for the tsar's downfall. My resentment subsided, for now.

Despite that chilling flash of rage, and his inability to see his father for who he truly was, Ivanushka had Anastasia's blood in his veins, and her goodness. I hoped in time his mother's side would win out in him, and that he would come to see his father, the tsar, for who he really was. Someday, he would also take his place. His brother, Fyodor, was safe for now. So, where else would I be? Of course, I would stay and protect Ivanushka. And by staying, I would join his cause, a true cause led by a prince of Russia—for her suffering, beleaguered people.

"I will help you, Ivanushka," I said with a resolute nod.

The tsarevich grabbed my hands, smiling at me, thanking me. The tent's walls convulsed in a wind that howled in my ears. Again I met the unwavering, still-darkened gaze of Vasily Adashev and knew he understood what had to be done. I let the unspoken words—a promise—pass between us: to do whatever was necessary to stop the tsar.

Interlude

THE LADY OF Death is growing stronger. Her body is more substantive, she stands straighter, is younger for longer. She must try to venture to the World Tree again.

As Selica steps into the swamp, a head pops out of a thicket of decaying roots and shrubs. Small, birdlike, with pointed ears and greenish hair, disheveled and dripping algae and a spider or two. The chin is pointy; a black beetle rests there. "Why would you leave this exquisite swamp?" the creature squeaks, and twirls, claws swaying above her, seaweed sliding down her wrinkled body. She is back where she belongs in her swamp.

Selica shakes her head; Kikimora has been incessant with her talk ever since she arrived eight years before. "I have no time for your nonsense. Be thankful you are here."

Kikimora stops twirling. Moths flutter from beneath her hair. "*I* poisoned the tsaritsa with my sap, my own lifeblood. *I* won my rightful place in this swamp—"

"Which I can banish you from anytime I please," Selica says, teeth gritted. "Besides, it was not difficult. Yaga isolated herself from both mortals and immortals. She would have failed to recognize any creature, much less one like you, born of the swamp."

"I had to do much to make myself Anastasia Romanovna's Great Mistress—"

"Enough! Go frolic in your hard-earned swamp, or I shall take it away."

Kikimora does not linger. She dives under the murky water and does not reappear.

Thanks be to Nav. Selica swims to the other side of the swamp, then glides across the plain. She stays solid, doesn't flicker, doesn't go out, even when she walks across the frozen river drizzled with a frost that nips at her skin.

The Tree is a riot of bursting light. Selica raises her arms, opens her mouth, and drinks in the human souls. Their light pierces her, then scalds her insides in a surge of sizzling energy, replenishing her until she is truly breathing. Truly herself.

The souls not only give her strength and youth, they are her way to someday walk among the living. If she can drink in enough of them to become truly alive.

Selica has labored tirelessly to usher the souls into Nav. It took time to find a mortal who could kill on the scale she needed. But Koshey found him. All Tsar Ivan required was a little push, so his true self would be revealed, so he could steal more lives. All Selica had to do was get rid of his pretty wife and Yaga, then summon her husband to freeze Nav's passageway and river, to bring winter and desolation to Russia.

Selica takes a step toward the plateau. Weakness tries to drag her down, as if she has suddenly thrown on a sumptuous gown of brocade and jewels too rich and heavy for her. But she does not fall. The weakness recedes. She *is* stronger. And will be stronger yet.

"It is simply not time. But it will be soon."

Selica looks longingly at the plateau, then toward the frozen cut in the fabric between lands. As she turns back to the darkness, she doesn't remember a time when she has wanted to be among the living so desperately as she does now.

Harsh laughter rose above the screams of the villagers—the oprichniki.

I whispered a few words to the local animals, then gave a whistle that threatened to split the night open. Our horses halted, kicking up flecks of ice and dust.

Just as I slid off Dyen, I spied several oprichniki coming toward us. This was quickly becoming my favorite part. "Well, well, well, we meet again!" I said. I intended to have a little fun with Tsar Ivan's bullies. The cats' meows were barely noticeable, but they were there. They had listened, and they were on their way. I had nothing to fear.

"Who are you?" demanded an oprichnik. "We have not met."

I gave him a dramatic bow. In my mask and trousers, with my long and wild hair pulled back, I probably looked no different than our men. "My apologies! That must have been your friends in the North. I am sad to report they are all dead."

"Dead?" The oprichnik blinked.

"The correct word"—Vasily was suddenly at my side—"is drowned." His eyes gleamed a startling blue when they met mine through his mask.

"Rotting at the bottom of the sea," Marya added, as she and our men surrounded the oprichniki, who drew their swords.

"Who are you?" the same oprichnik asked again, this time, uncertain.

"They have not heard of us," said Marya. A taunt pushed into her words. She turned to Vasily and me. "What do you think of that?"

"We should show them who we are," said Vasily. "So they remember."

I glanced around, at our men in their masks, the same ones worn at rambunctious entertainments all over Russia. Our men were no different than the jesters, with their own parts to play, their own disguises to hide behind. They were also wanderers, soldiers drifting across the land. I smiled at the oprichniki. "We are the Skomorokhi Knights."

"Yes," Marya said, lips curving, liking the name. "The Skomorokhi Knights."

Vasily's teeth flashed through his mask as the oprichniki lifted their swords a little higher, with a little more warning. But it was too late.

Dozens of black cats were ambling toward us, glaring and hissing at the oprichniki. I shivered at their brilliant yellow eyes, sparkling like poisonous gems. I found a button that I had sewn into my pants to ward off bad luck and held on to it. Black cats in one's path never boded well; their presence signified an unfavorable ending.

The cats flew at the oprichniki as if possessed, their claws and fangs out. The men tried to shrug them off, but the creatures pawed and scratched at them so viciously, so efficiently, that not a single inch of skin was missed. All the hooligans could do was scream and scream. As they should. A slow smile spread across my face. Fate was just, for once.

Marya lifted her mask. "You have quite the influence over beasts, dear Yaga."

"And it was as if my horse had grown wings!" said Vasily. "Be careful, Yaga, or I shall get used to your magic . . . and you." The last part was said too softly.

For a second, I thought he was jesting. But he did not laugh, and I gave a shrug. "A simple, ancient remedy. As for the animals, we understand each other, that is all."

More screams pierced the air.

"Let us leave your cats to their work." Vasily gestured, his gaze lingering on me.

As we hastened through the village, all I could do was stare. Corpses lay everywhere, their entrails exposed, the blood still oozing. Gore seeped into the snow, leaving splotches of dusky red. Some izbas had been devoured by flames, others hacked into, swaying, falling apart. Doors and window shutters swung in a bitter, rising gale. Icons and other treasures that could only belong to the poor were strewn all over. A discolored saint peered out from the dead grass, a string of freshwater pearls lifted off a pillar, cheap gold glinted in the frozen earth. I almost shut my eyes to the horror, but I forced them to stay open—to see why I had come back, why Tsar Ivan had to be stopped.

A hand, warm and secure, gripped my arm where a snake coiled in ink on my skin. One pull, and I was stumbling back. My hair, undone, lashed at my face.

I pushed it aside, wrestled from the grip—Vasily's—to see the oprichniki back to back, their blades raised, a cloud of dust and snow hurtling at them. No, not a cloud but a herd of stampeding animals. More cats, dogs and goats, roosters and chickens, even sheep, horses, a few cows. The men panicked, blustering nervously.

"Quick, quick! Gather together!" I heard them say as they drew into a tight circle, their blades wavering and sweat running down their faces.

I saw fragments of it. A black felt hat falling from a hairless head, a fluffy hen landing in its place and pecking until blood gushed forth. A horn going through a man's chest, all the way through. The punch of a hoof. The glint of sharp, little teeth belonging to a pair of mice, closing around a ringless hand, a fleshy arm, a pantless leg.

By then I was already hastening back to the izbas and what peasants were left alive there, my satchel gripped tight in my hands. In it, clean cloth and a little water, leaves of witch hazel and stalks of horsetail, my charmed infusion against festering wounds, herbs and roots against pains and fevers, and, of course, my healing ointment, meant to soothe anything from scrapes and scratches to gaping, hemorrhaging wounds.

I discovered later that Marya, Vasily, and their men did not kill all the oprichniki. Those left alive were allowed to go, barefooted and coatless, to spread the word about the Skomorokhi Knights—to the other oprichniki, and to the tsar.

Once I had aided the villagers with their wounded and our men had gathered their dead, once we had prayed with them in front of their icons and had our fill of their food and drink, we headed back to camp. It had taken a little over an hour to reach the village. The journey back was longer and more difficult in the soaring drifts of snow.

In my hut, fragrant with mint and rosemary, a fat candle burned. It illuminated the room just enough to see through the dimness but no more.

Since Noch had returned with Little Hen, people at camp had come around to my hut. They did not stop and stare at Little Hen, where she had settled on the edge of the wood, as frequently or as openly. Women and children had even started to enter Baba Yaga's infamous hut for assistance with an array of maladies, as long as Little Hen did not show her legs. The warmth inside provided them with a welcome respite from the cold, though not my food—too many herbs, they said, but they really feared finding human bones in it. On a particularly icy night a day or two ago, Bogdan and Miroslav had even fallen asleep on my pech, despite the rumors I stuffed it with children.

That night, Marya lay moaning and groaning on my pech. She was a few centuries old, and not having a god's blood in her veins, her joints were those of a very old woman, especially when they were tested and tried in the heat of battle. I sat next to her with a pot of a greasy wormwood and red dead-nettle ointment I had concocted for her, smearing it on her arms and legs as I chewed on a nettle leaf. The peppery zing in its flavor kept me awake.

The hut was as quiet as the snowfall outside, except for the chickens, who pecked and scratched at the wooden floorboards, jolting Little Hen from her slumber every now and then. Dyen and Noch were out hunting again.

"You *are* a goddess, Yaga. No one has ever made my pain disappear like you have. As you can tell, those rumors about my possessing magic are utter fuckery." As soon as the ointment had touched her skin, Marya had relaxed into the pech, stretching out like a cat. She looked up at the slanted ceiling, from which my herbs swayed with Little Hen's gentle rocking. "This hut is glorious—she's not like the rumors at all."

Little Hen gave a little hop, warming under Marya's praise. It warmed me, too, since it came from my first immortal friend that was not Koshey. I smeared some ointment onto Marya's leg. "You mean she's not hung with human bones and—"

"Your hairy body stretching from corner to corner?" Marya laughed, a wonderfully lively sound. "No, not like that at all. What does Vasya think of your hut?"

I ignored the diminutive of his name, as I had refused to use it despite his protestations. It reeked of intimacy. I shook my head, recalling Vasily's wide, almost blue eyes when he had first beheld Little Hen.

"So, it is true?" he had said, quite dumbfounded. "You have a hut that actually stands on chicken legs?" In response, Little Hen shook threateningly over him. The color drained from Vasily's usually ruddy face, and he jumped back. "It wants to kill me!"

Little Hen lunged at him again, and I hurried to pat her legs. They still had frost on them. "Well, of course she does. You called her an *it*. Come, pat her a little, and tell her something nice."

Vasily's boldness returned. Not five minutes later, he had won her over with his gentle caress and endearments, declaring that once the tsarevich was well enough to leave his tent, he simply had to meet Little Hen.

Back in my hut, blood hastened into my cheeks, still swollen from cold. He had looked at me after and had asked, "Are you made of magic?"

I answered Marya's question with the truth. "He charmed her into liking him, of course."

"He charms all women," Marya said, her keen eyes missing nothing.

"Not all." I may have had many men throughout my long life, but only one had charmed me, and he was immortal, and my enemy. Aside from a quick quenching of desire, mortal men held no interest for me. They were here one moment, gone the next.

No, Vasily is different, said a tiny voice inside me. True, Vasily was a little bolder, a little more self-possessed, maybe a little more handsome, with eyes that were quite nice, and he certainly was considerate, and thought me magical . . . What was *wrong* with me? Clearly, I was lonely or deranged or both. Maybe I would bed him just to satify this . . . need, then forget him and his nice eyes as I forgot all men.

I rose from the pech and went to put away the pot of ointment.

"What are we going to do, Yaga?" Marya's voice was small.

I wiped my hands on a rag, absently staring out the window, at the whiteness beyond, swirling and swishing and lending a cozy feel to Little Hen. But I was cold. I recalled how Vasily had stood up to Ivanushka, the silent promise we had made to stop the tsar. Little did Vasily know of the immortals who were inciting Ivan to violence, or he would not have been so enamored of my magic, or of me. I thought about Vasily's dead family, of his fight against the tsar and the oprichniki, all for Mother Russia, and my hands warmed as if he had caught them in his. No, he would not like me then.

And I still did not know what to do. I would certainly help Ivanushka and his Knights on their expeditions against the oprichniki, heal what peasants I could—but beyond that? I had hoped Kupalo's vision would have made sense by now, but aside from gleaning that Tsar Ivan had gone mad, that Koshey and Morozko were serving him and the woman in Nav, I still knew next to nothing. And to save a few mortals, even a prince, could not be the only reason for the vision. We could try to go to Moscow and kill the tsar, but Ivan hid behind an army of killers and, even if we could kill him, the immortals would just replace him. No, I needed to try to reach the gods again.

"How much do you know of our world?" I asked Marya, sitting beside her on my pech. This was the first time we had been alone and could speak candidly.

She raised herself on her elbows, meeting my gaze. "Some."

My heart gave a little flutter. Except for Mother, Dusha, and Koshey, I had not known anyone that I could unburden myself to. But could I trust Marya? What if she was another servant of darkness? Then I thought of her fighting the oprichniki, endangering her life by doing so—for an immortal could still die. And I thought of her and the mortal Varvara, their tender gazes, their clasped hands, the kiss they would share every time Marya left for an excursion and came back. How could Marya serve a cause destroying ordinary Russians if she was in love with one? It made little sense.

I would trust Marya until she gave me a reason not to. So I told her my story—not all of it, but just enough. My summer at Ivan the Terrible's court in Moscow, Anastasia's death and my self-imposed exile in the taiga, my time with Dusha studying earth magic, my reaching Kupalo and the vision in the pool, my return to civilization, and my resolution to reach out to the gods again, I just did not know which one. By the time I had finished, the snow outside had stopped. It left a shimmering darkness behind it.

Marya was quiet for a long time. Finally, she said, "Thank you for trusting me with your story, Yaga." Then, "I cannot help you get through to the gods. I myself had only one experience with them, and I think you already know about it."

I nodded, slowly, having heard the stories of how she had become immortal. It was said that while fighting the Mongols and their Golden Horde, she had seen Lord Perun up in the clouds. For once, he had come back to the Land of the Living, to engage in a battle. Perun let his thunderbolt arrows fly, until one hit a warrior princess by the name of Marya Morevna, in her chest, in her very heart, stopping it from ever beating again.

Marya lifted her rubakha and showed me the silvered scar right below her left breast—in the jagged shape of a lightning bolt.

"I will tell you my story, the one you have not heard, and it may help you." She pulled her rubakha back down. "I had a husband, when I was young and mortal."

My face must have betrayed my surprise, for she laughed, softly for once. "I was a princess, of course I was married. It was loveless and empty, not like what I have with Varvara at all. I was frequently away from the castle we called home, battling the Mongols across Russia, where I met someone you are acquainted with."

"Koshey," I said without hesitation, for who else had frequented the battlefields as much as she had? Instantly, I was on my guard. Little Hen also, for she clenched beneath me.

"I imagine I fell in love with him for very different reasons than you.

And yes, he told me all about you. I must admit, I was jealous. You were the daughter of a goddess, unattainable for him, wild and free and filled with light. I think that is what he wanted, though he knew he could never have it, or you."

I could barely breathe under her gaze, hard now, as if, having remembered her jealousy of me, it lingered in her eyes, and her soul. "He said nothing about you."

"Why would he? I did not matter to him." Marya smiled, but not bitterly. "I loved him for being a brute, for knowing his way around a battlefield. Not like my Vanya, weak and horrible with the sword, even worse in bed. Despite this, like many husbands in Russia, Vanya still treated me as a servant; Koshey, on the other hand, treated me as his equal, as the warrior I am. But as you know, nothing with Koshey lasts. He tricked me into believing he would help my army in a major battle where we were outnumbered. Then he left me high and dry, my army slaughtered. I cursed him, hated him so much I resolved to kill him. I pretended to still be in love with him and contrived a trap for him. It worked. I chained him deep in my castle's dungeon and told Vanya not to open the door while I went off to war again. Really, I went in search of Koshey's heart."

Though I knew the end of the tale, that Marya would not find his heart, when she came to a pause and seemed not to be able to bring herself to speak any more, I grew impatient. "Well? What happened?"

"What else? My foolish husband let Koshey out. He told me later that he was so overcome with curiosity he could not eat or sleep, he simply had to know what I hid in my dungeon. After he had opened the door, it was not hard for Koshey to convince Vanya to give him a meal fit for a grand prince and three buckets of water. His strength returned, he tore through the chains, and he disappeared. But not before hacking poor Vanya to bits and placing his remains in a barrel for me to find—on my dining table."

I had covered my mouth with my hand. Still, I could not suppress the gasp.

"Now, Vanya may have been a fool, but he did not deserve to be hacked to bits. I wished I could undo what Koshey had done. At the time, I had heard of the Water of Life, then thinking it was mere holy water. I visited every holy fool in the land. Finally, I came to a man with orange hair, mad green eyes, and no beard. I told him my story, not leaving anything out, and the orange-haired fool gave me a vial, instructing me to sprinkle it on Vanya's remains. The next day my husband was alive and whole."

I shook my head, confused. "I thought the Water of Life could not bring mortals back from the dead—"

"It cannot." She looked at me pointedly.

Who could bring mortals back from the dead, if he wanted to? Only one being.

"Lord Volos," I whispered—the custodian of the dead, the god missing from Nav. But he had always taught me not to interfere with the natural process of things. Apparently, he had changed his mind.

"Yes, it was he—in disguise."

"But why would he help you?"

"I soon found out. I went off to war again, to the battle at which I met Perun. After I had been pierced by his thunderbolt arrow, I should have died. Yet he appeared to me in a dream. He told me of my immortality, that the holy fool had been the Lord of the Dead, wreaking havoc in the Land of the Living by making the dead come alive to show his power to Perun. Perun, in turn, wanted to show Volos that he could kill his dead *and* make a mortal woman immortal. For the price of my immortality was my husband, who died exactly three days later to the second. So, there you have it, Yaga. Volos is alive, and in the Land of the Living. And if you reach out to him, perhaps he could tell you about the woman in Nav who has taken his place, why Koshey and Morozko are serving her, how to stop the tsar and them. But he will not be easy to find."

After Marya had gone back to the tent she shared with Varvara, I went into the woods. I started a fire, soaked up the energy from the sky, the snowy trees, and the earth, and reached into the Otherworld for the first time since returning to civilization.

I believed that, while Volos hid behind a human form, I could reach him through the spiritual realm. But though I felt the forest spirits, even the ghosts beyond, I could not travel any farther into the dimensions. I had lost my strength in these months, and I would need what dear Dusha had always taught me—knowledge, practice, and time. But time was exactly what I did not have to find yet another god who refused to be found.

Interlude

DAWN IS TOUCHING the sky, but the snow whirls on. It started a little before Koshey Bessmertny left Morozko, after learning Yaga had not gone back to the taiga despite his warnings. What will become of her? He has been ambling through the wood near the tsar's fortress, his chest aching, as if his heart is really there. The human part of him, still breathing, still existing. He doesn't turn into a bird quite yet.

The woodland is cold and lifeless at this time, when night morphs into day. Not a rustle, not even under his feet. He thinks that above the smoky clouds he sees actual smoke, as on the dawn of that battle long ago. The silence is the same, too. It is the silence of snowfall, of tragic things coming to pass. Can he smell flames, burning flesh? The battle happened hundreds of years ago, in December 1237, but it feels as if it is happening now.

Tsar Ivan's ancestors rule a Moscow in its infancy. There is no Russia yet. Her lands are occupied by the Mongols. Old Ryazan is a city on the Oka River, two hundred kilometers southeast of Moscow. Its walls are shuddering as it holds its breath, having been besieged for a week.

The city's streets are empty. The Russians are hiding in their izbas, shaking, sick at heart. The walls should hold, *they think.* They will most definitely hold.

It is snowing. Black smoke blankets the sky, blotting out the gold cupolas of their glorious cathedral. Fires are breaking out. They are destroying their indestructible walls. Only the strongest and bravest men are out on the streets. They follow a soldier, the strongest and bravest of them all. Tall, black-haired, black-eyed. His uniform is torn, and he is tired. But a fervor grips him. He will not give up his city. The invaders shall perish first!

After all, he comes from a long line of bold men who fought for old Rus'. The soldier himself has fought in many battles, and in defending this land, he has grown to love it more than anything else. Not just because it is his motherland, but because it is the land of endless horizons, of majestic mountains and forests and plains, of untold beauty. This soldier, this defender of Mother Russia, is called Konstantin.

He is nearing the wall when there is an explosion. His men fall back; wood and stones pelt them. They are on their backs. Some are wounded, a few are dead.

"Keep going!" Konstantin is on his feet, breathing in the ash and sulfur, pushing toward a wall now engulfed in flames.

A horse leaps over the wall, then another and another. The horses have shorter legs than any Russian has ever seen yet larger heads. The riders' hair streams like water down their backs, their knee-length coats like bright blue lanterns, illuminating faces red with heat, with bloodlust, cheeks slashed with scars that look as if they still bleed. They aim their bows at Konstantin, at what men he has left, and arrows fly through the air.

Konstantin runs between the ranks of invaders, hacking at them with his sword.

The snow, thick and wet, intensifies. Strangely, it does not put out the fires. Nor does it dismay those dauntless Mongol warriors. There are so many of them that Konstantin cannot see past their blue-clad, fur-lined bodies. They have made their way past his men; they are swarming his city, and the wall is crumbling.

A kettledrum beats like a death knell. It is louder than the bells of the churches.

The cavalry rolls in. Riders with metal-plated armor ride through the ruined wall, brandishing battle axes, maces, lances.

Konstantin dodges horses and men, falling planks and stones. He slips, goes down in a pool of blood. His men lie motionless, their bodies flayed open, burned, slashed into pieces. He tastes tears on his lips, struggles up, stops. A horse is gallop-

ing toward him. Though he is faint, his vision clouding, Konstantin grabs a club at his feet. He swings, once, the club connecting with the horse the instant it would have trodden on him. The rider falls. Leaping to him, Konstantin sinks his sword into the man's chest. A spray of red on his uniform. It is a small, meaningless victory, but Konstantin smiles.

The dying man opens his mouth, sputters. A radiant smile fills his bloody face. It puzzles Konstantin. The man points. "What about me?" Konstantin demands, feeling a mad need to know. But the man closes his eyes and dies.

Pain blossoms in Konstantin's body. He looks down, half expecting to be run through with a sword. But he is getting smaller. His bones creak, his head aches. He is being squeezed into a tiny version of himself. Konstantin is screaming. At least, he thinks he is. He is small, so small, and his eyes are large, so large. Huge wings appear on either side of him, black and oily. Then he is lifted into the air, and he is flying.

His heart beats really fast. He is panicking. But there is nothing to be done. A greater force is propelling him into the sky. As he looks down at the burning remains of his city, he thinks he will die of grief. Instead, he flies over drowsy villages and dense forests, until he comes to a glade with a hut that stands on chicken legs. It is surrounded by a fence crowned with skulls. A woman stands there, feeding animals. A wolf, some hens. Konstantin's heart beats even faster as he flies over her.

She stares up at him, her gaze fierce, her hair wild, her imperfections curiously charming. Konstantin has known plenty of maidens. But none of them has taken his breath away like that. He is not yet aware she is a half goddess, the vedma Baba Yaga.

Behind her hut, he bursts into a different world, a dim, dying world with decay in the air. He sees a gnarled tree. A river, throbbing black. A plain with translucent figures. And an overgrown swamp. In the middle of it, on a speck of earth, sits an old woman on a golden throne. Konstantin lands on a half-submerged log floating in front of her.

The same pain as before blossoms in his body, only he is becoming larger. He is screaming. Really screaming, his throat raw, tearing with an explosive sound that rocks through him. He senses his arms, legs, chest. He is a man again. He is himself.

Konstantin looks up at the woman. "Where am I?" he asks in a scratchy voice.

The hag gazes at him silently. Hissing snakes crawl all over her arms, slick and black with zigzags of poisonous yellow. She pries them off, the dark fabric covering her nakedness unraveling a little, and comes down from the throne. Her body flickers like a ghostly apparition as she drifts over the moss-green water and lands on his log. "What is your name, soldier?" She is in his face, so he tells her. "You will serve me, Konstantin." Her withered lips twist into a lopsided smile. "You killed my soldier."

"The Mongol." A flash of anger. "Did you send them to attack us?"

"My soldier follows whatever cause he believes in. That one happened to be a Mongol." She tilts her balding head; spots of age freckle her scalp. "How did you kill him?"

"With my sword."

"My servants are immortal, Konstantin. Yet you killed my soldier despite that." Her eyes glint like tainted emeralds. "Only a man meant for me could do so."

Konstantin opens his mouth, to insist the hag return him to Ryazan, when she starts to chant. His head splits. Color bursts into him. She thrusts her hand into his chest and takes out something bloody and pulsing. Is that his—?

The hag holds up a long needle that absorbs the pulsing thing. She takes out a quivering egg and buries the needle inside the egg, tossing it into the air. A mallard, languishing in the shadows, leaps up, opens its flat bill, and swallows the egg. A long-eared hare sprints toward the mallard. In a blink, the mallard is eaten, too.

The hag grins and scoops up the hare into her arms. "You belong to me now."

Konstantin is not sure if she is speaking to the hare or to him. He only feels the empty cavity that is his chest.

The woman is back on her throne, stroking the hare with brittle nails. At her feet is an iron chest studded with nails. "Your heart is no longer yours. It is separated from your body, along with your soul. You have no choice but to serve me."

Beneath his grief, Konstantin senses his old fervor. "I would rather die."

"Is that so?" She tilts her head again. "Or would you rather live?"

Now, Konstantin has been strong and brave not because he did not fear death. He simply never thought of it. He considered himself a tireless soldier who would never die. Finally, he thinks of it, and he is afraid. Would he cease to be, become entrapped in this strange land, or drop down to Hell with its many fires? Either way, he wants to live. He definitely wants to live. Before he can consider the price, Konstantin is nodding.

"Who are you?" he asks through numb lips.

"I am the Lady of Death, and this is my domain. I do not care whose side you choose—that of Rus', the Mongols, another foreign land. As long as I have my mortal souls, you can live on. You have the blood of Chernobog, the Lord of Darkness, in your veins now."

"But you have my heart!" Konstantin's cheeks are streaked in tears of sorrow.

"You are better off without it." Her smile distorts her wrinkled face. "You serve death now, soldier. Human emotions only burden."

Days later, Konstantin is walking through a city—his city, Ryazan. Yet he doesn't recognize it. It is a destroyed city, filled with ghosts. Where are its holy churches, its posad? Where are his men? His mother, Natalya, was old and feeble. Did she die alone? Everything is ash. And there is no one left to mourn it except for him. He cannot bear it. If he sees any more, he will die. But the hag's curse holds. Konstantin turns from the wreckage, and he is a raven, hurtling back into the sky. Emotions only burden.

Konstantin is now called Koshey Bessmertny because he is so tall and so thin, his bones show through his skin. And he is deathless. The legends around Koshey have swirled. Some are true, some are utter nonsense. Only one fact is certain: 1237 is a year Koshey has not forgotten. He never will. Nor will he ever reveal his servitude to anyone, it being his burden, his shame, his weakness. He will carry it with him forever.

Back in the woodland, Koshey raises his arms as though in supplication to the gods who have forgotten him. He senses the familiar ache in his shoulder blades as black feathers sprout from his skin and become wings. His fingers curl into claws, his mouth into a beak. And Koshey knows he will do what he has always done—survive.

22

FOR THE NEXT few weeks, hard on the heels of Tsar Ivan's men, I journeyed through the frozen North with the tsarevich and his Knights.

Usually, the invaded village or town would already be crawling with oprichniki upon our arrival, though Ivanushka's messengers or Noch tried to notify us ahead of it. Most times, we were able to save at least some of the inhabitants with the help of my animals, my charms and potions. Other times, we were too late. We would return to the camp we had made without speaking, indeed, without looking at each other. Words were dangerous, for Vasily was the son of a traitor, I the rumored Baba Yaga, Marya a warrior princess who was not supposed to exist, and Ivanushka the tsarevich. One word, one glance, threatened to upset the delicate balance between us.

On a particularly hushed night, when not even the trees rustled, we returned to camp in the grip of horror. By the time we had arrived at the last village, there had been no one left alive. The men dangled from posts, beams, chandeliers; the women lay naked in animal pens, viciously torn apart by sharp teeth and pierced with arrows.

I kept seeing their mangled flesh, their deformed features, long after we had taken our leave of that grim place. No matter what I did, it never seemed enough.

Vasily, Marya, Varvara, and I gathered in the tsarevich's tent, but none of us could stomach the meal Varvara had prepared for us. I glimpsed Varvara putting her arms around Marya, and suddenly, all I wanted was for someone to hold me. My gaze flicked inadvertently to Vasily. I shook my head, then started to pace.

The tsarevich watched us from his chair. "We will do better next time," he said.

The innocence of his statement elicited a snort from Vasily, sitting opposite Marya and Varvara on the rugs and furs. He drained his wine and wiped his mouth. His blond beard was thick now, his face somehow harder, older, the lines in it deeper. "Maybe we would do better if you did not run off to your father every chance you got—"

"What did you say?" The metal plates on Ivanushka's leather kuyak flashed as he sat forward, too young, too defensive. "You are forgetting yourself."

"On the contrary," Aleksey's son said, with an edge. "I am remembering you sit at the side of a murderer."

"He is my father and your tsar."

"You render our work meaningless when you pretend—"

"To pretend is to keep me alive—"

I met Marya's gaze, and she shrugged, as if to say, *Well, what did you expect?* Mortal men often descended into such quarrels, trading accusations like bartering fishmongers. "Please," I tried, "do not argue—"

The tsarevich held up a hand. "We found out about the last attack from a messenger. Where were your beasts? Is this really all the powerful Baba Yaga can do?"

"Yaga," I corrected him, not in the mood for his petulance. "The animals have done their best, Ivan Ivanovich. As I have told you, there are limits even to my powers. You cannot expect me to perform miracles, though I would say I *have* performed one on you." I stopped near him, my eyes shifting to his abdomen, healed in under a month.

He had the decency to look ashamed. "I was not suggesting . . ."

"Besides, your messengers have also been found lacking," I said, immediately regretting it. After all, we were not just up against a mortal tsar and his band of killers, but immortals, maybe even gods. I took a deep breath. "We should not argue. The fact is, we have a very clever enemy, an enemy that might be watching us—"

"Yaga is right." Vasily stood with his empty goblet. "Just the other day, a dozen or so ravens were circling our camp. Could someone have—a skill—like yours?"

I went cold all over. Ravens—Koshey's, or a coincidence?

I glanced over at Marya, but she didn't meet my eye. The night she had told me about her and Koshey, she had returned the next morning to ask me not to reveal her true identity, not even to Varvara. *I am a myth*, she had said. *I would like to stay that way. It is easier.*

Marya would be of no help. It would be up to me to cleanse the camp with my vodka ritual, to keep the ravens—maybe Koshey and Morozko—away, and to perform a protective ritual around the camp's perimeter, against prying eyes. If one of them discovered Ivanushka fought against the oprichniki and therefore against his father, we would be lost. The fact that it had been quiet gave me hope the ravens were a mere coincidence. I assumed Koshey and Morozko had better things to do than to follow a fifteen-year-old boy, even if he *was* the tsarevich. I also assumed Koshey's power over birds was limited by distance and connection, like mine. And that Morozko could not be everywhere, unlike his snow.

Still, I had to warn my friends, especially since Marya refused to. But how? We did not speak of my immortality. How was I to explain the actual world we lived in, the gods and creatures inhabiting it? That an immortal called Koshey Bessmertny plotted against me, that the Lord of Winter dispensed warnings to me, that a creature in Nav was controlling them both and stealing human souls on top of it? They would think me mad. But I had to tell them something.

"It is not just the oprichniki we need to fear," I said carefully. "It is also the tsar's advisor, Boyar Konstantin Buyanovich."

"Why?" asked Ivanushka. "Besides the hunger for power that is the trademark of all my father's advisors."

"I believe he possesses a similar talent to mine." I fixed my gaze on the carpet. "He has used ravens as his spies in the past. He might be using them now. And he . . . well, he is beholden to a . . . foreign power—"

"Who?" Vasily towered over me.

"I do not know," I said, for I did not know who the being in Nav was. "I . . . just know he doesn't only serve the tsar, and is purposely inciting Ivan and his oprichniki to violence. I learned of this treachery after I had left court. Either way, it is only a matter of time before Konstantin Buyanovich discovers—"

"You could not have told us sooner?" Vasily's voice was blade-sharp, surprising, as he had never before aimed it at me.

I gave him what I hoped was a piercing look. "I am telling you now."

"After we could have already exposed ourselves to him?"

"Vasily Alekseyevich," Varvara spoke just as sharply. "I hope you are not accusing Yaga. She has only tried to help us, healing His Majesty and most of the camp, and enabling you to fight the oprichniki more effectively."

Marya met my eye—guiltily? "Varvara is right. We should not blame Yaga."

"We should not." Ivanushka leaned forward in his chair. "I am sorry, Yaga."

Vasily slammed his goblet onto an oak table near the rugs, making Varvara jump a little. "We need to move the camp," he said.

"Not before we agree on a few things," I countered. "We must stop arguing, and Ivan Ivanovich must not set foot outside camp without his mask. Finally, each of us must agree to do her or his part. Ivan Ivanovich will go to the tsar as often as is necessary to avoid suspicion. Meanwhile, we will continue the fight against the oprichniki here in the North." *And I*, I added silently, *will continue to try to find a way to stop Ivan the Terrible and the beings hiding behind him*. To do that, I had to find Volos.

"I agree, Yaga." Ivanushka glanced at the others.

"We agree, too," Marya said, on behalf of her and Varvara, who nodded. Once Ivanushka had looked away from them, Marya mouthed to me, "I am sorry."

"I also agree," Vasily said suddenly. He strode to Ivanushka and bowed to him deeply. "I should not have overstepped, my lord tsarevich." Then, just as suddenly, Vasily turned his eyes on me, intent, a light within silvering the gray. "And to you, Yaga. I . . ." He cleared his throat. "I admire you greatly," he said, then muttered something about preparations for our departure before rushing out of the tent.

As we made our own exit into the still night, Varvara took my arm. "I have never seen Vasya like this," she whispered. "You have bewitched him."

I was about to tell her Vasya could go to Nav for all I cared, when we nearly walked into Marya, who had left earlier to check on the preparations. "Yaga, may I have a word?" she asked almost timidly, with an apologetic glance at Varvara.

Varvara smiled, letting go of my arm. "I should make my own preparations."

Once we were alone, just outside Ivanushka's tent, Marya turned to me. "You must think me horrible for not coming to your aid in there."

I took a breath of the chill night air, realizing I was no longer angry at Marya. We were both immortals among mortals, both women among men, both trying to find our place in the human world. I could not blame her for protecting herself as well as Varvara. I put a hand on her arm. "You are only doing what you think is right to protect you and the woman you love, my dear Masha. I could never think you horrible for that."

She relaxed under my touch. "Have you tried reaching out to Volos yet?"

I sighed, the cold air burning my throat. I had been trying to reach Volos for the past few weeks with no success. I shook my head, unable to speak for fear of weeping.

Marya gave a nod. "How were you able to reach Kupalo?"

"I waited for the summer solstice to perform the ritual in a banya." I felt the irritating prick of tears. "And we have no banya nor a year to wait."

"Both the summer solstice and the banya brought you closer to Kupalo. Though he is no longer in the Land of the Dead, Volos is still the god of the dead, and if you went to a place with the dead—"

"I might reach him," I whispered.

I was already hastening toward my hut when Marya called after me. "Yaga?"

She unfastened her glorious braid, plucked one dark hair, and held it out to me. "Since I have a connection to Volos, this small piece of me might help."

Black clouds extinguished the moonlight and stars as Dyen and I rode through the even blacker forests back to the village-turned-graveyard we had left with such heavy hearts earlier that night. I wished myself back at camp.

Vasily was nothing if not efficient. By the time I had left, the entire camp was almost ready to leave, as travel by night was safer. When he learned where I was going, he looked at me long and hard.

"You did not just forget something there, Yaga." It was a statement, a fact. He did not believe my lie. "And you will not let me come with you?"

I hesitated, then shook my head.

"I am sorry . . . for what I said in Ivanushka's tent." He took my hand in his rough one, drawing me close. "Be careful, Yaga, and come back to us . . . to me." He squeezed my hand once before letting go. But his eyes had been full of fear. Except for my companions, no one had ever feared for me. And what had he meant—come back to him?

I had had little time to think about it. Though our camp would shortly be on the move, I still performed my cleansing and protective rituals—a leaf of rosemary, three cloves, a sprinkling of sage, and a pinch of salt, in addition to the blue and red erek blossoms to hide us from prying eyes, all strewn around the camp's perimeter, along with the vodka, and chanted over. Though everyone was by now used to my odd, witchy ways, they gave me bewildered looks as a gust of wind whirled at my words. I had simply laughed it off—if that was the price of keeping them safe, then I cared not.

Now I slid off Dyen, keeping one shaking hand on his neck. For I had inhaled the air, and it smelled of blood. It smelled of death. It smelled of Russia.

I will be by your side the entire time, said my faithful wolf.

"I know you will." I stroked his neck.

Me too, Ya. Noch swooped down. She brushed her feathers against my cheek in a gentle caress before settling onto Dyen's back.

I thanked them both and started down the road into the village.

It was quiet at the end of the road, the only sound being the rags billowing on the dead men swinging in the light wind. The men had been strung up on a post and left there to rot. We had tried to bury most of the dead but had not reached this part of the road.

A wave of nausea spiraled through me as I sat in the dirt. Marya had been right—as in the banya, I had no need of a fire in this place of death, this deep in the night, these hours reserved for the Lord of the Dead. And Volos was associated with the hanged.

I faced the dead men where my fire would usually burn, and I scattered the ingredients for my ritual in a circle around me—the last of Nav's soil from my stores, along with the bark from the World Tree, a few chicken legs for divining, a magpie feather to call up the dead, and Marya's hair, to connect me to Volos.

I channeled the energy from the night, the wind, the frost, the very stars. I breathed in the smell of blood, of death, and I stretched my arms out to it all. Their weak energy trickled into me like very cold water, filled with ice and tragedy.

I closed my eyes and reached for the Otherworld, past the spirits, past the dead—all those people trapped here with their lives cut too soon and too violently to rest in peace. And beyond them to the other dimensions, including one that was green and slightly fuzzy. It felt like summer, warm and fragrant.

A face, lined yet shockingly youthful, turned toward me with wide eyes. I saw white hair and a white beard reaching bony ankles. I peered at the man, who was foreign and familiar at the same time. I could tell it was Volos in disguise, and from the large window behind him, from the moon and stars dimly visible in the sky of those parts, I knew Marya was right—Volos was in the Land of the Living. What's more, what's so inconceivable for our barren, wintry Russia, was I thought I also saw green outside the window. A tree? Leaves?

This time, the push I felt was not just jarring. My body seemed to splinter from the impact. I grabbed my head. The scream that had torn through me threatened to split me open. It threw me into pure blackness, a gaping hole, cold and empty.

I came to with the steady gait of a horse under me, her hoofbeats loud in my ears, still ringing with my own scream. I did not open my eyes quite yet. Strong arms held me by my middle, gently, as if afraid to be caught there, but tight enough to ensure I would not fall. My long, wild hair was a curtain of the same blackness I had surfaced from.

I had reached Volos, though he had not looked like himself. A fissure of hope lit within me just as dread extinguished it. Unfortunately for me, Volos had chosen a clever disguise. His appearance was no different than the hundreds, the thousands of holy fools across Russia. Still, I *had* caught him. And that unlikely spot of green . . . I would find him. In any case, I would try. Blackness spread across my vision, and I was falling back into unconsciousness. But not before I felt a kiss, on the top of my head, fierce yet tender.

And I knew, I just *knew*, it was Vasily.

Later, I learned Noch had flown all the way back to camp, and Vasily had immediately set off for the village we had left not hours earlier, where I had lain unconscious by the swinging corpses while their souls wept bitterly over me.

23

FEBRUARY 1569

WE MOVED OUR campsite to another location, where I repeated my cleansing and protective rituals against prying eyes—and immortals. In February, Ivanushka went back to his father, while Marya, Vasily, and I tracked the tsar's men on their tear through the North.

Thanks in part to my animals, we intercepted the oprichniki attacks on the unsuspecting towns and villages—or helped the survivors if we did not learn of them in time—and we raided the oprichniki vehicles, piled high with supplies and pillaged goods, always returning what was stolen to the people.

Wherever we were, I tried to heal as many as possible. And not just the wounded and dying, but women, helping with their babes, their husbands, their lovers. Whether it was in the heat of birthing chambers, in low-ceilinged rooms with spinning wheels, in darkened bedchambers with fussy, wakeful children, or in the dilapidated huts of very old women, I asked what holy fools they knew, where to find them, what they looked like.

In the months that followed, I sent Noch and her fellow owls to look for the white-haired, long-bearded man I had seen through my ritual, for the face that was not young and not old. For Volos. And for that spot of green.

Vasily and I also looked for the god. We would take his horse and Dyen and travel to every holy fool the women I spoke with named. But none had Volos's disguise.

Despite his curiosity, Vasily did not ask for an explanation for our search. After the night we had quarreled in the tsarevich's tent, he had shown a surprisingly unquestionable trust in me. He was willing to follow and help me without needing to know why. This meant he believed my reasons to be valid no matter what they were. But though we looked for him and I tried to reach him again through ritual, Volos eluded me. I knew I had to keep looking, had to keep trying. I had to have hope.

Volos was the key to learning about the woman in Nav and why Koshey and Morozko were tearing Russia apart for her. Only then could we truly fight Tsar Ivan and his Oprichnina, and eventually release the people from their tyranny and oppression.

The Skomorokhi Knights found no shortage of skirmishes to fight.

The people started to recognize us, having heard of our work. We were the masked and wandering soldiers not unlike the traveling jesters they knew and loved so well. Cheers rose when we passed their ravaged farms and estates; applause broke out when we came to their besieged towns and villages.

Apparently, Tsar Ivan had also heard of us. Ivanushka had recently written from the Aleksandrovskaya Sloboda fortress, telling us of Ivan's tirades about "the Skomorokhi fuckers threatening the very foundation of the Russian state!"

I was relieved. The fact that Ivan knew of the Knights and yet Ivanushka was still free to write signified that Koshey and Morozko did not know of the tsarevich's involvement. Or if they did, they said nothing of it to the tsar.

After each successful raid, we started to meet in the tsarevich's tent, it being the largest and most spacious. From my place by the oak table on one such night, I caught a glimpse of Marya and Varvara reclining on the furs beside the twentysomething Gorya and Fedya—young, rambunctious brothers and Marya's favorites, having fought in many battles with her. They raised their cups of mead, brewed by Varvara and the elder Yaroslav, who had since gone to bed. Sanya and Agniya were in the far corner watching their sons Bogdan and Miroslav chase each other throughout the tent.

A rush of icy wind blew inside, and the now quite handsome Mitka appeared with a pretty blond maiden that he had likely picked up from a nearby village—a frequent occurance always accompanied by rather boorish boasting. He smiled too brightly as he headed toward Stepan and Pyotr, who were speaking in low tones to a few other men near the food and drink. Vasily towered over the group of men as he recounted some exploit, judging by his animated gestures. Still, once in a while, that perceptive gray gaze shifted to me.

I picked up my mortar and pestle, trying not to read into the gaze. Or breathe too deeply of the salted fish and cabbage wafting from the other side of the tent.

A few of the camp's women came to consult me on remedies I had given them or to share gossip. A woman named Olga thanked me for a thistle and wormwood potion that had cured her daughter's fever. Yaroslav's granddaughter Yelena complained in whispered tones that, yet again, Stepan was ignoring her. Yelena was pretty but shy. I told her I would give her an amulet with dried odan and ibragim that would catch his eye, though it could not make him fall in love. She would have to do that on her own. She thanked me, flushed and happy. As she rose, Vasily approached.

"You are never still," Vasily said, sitting beside me once she had left. "Or alone. I have been waiting for you to be by yourself for an hour now."

"Why?" I turned to him with a smirk. "Do you suffer from some malady?"

"Perhaps." His eyes lingered on me, turning more amber than gray as he laughed.

It was always his laugh that drew me in. It gave me relief from the oppressive darkness that clung to me, even in this bright, crowded place.

Vasily's arm brushed against my shoulder. Though we should have been at ease, having seen the horrors we had, I shifted away, trying not to think of his arms around me when he had carried me back to camp. Or the way he had kissed my hair. I wanted to ask Vasily why he had implored me to come back to him. He admired me, apparently, yet he had not tried . . .

Stop it, Yaga, I scolded myself. *He is mortal, and too young for you.*

We watched Sanya and Mitka take their turns doing impressions of the mad tsar, ranting and raving about the Skomorokhi Knights, witches, spells.

"Tsar Ivan loves to believe himself surrounded by spell casters," Vasily said, his gaze distant. "He can blame them for every injustice, any wrong perpetrated by him or by God. Do you know he accused my father and Sylvester of being sorcerers, of poisoning the tsaritsa of Russia?"

I shook my head but was not surprised. The tsar and Koshey had also blamed me for Anastasia's death, as well as associated me with Aleksey and Sylvester. It was but one step further to accuse them of witchcraft.

"Bloodthirsty hounds! Vile dogs!" Vasily bounded to his feet, his voice booming like the tsar's. He shouted the rest over the clapping and cheers: "Lithuanian spies!"

Russia was still senselessly at war for the Livonian lands, the tsar paranoid that another noble would forsake him for Russia's biggest competition for those lands—Lithuania. That was what his onetime friend, Prince Andrey Kurbsky, had done in 1564. I couldn't blame Andrey. After all, it was safest where the bloodthirsty tsar was not.

I complimented Vasily on his impression of Tsar Ivan as he dropped back down beside me, ever closer. Only now did I notice he had removed his armor, and his midnight-blue kuyak was unbuttoned. Behind the mail shirt and the linen rubakha, I could see the bare skin of his chest, the dark hair turning golden in the candlelight.

Stop these foolish thoughts. My pulse sounded hot and fast in my ears.

I hated how I wanted to pull Vasily to me and kiss him, right there, right on the mouth. Ridiculous! He was only mortal, practically a boy, not yet thirty. Unless . . . the idea *had* occurred to me to bed him. Perhaps my maidenly crush—for that was all it was—would leave me be. But what would Ivanushka say if I were to bed his best friend? No, I would just have to become a cold, hard-hearted goddess. Except Vasily was making that very difficult. And I was half-mortal, and not hard-hearted at all.

"I cannot stop thinking about my mother," Vasily said. "My father also. Especially how they died."

Somehow, everyone had left, and only we remained in the quietly dying candlelight. I wandered over to a pitcher of mead, filled a cup with it, and sat down on the rugs where Marya and Varvara had just been. "Tell me about them," I said, leaning against the silky furs, not wanting my cold bed, wanting to be with Vasily.

"A messenger had arrived, riding so hard he had lost his hat," Vasily spoke from his place by the oak table, his voice soft and distant. "There was ice in his curls, and he bowed to my mother as though Father was the tsar himself. She didn't shed a tear. She had considered him gone already." Vasily's gray gaze was sorrowful. "You met my father—what was he like . . . at the end?"

I remembered Aleksey, that house-turned-prison. "He was much like you. The same eyes and hair, the same bearing. He was kind like you, too. He took care of everyone, opening his doors to the infirm, even as he knew there was no hope for him."

"That does sound like Father." Vasily smiled a little. "And thank you."

"What about . . . your mother?"

"She did not live long after that, tsarstvo nebesnoye to her." Vasily crossed himself, the first time I had seen him do so. "I had been no older than the tsarevich when she died of a broken heart. I put her in our chapel, the one she used to spend her time in on her knees, and I prayed over her as I had never prayed before—for three days and three nights. After that, I never prayed again."

My heart ached with my own loss, too fresh, even centuries later. "I know your pain," I said, surprised at my admission. "I lost my mother at fifteen, too."

"I am sorry, Yaga." His eyes invited me to say more. No one ever had. Whether mortal or immortal, people did not like the sight of grief. They feared it.

I took a breath, painful and strange, not having spoken of Mother to anyone except my companions. There was something about Vasily that made me speak now. Perhaps it was that, in his silence, he made space for me. I took a sip of mead, the taste of spice and honey giving me strength. "She was a . . . healer, too," I began. "We lived in a village near Moscow that we called home."

"Home," repeated Vasily, wistful. He leaned back against the table. "Tell me about your home." He closed his eyes, as if to envision it.

The memories flooded back then, of Mother, of that village, my family.

I told Vasily of the massive pech in our izba, of the red horses patterning the oilcloth on the table, the six-petaled rose carved into our rooftop in homage to Lord of the Sun, Dazhbog. I told him of how I used to duck into the overheated izba of old widow Nadya Samaravna for a cup of kompot juice, from the apricots, plums, and cherries we had picked under a crisp, late-autumn sun. Of how I used to sleep in the feathery bed of our pretty neighbor Taya and her twin girls when Mother would be absent on her travels and I too young to go with her. Of how I got older and started to visit the villages with her to heal the peasants. Then I told him of Mother. How she taught me about herbs, rituals, potions, charms. How kind she had been, how wise and knowing.

"There was a fire—" At some point, I had started to cry. I could taste the tears on my lips. "I did not think she would die. But . . . she did." And what had I done to find her? I had not even tried the ritual that would allow me to descend into Nav's dimensions. I had barely been able to access the Land of the Living's dimensions.

I was lost in self-reproach. I did not notice how Vasily took the cup from my shaking hands, lifted me up, and put his arms around me. They were expansive and so *there*. The shadows seemed to recede from us a little, the candlelight becoming stronger. Or maybe it was just him, melting away the guilt and the darkness with it.

We sat down and drank together. "You have a sister, do you not?" I asked Vasily, remembering Aleksey mentioning a Marinochka.

Vasily leaned against a heavy chest and gave a sigh. "I did, once. But she did not live long, either." He looked away. "That first winter without our mother, we stayed in our old family home. No parents, no servants. Just the great estate, decaying and dying all around us. It was cold, so cold. We would huddle together for warmth, wrapping ourselves in furs, coats, whatever we could find. But she was a sick little thing. One night, she died in my arms. Tsarstvo nebesnoye to my little angel, my Marinochka."

I had the sudden urge to hold him again, even a small part of him. I reached for Vasily's hands, and I took them. His eyes shot to my face, but he didn't pull away. His grip tightened on my fingers with an intensity, a desperation, that left me breathless.

"I buried her in my mother's garden, under a tangle of dead weeds that had once been white lilies. My heart broke at the sight of that tiny mound, just as the sun slid over the horizon, awash in a bright, bloody red." Vasily said the last in an aching whisper.

He bowed his head over our clasped hands. I felt his tears, hot on my skin.

In a few minutes, he continued, but in a voice that was brittle. "I went to live with a close relation of mine, but he was executed soon after my arrival, along with his wife and children. All those little ones, all dead. I buried them myself."

"How did you escape the tsar?" I could hardly speak.

"I had gone on an errand. When I returned—" Vasily straightened. His normally clear gaze was clouded with tears. "I lived with an uncle after that, a war hero in Tsar Ivan's army. He was eventually rounded up and killed, along with my other relations, on charges of treachery and sorcery. Really, it was because he was an Adashev. His young son was killed, too. Oh, Yaga. Every time I close my eyes, I can see it all over again. A slash! And the blood, gushing from that little throat, the boy crumpling against me. Small, so small. If not for the tsarevich, it would have been my fate also."

I stared at him, aghast. "Ivanushka was at the execution?"

Vasily nodded. "When Tsar Ivan indicated I was next, the tsarevich bounded up to me and said, 'Father, can you spare this one for me?' I stopped breathing in fear."

My chest was tight with anticipation, and something else. A new kind of intimacy. I was not only letting Vasily into my life, my loss, but he was letting me into his.

"Ivanushka told the tsar he wanted his first kill to be undisturbed. He took me to the back of my uncle's house, raised his sword, and . . . he whispered for me to run. Just like that. No fear, no trepidation." Vasily's smile did not last. "I have often wondered why he did it. My life isn't fair, you see. It is a stolen life, lived on borrowed time—"

"Don't say that, Vasya," I said, too quickly, realizing too late I had used his diminutive, something I had told myself not to do for fear of intimacy.

Our gazes met in shared pain, in the need for comfort, for simple contact. Gently, slowly, Vasily turned my hands over. Looked closely at the inked crescents on the insides of my wrists. Then he pressed his mouth to each one, sending a burst of heat up my arms, into my cheeks, through my belly. He looked up at me, his eyes too bright, too filled with heat. I craned my neck, to meet him, to taste him . . . But what was I doing?

My head snapped back. I freed my hands, still feeling his mouth on my skin. "You are here for Ivanushka. He needs you." I *need you*. Did I?

"That is why I fight," Vasily said, the moment of weakness, or desire, gone. "For Ivanushka. For my family. For all those murdered women and men, girls and boys."

I marveled at how alike Vasily and I had turned out to be. We had our causes, and we fought for them. Vasily's determination to make a difference in our country, however small, made me not only understand but admire and respect him. I raised my cup in a toast. "Think not that

21

THE MOONLIGHT SURGED from the depthless, obsidian sky,
frosting the galloping horses in front of Dyen and me silver. They
skidded and swerved on a path riddled with ice, in the face of a wind as
raw as it was savage. On either side, the pines were blue fading into
black, a trailing bruise. My mind split with images of blood. What if we
were too late?

Not an hour ago, Noch had flown into the tsarevich's tent, having
recently returned from the taiga with Little Hen. My owl's wings flapped
with a rare frenzy, an even rarer urgency. A band of oprichniki were on
their way to a small, defenseless village not far from our camp—which
meant another attack, more bloodshed.

"There is no time to lose," Marya said with bright eyes. "Vasily and
I will go."

He gave her a quick smile. "You read my mind, Masha," he replied
familiarly with her nickname, then thrust his head out of the tent and
shouted for his horse.

While Ivanushka's recovery had been speedy in the past few weeks,
with the prince now able to move around his tent, it was still too early

for him to return to fighting. And, if it were up to me, he would never fight again.

The tsarevich put a hand on Vasily's arm. "There seem to be more oprichniki than we have dealt with before, Vasya. You and Marya cannot handle—"

"They can, for they have me." I stepped forward. "But first, where are your horses?"

They did not hide their bemusement. But Ivanushka pointed the way, and I slipped out into the night. I found the horses easily, in a shadowy corner of the camp, where they were bent over their oats. I ground a pinch of diagel herb in my mortar and pestle, and added it to the trough. The horses jostled against one another, squabbling and stretching their necks. I was rubbing a dollop of deer fat into their bellies when Vasily approached with a look of wonder. He watched me, surprisingly, without a hint of humor.

"It is . . . a ritual for moments of danger and additional speed," I said, if only to say something, still rubbing at the horses. "You shall see."

"Really?" He tipped his head back, still watching me. "No, I have definitely never seen the likes of you."

If he only knew. But I just laughed, mostly to hide my confusion. Men ridiculed me, doubted me, feared me—yet they never treated my magic as a thing to be in awe of.

"What are you doing?" Marya asked, joining us. "Are we not going?"

The horses were saddled, the men readied, and we had set off on my first excursion outside of camp, with my very own skomorokh mask.

We burst through the last of the trees and undergrowth into a tiny village.

One dusty road with izbas on either side. That was it.

The villagers were streaming out of the izbas with tearful children at their heels, their dogs leaping and barking, their cats screeching.

Flames flickered, bathing the darkness a feverish orange. Yet my fingers were icy cold. I glanced around for the Lord of Winter, but Morozko did not seem to be here.

concerning these evils I will remain silent before you," I quoted the tsar's former friend Prince Andrey from a disseminated letter he had written to Ivan some years ago. "To my end will I incessantly cry out with tears against you."

This time, Vasily's smile did not reach his eyes. They had gone back to the dark gray of fierce storms and heavy clouds and gales that turned everything upside down.

Not glancing away from each other, we clinked cups, and we drank.

Interlude

SELICA IS TRANSFIXED by the light streaming into Nav. It is warm, so warm, especially on the plateau before the passageway to the Land of the Living.

Her blood responds to the light; it sings with the souls of the dead inside her.

Selica has taken to walking to the World Tree every day, drinking in the mortals until her hag-like form retreated, hopefully forever, her body more substantial and more beautiful than ever. Once her skin had started to glow silver from the souls, she knew she was strong and alive enough to try to venture into the Land of the Living.

Now, Selica takes a step toward it. She is hesitant, almost shy.

You are destined for darkness—

Selica glances back, but there is no one behind her. She takes another step.

—cursed by Lord Chernobog.

She stops abruptly. Remembers that day in all its aching details, though she lived it nearly one thousand years ago. Selica can practically see the pale meadow that sickens her with loneliness, the trees extending their bare branches toward her, the thawing cerulean river, inviting her for a taste. A devastatingly cold spring day.

"I do not want to marry him," she says thinly.

Her mother looks at her without pity. "You have no use to me otherwise. I already have a daughter to follow in my footsteps."

Selica burns with jealousy at the mention of this newest child, a child her mother apparently lives with like a mortal in a place called an izba—a home, a real one.

"You are of Chernobog, of darkness. You cannot change who you are, just as you cannot do the work my little one and I do. She is of light, your opposite in every way."

Selica glances down at her dress. She wishes to be the pure white of it. She wishes to be of Belobog, like her sister. Then her mother would love and live with her, too. Selica has not yet learned that if she desires something, she has to take it. She has to choose her fate, instead of following the outdated, fatalistic belief system of a goddess past her prime and letting fate choose her. In the still wintry breeze, the satin ribbons unfurl from Selica's hair. Their blackness reminds her who she is, who her mother is.

Selica has not seen her in years. The last time had been at the quartz palace in the Heavens for a few paltry hours. "I have little time," Mother had said. "The humans need me." I need you, Selica wanted to scream. But what would have been the point? And Mother had not visited her in that cave at all. "Poor little goddess," Simargl teased mercilessly, "forgotten, buried, erased." Her mother had only come to announce her marriage, to shackle her anew, this time to a husband and his lonely house.

Though she had been rejected long ago, Selica could not suppress the bitterness that rose up inside her. Her mother was her jailer, taking her from one prison to the next.

Now her mother flicks aside a lock of Selica's hair. Distaste is writ all over her face. "Marry him," she says. "Everything in the Universe has a purpose. The purpose of my daughter and me is to provide mortals with succor, to protect women and their destiny. As the Goddess of Rebirth, your purpose is to kill your husband."

"Yes, you told me, every year—"

"You must do so without fail. It will make way for spring, for the rebirth of the land. But do not worry. Your husband will return to you with every winter."

Her mother had failed to mention that Selica would have to take her own life by burning, then by drowning, before killing her husband. Every year. To be reborn, to be strong, to have the touch of death. Simargl had been right about this, too. She would be reborn a monster, a murderer, her own weapon.

"But I do not want to kill at all." Her voice is small.

Her mother laughs. The lingonberries in her wreath nod, also laughing. They are as scarlet as mortal blood, the blood in her sister's veins. "The Universe does not care what you want. It is how you are made, what you do. It is who you are."

Selica feels small. "Are you to sacrifice me, then, Mother?"

"Yes." Her mother's hazel eyes have never looked so green. "The Universe and the Lord of Winter must be appeased. You are the daughter of gods. You were born of obligation. Reconcile yourself to your fate, your darkness," says that great and powerful mother of hers, Mokosh. "Come, no more delay. Morozko is impatient for his bride."

Every word had been a dagger to Selica's heart. She had even expected to see blood on the white of her dress. Only her blood would be the deep black of ravens, of nightmares, of death. Selica has no memory of her wedding.

She shrinks from the light. This is what her mother did. She shamed Selica until she became an insignificance, a pebble in Mokosh's woven lapti shoes. Cursed by Chernobog, Selica has no claim on the light nor on the Land of the Living. Her sister is the one who belongs to Belobog, who deserves their mother's love and devotion, all the adoration.

"To Nav with you!" Selica cries out as she retreats back into the shadows.

She hates to utter her sister's name. It is a curse, a pestilence, her heartbreak. But she says it now, and it comes out in a terrible whisper that portends terrible things: "Yaga."

24

SUMMER 1569

JUNE WAS THE time for weddings. But as in years past, this summer was barren, the rosebuds browning before they had a chance to bloom. A steady, cold gray rain fell. Its dampness seeped into me, even as I sat in the tsarevich's tent at the oak table laden with spirits, sweet wedding rolls and loaves, and an assortment of cheeses and grains.

Yaroslav's granddaughter had had a whirlwind courtship with Stepan. As soon as the girl started to take my advice, Stepan forgot all about Mitka's maidens in favor of Yelena's fabulously red hair, cornflower-blue eyes, and innocent nature. Before we knew it, Stepan was asking Yaroslav for Yelena's hand in marriage. Now we arranged the bride's snow-white veils at the head of the table, the women gasping and fussing and kissing Yelena's cheeks, her father proud at her side with barely held back tears.

She was still awkward with youth, yet this only added to her beauty, along with her freckled cheeks, long braids, and daffodil-yellow sarafan, to which I had discreetly fastened a few eyeless needles, while Marya and Varvara placed garlic and flaxseed in her shoes—against troublesome spirits and the evil eye.

None of us had the heart for something as joyous as a wedding, especially after the grueling last few months—the nonstop riding through the North and the changing of camp locations to be nearer to the towns and villages most in danger from the oprichniki. Then ritual after ritual in hope of reaching Volos again, visiting one holy man after the other, to no avail. I was starting to feel the strain of it all on my body, and in my spirit.

Because of the foul weather and his father's even fouler temper, the tsarevich had not returned from Aleksandrov—worse, we had not heard from him, had even sent Mitka to Aleksandrov to find him. Especially when we started to receive worrisome reports that Ivanushka had been sighted on the tsar's expeditions against the people.

Why wasn't Ivanushka standing up to Ivan and refusing to partake in the expeditions? Was he still blaming the oprichniki? I wanted to protect the son of my Anastasia, to fulfill my promise to her. But I did not know what to think of the son of Tsar Ivan.

Back in the tent, Yelena beamed with happiness, and I resolved to hold on to that smile—it spoke of love and good, the opposite of Tsar Ivan's hate and evil.

The groom, handsome in his ivory kaftan, came in with the men. I kept my eyes on the bride, knowing Vasily was there, knowing his gray eyes had found me.

He slid in beside me on the bench, his embroidered scarlet kaftan grazing my arm. I ignored the spark of warmth, how that costume brought out his tall figure, how his blondish-bronze hair swept into his eyes too charmingly. He had become a lion of a man in the near half a year I had known him, in bearing and in appearance, especially with those broad shoulders and thick beard.

There had been a shift between us the night he told me about his family and his escape from Tsar Ivan. When he was near, my heart was full for the first time in years, like I wasn't alone, certainly a new experience with a man, mortal or otherwise. It was not a crush, nor was it only about comfort or relief from pain. Our camp had become a sort of home for us, two beings adrift and lost in the world. It made me question my philosophy on love. Maybe belonging to someone was the key to life, the key to happiness, even if it did not last forever. Maybe I could have what Marya and Varvara had, too. Still, I did not let myself get as close to Vasily as I had on that night.

Especially since he looked at me with even more intensity, sought me out and stayed beside me. Thankfully, I no longer kept a dried bat in my clothes; too pungent.

Vasily smiled at me now. "You look well, Yaga," he said.

My lips twitched. "Don't we all? A far cry from the dust and filth of the roads."

"No, *you* look well. Really . . . beautiful." He shook his head and scrubbed the back of his neck. His smile fell away. "But this wedding could not have come at a worse time."

I took his hand under the table, still warm from his compliment, and gave it an *I feel the same way* squeeze. "I know."

Vasily brushed his fingers against the crescent on my wrist.

My heart sped up. I had just taken a drink of wine from my goblet when a movement at the tent's entrance caught my eye. The flap of a wing—Noch.

"I will be right back," I hastened to whisper to Vasily before hurrying out of the tent. I had sent Noch on yet another mission to find Volos, and I was eager to see if she had found anything new. Likely not, since there was still no sign of the god.

Outside the tent, the rain had slowed. It fell in silent, icy droplets onto my face, leaving not only my skin numb, but everything inside me also.

You will not believe this, Ya. As soon as Noch saw me, she flew over. *You shall love me forever.*

"I already love you forever. What is it?"

I was almost to the taiga— Before I could ask, she flapped her wings. *Dusha is well. But on my way back to camp, I flew over a number of villages where there was talk of all kinds of oddities—flocks of sheep and cattle missing, as well as hay and crops from harvest, mirrors, coins, herbs, even chickens, all gone.*

My hands went cold. Volos loved to steal, sheep and chickens especially.

Of course, I investigated further. A man called Nikolai Salos, otherwise known as Mikula, has moved into a singularly strange house in one of the nearby villages. Snow cannot touch this house, and there are green trees in a yard filled with sheep!

That spot of green . . .

Some say this man is a holy fool, others a madman.

"What does this holy fool look like?" I asked, hardly daring to think, to hope.

He fits your description perfectly, Ya. As tiny as his house, white hair and beard, his face both old and young, almost . . . childlike.

And I knew Mikula was none other than Volos—the Lord of the Dead.

"It is him?" Marya's voice came from behind me.

I had not realized that she, Varvara, and Vasily were also outside.

I nodded once, though I could not speak. I had found Volos. All I had to do was ask Noch where he lived. All the months, weeks, days of searching for him, and now I had him. It left me dazed, and somehow strangely empty.

I blinked up at them. "I must go," I finally said.

Marya took my hands in her strong, comforting grip. "You must, dear Yaga. And you must convince him to join us."

I was light-headed at the enormity of the task. Not only to confront a god in hiding, but to obtain answers *and* enlist his help. I tightened my hold on Marya, wishing she could accompany me. But she was not of the gods. Volos would not appreciate her presence, at least not right now. Vasily could not accompany me, either—being mortal, he could not understand my world no matter how much he tried.

Varvara said nothing. She simply put her arms around us both.

Then she and Marya returned to Ivanushka's tent. The wedding feast was now in full swing, a last burst of frivolity before the more solemn church ceremony and bedding began. The clink of goblets and laughter reached us even here. Only Vasily and I remained outside, with a space between us that had suddenly grown.

Finding Volos changed everything. Immortals changed everything.

The fight against Tsar Ivan was about to take a perilous turn—I had to be strong, had to focus, now more than ever. Distractions would lead to missteps, miscalculations, missed opportunities. They would lead to mistakes that could cost us everything. And I had to keep Vasily out of it, had to keep him safe, from me and what I carried with me.

"What are you so afraid of, Yaga?" Vasily closed the space between us, his breath rushing at me. "Why do you still refuse to let me in?"

"Because there are things you cannot understand about me—"

"That is an excuse, Yaga." His hands were on his waist, on the white-gold sash of his kaftan. "I want you, all of you. I do not care where you come from, what you do, only that—" He broke off, looked away. "Only that you want me, too." His eyes, when they had shifted back to me, were that dark, dark gray, the gray of the skies above us.

I licked my lips, tasting rain, and I reached for Vasily.

I touched his face, stroked his cheek. The beard beneath my hand was damp and rough. My blood was on fire, my heartbeat thudding in my ears. Before I could change my mind, I grasped him by the collar and pulled him toward me, pressing my mouth to those slightly parted lips with all the heat inside me, all the wanting of the past months. His eyes widened in shock. But they fluttered closed. He opened his mouth, letting me in, and he kissed me back with a fervor that stole my breath, and what remained of my heart.

I pulled away, both of us breathing hard, both of us unsteady, unmoored.

I wanted to tell Vasily that I did want him. That I was maybe even in love with him. That I would tell him about me, this time, all of me. But I could not love a mortal man. I could not love anyone. I was a half goddess, the daughter of Mokosh, Baba Yaga. No man fit into my life, the direction it was taking, back to the gods, back to my world.

"I am sorry, Vasya," I whispered. Then I turned and fled.

25

T HE HOLY FOOL Mikula lived in a tiny stone house at the end of the most winding street in the tiniest northern village I had seen. It took Dyen and me a day of travel from camp to reach it.

I smelled pure air and saw the mountains, rising above a scattering of homesteads and izbas veiled in the violet shadow of afternoon. The air cleared my head and, with it, the image of Vasily, the hurt in his face, that kiss, the one that kept coming back to me, unbidden. It had left me wanting more, but I could not succumb to my infatuation. I resolved not to allow my foolish heart to distract me from my work.

As Noch had described, Mikula's house was surrounded by blooming green trees despite the snow. Behind the wooden gate, sheep congregated, so fat and fluffy it was as if the very clouds had descended from the sky. Among the sheep, with a tall shepherd's staff, stood the tiny, naked, white-bearded Mikula with his lined yet shockingly youthful face—the same face I had seen through ritual when I had reached Volos.

I slid off Dyen and approached the gate, taking hold of the wooden planks with hands that were stiff with cold. I pressed my face between the planks. "Are you Mikula?" I called out to the man, who looked up with a quickness belying his age.

"Who is asking?" His voice had a touch of airy, childish laughter to it.

"The daughter of Lady Mokosh—Yaga."

"Don't you go by a different name these days, daughter of Mokosh?"

I opened my mouth, then closed it. "Baba Yaga," I finally answered.

"Baba Yaga . . ."

I held my breath, half expecting Mikula to turn into Volos right then and there.

"Nay, I know you not!" He spun on his heel and kicked the gate closed.

I blinked after him in dismay. Mikula did not sound like the holy fools I had once known, dour men who rarely spoke of anything other than their almighty. His quick words, flicker of a smile, and agile movements were all veiled in a strange, shifting whimsy wholly uncharacteristic of holy fools. I wondered how Volos had kept up the ruse for so long. I pounded on the gate so hard my fists ached.

The gate opened a crack, keeping Mikula hidden. "You are scaring my sheep," he said. "Are you to go after my cattle next?"

"I need to speak to you—I know you are Mikula . . . and I know you are Volos."

"Ha! You are a strange bird! I am only a man, a Christian, a holy fool. I went through great pains to obtain my sheep. I refuse to let Baba Yaga cause them undue stress. Good day."

"Great pains? You stole them, Volos. That is how I recognized you."

A giggle, then nothing.

I pushed past the gate into the yard, empty of Mikula. At the sight of Dyen, the sheep shuddered and pressed their fleecy bodies against me, barring my way.

Dyen growled with a show of fangs. *They are getting on my nerves. I shall have to eat one to shut them up . . .*

"You shall do no such thing," I said, and charged past them with my hands over my ears. Unlike ordinary wolves, Dyen could control himself. Mostly.

Mikula's dwelling was not a typical house, being larger on the inside than it appeared on the outside. The hall I entered was spacious with floor-to-ceiling windows. But it was all the greenery that really caught my eye—the same greenery I had seen through ritual. Swaying palms and verdant bushes, flowering blossoms bursting with fresh pinks and whites. I inhaled the long-forgotten fragrances of tea roses and peonies.

Vines crept out of the stones in the floor, the whitewashed walls, the rough-hewn furniture. My ears filled with the rush of water, from the translucent streams weaving through the space to the bubbling brooks pooling in the corners.

It was living, breathing summer, hidden in one tiny house.

My wonder peaked when I saw a throne of branches that twisted like snakes. On it sat Mikula with his shepherd's staff. But he had a very different face and beard now, each one half-young, half-old. It was Volos—the Lord of the Dead.

I blinked rapidly, not quite believing it was him. "Lord Volos."

"So, you found me, Yagusya."

I didn't remember the last time I had seen him, but I remembered the first time Mother had taken me to the Land of the Dead when I was no more than seven years old.

How the darkness of that place clawed at my wide eyes, its dank air at my little throat, its silence at my ears. Mokosh and I had met a frazzled Volos by the passageway. Something in the soil had maddened his flock of sheep. They had been assaulting the mortal souls, devouring his pet vines, and generally wreaking havoc.

"Look!" I had cried out, seeing a blue-backed swallow fly over the pulsing black river. No sooner had I reached the water than cold fingers grasped my wrist, pulling me back.

"You cannot cross this river, Yaga, or you will die," Volos had said in a severe voice. "As a daughter of Mokosh, you are given talents humans can only dream of. But magic cannot be hoarded. Be thankful, child, or it shall be taken away."

"Look at you," said Volos back in his house. "How far you have come, Baba Yaga." His aged eye was detached, the young one piercing gold and assessing.

Suddenly, my chest was tight. If he had stayed in Nav, none of this would have happened. "And look at you. Why aren't you on your real throne, Lord Volos?"

"I am where I should be. As god of the living, I can grow vegetation here just as well as in the Land of the Dead. Besides, I prefer it in the sun, among mortals who worship me." A vine slithered up to Volos, and he stroked it absently.

Magic cannot be hoarded, he had warned me. Yet here he was, hoarding. And I heard the same longing for life and worship from him as I had heard from Morozko.

I needed to talk sense into Volos. But I had to tread carefully, for he was a jealous, treacherous god. Russians with land and beasts still feared him, sure to leave him an offering or two in the fields at harvest. I myself didn't fear Volos. He was neither good nor evil, standing apart from other gods, self-interested, self-serving. And he had had a relationship of mutual benefit with Mother in the past, she helping him with his flock, he with her herb making, the intention in her rituals and spells and charms.

I said, "You may be growing vegetation in your house, but the land lies barren. Not like when you were on your real throne, and both the Earth and Nav flourished."

"Of course. What vegetation grew in the Land of the Dead also grew in the Land of the Living, where Lord Kupalo tended to it—"

"Then what made you leave? You were banished again, weren't you? Only this time, it wasn't by Perun . . . but by some being, some minor goddess. Who is she?"

Volos clucked his tongue. A sheep lumbered over to him, chewing hay and bleating forlornly. "A woman sold into marriage to a cold god who refused to see her and used her little better than a servant. To die every year, to burn, then drown, to be reborn so she could kill her husband and make way for spring. No, I do not blame Selica."

So that was her name. Selica. There was a rush of blood to my skin, of impotent rage at this being who called herself *Lady of Death*. But. To die every year. To kill. To be sold into marriage. To be used as a servant by a cold god. There was only one god cold enough. "Morozko has a wife?" This explained why Roz was so invested—he was serving his own wife. I wondered when he had become the servant and she his master.

"Do not look so pained for her, Yaga," Volos said, seeing what must have been pity on my face. "Selica killed Tsaritsa Anastasia. Was she not a friend of yours?"

A rushing filled my ears, my vision oscillating. "How?"

"A servant of hers did the deed. I believe she was the tsaritsa's Great Mistress."

Kira Armikovna? But how? When?

"She is none other than Kikimora," Volos said, as if I had asked out loud.

I had heard of this creature, this monster. Known for her birdlike appearance, Kikimora plagued the dreams of mortals who succumbed to sleep near whatever swamp she happened to be haunting. But how could the pretty, blond Kira Armikovna be Kikimora without her trademark green skin and hair? I had heard of some immortals being able to hide their true selves, but I had thought this a myth. But then I recalled the green footprint I had seen, the drop of the same green on Anastasia's gown, the spiders and my dead animals, and her inexplicable hatred of me, and I realized with a shudder that it must be true, though I didn't know how. Curse her. Curse her for her duplicity and treachery. And I cursed myself that I had been unable to discover her perfidy before it was too late.

"Where is Kikimora now?"

"In the swamp of Nav."

At least she was not at large in the Land of the Living. "And what did Selica and Morozko do to you?" I asked numbly.

Volos shrugged. Tufts of hair burst from a bony shoulder on his aged side. A luxurious brown bear pelt covered the rest of his body, including the private parts, thanks be to the Heavens. "Selica came armed, that is all. Her touch is deadly after her death and rebirth. She said she did not have to kill me, as she had her mother. Instead, she offered to return me to the Land of the Living, provided I let her take my place. I was too happy to oblige. I invented a personality, and ta-da! Here I am. I have had to reinvent myself over the years, of course. But I am fond of Mikula the Holy Fool, a mortal man, a Christian. A clever disguise for an old god, yes?" Volos shifted on his twig throne.

"What do they want, Selica and Morozko? And why is Koshey involved?"

"Koshey Bessmertny has pledged himself and his life to Selica and her cause. I have heard she has something of his."

"His heart," I breathed. I had always assumed he had separated his heart, his soul, from his body. I thought of Marya, who had looked all over the Land of the Living for it, when it had been in the Land of the Dead the entire time. Or wherever Selica had hidden it. Perhaps Koshey was so scared of being mortal, of dying, that he had traded his will, his very life, for immortality, and did her bidding blindly. To be Bessmertny. Deathless.

Volos rubbed the sheep's back with his foot as another sheep ambled over. "As for Selica, I assume she has come to regret her decision to take my place. You see, Yaga, even the dead desire the light. Why else would she need the human souls she is pushing Ivan to take? If she amasses enough, she may be able to become a living being and return to the Land of the Living. I myself chose to catch one of Perun's thunderbolt arrows rather than do so. But I imagine Perun's arrows are hard to come by these days."

I took a deep breath. "Lord Volos—"

"You are about to ask me to intervene, to convince the other gods to do the same, to stop Selica and Ivan the Terrible in their reign of terror, yes?" I opened my mouth to say, *Yes!*, when he said, "No, dearest Yaga, I cannot. It would only serve to expose me."

I thought fast. Volos was too selfish to care for the country. He was too cowardly. *All gods are cowards*, Mother had told me once. *Some of us are simply better at masking it. Not Volos. He suffers from an easily wounded vanity.* The kind of vanity that could be shamelessly flattered to obtain what one desired.

"Are you not the mighty god who fought Perun for the sky in countless battles, even the one that forged old Rus'?" I kept my voice demure for the greatest flattery. "Who was never afraid to take anything of Perun's, not even his beloved Dodola?"

Volos's eyes fluttered; he scratched one of his horns. "Ah, my Dodo, a sweet thing, though she did flood Nav when she was there. My Lady of Rain. Hmph! Lady of Tears is more fitting. She wept entirely too much. We were not meant to be."

Well, you did abduct her. I arranged my face to look baffled. "So, it is true?"

"It is all true, my dear." His gold eye bulged in pride.

"You lost, yet you always returned, you always fought on."

"I was never afraid of him. But when I think of that place where he imprisoned me . . . I eat." Volos produced a turnip from a woven basket by his throne and bit into it viciously. "Selica saved me from that death by giving me life."

"You may not have been afraid before," I said quietly, "but you are now."

Volos leapt up. His turnip flew into the air. "Of Perun? Why, he has not been seen in hundreds of years! Cowering in the Heavens, I am sure. No, Yaga, I am not afraid. Not of Perun, not of the tsar. I simply prefer to live in the light."

"You are hiding, then—in Perun's world." *Like the coward you are.*

"It is not *his* world. *He* is gone!" But he knew what I said was true.

"Not seen is not gone. Face it, Lord Volos, you live in his world."

Volos sat down wearily. The vine slithered back to him. The sheep bleated at his feet. "You make . . . valid points."

"So will you help me?" I asked, not letting my eagerness show.

Volos broke into a wide smile. One side of his mouth had strong white teeth, the other empty cavities and gums. "I know not. We shall have to live and see."

"For how long?" I asked. "And do you know where my mother is?"

"My sheep need me." I opened my mouth in protest, and he held up one trembling hand. "*I* shall be the judge of how long the living and seeing shall take."

He ushered me out of his dwelling, the door hitting my behind painfully on the way out. I wanted to pound on his door, break it down, but what would that do? He had given me some answers, though not all. It was always thus with gods. If I pushed too hard, he would refuse to help me. Yet I would still be returning to camp with nothing. Knowing about Selica, Morozko, and Koshey was well and good, but it did not offer me a way to stop or even fight them. In the meantime, Tsar Ivan and his oprichniki would continue to murder and spread terror, to oppress Russia and her people.

Tired and disappointed, I climbed onto Dyen and let him take me back to camp as twilight deepened into a very black night. And as dark forests replaced villages, I replayed the events in Moscow, Anastasia's poisoning by the monster Kikimora and my unsuccessful efforts to help her, the idea of what we were truly up against sinking into me with all its difficulties. Not only a tsar hiding behind an army of murderers, but a vengeful goddess killing to live with two immortal servants sworn to oblige her—and the half-mortal Baba Yaga in the middle of it all.

26

NOVEMBER 1569

"THE CHILD IS strong, Lenochka," I assured Yelena, who lay on her pallet propped against a mound of pillows as the snow came down outside the tent. I kept my hand on her swollen belly and was rewarded with a tiny kick. "Your little one does not like to be still."

It was now November, and Yelena was in her sixth month of pregnancy.

As soon as she had failed to come for bleeding rags, I knew she was with child and immediately dragged a jar of hemp oil to her tent as an offering to Mokosh.

I brought my ear to Yelena's stomach, opening my senses to listen for the babe's heart. I heard the little flutter against my eardrum and was thankful. I bowed my head and whispered a little charm over Yelena: "The first mother is the Holy Mother of God; the second, Moist Mother Earth; the third, the mother who gives birth in pain. Keep our newest mother safe." Though it spoke of new gods in addition to the old, I liked to use the charm; two mothers watching over a young mother was better than one.

Looking at Yelena's rounded belly, her glowing eyes and cheeks, her air of womanly confidence, I felt a stab of envy. I swallowed against the unfamiliar sensation. But I was suddenly painfully aware of the emptiness of my own womb, of the sad fact that pregnancy was an impossibility for me.

After I had witnessed my first birthing not ten years into my life, Mokosh had explained to me the intricacies of lovemaking and childmaking. "Though immortals can birth other gods and half gods," she had said, gently, "it is not simple for us, with mortals above all. Most of the time, it happens not. It is even harder for half gods. If it happens, it does so for a reason. It is willed by the Universe." I had known many men over the centuries, both mortal and immortal. Not once had my trysts ended in anything other than fleeting pleasure or pointless regret. I knew it would never happen for me.

It was just as well. The only man I liked was barely speaking to me. For I had not run into Vasily's arms upon returning from Volos. I believed I had done the right thing. I could not afford to be distracted, not by Vasily and certainly not by love.

At first, he had made friendly overtures, clearly hoping to rekindle what had passed between us the day we kissed. But though it pained me, I responded only with cool reserve, and withdrew from him, until he stopped seeking me out, stopped riding with me, stopped speaking to me. I could tell he was hurt and confused. He had helped me in my search for Volos for months, asking no questions, and now felt cast aside. We had spoken little in the past months, and I had largely avoided camp, keeping to my woods and my magic, healing in Little Hen or in the tents of the women, and accompanying Marya to the nearby towns and villages. It was a precarious time. Ivanushka had still not returned to us, nor had Mitka sent any word.

I still had not heard from Volos, either, though I had since tried to reach him through ritual. I also tried to reach Lord Kupalo again. But neither god answered, even as the situation in Russia did not improve. I had told Marya about my conversation with Volos, and while she understood I had done my best, I had seen the disappointment in her face. All because Volos was too busy living and seeing and tending to his stolen sheep.

I summoned a smile for Yelena and gathered my healing implements. "Get some rest, Lenochka. I shall return later." No sooner had I spoken than a clamor arose outside, urgent voices and footsteps, a horse wheezing and fighting for breath.

With a few last words to Yelena, I rushed out of the tent, both praying for news and dreading it.

Through the wintry-white haze, I saw a man tumble from his horse. It was Mitka, finally back from Aleksandrov.

The men were quiet as they crowded the boy, nearly senseless in Sanya's arms. His blond hair was plastered across his forehead in dark, wet streaks, his coat threadbare and dirty, his cheeks hollow. He was a shadow of his old sparkling self.

Vasily was gesturing at Sanya. "Get him into the tsarevich's tent." His gaze landed on me, lightening for just a moment, before returning to its usual cold slate gray.

"Take off his wet coat and wrap him in furs," I instructed Marya, turning toward the fire where Yaroslav did his cooking. There I managed to scrounge an infusion with the ingredients from my satchel— honey to warm, rosemary to stimulate the blood, basil to keep colds away. I brewed and strained the mixture, but not before adding to it a dash of snow, to purify and clean Mitka of his travels. I charmed the infusion to prevent illness and fever, then carried it in an iron cup to Ivanushka's tent.

Sanya and a few other men hovered at the entrance, and just inside, blue-lipped Mitka shuddered, even as Marya and Varvara covered him with furs. They left quietly as I approached. I rubbed at his arms for circulation and handed him my concoction.

Something had happened at the tsar's fortress.

My eyes strayed to Vasily. The flames of the bronze candlesticks quivered like frightened children as he paced past them. Every so often, he would meet my eye, scrub the back of his head, and keep pacing. Why was it that even in such dire circumstances, even with a broken boy in front of me, I could still feel our kiss? Why did my gaze keep drifting to his rubakha, haphazardly pulled into his trousers and undone at his chest? Had he been sleeping? Because of the snow, we had been unable to leave camp that day.

For gods' sakes, Yaga, focus.

Mitka raised his head slightly, the concoction beginning to do its work. "It is hardly a palace," he whispered, the hush in the tent more horrible than the one outside. "Aleksandrovskaya Sloboda is a fortress, remote and isolated. No one is aware of what goes on there. The interrogations. The torture. The murder. The air is . . . heavy with the stench of flesh, of the decomposing dead. The corpses are left outside to rot, you see, the tsar not believing that traitors deserve a Christian burial."

A shiver of horror rippled through me. But then, I had seen Russia's villages.

Vasily crossed his arms at his chest. "How did you get inside?"

Mitka drank more of my infusion. Color sprang into his cheek. His voice became stronger. "I decided the best way to reach Ivanushka was from the inside . . . as a guard."

Vasily stared at him. "You became an oprichnik?"

"It was the only way I could think of reaching Ivanushka. But the things I saw . . ." He shuddered. "The tsar is never more cheerful than when he is in his dungeons, taking part in the terror. Blood spurts at him, and he is so excited, he shouts, *Goida! Goida!" Hurrah! Hurrah!* "A day does not pass without the murder of at least a dozen people. The oprichniki who do not do his bidding are executed. But there is one man who does whatever the tsar commands, the bloodiest deeds he can envision, without fail—Malyuta Skuratov." Mitka's voice had descended to a whisper. "He is the tsar's hangman."

My skin turned to gooseflesh. "Did you find Ivanushka?"

"Yes." Mitka met my gaze. "But he is not himself. The tsar has been forcing him onto his expeditions. I know because I went on one such expedition. They didn't care about me, so I myself was not made to do anything. But Ivanushka was. I . . . saw him kill, and not just once. Many times, many people." Mitka swallowed. "He seemed hesitant, sick after, loathful of what he had done. I resolved to speak to him. But he was always either with his father or with the oprichniki. The few times I could get him alone, he said he had no choice and seemed hopeless about being able to get away. Every movement of every day is accounted for. The tsar runs the fortress like a monk, forcing everyone to rise early, to attend church services, even to refer to one another as Brother."

They *were* brothers, in their own way, for they shared their desire for murder as zealously as monks shared their faith. But Ivanushka, a killer?

"What about the tsarevich's brother, Fyodor?" I asked.

"He is safe, in prayer and contemplation at some monastery or other."

I let out a breath, now wanting to find out more about Ivanushka's mindset. I leaned toward Mitka. "Does the tsarevich still blame the oprichniki?"

Mitka gave a shrug. "He has been forced to see his father's true self, but he is afraid for his life—"

"We are all afraid!" Vasily burst out. "Look at Stepan, about to become a father, yet fighting on. And Marya and Varvara, exhausted, yet here. Still here. And Yaga . . . taking care of all of us." He said the latter with his eyes on me. "Ivanushka used to fight, too. And now what? He prefers to fight at his father's side? He is killing his own people? If so, he is a traitor . . . to us, and to the motherland." Vasily continued to pace, keeping his distance from the tsarevich's chair, which sat empty in the corner.

"He has tried to speak to his father on several occasions, the most recent of which is why I returned now without him." Mitka drained the rest of my potion. "Tsar Ivan has secretly been evicting hundreds of families from the cities of Novgorod and Pskov."

"God forbid he wants to lead an expedition against them," whispered Varvara.

That would be serious indeed, as Novgorod and Pskov were some of the oldest and richest cities in Russia, given that they traded with Europe.

"Ivanushka asked the tsar about the evictions, begged him not to send an expedition there. Though the meeting was cloaked in secrecy," Mitka said with his old twinkle, a shadow of a boast, "I managed to slip in and remain hidden."

Vasily strode over to us, stopping directly behind me. "And?"

"The tsar was outraged. He mentioned a letter, proof of some alleged conspiracy in Novgorod, to bring its territories under Sigismund Augustus—"

The king of Poland and grand prince of Lithuania . . . It was no wonder the tsar was paranoid. The northwest cities of Novgorod and Pskov were far from Moscow and too close to Livonia, the foreign lands west of Russia. Lithuania, the foreign power fighting Russia to gain Livonia, was also a formidable neighbor. Still, wasn't it something that a treasonous letter had been found so easily and so conveniently?

Vasily was evidently wondering the same. He pulled at his beard, his gaze intent on Mitka. "Is the letter their only proof?" asked Vasily.

"And what about Pskov?" Stepan stepped toward us.

"In October," Mitka said quietly, "the tsar supposedly learned the guards defending Pskov's nearest fortress opened its gates to the Lithuanians."

"Impossible," Vasily whispered, echoing my thoughts. He was so close that I could almost lean against him. And I badly wanted to fold into his arms.

"No Russian would ever do that," added Marya, "not even under threat of death."

Mitka shrugged. "The tsar insists there is treason there. Apparently, the Novgorodians are complaining about the taxes in support of the army fighting our wars, about the army billeted there, about trade coming to a standstill. The tsar is broken and vengeful, especially following Tsaritsa Maria's death—many believe from poison."

I drew back in shock. "Tsarstvo nebesnoye to her," I joined in with the other whispers in the tent before making the sign of the cross.

"And everywhere there is Konstantin Buyanovich." Mitka turned to me. "You were right about him, Yaga."

The blood had drained from my face, and I was very cold. Koshey did not surprise me, given his service to Selica. But I could barely process the newest tsaritsa's death, thinking of her and Anastasia both. Nor could I accept the fact that Ivanushka was now complicit in his father's crimes. He had finally seen through to the tsar's evil, had even stood up to him about the two cities, but he was too frightened to refuse to join him on his expeditions, to descend into his dungeons, to kill for him. Was Ivanushka his father's son through and through? Was there nothing left in him of my Anastasia?

Even worse was the threat to Novgorod and Pskov—major cities with thousands of inhabitants. Their destruction would be an incredible escalation. If Tsar Ivan commenced his reign of terror there—and he would, eventually, for once the idea of treason and conspiracy was on his mind, he was loath to let it go—what would be left?

I had been patient with Volos, but we had run out of time. I had to get through to him. Tonight.

I sat in the snow, the woods white and silent. I knew that this time, I would reach Volos. Maybe it was the dire need. Or the vibrancy of my memory of the god and his dwelling, the fact that I knew where he was. But I drank in the energy all around me as if it were the last time, filled myself up with it until I sizzled magic, and went into the Otherworld, then past it, farther and deeper into the dimensions, until I was back in Volos's dwelling.

Though blurry, I could see through to the fragrant, living green of it—and to the half-young, half-aged face of the Lord of the Dead.

He was sitting on his throne, majestic as ever, with his staff gripped in his strong hand. Unlike our surroundings, Volos was as clear as glass.

I had not spoken in the dimensions, and I opened my mouth uncertainly. But the words came. "You must intervene, Lord Volos, before Ivan the Terrible destroys Novgorod and Pskov, and everyone in them."

Even the god of death looked alarmed at the idea that Ivan would commit such horror. Volos put up his old hand; it shook. "What would you have us do?"

I had not yet figured out how to stop the tsar entirely, not to mention the immortals who hid behind his violence. But I could slow Ivan down. To do that, we would need to draw him out; we would need a distraction. As I looked at Volos, I saw Mikula the Holy Fool. The Christian.

The magician. Ivan had always been fascinated with those he considered holy. Fools. Kolduns. Vedmas. Baba Yaga.

Not many are as holy as me, Ivan had told me once. *Still, many try.*

How fascinated he had been with me that summer in Moscow, even believing me to be as holy as him. How small he would look in the vodka bath I would draw for him, how ordinary he would seem when he prayed to his saints in his church.

I drew in a sharp breath. *When he prayed to his saints.*

That contrast—between the glittering tsar in front of his court and plain Ivan in front of the Christian lord's resplendent wall of icons. It was the holy that had always secretly intimidated Ivan.

"I believe the tsar still fears his god," I said to Volos.

He hacked out a laugh. "Ivan strings up priests and monks by the dozens. What makes you think he fears anyone, least of all his god?"

"I knew the tsar once. He does not believe those priests and monks to be holy, only pretending at holiness. But if he does consider someone holy, and close to his god, there is no end to his fascination . . . or his fear."

Volos's gold eye glinted. "Mikula the Holy Fool?"

"Precisely." I took a small breath, darkness suddenly creeping into my vision. I forced myself to keep going. "If Tsar Ivan believes Mikula to be a holy man, if he fears him as he fears his god, we may succeed in influencing him. Confronting Ivan about his actions will draw him to us. It will put the fear of his god in him and slow his rampage, which will in turn slow Selica and rob her of the souls she needs for the Land of the Living—maybe enough for her to stay in the Land of the Dead. At least for now, until we can find a more permanent solution."

As I had expected, Volos sat up straighter. If the tsar attempted expeditions to Novgorod and Pskov, Selica might amass the souls she needed. And Volos preferred her in the Land of the Dead, so that he could stay here.

"All right, Yaga," he said slowly. "What do you suggest?"

"For you to install Mikula as the holy fool of a town on the road to Novgorod, as the tsar is sure to go there first. If we prevent him—"

But Volos was shaking his head. "That will not carry the legitimacy of a large city like Pskov or Novgorod. And I need legitimacy. A city in the North, too. Pskov will allow more time for Mikula's holy reputation and deeds to spread. If the tsar fails to hear of him by Novgorod, he will most certainly hear of him by Pskov."

I swayed, the weakness returning. "You are willing to risk Novgorod—?"

"Novgorod is more than six hundred kilometers northwest of Tsar Ivan. With the weather and the holidays, and with the number of men he will need for such an undertaking, we have time. Besides, you and your Knights are perfectly capable of protecting the citizens of Novgorod should matters come to a head before I am ready, before Tsar Ivan hears of Mikula the Holy Fool and judges him worthy of holiness, of his fascination and fear."

The darkness gathered about me. "Just resist," I fumbled for words, "stealing their sheep." The last I felt was a violent push, and I was spiraling through the dimensions.

When I found myself back in the woods, I knew I had to share my plan with the others. I knew I would need their support for it to work.

Despite my lingering weakness, I returned to Ivanushka's tent, empty now save for Marya and Vasily. They looked up at me, surprised. It had been a long time since I had joined them. I strode over, snow melting on my cheeks in the warmth.

"Mikula will help us," I said, revealing how we would lure the tsar to us, how the holy fool would put the fear of the Christian god in Ivan and slow him down, dampening his thirst for terror and hopefully preventing the massacres of Novgorod and Pskov.

"Well, it certainly is ambitious, Yaga," said Marya, "but we are behind you."

Vasily stood. Like in this same tent not an hour before, when he had met my eyes for the first time in months, he looked at me now, really looked at me, not evading or shifting his gaze away. "What do you need me to do?" he asked.

Perhaps the direness of the situation was thawing his coldness, or maybe we did not matter in the enormity of the unfolding events. Either way, as when we had searched for Volos, he did not ask questions. He simply trusted in me and what had to be done.

But the funny thing was, I wanted to tell him—this time, really tell him—everything. About Volos, the gods, me. Maybe I would. Maybe I had been wrong and my pushing him away *was* an excuse, and maybe it was fear. Fear that my feelings for him were real, fear of what they would mean, that I had to actually let someone in and see me, all of me. I remembered both my mother and Dusha telling me the importance of my mortality in magic and in life. When I had found Volos, I had reverted back to choosing between gods and mortals, choosing my divinity to the exclusion of my humanity. But why did I have to choose? Especially since I could not keep Vasily from my world. He was in it, whether I acted on my feelings or not.

"We need to change locations," I said, finally, "to be as close as possible to Novgorod without attracting attention, so we can watch over it in case of any oprichniki."

Vasily nodded. "Of course, we cannot let the tsar and his thugs destroy our cities. We have to do everything to prevent it . . . and stop them. I will make preparations."

"And one more thing," I said. He stopped at the entrance, turning back to glance at me, and I added, "Thank you, Vasya," and gave him a tentative smile.

He opened his mouth, then cleared his throat and gave me another nod before hastening out of the tent. But I thought I saw his lips curve up, ever so slightly.

I turned back to Marya. "Don't you dare say anything."

"I wouldn't dream of it," she replied with a twitch of her lips.

Interlude

SELICA IS A breath away from the light—and the Land of the Living. The frosted-over tear in the fabric between lands is icy under her fingers. It melts at her touch as though her skin is made of sunlight. This time, she remembers her husband's voice, centuries ago now, when he asked her, *"Are you certain?"*

"Do you want to continue dying over and over?" she counters.

"The Universe and our Chernobog blood have willed it."

"You are wrong. We are masters of our own destinies." Selica watches her black ribbons flutter in the cold March breeze. For her final transformation, she has worn her wedding dress and juniper in her hair. A celebration—of her liberation from the Universe and her husband. *"Are you not tired of being dead for half the year?"* she asks him.

Roz takes a deep, weary breath; the torch in his hand wavers. "Yes, I am tired. But maybe we will grow used to it. It has only been fifteen years since our marriage."

"I have no desire to reconcile myself to a fickle fate dictated by out-of-touch gods. Or by blood. I prefer to pave my own way. Nav's throne will give me, us, the power over death to make our freedom from the Universe and the gods a reality."

"But must I . . . ?" He gestures to the mound of branches and leaves below Selica, the wooden stake at her back, the coil of rope tying her to her destiny.

"As you well know, my transformation demands death by burning and rebirth by water, to give me the touch of death strong enough to kill a god." A monster. A killer. Goddess of Rebirth. *"Be thankful it is not you on the receiving end."* The spray of water is chilly and hostile on her skin. Yet each year she has set up the sight of her burning near the riverbank because she hates the acrid smell of the flames, the stench of her own flesh. Drowning is a mercy. *"Now, come, dear husband, light me up."*

A touch of the torch, and the fire catches on. The leaves and branches beneath her begin to smoke, releasing spurts of gray into the air. Then the flames are everywhere. Blinding, hot, unbearable. Her eyes sting, her throat aches, her head swims. Flecks of ash stick to her tongue. She spits out hacking coughs as the flames devour her dress and start on her flesh. Pain. So much pain. Her own screams pierce her ears, detached, terrifying in their isolation, as though coming from a place outside of her.

Blackness creeps in. Before she loses herself in it, Selica tips her body into the river, stake and all, and the just-thawing waters smother her.

It is but a moment before she opens her eyes. In reality, it could have been hours. Selica is lying on the riverbank. The sky is bitter blue, the white disk of the sun careening between a gaggle of fat-bellied clouds. So like her wedding day.

"Oh, thank the gods!" Roz falls to his knees beside her. *"I was worried you would not wake up, my snegurochka, my snow queen."*

His bouts of drama hold no meaning to her, for he does not really feel, not like she does. As he blathers on, Selica stares at the picture in silver ink on his head, of wind blowing at her. Can she sense it? She breathes in the air, filled with the sweet promise of spring, and of revenge. She lets his bearish arm grasp her waist and pull her up.

"Let us find my mother, dear husband."

It is not hard to locate the mortal village where Mokosh lives with her youngest daughter, their warm izba with the spacious bedchamber and its great canopied bed. The linen hanging brushes against Selica's arm as she bends over her sleeping mother. Her body is perfectly straight, her hands folded at her chest, as if she lies in a human coffin.

For the first time, doubt stirs in Selica's heart.

But the happy, sunny izba extinguishes this doubt, especially when compared to Selica's sad, dark prisons. This is the woman who rejected and abandoned her. Replaced her with another, lighter daughter. Forced her into a loveless marriage with an icy oaf. Encouraged her to hurt herself over and over. Made her into a killer.

No, this woman did no more than give birth to her. She is not her mother. Selica leans down and kisses Mokosh's forehead. Death burns on her lips like an endearment, or a hastily whispered curse. Instantly, the black hair grays, the snow-drops in the wreath wilt. The skin wrinkles, ages, decays to a skeleton. Then to dust, then to nothing.

As Selica steps out of the izba she is glad. No tears come to her eyes nor guilt to her heart. Mokosh had expected her to kill. Now Selica has. She shivers, the wet shreds of wedding dress sticking to her skin. Despite the bright morning, snow covers the ground. The silent izbas with their sleeping occupants loom on either side, casting cold shadows over her. Something is missing. Or rather, someone. Her sister.

"Was that necessary, my precious snegurochka?" asks Roz.

"Mokosh would have tried to stop us. With her gone, and the other gods too far from Earth to notice, it will be too easy to replace Volos." Selica glances around. Where could a fifteen-year-old half mortal have gone so early without her mother? She will not be safe if her sister lives. But her power over death does not last long. Selica wants to scream. Instead, she blows on the palm of her hand and a flame sprouts there. "Burn it all," she whispers to the flame, and lets it drift.

The gods trudge on. Behind them, the village fills with yellow and orange light, flickering and dancing, as it spreads from izba to izba. They walk through a tangled wood to a frosted-over glade, where Selica feels for the hidden tear in the fabric between lands.

"How are you so convinced that Volos will give up his lands and throne to you?" These are Roz's first words since they left the village.

"He has wanted to return to the Land of the Living ever since Perun banished him to Nav after their last battle for the sky," Selica says, as she finds the tear and pulls it open. "When I take Volos's throne, he will be able to return to the living."

They step through the passageway into the darkness and walk to a jet-black river.

Roz points his scythe at the water, and a bridge of ice stitches itself across. "Welcome home, my Lady of Rebirth . . . and Death," the Lord of Winter says, resigned.

That was centuries ago now. Selica cannot believe she had ever wanted the throne of Nav. Back then, she had truly thought it would give her power and independence, that she would get rid of her husband and the need to kill him and usher forth spring. She had been a young, naive goddess, totally ignorant of the fact that as soon as she sat on that throne, she belonged to the dead. That the land shackled her to old age and infirmity, to the darkness.

Enough, Selica tells herself, and forces her way into the Land of the Living.

Suddenly, she is choking, grasping her throat, pulling at her skin. There is too much air and sound. The light slices through her. Yet even as she chokes, momentarily deaf and blind, Selica swears Yaga will suffer. Her sister will learn what it is to be the favored daughter of the light.

27

DECEMBER 1569

THE MEN HAD donned their Skomorokhi masks, their hides and pelts, and they danced around the raging bonfire, singing kolyadki carols and making merry. The budnik ritual log burned bright and cheery for our ancestors, dressed in a strawberry-red shirt and adorned with the dead flowers the women and I had gathered in the woods earlier.

Free from the requirements of church and court, the people at camp had insisted we follow this beloved pagan tradition and kindle a ritual log, too. For common folk still celebrated the winter solstice and the Kolyada festival that came with it.

Marya and I sat on a tree stump a little farther from the festivities with cups of mead that Varvara, now dancing with Yaroslav, had brewed with extra cinnamon and cloves. My head was already pleasantly light, and I let my eyes stray to Vasily. He stood by the fire with Sanya, Stepan, and a few other men. He wasn't wearing a mask, and the firelight set his face aglow, made it more intense and more vibrant.

After Mitka had returned from Aleksandrov, weeks ago now, we made camp in a wood about half a day's ride from Novgorod. Vasily and

I had grown friendlier since, even riding into the city on a few occasions for food and supplies.

Volos had been right about the holiday season, as well as the storms and snows that had blocked most of the roads, preventing any further travel. I tried to use this time wisely. I practiced my rituals to keep up my strength. Before the storms, I had heard talk in Novgorod of a holy fool called Mikula who had the ear of the Christian lord and who lived in Pskov in a house with blooming trees that snow couldn't touch. I entrusted Noch and Dyen, as well as the animals near the city, to keep watch for signs of the tsar or his men.

In the meantime, I continued to care for the people at camp. Yelena's pregnancy continued uneventfully, and I tried my best to heal Mitka and keep his spirits up. Though physically recovered from his trip to Aleksandrov, he was not the same bright boy he had once been. He sat far from the fire now, alone, nursing a cup of mead.

My eyes strayed back to Vasily. In that moment, his gaze met mine. It was amber from the flames and burned into me with an intensity that sped up my heart.

Marya, clearly noticing our shared glance, patted my knee. "I've never told you how I met Varvara, have I?"

"You have not," I said.

Marya smiled, playing with her braid. "Well, it had been at the start of the Oprichnina, in '65. The town Varvara lived in, where her father had an inn, was among the first attacked by the tsar's men. That day, Gorya and Fedya and I were fighting the oprichniki in the streets. From the doorway of an inn, I saw an oprichnik grab the waist of a woman with hair like the sun. He was about to . . . Well, you know what they do to women."

I felt the prickle of anger, of fear for Varvara. "What did you do?" I whispered.

"I ran up to the bastard and slit his throat." Marya's laugh was short-lived. She peered into my face. "I saved Varvara from the oprichnik who had killed her father. And she saved me right back, by coming with me.

Before her, I had not loved anyone who truly loved me for who I am, who gave me belonging, their very selves. Centuries of lovers! And not one man or woman fit me like Varvara. Well, you may have had centuries of men, but not one has wanted to know you like Vasily. And once in a while, Yaga, you have to let someone save you, too."

Silvery gusli strings wafted toward us through the swell of gray smoke. Vasily now stood at its edges, hanging back from the men, as if waiting for me. Marya was right. Centuries on this Earth, and I had never met anyone like Vasily, had not felt what I had with him, had not wanted to share so much of myself. I didn't want to refuse him anymore. I had run out of reasons, was through making excuses, finished with fear.

I drained my mead and stood. "I think I shall go and see what is happening by the fire."

"I think that is the best idea you've had in a long time." Marya's smile was sharp.

I shook my head at her. But I was smiling.

The sky was hazier, promising to shed snow, as I came up to Vasily. He put his cup down on the ground. But he kept his eyes on the fire, which was crackling and hissing with the surge of song. Now that I was here, so close to him, I didn't know what to say or do. A fleck of ice landed on my skin with a clinging touch.

So I simply said, "Would you walk with me, Vasya?"

Vasily's face was guarded. "All right," he said finally, and we started to walk.

I took a deep breath as more icy flecks sifted down. I had to get the words, their truth, out in the open. I had to tell him. "When Mitka came back, and I had put together my plan, I . . . wanted to tell you first. I wanted you by my side despite all the reasons not to. That's when I knew that, no matter the reasons, I . . . I do want you, too, Vasily. I want to let you in. I—"

"You shut me out, Yaga. You acted like I meant nothing to you—"

"I know." I swallowed, seeing his face shadow with the hurt, the pain, I had caused him. "I thought I was protecting you, that you couldn't handle—"

"Handle what?"

Again, I had the incredible urge to tell him everything. But I settled for, "Being with someone like me."

Vasily took a breath and shook his head, as if what I said was too inconceivable for belief. I was about to say more, make my case in the strongest way I knew how, but then he took my hand. "I can handle it," he said, his voice giving and becoming softer.

We were passing the tents now. Sprigs of holly and bits of ivy were affixed to the canvas walls, branches and twigs twisted into angels and stars. The fire was farther, the talk and laughter, too. It was quieter here in the snowfall. I looked down at our entwined hands, and my hand seemed to me like that of someone else. Surely not that of Yaga, an immortal half god cursed to an eternity of solitude and loneliness.

I stopped and turned to Vasily, the snow sifting faster and faster. We had brokered some sort of peace between us, but I needed to ask him this. I needed to know. "I have lived . . . very long, Vasya. Are you sure you don't want to experience life with someone as new as you, someone who has not done it all and been disillusioned?"

"*Have* you done it all, felt it all?" Vasily pressed my hand against his chest. "My heart is beating so loudly. I thought you could hear it."

I could, even through his fur-lined shuba.

"Has yours ever done that?"

"No," I admitted. The snow was blotting everything else out.

Vasily lifted my hand to his cheek. My fingers tangled with his, feeling the flush on his skin, the roughness of his beard. "I hope that is because what you feel with me, you have not felt before," he said. "God knows I have also been disillusioned, lonely, lost. I no longer remember the faces of my family. My family! Father and Mother, even little Marinochka. Battle seems to have erased them." We stood in the same place, our hands and eyes tangled. "But when I am with you, I don't feel lost or disillusioned. No, I . . . see life differently. I have hope."

"Even in the past few months when I treated you so horribly?"

Vasily was quiet for a moment. "You are here now. *We* are here now—"

But I didn't let him finish; I pressed my mouth to his mouth, and I felt the rush of sensation and pressure on my lips, the thrust of his tongue finding mine, the burn of his beard on my cheek. It was I who had gotten him alone, it was I who had kissed him, and it was I who was adrift now, losing any sense of balance, pulled in deep. Maybe he was, too.

We careened and swayed, feet unsure, through the snow and dark, into Vasily's blackened tent, knocking over a chair—a motion of his arm and it flew backward, landed with a crash. Then the push and pull, this time of our trembling hands on each other, tugging off coats and trousers, his kaftan and the zipun underneath, my linen shirt, our rubakhas. A flash of white as they went flying, inflating with air, then deflating.

We were naked in front of each other, revealed completely. Our hair dripped, clung to our skin, the melted snow falling to the ground like rain.

A shiver ran along my spine. Vasily was looking at me, *really* looking at me, his eyes large and liquid amber. He approached me slowly.

With roughened fingers, he traced the pictures inked into my skin. A row of full moons on my collarbone, the snake on my arm, a smattering of raindrops under my right breast, the three bees at my waist. A sharp intake of breath when his hand slid lower, his fingers dipping inside, as he kissed me, hard and urgent, on the mouth.

Then the rug was under my back, the furs slinking past, and the solid weight of him pressed into me. Our bodies entwined too easily, too instinctively, as if we were meant to weave into this feverish embrace all along. My back arched as his fingers trailed the inside of my thigh. I drew him in with one brisk motion that made us both gasp.

Vasily and I fell into each other without reservations. And we took equally, our limbs twisting to probe further, reach deeper. The rhythm pulsed with a surge of warmth from me to him and back again. It heated my blood until his very touch burned into me.

He closed his eyes when he caught my mouth with his. A slow, deliberate kiss that shattered me. And I was spinning, as if twirling with my arms spread in the air, earth tilting, sky crashing in with light. Before I knew it, we had broken apart, spent and panting, wanting, needing more. Our eyes were still tangled, yet the melted snow was seeping into our overheated skin, the light fading, the air too cold and raw and real.

"How does it feel to live without fear?" Vasily was leaning on one elbow, his eyes sharp with challenge. We were still naked, still lying together in a crushed heap on the furs and rugs taking up half his tent. I felt his thumb on my lower lip, then a kiss on the corner of my mouth. "This is how I live," he whispered, "how I have always lived."

In the tent, it was no longer black but grayish-blue. Morning approached. Snow pelted the canvas, a pitter-patter that sank my heart with a strange sadness.

"You are braver than me, Vasya," I replied, unsmiling, watching the walls rustle like dry leaves trodden on too quickly. "I should go." I stood abruptly, dizzy with the implications of what we had done now that the mead had faded and despite my vow to live without fear. In the morning's light, that fear crept in a little. I wanted to tell Vasily the whole truth about myself, but I worried what would happen. As if in answer, the cold suddenly stung; my breath curled in the air. I needed to return to Little Hen before anyone saw me in this tent. But looking at Vasily, my heart filled with warmth, with a sense of belonging, a totally foreign feeling after the act of lovemaking.

"Come back to bed," Vasily said, oblivious to the warring going on inside me. He leaned back, stretched his legs. "It is still dark. It is still night."

I bit my lip, swollen from his kisses. "No one can see us together, Vasya."

He raised himself on his elbow again. "Why not?" Was his voice guarded?

"What would Ivanushka say if he found out?"

Vasily lay back, silent. "Perhaps I care not."

I approached his bed. "I will not defend Ivanushka or what he has done. But we should not blame him until we have spoken to him. And . . . if this is real"—I gestured between us—"we should tell Ivanushka ourselves, instead of him hearing it from someone else."

"It is real." Vasily rolled over to look at me. "But perhaps that is wise."

"Of course it is," I smiled archly, forgetting why I had stood in the first place. The anxious thoughts had vanished. "It came from me, after all."

"Yes, Baba Yaga herself . . . whom I have now bedded."

I straightened, pulled my hair back, let him see me. My body may have been far from the ideal of the times, but I liked my breasts and curves and browned skin, the pictures inked into it. "Be careful, Vasya, or you will not get to do so again."

"You believe that?"

I placed my hands on my hips and leaned toward him. "I do."

Before I could pull away, Vasily grasped my wrists and guided my arms over his shoulders. I felt the ripple of his muscles, the curve of his body. His face was so close I felt his breath on my lips. But he didn't kiss me, though my body burned for it.

"Maybe you are not as wise as you think," he whispered, as if he heard my thoughts, sensed my body even without touching me in the places I wanted him to.

"You are arrogant and much too satisfied with yourself," I said, still burning up.

"Arrogant, maybe." Vasily smiled, eyes intent. "But not satisfied. Not even a little. Come back to bed, love, you are wanted here. Nay, you are needed."

He grabbed me by the waist and lifted me off the ground—into his bed, where he enveloped me in his arms and finally kissed me.

Storms battered us in the weeks that followed, there seeming no limit to the cold and desolation. The short, dark days went by deceptively slowly, filled with inconsequential tasks. All Vasily and I could do was catch each other's glances, graze each other's hands, and steal a kiss or two.

Those were filled with a heat, with a longing, that left me dizzy and sick at heart. The winter nights were long, yet how quickly they passed. During the evening festivities, Vasily and I would find one another. We spent every night in one another's arms, falling in and out of each other, in and out of sleep, then back again.

But how long could this last? It had been much too quiet, which did not make me feel at ease, especially with Little Hen's constant restlessness. She quivered up and down and paced through camp. Maybe it was the children, who slept in her warm confines every night now that I had taken to sleeping with Vasily. Or maybe she was also uneasy.

"Something is not right," I said one night as I lay against Vasily's chest. "Yes, Tsar Ivan is obsessed with pageantry and so is likely preoccupied with the holiday celebrations. And yes, the roads have been blocked by the storms. But in the quietest of waters, Vasya, there is evil," I said, shuddering as I remembered Mother's saying.

"I know it." There was a beat of silence. "But if there were trouble, wouldn't your animals notify us? Wouldn't your holy fool send word? We would hear from our messengers, the people. Someone—anyone—would come."

He was right, of course. And Volos had warned it would take time to install himself as the holy fool of Pskov, worthy of a tsar's attention. Likewise, it would take time for Ivan to reach Novgorod. And when he did, we would need to act fast, maybe fight his men, if it came down to it. I was suddenly very aware of Vasily's arms. I had seen him in battle many times, but envisioning him fighting the oprichniki now made me shudder all over again despite the warmth of the tent with its hazy, candle-lit glow.

"What is it, dorogaya?" Vasily shifted on the bed to look at me.

"I am . . . afraid. For what is to come, yes, but also . . . we have just found each other." I tightened my hold on his arms.

"Do you fear for me, Yaga?" Vasily smiled at me teasingly. "You should be more afraid for the oprichniki about to get near my blade . . ." But he glimpsed what must have been my pale face for he took a breath, not smiling anymore. "You will not lose me," he said, his voice sure, unwavering, like him.

But of course I would. Even if I could keep him safe, even if we stayed together, Vasily was mortal. My throat constricted. Though it was too soon to make promises, the truth was, I never wanted to lose him. He made me feel whole, like coming home. I had fought these feelings for so long, had finally allowed Vasily in and saw what we were together, that the idea of losing him, this, now, filled me with panic. And I worried what would happen when he knew who I really was. Despite all this, I found myself whispering back, "You will not lose me, either."

28

JANUARY 1570

O N A MORNING sometime in the second half of January, I
stepped out of Vasily's tent to a world awash in whirling whiteness.
I could not see past my boots.

This latest storm had started several days before and not stopped. It
seemed more violent than the others, longer, more extreme, even for a
Russian winter. The flakes were large, almost as big as my fist, the snow
spiraling in strange twists, as if enchanted. Was it Morozko? Had they
discovered us? I had to go into the woods to see; if nothing else, I would
be able to gather some snow there, where it was most pure, and perform
my identifying spell.

I swayed with a particularly strong gust of wind but kept going, past
the tents, to where I knew the edge of the wood to be.

It was also strange that Noch and Dyen had not returned. My companions had been between Novgorod and camp many times since
November . . . Still, when was the last time I had seen them? Surely it
hadn't been weeks. But it had to have been. Why had they not come
back? And we had not received any other reports, not from the animals,

not from our messengers, not from anyone else. I had assumed it was because most in Russia—including the tsar—spent January on holiday. Winter in the North, even without the severeness of the last years, also lasted long, with snow preventing even soldiers from traveling. And my companions frequently left me for significant stretches of time. But I also had not heard from Volos, and that was now worrisome.

Finally, I saw the near-blotted-out outlines of the trees above me. I leaned down to the powdery whiteness to scoop up some snow when, suddenly, I felt my head go light as a wave of weakness passed over me. I saw something flash ahead—glass or ice or even an icicle? Could it be Morozko's scythe? Despite the weakness, I started to run toward it, farther into the wood, the snow swirling about me like a mad vortex.

I gasped for breath. Staggered as if drunk. I was cold, so cold, yet my chest tightened with a furious heat. I tore open my dublenka, taking deep breaths of the bitter air, so heavy and thick with the abnormally large snowflakes, I could see nothing.

"What do you want?" I shouted. My voice was drowned out by the snow, but I kept shouting. "You are there! I know you are, you bastards!" I stared up into the shifting white sky. "Roz!" The outlines of the trees spun, the sky and earth blending, impossible to distinguish. I fell into the snow, panting, still repeating his name. "This is your storm, isn't it?" I swallowed against a raw throat, the realization hitting me all at once: that the storm *was* enchanted, that we were trapped here, that Morozko and maybe the others knew where we were. "You will not allow us to leave." I was sobbing now, the tears freezing as soon as they slid down my cheeks. "Is the tsar in Novgorod? Is he? Is he?"

A black raven landed beside me. Its eyes were the burnt orange I knew so well.

"Koshey," I whispered, the angry heat rekindling in my chest, so infuriated was I at the raven's silence. "Speak, you coward! I know you can!"

But the bird simply flapped its wings and shot back into the sky, reducing to a blue-black blur before I could try to stop it. I hadn't realized that I was now shuddering, that there was ice on my cheeks and eye-lashes, that my lips could barely move.

And that someone was calling my name, over and over.

Out of the whiteness the figure of a man materialized—Vasily.

"What are you doing here, Yaga?" he said in a broken voice, as he gathered me in his arms and pulled me to his chest.

Vasily carried me through the snow and trees, back to his tent, where he gently lowered me onto his bed and wrapped me in a pile of furs.

"Oh, my love—" His eyes were wide and very dark. "Your lips are so blue—"

I could not speak, could barely breathe, the shuddering of my limbs so intense I heard the chatter of my teeth. I could not feel my toes or my fingers. "H-help me take off my clothes." Vasily did so and, taking off his own coat, put his arms around me tightly.

Once the warmth had brought some life back into my body and I could form words without shuddering, I said, "I need to speak to you, Vasya."

"Not now, dorogaya, not now. You must warm yourself first."

But I could avoid it no longer. "When I told you I have lived long, I did not tell you how long." I was thankful I could not see his face, though I felt his body stiffen a little. "It is not just thirty or forty or even fifty years. It is hundreds of years. I . . . was born before Vladimir the Great, before he brought your god to Russia."

Vasily leaned back and peered into my face. "You are serious. I . . . knew you were a vedma in possession of magic, but how is it . . . this possible?"

I took a breath; it hurt. "My mother was a goddess, an immortal."

"What does that mean?" he asked in a quiet voice. "You cannot die?"

"I can—my father was mortal—but it is not a simple matter."

Vasily let his arms drop. He brought his hands to his waist and started to pace. "Why tell me now? Why tell me at all?"

In a way, his acceptance of my words as truth, not some ridiculous lie, was a relief. "I have reason to believe the tsar may already be in Novgorod, or on his way there."

Vasily took a step toward me. "How do you know this?" His voice was still quiet, but there was now a tense current underneath it.

"I do not know for certain." I swallowed, tasting a bitter mouth. "But I thought I glimpsed a god"—I ignored the widening of his eyes—"who would not be here unless he and our enemies know about us, about where we are, which could mean . . ."

Vasily's face was as white as the snow outside. He made a motion toward the tent's entrance. "We must—"

"Wait, Vasya." I licked my lips to bring some moisture there. "I also have reason to believe we are trapped here, and even if we try, we will not be able to leave."

"The weather?" Vasily came to a standstill. "The snowstorm? They started—?"

"Among other things."

"What things?" he asked, too sharply.

"Not only does Konstantin Buyanovich have power over birds, he can become one. I believe I just saw him here, as a raven. He, too, is an immortal. Like me."

"And you didn't think to mention this fact earlier, when you spoke of his treachery before?" Vasily's features contorted through the dimness.

My cheeks felt red and swollen. "I thought you would not understand—"

"What foreign power does the bastard work for, hm? You said you did not know, yet I have a feeling you were withholding that also."

"He works for immortals, all right? The god I thought I saw, the Lord of Winter, and . . . a death goddess." At his blank, pale face, I said, "See? This is why I did not tell you. Your anger is proof you cannot handle it. And it would not have changed anything."

Vasily crossed his arms, evidently recovered from his shock. "And you expect me to tell you it is all right, your assuming I would not—" He sighed. Placed his hands back on his waist. Looked down. "Fine. Perhaps I do not understand everything. But what about Konstantin Buyanovich?"

"What about him?" My voice was now equally hard.

"Why not tell me more about his nature before? Unless—" His gaze on me was piercing. "Are you protecting him? Were you . . . involved with him, back at court? Did you, did you love him?" His words came out in sharp bursts. "Do you still?" When I said nothing, Vasily whispered, "Answer me."

I rose. My still-raw skin stung, so soon exposed to the cold again. I hastily threw the furs over my shoulders. "Not that I owe you any kind of explanation, but we were together once, long ago. Hundreds of years ago. That is not the reason I did not tell you everything about him. I thought I told you enough to keep us safe without revealing . . . how I knew what I knew. If I were truly protecting him, I would not have said anything about him at all. I did not tell you because—"

"Let me hazard a guess." Vasily brought his livid face close to mine. "I am but a stupid mortal man who knows nothing. Is that it?"

I brought my face, just as livid, even closer to his. "You got it right, *finally.*"

As we stared at each other, Stepan's voice broke in, loud and frantic. "Vasya!"

We both turned toward the tent entrance just as it flapped open and the man himself appeared, all covered in snow. "Do you know where—?" I saw his eyes widen beneath his hat. Stepan stared at us in shock. Now the whole camp would know about Vasily and me, and from the man's face, the news would be received with consternation by some. "I . . . am sorry to interrupt."

I looked down, at my barely covered body, and sighed in irritation. "Well?"

"Something is wrong . . . Yelena is having pains. But it is too early, isn't it?"

A month, if not more, too early. I was already reaching for my clothes. "I will be there this minute."

Stepan nodded, his hat nearly rolling off his head, and rushed out.

"Are you satisfied?" I demanded when Vasily and I were once more alone. "Now the entire camp will know about us."

"That is the least of our worries." He sat on the bed, watching me dress. "If you are right, and Novgorod is under attack, what will we do if we cannot leave?"

"Well, I shall go tend to Yelena first, then we shall see."

It turned out that while Yelena's pains had intensified, the babe wasn't coming quite yet. But by the time I returned to Vasily's tent, he was gone.

A FEW DAYS LATER, Yelena went into labor. As soon as I heard, I gathered my herbs and implements. The storm had not eased. Its large flakes pelted Little Hen so that she shook and curled into herself, becoming smaller. There was no sound, no light, just snow.

I swallowed, tasting the same dry, bitter mouth that had greeted me that morning.

I reached for the cup of mead that Varvara had left by my pech the night before. One sip, and I was pushing it away. Had it spoiled? Ridiculous! Mead cannot spoil, not like this. Still. The spices tasted . . . wrong. And I was so thirsty. I glanced around my hut—no water to be had. And since the weakness in the woods, I had been so tired.

But then, it had been an exhausting few days.

Vasily and his men were trying to get past the storm, past the edge of the woods, but as I had feared, the storm kept sending them back to camp no matter how far they walked. I also attempted to get through the enchantment, but herbs and rituals could only do so much. We had nothing left to do but pray there would be someone left to save when it was all over. I went cold at what new horror we would find in Novgorod.

Vasily and I had not spoken further, had barely seen each other, especially since the men were working around the clock to break through the storm. But today they planned on stopping early so Stepan could be present for Yelena. As I went back to my preparations, I caught a glimpse of the wooden horse, Mother's symbol, on the wall. My hands, hovering over my satchel, started to shake. This time, not with the cold. When had I last bled?

Between Vasily, Yelena's pains, and my increased worry about the tsar's whereabouts, I had quite lost track of my cycle. But no matter how much I thought, I could not remember. Until a few days ago, Vasily and I had slept together every night since that first night. Which meant I had not bled at all. Which meant . . . I was weeks late.

But it couldn't be. How could it, after centuries of barrenness?

A gust of wind blew and Little Hen tensed, then jiggled, as if to shake a fist at the storm. It was good to see her weathering all our difficulties with her usual pluck. I patted one of her walls and finished my preparations. I would deliver the babe, and then I would find Vasily.

Yelena and Stepan's tent was crowded, the air heavy with perspiration and nerves.

"Out," I said to all but Marya and Varvara. I lowered my hood and strode to a tousle-haired Yelena, pacing with her large round belly straining beneath her shift. Marya fetched water while I made a drink of catnip and chamomile, charmed to calm labor and birthing pains. "Drink this," I told Yelena, giving her the cup of potion.

As the mother-to-be groaned and cursed, I thought about how the tsar's men were probably in Novgorod by now, wreaking their havoc. And Roz's storm still held us hostage, preventing us from doing anything no matter our proximity to the city. Selica, for I knew it was she, had done this on purpose. She wanted to punish us by keeping us from Novgorod long enough that we would be too late to help anyone.

Either way, even if Volos was not ready, we had to make our plan work, had to make it in time to Pskov to try to set the trap for Tsar Ivan and prevent more bloodshed.

But how was I supposed to do this if there really was a child? If I were pregnant, the Universe had willed it so. But what could the Universe want with me and Vasily? Would he even want a child from me? Either way, it was the worst possible time for it.

I sat on a small stool beneath Yelena. "All right, Lenochka, push now." I counseled her though the pain as each contraction came faster and faster. The baby's head appeared, and I shouted for Yelena to push, push, push! Suddenly, a whooshing, and the child slid out, all stunned and blue and—most importantly—alive.

Yelena had given birth to a healthy baby girl.

To my surprise, she let me name the child. And I called her Anastasia, after my dear friend the tsaritsa.

I have no idea when I finally made my way to Vasily's tent. Everything was white with snow. But the world seemed darker, quieter, so I assumed it night. I had scrubbed my hands and face, and once inside his tent, mercifully, I shed the bloody clothing. I paused, debating what to do, if Vasily was asleep or not. Then I climbed into bed beside him, holding my breath, nervous all of a sudden.

But he pulled me toward him and wrapped his arms around me, tight and warm with his particular, very intense heat. "I have been waiting for you," he said, wide-awake.

"You have not slept?"

"No." He sighed. "I just came back. A few of us were still by the woods. We will try again tomorrow. I want the men to get some sleep," Vasily said into my hair. "How is Yelena?"

"She had a girl . . . and I got to name her Anastasia." I smiled into the darkness, remembering my own Anastasia, her beauty and goodness. I was warmed to think of her watching over her little namesake. The silence turned my thoughts to my own child, if there was one. I took a breath, gathering the words, waiting to say them and make them real.

"A good name," Vasily said, and the moment passed us by.

It was just as well. I still did not know, not for sure. And though he no longer seemed angry, I did not know how to feel about a child, or how he would feel about it.

"I am sorry, Yaga," he whispered then.

I let out a slow breath. "It is I who am sorry, Vasya." Though loath to pull myself away from him, I shifted so we faced each other. "I should not have assumed the truth would be too much for you—"

"No, you shouldn't have." His eyes were closed, but I saw the flash of his teeth through the dark.

"Can I—" I hesitated. "Can I tell you about me, Vasya? Everything?"

A beat of silence. Then softly, "Yes." He opened his eyes. They were dark gray but for a glimmer of light. "Tell me," he said.

And I started to talk. I didn't finish until morning had come and, with it, more snow, more of Morozko's storm. But Vasily and I had made it to the other side of the night with a closeness, a realness, that only lives in openness. Though I suspected there was yet one more secret between us. I just had to be sure, and then I would find the right time to tell him— even as our enemies drew closer, threatening everything we held dear.

Interlude

IN THE SHADOW of the mighty Gorodishche Castle, Selica watches twilight douse the white land in velvety blue. Even darkness is beautiful in the Land of the Living. She opens her mouth and savors the snow that drizzles her tongue. How wonderful it is to feel again.

The castle behind her is in ruins, its copper and ivory-hued brick corroding. Tsar Ivan has chosen this campsite not only for practical reasons, it being a spitting distance from Novgorod, but for symbolic ones. It was where the Vikings had asked Rurik, the founder of Russia and the tsar's ancestor, to rule over them all those millennia ago.

In front of Selica, there are fluttering tents and restless men and smoke twisting into the sky. Supper is cooking on spits still bloody from the night before. Yet Selica can hear the pacing in the depths of the castle. She sees the tall figure, the long shuba gliding over the stones.

As soon as Selica had freed herself from Nav, she had joined Tsar Ivan and his men on their journey north—or rather, northwest, not taking the roads southwest through Moscow, as was the way to Novgorod, but through the forests, purposely in secret, the men armed only with muskets to keep their destination hidden from the people. The capital and the boyars there will not support the plan to sack Novgorod.

Did she look away when the oprichniki slit the throats of the peasants in the woods? To her shame, she did, though the more of them descended into Nav, the longer she could stay in the Land of the Living, being strong enough now to channel their light from a distance. Alas, it is quite different from the actual act of killing, which had made her sad. But there is no choice, not for her, not if she desires a new life.

The footsteps bring Selica back to Gorodishche. Tsar Ivan had not asked her name or questioned her presence. She was already in his mind, in his heart, in his soul.

Selica is glad Koshey is not here now, irritating her with his warnings, his disapproving looks, condescending as only a man used to lording over women is.

"Why must you pace so, Ivan?" she says to the man. "I can feel the tremors of the castle. If you do not desist, it will crumble upon us, and then where will we be?"

"What am I to do?" comes his voice, low and lost like that of a plaintive child. "I have interrogated, even tortured, those too-proud citizens of Novgorod. Each man, woman, and child that I could get my hands on. They say nothing, except that the letter was planted. That it never existed. That their Archbishop never wrote such a thing, never conspired with the foreigners, never was a traitor. But you saw him on that bridge."

She had. In the wake of their arrival in Novgorod, the tsar took the tsarevich and several men to the Cathedral of Saint Sophia, behind the walls of the city's Kremlin. The Archbishop of Novgorod came out to meet the tsar, supposedly to bless him and his entourage. Yet the clergy had been armed to the teeth with gilded crosses, miracle-working icons, and holy banners, which they had held out before them like muskets.

"First impressions are usually the clearest, the most true," whispers Selica.

"I told him he worshipped the Devil," says Ivan, "his cross a weapon seeking to hand Novgorod over to the foreigners. Traitor, he is a traitor."

"One traitor means others are not far."

"Quite right." He turns his creased, sunken face in her direction.

Selica cringes. Now that she is young and beautiful, she cannot stand the sight of age or decay. She need only say one word that will tip the scales in her favor and against the poor tsarevich, who keeps reminding the tsar of mercy. She says it. "Treachery."

"Treachery," Ivan repeats, eyes bright. It is a word he is more familiar with than mercy. "Treachery surrounds me," he says, as he has always said. There is also something about secret messages sent to foreigners and punishment.

But Selica has stopped listening to the mad old loon's ravings. "You have come here to punish, prince. So punish. Do not be a coward, a weak man. Be the fearsome man I know you can be. Teach Novgorod and its people a lesson they shall never forget."

There is no way back. Only into the future, where she can live free from the Universe, gods and men, Mokosh and Yaga. Entirely free and above everyone. Selica smiles slowly, watching understanding dawn in Tsar Ivan the Terrible's face, watching his resolution crystallize like ice over the rivers of Mother Russia. He will punish them. And she will live. A monster and not. A woman and not. Herself.

30

FEBRUARY 1570

IT TOOK DAYS for Morozko's storm to stop. And by then, February had already arrived.

It happened suddenly. One moment, I was scattering hawkweed, dandelion, and sow thistle along the edge of the wood, the wind and snow blowing in my face; the next, I was blinking away snowflakes as the wind blustered into nothing and the sky cleared.

"It is as if an invisible hand has waved it all away," Sanya said in wonder; he had been digging through the accumulated snow beside where I stood.

If you only knew. But I just nodded, trying not to breathe in the smell of garlic wafting from him. There was no longer any point in denying I was with child. I still had not bled and was constantly drained and nauseous, sometimes sick, both averse to food—particularly meats—and ravenous. Even asking a trusty oak for new energy, something that had previously guaranteed a return to health, proved futile. Yet I hid my condition, even from Vasily, not wanting to burden him with the news as we continued to labor tirelessly to get past Morozko's storm. But every day that went by, I had less and less hope.

Was this why I kept dreaming of that mountain of glass? Only in these dreams, the glass dissolved under my feet, and I fell into a bottomless land for an eternity.

I watched the edge of the wood, growing uneasy. Where was Vasily?

He had taken another search party into the forest, hours ago now. Fear clutched at my heart. If anything were to happen to Vasily, and before I had a chance to tell him about the baby . . . I would not soon forgive myself.

The air had become strangely warm, as if a thaw had swept through.

Yaga! A howl, and Dyen was bounding up to me. *Thank the gods!* He jumped on me, licking my face and hands. *I could not get through the snowstorm. I was afraid . . .*

I threw my arms around his neck, pressing my face into his fur. "Me too, my friend." I could not say more; relief was choking me. "The storm was courtesy of Morozko," I said at last. "Where is Noch?"

Right behind me, said Dyen. *But, Yaga . . .* His voice was small, barely there.

I swallowed past the dread. "The tsar is already in Novgorod, isn't he?"

Dyen turned sad, shining eyes on me. *He has already left, along with his oprichniki—and a woman. The one you described you had seen on the Throne of the Dead.*

"Selica is with the tsar," I whispered, "which means she is in the Land of the Living." Volos had predicted it, yet I was still unprepared for it. We would need to account for her in our plans.

The city is in ruins.

I breathed through the nausea, the guilt that we had not been able to help Novgorod.

I saw the tsarevich . . . the tsar forced him to participate in the massacre.

Nausea roiled through my stomach. "Where have they gone?"

They were headed southwest . . . toward the Livonian border.

"To Pskov," I said in a low voice. "How quickly?"

We have time. They have a lot of men and are basking in their victory.

And Pskov was more than two hundred kilometers from here. We did have time, though we still had to look for survivors in Novgorod before we set out for Pskov.

Just then, Noch swooped down. Her wings fluttered against my face gently.

"I have to ask you for a dangerous favor," I said to her once we had exchanged greetings. "I need you to follow the tsar."

There are ravens circling his camp, said Noch, *but I will try.*

"We need to know when Ivan and his entourage are approaching Pskov. And if Mikula the Holy Fool is mentioned in his camp." I stroked her wing. "Be careful, Noch."

She spiraled into the sky, Dyen darting past me toward camp, just as Marya and Vasily climbed out of the snow-covered undergrowth. The rest of their party followed—Stepan, the brothers, a few others—all with horribly blank expressions and hollow eyes.

I opened my arms, and Vasily, haggard and sunken-faced, walked into my embrace without a word. He grasped my waist desperately, as if he needed something to hold on to, something to ground him. I don't know how long we stood like this.

"We reached the nearest village," he whispered when we had pulled apart. "Izbas smashed to bits, the church stripped, everything in ruins. Signs of hanging, torture . . . Then we saw the corpses. Women. Children. A massacre." Vasily wiped at his wet cheeks. He rarely made the sign of the cross, but he did so now.

I clutched at my stomach. Horror burrowed into me, like cold into bare flesh. I could barely inhale without vomiting. Covering my mouth, I plunged into the wood and was sick there as never before.

We prepared for our departure, yet the nausea gave me no peace. It became harder and harder to hide it from the others, especially from Vasily.

I knelt on the wet, blackened ground of the wood. Vasily held my hair from my face, my body expelling the sickness until, spent and sore, I sat back on my heels.

Vasily came around to face me.

I avoided his gaze, scooped up some snow, and rinsed my mouth of the bitterness.

"You have been very ill," he said quietly, crouching down beside me, "and not just now." His eyes on me were steady. "I have seen my mother ill, just so."

I exhaled slowly. "This is the worst possible time for it, I know, but—"

"You are with child."

All sound seemed to have died away, even from camp. "Yes," I said, suddenly fearful that Vasily did not want this child and, just as suddenly, knowing I did.

To my surprise, he took my hands in his, stilling my fretful fingers, and kissed the back of each hand slowly, affectionately, before looking up at me. That is when I realized he was smiling. "I am very glad," he said. "Very glad." Then he was pulling me up and into his arms, stroking my hair, kissing me, whispering his endearments.

The tension fled from me. For a moment, only we existed, here in this snowy wood. Vasily was not a traitor's son and an outlaw; I was not a goddess but simply a woman. It felt like we were an ordinary mortal couple, expecting an ordinary mortal child.

But of course, we were not ordinary, not even a little, and we were not in an ordinary Russia. Slowly, regretfully, I pulled away from Vasily. Because of the preparations, we hadn't been able to talk. Now I told him what Dyen and Noch had related to me. "The tsar and his men have left Novgorod. They are on their way to Pskov. Our plan is moving forward." He opened his mouth, but I raised a hand to his lips. "There is more—Ivanushka is with them, and he participated in the massacre."

Vasily stood very, very still. His countenance had hardened.

"Maybe there is a way to get him back," I said. "To save him as he once saved you." Ivanushka could not be the prince we had hoped for, but he could still be better than Ivan. Anastasia's blood was in him, after all. And I owed it to her, to my dear, departed friend, to give her son and heir a chance to explain himself.

Vasily moved away from me. "He is weak," he said, not masking his accusation or disgust. "His hands are forever stained with innocent blood.

Yes, he may have saved me once. But he is a murderer now, just like his father and their oprichniki."

Ivanushka was indeed weak, his desire to live and save himself stronger than his principles, like Koshey's. I knew Vasily could never understand this. He would rather give up his life than spill innocent blood. I approached him, put a hand on either side of his face. I could have said much. But I said only, "I love you, Vasily Adashev."

"And I you, Yaga Mokoshevna." His gaze had softened to a light gray. He gave a heavy sigh. "There is nothing I can do to convince you to stay behind, where it is safe, is there?"

"I cannot rest," I said. "I will not."

Vasily knew me too well to argue more. He took my hands and bent down to kiss them. "All right," he said, though we both knew his words were empty.

I was going to Novgorod and Pskov, and he with me; whether we could stop the tsar or not remained to be seen, for now his death goddess was with him.

31

I T WAS NOT until the following morning that we finally sighted the pale yellow and pearl-gray domes of Novgorod the Great, as its citizens affectionately called it. I did not recognize the once bright city. Its ivory watchtowers and white-walled churches appeared curiously worn, the brick red of its Kremlin walls faded.

Everything was empty. There was no sign of the tsar or his entourage.

I rode Dyen, who walked at an unusually slow pace. I had told him about the child before we left, and he, like Vasily, had not been happy with my going anywhere. Besides Marya and the brothers, as well as Sanya and Stepan, we had taken a larger than normal party in case of trouble, leaving the others back at camp. Vasily had ridden beside me the entire way, glancing at me worriedly, trying to reassure me with his gaze or a quick smile. But there was no reassurance to be had. Not here. Not now.

Dyen went around a pile of wooden planks in the middle of the road, likely the remains of the guard posts and barriers erected by Tsar Ivan's oprichniki. I did not doubt the people had opened the gates of their city to the tsar in welcome, only to be barricaded inside.

Something glinted in the earth. I drew in a sharp breath when I understood it was an iron shackle, binding a severed arm. The yellowing skin was streaked blue-black. Another glint, another shackle, this time binding a leg. I had taken in too much air soured with death. As if I found myself in a desecrated grave, the dead exhumed and torn through. My stomach seized with nausea. A tug on Dyen's mane, and I leapt off his back.

Then I was on my knees by a ditch, heaving until there was nothing left. I wiped my mouth on my sleeve and stood. My gaze inadvertently lowered to the bottomless ditch—and the rows of dead bodies lying there. Flesh mangled, decayed, blackened. Clothes shredded and smeared with dried blood and dirt. Eyes unseeing or missing.

I crumpled. I felt hands on my waist as someone pulled me up and dragged me away. A pair of strong arms wrapped around me—Vasily, of course. I clung to him, sobbing uncontrollably into his chest. I couldn't speak; I could barely breathe. My head spun, grasping for any sense of logic, of reality, then hopelessly losing it. I had thought myself prepared for what I would see, had known it would be worse than anything we had encountered before. Vasily and Dyen had said as much. But it turned out nothing could inure me to the death and destruction that Ivan and Selica wrought.

The rest of the countryside passed by in a haze, the once prosperous manors gutted and glum, doors swinging on their hinges, open to let anyone in. Their owners' bodies swung in the air, their animals slaughtered in crusted-over puddles of blood. Crucified abbots and monks crowned entrances of churches and monasteries. We saw crosses, sacred cups, and shreds of velvet scattered on the road as we rode past the Kremlin gates into the city.

"The Kremlin must have been plundered," Vasily broke the silence. His voice was hushed as he spoke to me and Marya, who was riding next to him. "Look at all these treasures . . ."

"Piled too high on the oprichniki's carts, no doubt," Marya said bitterly.

I felt Vasily's eyes glide over my face. "Are you all right, dorogaya?" he asked quietly, leaning down to me. "Do you need to rest?"

I shook my head. "No, Vasya. I am fine." *Fine. Fine. Fine.* If I said it enough, perhaps it would be true. I steeled myself, trying consciously to become numb to it all.

"Look at that!" Sanya, riding behind Vasily, pointed. "My God!" He swiftly made the sign of the cross.

I heard our party's sharply indrawn breaths, gasps, swears.

The Cathedral of Saint Sophia stood without its bell and without its bronze doors. I went cold.

"To think that bell had summoned the people of Novgorod to church for hundreds of years!" said Sanya. "Removed, gone, just like that!"

Tsar Ivan *would* want to haul the fragments of Novgorod's cathedral back to Aleksandrovskaya Sloboda. Mitka told us Saint Sophia had been where the supposedly treasonous letter had been found by the tsar's men, providing them with the excuse to attack Novgorod, baseless as it was. I shook with rage at Ivan for his senseless persecution of our people and cities, at Selica for shrouding our country in death, for letting a madman loose on her. We rode across a bridge into the marketplace, the blood-stained square chillingly devoid of life. I slid off Dyen with my satchel.

Glass crunched under my boots as I threaded through the bodies lying on the streets.

Every once in a while, I bent down and checked a pulse, or knelt beside someone stirring and craning their neck. No matter who they were, their eyes were hollow, distant, as if they had been to the Land of the Dead—or their hell—and back again.

I looked up to see my owl flying toward me. Thank the gods Noch was safe. She landed on my arm, hard, her talons sharp even through my coat.

He plans to reach the outskirts of Pskov with Selica and his men on the morrow.

I turned to her. "So soon?"

Calm yourself, Ya. They say he intends to hole up in the Monastery of Saint Nicholas first, then drown the city in blood the following day.

This meant we had to travel to Pskov immediately—tonight—so we would arrive there no later than tomorrow afternoon. This would give us just enough time to find Volos and finalize our plan, especially now that we had to account for the death goddess.

The name of your holy fool has spread like wildfire across Tsar Ivan's camp, Noch said, anticipating my question. *Apparently, he talks of no one else, and is considering seeking him out upon his arrival. I suppose you want me to go to Pskov, Ya.*

"I do. Watch over the city, Noch. And listen."

You realize when all this is over, I shall no longer do your bidding.

I laughed—really laughed. "I do realize it. I will savor every minute."

You should savor every second. Then she was hurtling back into the blue twilight and disappearing behind clouds that feathered raven black.

The laughter died on my lips. Our plan was significantly harder to execute now that Selica was with the tsar. But as with Ivan, all we had to do was slow her, by returning her to where she had come from. As the Lord of the Dead, Volos could create a tear in the fabric between lands from anywhere. But she was strong and would not go willingly. We would need to somehow drain the strength she had gained from the souls. With Tsar Ivan cowed, it would take her years to return to the Land of the Living. By then, I could only hope we would find a way to destroy her for good.

In the meantime, how to weaken her? Maybe the other gods could help . . . Maybe Perun could help. Suddenly, I remembered Marya's story, how she was shot with Perun's thunderbolt arrow. It would have killed her had Perun not made her immortal. Selica was already immortal, so the arrow would likely not kill her. Though who knew? At the very least, it could injure her, allowing us to force her back to Nav.

Now I just had to convince Volos to accept the help of his greatest enemy—something he had never done before.

M Y FAITHFUL WOLF carried me on his back the entire distance from Novgorod to Pskov, where we would try to put the
fear of the Christian god into Tsar Ivan, enough to slow him and Selica
down, avoiding another massacre.

We agreed to split up to avoid entering the city with our entire party.
Leaving a few men outside to keep watch with Dyen, we journeyed to
Mikula's house, which Noch had told us the location of.

Vasily and I made our way through the streets, my hood pulled forward to avoid recognition. Hundreds of bells rang. The setting sun, out
for the first time in weeks, melted into a blaze of raspberry-hued cloud,
bathing the city's limestone walls in red.

I had expected Pskov to be empty on the eve of Tsar Ivan's arrival,
assuming its people to have barricaded themselves in their homes or
shops. But it seemed all of them were out in the streets praying. No one
paid attention to us as we went around a kneeling man with upturned
eyes, then a circle of women clutching candles to their breasts, their whispered words soft yet fervent. Two girls in yellow sarafans sprinted past, as
solemn as the boys they joined, who were raising silver crosses to their
lips.

What people spoke, they did so in hushed tones. I strained my ears to hear their words over the relentless tolling of the bells and the prayers, drifting over to me in murmurs.

"So, it is to be tomorrow. How ideal the Lord's Day is for divine retribution!"

"Mm-hmm, particularly during Lent. Farewell, my good man."

"And farewell to you. It has been a blessing to live and trade with you."

"They seem resigned to their deaths," I said to Vasily, inhaling the spice and smoke of incense from a nearby church, the entrance of which was filled with people.

"Resigned and patiently awaiting their punishment from their dread lord." Vasily's tone was mocking. *Instead of fighting back*, he seemed to say.

"Or is this their way of fighting back?" I wondered aloud. "Perhaps their subservience is a strategy, to impress the tsar with their loyalty. After all, he loves nothing more."

"Could be. Anything to prevent a massacre," Vasily said as we kept walking.

It was not long before the house with the blooming green trees slid into view. The melting snow turned to sludge along the same wooden gate I had seen before. And as in his last yard, fat sheep congregated before Volos's dwelling.

Vasily stopped with wide, disbelieving eyes. "Why, there are green trees here! What volshebstvo is this?"

Exactly that—magic. There were no green trees to be had in this Russia, especially not in this winter. But I said only, "That is Volos."

"The god you told me about? The one who's not really a holy fool?"

"Yes, the Lord of the Dead," I said to Vasily, who could not tear his gaze away from the house.

I took his hand and squeezed it. We were the first of our party to arrive, and we waited as Marya and Gorya and Fedya, then Sanya and Stepan, and, finally, Mitka joined us. Their reaction mirrored Vasily's, all of them except Marya, who had seen this house before, though in a different place. Still. Anything alive was something to admire, and she approached it as I did, drinking in the green of the leaves and the red of the roses.

She took my arm. "Are you all right?" she asked me quietly. Vasily and I had told Marya and Varvara about the child, and they had been delighted but infuriatingly protective of me.

"Yes, Masha." I gave her a quick smile. "Do not worry."

"I will always worry about you," she said, giving my arm an affectionate stroke before letting go. "Well?" She glanced from me to Vasily. "Shall we go in?"

Leaving our party before the gate, the three of us made our way into the yard just as Volos boomed out, "Out here."

We followed his voice around the house, to a yard framed by similarly blooming trees, with green grass and a shockingly blue sky. The air was fresh and clean and warm. Birds circled overhead, their feathers turquoise, as if having captured a bit of the sea in their plumes. They called out to one another in wild squawks, preened, shimmered. Other animals rustled in undergrowth fragrant with winter jasmine.

Vasily blinked around him in wonder. Marya and I just smiled.

Volos stood in his bear pelt by an expansive willow tree. "So, you must know now my fame has spread through the city."

"Even the tsar has heard of Mikula," I agreed. "My owl, Noch, has been keeping an eye on his camp. Apparently, Ivan intends to seek you out once he comes to Pskov. I will have Noch watching for him when he does." But Volos was now peering at Vasily. "This is Vasily Alekseyevich Adashev," I said, introducing them.

"A human man." Volos leaned forward with undisguised curiosity. "Well, you are like your mother, after all. And an Adashev, you say? Here I thought they had all died out. What curious company you keep, Yaga." His gold eye shifted to Marya.

"And this is Marya Morevna," I said, gesturing to her. I would leave it to Marya to reveal how she knew him, since her secret was not mine to tell.

She smirked, giving Volos a mock bow. "It is an honor to see you again, my *lord*. I am still here because of you—or, rather, Vlad the Holy."

"They know each other?" Vasily whispered to me.

"They have met before, yes." It seemed she was not hiding that part of her life.

Volos flashed his half-rotting, half-white smile, and I felt Vasily stiffen beside me, as it was quite a shocking sight the first time. "Vladimir the Holy was a diverting figure to play." Volos's gold eye was unfocused, as if looking back on all those years. "Too bad he had to perish of pestilence along with his entire village." His eye shifted back to me. "I understand how we will draw Ivan here. What about Selica? She is now at his side."

A bright yellow bird soared over us, and I went for it. "We obtain one of Perun's thunderbolt arrows—" Volos was already shaking his head; I spoke faster. "Selica will show herself when Ivan is cowed. We use the arrow to injure her before you open the passageway, and we force her into Nav. She will be unable to continue her reign of terror in her weakened state, especially with the tsar defeated, preventing her from amassing more souls. At the very least, it will buy us time to learn how to really destroy her."

Volos's gold eye was now piercing. "I refuse to deal with that old thunderer."

"Do you truly hate Perun more than you hate Nav? If she stays with the living, you will need to return to the Land of the Dead."

A beat of silence. "I suppose a battle for the sky is long overdue . . ." Volos paced beside his willow. "How do you expect *him* to show up?"

Volos could not bring himself to say Perun's name aloud. I primed my voice for flattery. "He will see your great work when you confront the tsar and reveal yourself. Perun will quake that you are in the Land of the Living, threatening him."

Volos produced a turnip from within his bear pelt and bit into it viciously. "You think he will be threatened?"

"He has been hiding from you as you have been hiding from him," I said, hoping Volos would not remember my words the first time we had met.

"I can attest to this." Marya blinked up at the god. "Perun himself has told me so."

"He did, did he?" Volos took a step toward us, still chewing his turnip. "So, I will draw the thunderer out of his Heavens with my mere presence. What then?"

"Once you confront the tsar, Perun will want to do the same. He cannot be happy with what is happening in the Land of the Living. The balance in nature and the Universe is being upset. And all gods are afraid of—"

"All gods except for me, you mean. I care not about the Universe's balance. I am not afraid."

"Of course." I gave him a deferential nod. "Either way, Perun will start throwing his thunderbolt arrows. When he drops one, as he inevitably will, Noch will catch it and bring it to us. We will be on the roof of your house with our men, hidden until this moment. Then I will draw out Selica while you open the passageway."

"And then you will pierce her with the arrow and force her into Nav."

"Wait," Vasily said, turning to me. "You are to confront this . . . death goddess?"

I kept my gaze on Volos, a pair of lilac-breasted birds flying over him. "Yes."

"Yaga," Vasily said in a low voice. "How can you consider—?"

I gave him a look of warning. "And I will think of a charm to weaken Selica," I told Volos, "if Perun's arrow does not do its work."

"Good." Volos nodded in approval. "I would not be surprised if that happened. Now go. Morning is wiser than evening, and I must prepare."

After our audience with Volos, Vasily and I wandered through the streets of Pskov, darkened yet ablaze in candlelight. Marya had stayed with the men, who unwound their bedrolls in the yard behind Volos's house. It was sometime after midnight when Vasily and I came to a little blue church the color of lapis lazuli.

"Let us go inside, dorogaya," he said. Then, timid, "If you do not mind."

I took his hand and led him into the church. There, I saw Vasily do something he almost never did—he got down on his knees, and he prayed to his god. I sat beside him, closing my eyes and praying to my own gods—to Mother, to Lord Volos, to Lord Perun. To Lord Kupalo and the other gods. Even to the spirits in the dimensions, as Dusha used to do. I prayed that our plan would work, that Tsar Ivan the Terrible would lose his appetite for murder, that his reign of terror and oppression would end, Russia and her people freed from his tyranny. And I prayed the Lady of Death would be returned to the darkness where she belonged.

33

WE ROSE IN Volos's yard early the next morning. The exotic birds were squawking and screeching overhead, dashing past in flashes of brilliant color, dazzling when compared to what we knew—black ravens' wings, colorless snowstorms, the blood-soaked earth.

My eyes widened in wonder as Vasily approached our bedroll, his arms overflowing with apples months out of season. My stomach seized with sharp hunger. "And here I thought you went in search of garlic," I told him, eagerly biting into a yellow-green apple and savoring the burst of bittersweet flavor as Vasily sat beside me.

"Though you make it near impossible, I can still surprise you every once in a while," he said, handing me a dirt-stained head of garlic. "Volos has quite a garden."

A smile flickered on my lips as I ground three cloves in my mortar, to ward off hostile spirits, along with three drops of vodka to cleanse and disarm, three koliuka blossoms to hit my target, and three roots each of hawkweed and weeper grass, to subdue and frighten. I bit into the apple, chewed a piece, then spit it out into my mortar.

Vasily raised an eyebrow.

"The apple represents the child, who will add to my strength with their life force," I said. Though I had hated my mortality, it now lived inside me stronger than ever, would even help me in the fight to come. I felt Vasily's hand momentarily lower to my belly.

We had returned from the church late in the night and lain together in the bedroll in just our rubakhas, Vasily's chest at my back, his mouth at my neck as we huddled together, not speaking, not sleeping, either, cold from what the next day would bring. I held on to that memory, of his hand on me now, as I chanted over the herbs, adding a few poppy seeds to keep away the dead, before putting the charmed mix into my pocket.

I heard the scrape of blades, and I was brought back to the yard. Next to us, Marya and the brothers were sharpening their shashka sabers.

"You think we shall scare Ivan the Terrible, Masha?" asked Fedya.

"Not *we*," she said with a bold laugh. "Me, maybe."

"Well, certainly not them." Gorya jabbed a thumb at Sanya and Stepan, steeped in prayer on their bedrolls, and Mitka, moody on the other side of the yard.

"Eh, let them pray and eat." Marya laid out her daggers side by side on the grass, tossing her braid behind her. "Now, which one should I take?"

Vasily leaned toward me. "The men we left outside of Pskov are in the city, along with your wolf." He swept aside my hair, even wilder and frizzier in these temperatures, and tilted my chin up to meet his gaze, pebble gray, unreadable. "Are you ready, dorogaya?" At my nod, he rose and helped me up, his hands lingering on my arms.

Marya and the men threw on their armor, their blades, and their muskets, and went up the outside stair to the roof. Vasily caught my hand in his and brought it to his lips. "I will be here if you need me," he whispered, disappearing behind a curve in the stair.

I went around the house, blinking away the too-bright sun, intending to speak to Volos about the preparations. No bells rang in the eerie silence, though the incense and candlelight had stayed from the night before, as if trapped in the air.

"Perun will know . . . he will finally know!" Mikula's laugh was strangled. "It is the end! Goodbye, Mikula! Goodbye, old boy!"

As I turned the corner, I saw the naked Mikula with a large blade in his hands. His white beard was crimson. The yard was not empty nor was it quiet. Sheep cried out in frenzied bursts like children consumed with pain. Some of them lay unmoving in expanding red puddles, their bellies slashed open. The grass was soaked in blood, vibrant, glaring. Mikula raised his blade, slashed. Raised, slashed. White, red, white, red. Blood splashed onto my boots. Stomach churning, I stepped back. "Volos, what in Nav are you doing?"

He did not look up. "A sacrifice must be made." Blood dribbled from his blade.

The few sheep still alive bleated weakly, watching as their father destroyed them.

Noch landed on my shoulder in a whirl of wings. *The tsar is here, Ya.*

"How far?" My hands curled into fists at the burst of adrenaline.

The tsar and his men just finished a service at the Cathedral of the Holy Trinity and were climbing into their sleighs when I flew away.

"And Selica?"

I have not seen her.

What if she would not show herself? But no. I had to trust she would. Mikula slashed at another sheep. I swallowed down my nausea. "What about Ivanushka?"

He is with his father. Noch blinked at me. *You should know—I heard the tsar talking about an inscription upon a sword he saw in the cathedral, hanging above the tomb of Pskov's first prince. He kept repeating it.* Honorem meum nemino dabo.

I shall surrender my honor to no one.

I tasted the acid from the apple I had eaten. What if I had been wrong, and the tsar no longer sought out the likes of me? No longer listened to anyone, not even his god? His intention to see Mikula the Holy Fool could be a front, meant to convince his people that he still sought wise counsel, holy counsel, as he slaughtered yet another ancient city of

Rus'. But I would not think about that now. I could not. "Is Koshey here?"

No. The oprichniki laugh that he had to go and deal with the boyars in Moscow like a nursemaid.

I thanked the gods for this small mercy, as it had allowed Noch to gather the information she had, Koshey being too far for his ravens to do much of anything.

Noch gave a hoot. *You should look beyond the gate, Ya.*

Glancing back at Mikula, who was slaughtering his last sheep with a flash of his blade and a cry, I approached the gate and twined my hands between the planks.

My ears strained against the deepening silence. The church across the street stood empty, no prayers to be had. But the people of Pskov did not hide. They had heard the tsar was coming to visit Mikula, and they knelt in front of their izbas with bread and salt in their hands, the tables behind them laden with foods.

"The tsar!" came from the street. Even from behind the gate, I heard the tables vibrating, the pottery holding the foods clattering. "The tsar is coming! Prepare yourselves!" A man, probably an oprichnik messenger, ran by the gate.

The people, unfazed, possibly frozen, moved not. Indeed, they blinked not.

"Keep an eye out," I told Noch. "Notify me if the oprichniki start killing." Before my owl took off for the skies, I asked her to summon others of her kind. Though it was day, she knew how to spread the word to her fellow owls, to awaken the sleeping, to rally the uncertain. With one last glance at Mikula, deep in sheep's blood, I took the stairs up to the roof.

And I whispered to the animals, to anyone who would listen, "Help us. Be there for us if, when, the tsar kills again."

"WE ARE IN position," Vasily told me, his voice that of a soldier, as he helped me to the parapet of the roof, where Marya and our men knelt at the ready.

I lifted a hand to Vasily's chin, his beard rough against my fingers. "Good."

I crouched between him and Marya just as we heard bell chimes. We looked over the edge of the roof. Several sleighs were pulling up to the gate.

Below us, Mikula rose from the blood-soaked ground and faced the gate. "Ivashka! Ivashka!" His voice was that of Volos. It rumbled like that of thunder made by Perun himself. "Will you continue to displease God by shedding innocent Christian blood? Take care, or a great misfortune will befall you!"

If Tsar Ivan heard Mikula, he refused to heed his words. The gate swung open, and the autocrat strode into the yard. I covered my mouth to stifle a gasp—at the lined face, receding hair, swollen lips, and bulbous nose. Though I had seen him in Kupalo's vision, in life, Tsar Ivan was indeed terrible, especially in his expansive shuba.

Marya and Vasily had aimed their muskets at the tsar. But killing

Ivan would do nothing; the death goddess would continue to kill, would force Ivanushka to take Ivan's place. No, we had to wait and see if our plan worked.

Ivan's oprichniki filed into the yard, followed by a dour-faced man with a bloodred beard who came to a stop at the tsar's side. Though he wore the same black robes as the oprichniki, he had a commanding presence. Recalling Mitka's stories of Aleksandrov, I knew him to be Malyuta Skuratov, the tsar's hangman. But I forgot all else when, from behind him, the tsarevich stepped out. He had always been slight and pale, but now, new lines folded and kneaded the flesh of his face, aging him painfully.

My heart ached for him, for Anastasia. But Vasily had been right; his participation in his father's expeditions of terror, culminating in Novgorod's massacre, changed everything. While I had set out to protect Anastasia's son, I had not vowed to protect a murderer, even if he was an unwilling one. And maybe there was nothing left to say, nothing that would release him from the weight of his acts.

"So, you are the famous Mikula the Holy Fool," Ivan said, unimpressed.

Mikula did not respond. Instead, he thrust something red and pulsing into the tsar's hands. Sheep entrails, still bloody, still dripping.

My stomach roiled at the stench, wafting even to us on the roof. I lifted a hand to the tiny swell in my belly, and my eyes found Vasily's. It was safer there, steadier. We didn't tear our gazes away until, gagging, Ivan dropped the entrails.

"What is the meaning of this? I am a Christian! I do not eat meat during Lent."

"You do much worse!" replied Mikula. "You feed upon human flesh and blood, forgetting not only Lent but God himself!"

I almost smiled. Volos was putting on quite the production.

But then the eggshell-blue sky darkened, the sun dimmed, retreating behind clouds that had become bruised and bitter. Lightning flashed, and a clap of thunder tore through the air. The tsar and his men threw their arms over their heads. Vasily and Marya, meanwhile, looked at the sky calmly, challenging it to do its worst and impatient with the time it was taking. I just prayed that I had been right, that Volos's confrontation with the tsar would draw out Perun from the Heavens.

"A thunderbolt will strike you dead if you or any of your oprichniki touch a hair on the smallest child in Pskov. We are protected by an angel of God for a better fate than murder." Mikula raised his arms. "Leave Pskov alone or contend with the wrath of God!"

In the flashing sky, a mouth stretched into a roar beneath a long mustache of gold and a head of silver. It was the highest of gods, Perun. He had heard me; he had come back to protect Russia, to confront the tsar and Volos.

Mikula's face turned ashen. He had also seen Perun, and though it was part of our plan, I could see he was afraid. He had revealed himself to his enemy after hundreds of years in hiding. Even if we succeeded with Selica, and Volos stayed in the Land of the Living, Perun would not soon let him out of his sight.

I searched the skies for Noch. Lightning and thunder made by Perun meant the god of thunder and war was flinging his thunderbolt arrows.

Tsar Ivan fell to his knees. He begged, he cried, he wrung his hands.

A flash of Perun's iron bow, and the wounded, black-fringed clouds lit up as he sent a thunderbolt arrow flying. The sky exploded in a blaze of lightning more terrible than before, followed by a booming that had even us throwing our arms over our heads.

In a sudden fit of animosity, Mikula rounded on Ivan. "Stop your reign of terror, or you shall lose all—country, heir, dynasty. The Ruriks shall be no more!"

My eyes widened at the terrible words, at the curse hidden within them.

The tsar staggered back. "Take me away!" he spat at Malyuta through pale lips. Genuine fear shone in his face, and defeat.

I searched the sky, this time for the Lady of Death.

Several oprichniki half carried the tsar to his sleigh.

I peered into the sky. Nothing but Perun and his clouds.

"Away, Son of Rurik, away!" came Mikula's shout.

The tsar recoiled again, this time falling into a swoon. His oprichniki caught him before his head could hit the bloodstained ground and tucked him into his sleigh.

Suddenly, Vasily grasped my arm. His gaze was fixed on the horizon.

A cloud of dust was stealing over the buildings of the city and plunging them into shadow. The wind pushed the dust in all directions. It was not until it got on my tongue that I realized the dust was actually ash. As it whirled, a figure in white darted from the gate into the yard—Ivanushka. He must have seen us, or somehow understood we were here. Despite my previous thoughts, I held my breath, hoping he made it. But just as the prince was reaching Mikula, Malyuta the Hangman grabbed Ivanushka by the shoulders.

The ash was whirling faster and faster now. Could it be the Lady of Death?

I rose. "Go help Ivanushka," I said to Vasily.

"I will not leave you here," he insisted as the cloud re-formed, then floated down to us. A figure was becoming defined in the ash. It was her. It had to be.

I grabbed Vasily by both arms and locked my eyes on his. "Go, Vasya," I repeated.

At the urgency in my voice, Marya hastened across the roof with our men, who slipped on their Skomorokhi masks as they went. Vasily relented. He gave me one last dark-gray look before he threw his musket over his shoulder and, unsheathing his sword, followed Marya down the stairs.

I turned back to the ash cloud—and the woman now fully defined there.

Wild black hair whipped about her face, blending in with her gown of snakeskins and ravens' wings. Her eyes were oddly shaped like mine. And her lips formed a single word: "Yaga."

"How strange it is to be facing you," the woman said, her voice a gust of wind. "Though the circumstances are less than ideal." She glanced down at the tsar, quaking in his sleigh and unable to see us past the raised parapet of the roof.

"Selica." I tasted rage. This was the woman who had murdered my dear friend, who was drowning Russia and her people in blood. The rage filled my lungs as if with blood itself until I couldn't breathe. Yet there was something about her, achingly familiar, like I had known her. Maybe that was why I said, "You must stop this, Selica."

She looked at me, her ashy eyes fathomless, and I had the illusion of spiraling into her. I glimpsed green walls and ivy creeping over windows. Then darkness so deep, so wet and wistful, that I thought I had plunged into the core of the Earth. I sensed, rather than saw, chains cold and heavy on my wrists. Then a place of ice and snow, of sorrow, and tears hardening the moment they fall. Then a burning so intense I thought I had burst into flames. I breathed in smoke, choking on it, before a rush of water engulfed me out of nowhere, and I was drowning.

The vision vanished. I stumbled back. "What did you show me?"

She tilted her head. "I showed you nothing, half mortal."

"I saw a palace, a place underground, a house of ice and snow. I was burning and drowning—"

A rasp of a growl. "Impossible."

But I recalled her from my last visit to Nav. Her agony, loneliness, desperation. Dying. Killing. Sold into marriage. Used as a servant. The last must have been Morozko's stronghold in the mountains. The rest . . .

"Those were the places where you were imprisoned, weren't they?"

Before she could answer, Noch swept down to me with a jagged shard clutched in her talons. It gleamed silvery-black, like clouds in the most violent part of a storm.

Selica and I seemed to realize it was Perun's thunderbolt arrow at the same time.

The ash was whirling, flying into my eyes and mouth, as I seized the arrow and called for Volos. He had to tear the fabric between lands, to create the passageway into the Land of the Dead, and he had to do it now.

Suddenly, a few paces away, a tear formed out of nothing. It was as if the space there had been torn through and ripped apart to reveal Nav's darkness. I lunged at it just as Selica lunged at me and the arrow in my hands. Without thinking, without even breathing, I launched the shard at the goddess as she stepped in front of the tear.

The ash was whirling so fast I couldn't tell what was happening.

Then I heard a voice—hers. "Help me." Followed by a quieter, "Sister."

She was alive. I froze, the ash still whirling about me. But I thought I saw the glint of the shard in one bony shoulder, the black gown torn through, the billow of white hair as one age-speckled fist latched on to the edge. Slowly, I approached the tear. The face that looked back at me was old and withered—a far cry from the beautiful woman who had first appeared to me in the ash. But she was more solid than she had been.

"What did you say?" I said in a whisper.

The old woman blinked at me from behind the tear's edge. "Sister."

"You are lying." She had to be. But that black hair, those eyes, that face . . . so similar to my own, so similar to that of my mother, Mokosh. My stomach twisted, and I fell to my knees in front of the tear. How could it be true? According to Volos, Selica had killed her mother. It would mean she had started the fire that burned down my village, my home, Mother. How could a sister of mine have done this?

"Murderer," I whispered through numb lips just as, in one agile movement, she took the shard out of her shoulder and threw it behind her into the darkness.

Then she leapt at me.

We rolled in front of the tear, Selica's bony body strangely heavy and her eyes a putrid green, as her skeletal hand reached for my throat.

Though she panted for breath, she was as strong as I had anticipated, even after being pierced by Perun's thunderbolt arrow. I bared my teeth as I gripped her shoulder, pushing her as far away as possible while reaching into my pocket. I gathered a fistful of the charmed mixture. But Selica's hand was now at my throat, squeezing, suffocating and casting a dark pall over me. Her knee dug into my stomach, and I cried out in pain. I thrust my fist out. As I did so, I released the seeds and herbs into her face.

She recoiled as if burned. Her cry matched mine.

Her face became more solid than ever, with more spots of age, more lines, more years. Suddenly, Selica whirled away. Raising her arm, she started to dissipate into the ash. I rushed to her, but too late. She had disappeared—not into the Land of the Dead, as I had planned, but into her ash. She was still alive, still here.

A flash of brilliant white, a lightning bolt splitting open the sky, and rain poured down. Heavy, cold, torrential. I blinked rapidly. The ash had vanished with the rain.

I ran to the parapet and leaned over it, desperately trying to see through the rain.

"Away, Son of Rurik, away!" came Mikula's refrain as he stood shaking in the middle of his yard encircled by his dead sheep.

Perun was gone, along with his lightning and thunder.

The clang of blades reached me then, as I glimpsed the shifting figures of the oprichniki and our men at the gate.

I saw Noch and her fellow owls circling and diving at Ivan's men. And Dyen and several local cats were leaping at the others. Next to my wolf, Marya thrust the blade of her sword viciously into the oprichnik opposite her, her braid flying as she ran up to another. The tsarevich, also fighting, splintered an oprichnik's staff with his blade. So, Ivanushka was still on our side, despite his cowardice. He said something to Vasily as they engaged in a knife fight with three oprichniki, Vasily sidestepping the swipes lithely, boldly, without fear.

All of a sudden, Malyuta grabbed Ivanushka by the shoulders and dragged him to the sleigh where I could just make out the tsar. I gripped the parapet, hard, but Vasily and the others were overrun by oprichniki. And the tsarevich was being forced into the already moving sleigh, its bells chiming madly through the rain. Ivanushka had evidently stood up to his father. He had chosen us. Only it had been too late.

AFTER TSAR IVAN'S hasty retreat from the city, the streets of Pskov filled with celebration. There would be no massacre, not today. Laughter and the clinking of cups drifted through the gate to Volos's yard, where, soaked and numb, I stared into the sky. The moon was a broken crescent, drowning in black speckled with Selica's ash, still hovering in the air.

Mikula stood next to me in Volos's bear pelt as we watched Marya, Vasily, and our men clear away the dead oprichniki and sheep, though their blood had long been washed away by the rain. Behind the gate, I could see the people in their rubakhas, their feet bare on the slick stones. Though winter still reigned, everything dripped. On Volos's land, the lush leaves on the trees shimmered like emeralds, the thorny roses sparkled like rubies. The chill had seeped into my very bones. I pulled Vasily's coat closer about me, breathed deeply of him. But it didn't ease my troubled thoughts.

"She's still here," I said into the night. I had not been able to banish Selica into the Land of the Dead, which meant she was still a danger to us and Russia.

"She is," Mikula agreed in Volos's voice. His eyes on me were keen.

"Nevertheless, I am proud of you, Yaga. You weakened Selica. She has lost her youth, her power, and will need time to recover. Meanwhile, thanks to me, Ivan is cowed, frightened, and defeated. Even if he kills again, his heart will not be in it. What happened here, your work and mine, has given the people hope. They will rise up against the oprichniki and end the Oprichnina."

I shook my head. "I should not have become distracted—"

If only I had pushed Selica into the darkness when I had had the chance. But the shock of her revelation had quite undone me. It seemed impossible that Mother could have a daughter like Selica. And that Mokosh would sell her own daughter to such a cruel fate, would abandon and refuse to love her. And would tell me nothing, no matter the danger. Instead, she had told me she did not involve herself in games of love with gods. Maybe it had been a new resolution following Selica's birth, or Selica's conception had not been because of love at all but duty. Either way, keeping her daughter a secret as she rotted in her prisons did not sound like the actions of the mother I knew. But no matter how unreal, I had to reconcile myself to the fact that Selica was my sister.

Mikula sighed heavily, an odd contrast to the playful nature of his face. "Perhaps I should have told you."

"Why didn't you?"

"I believed you had to find out for yourself."

"But you must have known what it would cost us—"

"Even still."

I pulled at Vasily's coat and let the breeze rush in, cooling my suddenly overheated skin. "So how do we fight Selica when her power returns?" *As it inevitably will.* I wished there was a way of finding her in her weakened state, but she would not be with the tsar now, knowing what we knew about her. She was also a dead god and, according to Dusha, unreachable through ritual. But then how to find her? How to stop her? Only one being knew and would be willing to tell me. "What if I try to reach my mother?" I said.

Mikula turned to me, surprised. "Mokosh is dead, dear Yaga."

"Or is she in one of your underground kingdoms?" I looked at him sidelong.

"She *is* dead there."

It takes great strength, Dusha had told me of traveling to those kingdoms, *for not only are they far away, they are in a land that is dead.*

"Tell me, Yaga, do you value your life?" Mikula suddenly asked me. "The lives of your companions, your friends? Vasily?"

I swallowed, thinking of the child in my belly. I knew in that moment—clear as day—that I would have a daughter.

"If you value your life and those you love, you shall not look for Mokosh."

Dusha had told me it was possible I would not find my way back from the Land of the Dead's dimensions—if I didn't lose myself there first.

"What now, Yaga?" Vasily approached, as if hearing my thoughts. "The tsar will not soon forget the Skomorokhi Knights, especially with his son jumping at the chance to fight on our side—"

"What did Ivanushka say to you?" I asked Vasily, remembering their exchange.

He gazed into the distance. "He said to give them hell." I saw his old, fond smile for Ivanushka. But it disappeared just as quickly. "The point is," Vasily went on, "the oprichniki will be looking for us and anyone sympathetic to our cause. We cannot travel all over the North as we used to, even if . . . we could."

I thought of our daughter, and I knew he was right. I had to do everything to keep her safe, to keep us all safe. Not only from the oprichniki, but also from the magic that could entrap me in the Land of the Dead's dimensions.

Everyone in the yard was waiting for my answer, even Dyen and Noch. Mikula's eyes flared gold, a warning, a shadow of divinity and foretelling.

"We shall stay in Pskov," I said finally. We had to settle somewhere, and Selica would not look for us here, not after the confrontation with Perun and Volos, not in her weakened state. We would also be at Mikula's side, the one man in Russia that Ivan truly feared. I met Vasily's soft gray gaze and knew he agreed.

I stood in that green yard with the people who had become my family, the sound of celebration swelling in the streets, and with it, the unexpected feeling that life would go unbelievably, unapologetically forward, even in times of darkness.

PART III

O Russian land, you must mourn,
remembering your early age, your early princes.

◆

"The Lay of Igor's Campaign," from
Medieval Russia's Epics, Chronicles, and Tales,
edited by Serge A. Zenkovsky

36

1570

W E SETTLED IN white-walled Pskov in a little izba not far from the enchanted, now-notorious house of Mikula the Holy Fool. After months of travel through the North, years of the woods and the taiga, to live in a city again was a strange experience.

Moscow had been dark and wooden and heavy with smoke, but Pskov was all light and stone and clear skies. There were walls every-where and sunlight that lingered, domed churches that never ceased their tolling, traders and merchants always hurrying, always accompanied by a stream of words we didn't understand, from faraway shores we could only imagine. Even the smell was different, briny with a punch of exotic spice.

In such a bright city, where shadows evaporated as quickly as the poor weather, and the rest of Russia seemed farther away than China, it was easy to pretend we had seen the end of the Lady of Death and Ivan the Terrible. But though the tsar was comparatively quiet, the ash that had appeared with Selica still hovered. It gathered with the dust on the streets, swirled into our izba with the slightest breeze, collected on the doorways and windows. It even got on my tongue, so I tasted the death and loss of Novgorod, of all the villages and towns destroyed by the oprichniki.

That summer, for the first time in years, it was hot. The sun was low, blazing hungry and furious, the sky a chilling, very sharp blue, expansive and frighteningly large. Never one for tradition, I wore a linen tunic and trousers, loose fitting to accommodate my now very round belly, my hair wild and free and curling. I learned quickly that the people of Pskov cared not who I was or where I came from. Not only because the city was constantly abuzz with strangers and foreigners, but because the people were loyal to their city and to each other. They protected their own. I could be myself in Pskov.

But when city life became too restrictive, Vasily and I would venture outside its walls to the long strip of land on the edge of the Velikaya River. The grass grew untamed there and the water rushed at our feet. And above us, the gold and pewter domes of the Cathedral of the Holy Trinity glimmered from behind the wall as we shared a basket of sweet bread, smoked fish, honey, and cheese.

"The city food is welcome," Vasily said to me on one such outing, "but I miss this . . . freedom." He had kicked off his boots and was looking up at the sky.

I sighed. "Me too, especially the air, the trees, Little Hen, and my companions." My hut had stayed in the northern wood where I had left her, sleeping and dormant. I missed her terribly, but she could not abide city life. Dyen and Noch could not, either, not after that summer in Moscow. They preferred the woods near Pskov unless I needed them. I turned to Vasily, propping myself on one elbow. "I almost walked all the way to the forest the other day."

He turned to me with wide eyes. "You cannot walk so far in your condition, my love! You must rest and—"

I laughed, putting a hand to my belly and feeling the answering flutter deep inside there. "The child is strong, Vasya, exercise will not hurt her."

"Even still." He sat upright and rested both hands on my stomach, bringing his ear to where the babe was rolling and flipping, and listening with delight. "Take care of our daughter, Yaga. And I do hope you aren't riding Dyen. He is a fine animal, but—"

I laughed. Vasily tried to curb his overprotectiveness about the baby, but he did not often succeed. Ever since I had told him we would have a little girl, he loved to speak of our daughter. But I knew all of a sudden what her name should be. "Vasya," I said, "can we name her Marina, after your sister?"

He was quiet for a moment, his head tilted down so I couldn't see his face. When he could speak, he said, "I would like that very much, Yaga. Very much." Then he leaned into me and, grazing my cheek with his fingers, pulled me into a long and lingering kiss. He broke away too soon, whispering, "Marry me, Yaga."

I laughed, twisting away. "You have asked before, Vasya, and I have told you before—I do not believe in marriage. It is not my rite."

"But it is mine," he said, voice low, gaze darkening. "I want to call you my wife, and I want . . . Marina, to have a mother and a father married under—"

"Your god," I finished for him.

"Your gods, too. Our friends, neighbors . . . ourselves."

I sat up so we were face-to-face. I lifted a hand and stroked one bearded cheek. I had never wanted to belong to a man, or him to belong to me, always believing marriage to be a mortal construction, one meant to confine women, to define how their lives should be lived, all in terms of ownership, an unequal balance, a drudgery.

But as I looked into that now-beloved face, I realized Vasily and I already belonged to one another, and instead of confined, I felt freer with him than with anyone else, even Mother, who had only known me as a child. With Vasily, I was unapologetically, relentlessly myself, as I was now. He knew me as no one did, and he accepted me, all of me, without questions. Perhaps marriage was not ownership so much as choice. To choose to define each other in terms of forever, even in times of darkness, even in death. Wasn't there a certain freedom in that? Freedom in certainty, and in love, which grounded even someone like me in the face of life's chaos.

I felt the bittersweet stab in my heart, the one that accompanied any thought of Vasily's mortality. And I let myself feel it, all of it, for it was proof of my feelings for him, and of our life together.

"I shall marry you, Vasya," I said with a nod.

He exhaled a slow breath, still guarded. "I don't want you to do so to oblige me. I . . . don't desire to force you. I just wanted to see if you had changed your mind."

But I was bringing my hand to his lips, his breath hot against my fingers. "And I have. I want you to be my husband, Vasily Adashev. I had not realized how much." Then I touched his lips with a burning kiss that silenced even him.

Days later, we wed in the little blue church we had prayed in before Tsar Ivan's failed expedition to Pskov. I covered my belly, so as not to scandalize the Father. The rest of the city had assumed we were already married. While a woman with child could be a vedma in Pskov, she could not be unmarried.

Yet, after, our wedding feast was deep in the seclusion of Volos's yard, where tables were laid with foods and wines from far and wide, and we could be completely ourselves. The bright-feathered birds soared overhead, twittering and singing, as fragrant pink and white roses tangled in blooming trees glimmering with fireflies.

I wore a loose ivory dress with sky-blue ribbons and juniper in my hair, while Vasily donned a white kaftan, his beard for once neat and trimmed. Marina gave a kick inside as Mikula welcomed us to the feast. "May I present to you—the bride and groom!" I could taste Vasily's kiss as he leaned down to me, feel his warm hand on my belly.

"Wife," he said with twinkling eyes.

With that word, marriage had become our reality. While I had had many loves and lovers, I could call Vasily, and Vasily only, husband.

There is nothing better in this life than to love another, I could hear my dear Anastasia saying even now. There was indeed nothing better.

Especially when we were surrounded by our friends, most of whom had stayed in Pskov. Yelena came over with Stepan and baby Anastasia, and I stroked the little pink face while giving Yelena a significant look and a hand squeeze. For she glowed with a new child in her belly. Her father rushed past with a tray of cups holding the mead and beer brewed by Varvara in the little tavern she had opened with Marya. Sanya and

Agniya beamed, their sons still unruly, chasing each other all over Volos's yard with an energy that made me quite exhausted. As Gorya and Fedya started to sing at a nearby table, already too drunk and too happy, Mitka came over to introduce us to the maiden he intended to marry, the shy yet pretty dark-haired Raisa.

I looked around that sunlit yard, and my heart was full. I had never expected to know so many mortals, to be accepted by them, to call them not just clients and patients, but friends and neighbors—my family. I had not known this kind of warmth, this fast and sure attachment and belonging, not since my birth village and Mother.

Varvara approached Vasily and me with smiles and compliments. She pressed her hands to my belly and commented on how the child moved! How restless she was! "Like her father," she said, with a glance at Vasily, who laughed and kissed her cheeks.

"Baba Yaga is married because of me, you know," Marya said low in my ear. "You look happy, as does he. This means everything to Vasya. And you and I deserve some happiness, at least for a time, no?" She smiled sadly at Varvara.

"You speak the truth as always, my dear Masha." I glanced at Vasily, his smile the brightest, the most carefree I had ever seen it.

I felt his arms curl possessively around my ever-expanding waist, his rough chin at my neck as his lips grazed the skin there, a promise of what came later, when all the feasting was done and all the guests left, and we strode under the stars back to our little izba, to our canopied bed, where we loved each other all night and all the following day, too, not leaving our house, not putting on clothes, and certainly not sleeping.

It was in September, when the winds blew over the Velikaya River and the skies were heavy with rains, that my time finally came. I had been dreaming of that strange, dark land from my nightmares in Moscow. Except now the mountain of glass was towering high above me, the iron-gray land clear and endless, when I suddenly saw a figure in a ragged sarafan with a face obscured by shadow.

"Mother," I whispered. I ran after her, and ran and ran, there being no end to the land, Mother still impossibly far and unreachable.

But I heard, "Wake up, Yaga," no more than air carrying the hint of words.

I did not realize I had been screaming until I was back in my body, back in our bed. I felt Vasily's hand on my forehead, then on my belly, which was straining against my shift. I heard him say something. But the pain was unbearable, tearing through me, spreading into my back. I forgot all, even to pray to Mother. But within minutes the pain had eased, and I lay back, panting, staring up at the wood of our bed's canopied ceiling.

Vasily's eyes were large and frightened.

I nodded at him, once, and he gave me a brief kiss before going for the midwife I had found in Pskov, along with Marya, Varvara, and Yelena. They arrived, with the potions and rubs I had prepared, with their chatter and prayers. But the contractions tore through me hour after hour, merciless, robbing me not only of breath, but of thought itself. Time passed in a blur of spiraling pain and soiled rags and the women's faces, peering at me in delight at first, then becoming pinched and pale and fearful. I kept picturing that mountain of glass, that iron-gray land, Mother below ground in a dead kingdom. All I could do was pray to her, until, finally, I heard a voice say, "It is time, Yaga."

The pain ripped through my body faster and faster, catching hold of me like the sea. There was an emptying, an unburdening, and a cry, thin at first, then strong and full-voiced, and I was looking into the face of my daughter—Marina Vasilyevna Adasheva.

MY DAUGHTER, WHOM I liked to call Marin, had my very pale blue eyes. As soon as she was born, there was an awareness, a knowing, in her gaze that raised the question: would she be an immortal like me? So few half gods had children that I did not know what the answer would be. This unanswered question haunted me as the days sped up.

The initial months were marked by the usual difficulties, an endless khorovod dance of sleeplessness, feedings, and a frustrated, never-satisfied newborn. But when Marina would nestle at my breast, I felt a contentment that my restless nature had not known before; and when Vasily would hold our daughter against his broad chest, his face tender with love, I was able to fall asleep with his low-voiced lullabies echoing in my ears.

Normalcy eventually returned, and Vasily and I drifted back to the world.

In the daylight hours, he busied himself with Pskov's shipbuilding trade. Other activities he carried out under cover of night with close friends from the Skomorokhi Knights—Marya and Sanya and the others. They would saddle their horses, kept in Volos's stables, and take to the road between Pskov and Novgorod, the estates and farms and towns and villages there, taking over the work once done by the Knights.

After one last burst of executions in Moscow, Tsar Ivan had withdrawn to his fortress, and the oprichniki were free to pillage and loot to their hearts' content. But Volos had been right—the people started to fight back, until the Oprichnina was finally disbanded in 1572. Yet the Russian army then filled with Ivan's corrupt favorites, committing the evils of the oprichniki, so Vasily and his band of vigilantes had no shortage of work.

Every time I saw Vasily in his kuyak and armor, grabbing for his sword and musket, I would whisper to my animals to help Vasily and his men. I rarely joined them. Instead, I opened our home to people in need of my healing, my knowledge of charms and rituals. As before, when Little Hen and I had lived in the wood near Moscow, I helped the suffering people with their illnesses and injuries, with their babes, love lives, and marriages. After Vasily and I would put Marina to bed, Marya would often come knock for him. They would head off to the stables, chatting and laughing, while I savored the few minutes to myself that new mothers learn to relish.

Marina grew into a serious child, always questioning, ever watchful. But she had Vasily's brightness, his bronze hair and bearing, and his arrogance, too—the way she stood and assessed the situation, even when she was no more than five years old.

"But why, Mama?" she asked one time as I rubbed a dollop of sparrow fat into Vasily's cheeks and hands as he went about sharpening his sword.

"Well, you don't want your father to get cold, do you?"

"Everyone is cold now," she said, serious, thoughtful.

She was right. The summer she had been born was the last true summer before Russia once more became buried in ice and snow, the winter months severe, the summer months cold and sunless. The Lord of Winter was once more in control, nature brought to heel. And though we had not heard from my sister, the ash she had brought with her from Nav still lingered, still tasting of death and sorrow.

That's when I knew I had to do everything in my power to make sure Marina did not grow up to be as ignorant as I had been. She would know my world, its gods and creatures, my herbs, and my magic, if she had any. Not long after that, I took her into the pine forest near Pskov. Though it was late summer, autumn already spiked the air with its peculiar sharp and earthy scent, with its mists and coolness.

"I like it here, Mama," Marina said, peering into the trees. "It calms me."

"As it does me, milaya, my sweet." I took her tiny hand in mine. "Shall we walk?"

An unexpectedly bright smile spread across her face, and she sprinted into the wood, her long, wild hair streaking behind her. And I gave chase, home at last.

When Marina was six and a half years old, in the spring of 1577, Vasily bought her a toy sword from a merchant passing through Pskov. "What is that?" I eyed the wooden thing in distaste. "I do not want my daughter to battle like you and Marya."

Grabbing my hand, Vasily tugged me to him. His gaze pulled me up short. It was soberingly dark. "Come, Yaga," he said in that serious tone he had now. I sometimes forgot that while I stayed the same, he was changing, a man in his thirties, a little more weathered and showing his years. "Do you really think we are done fighting?"

We tried not to speak of Tsar Ivan, of Ivanushka, of the Oprichnina; neither did we speak of my sister and what was to come. And it *was* coming. *She* was coming.

I had been teaching Marina about my magic and had even enlisted Volos's help in her education. To my relief, she took to it, the immortality in her blood awakening.

One day not long ago, when I had brought Marina to the god's house for their study, he told me Ivan had reinstigated the war for Livonia. "The mighty autocrat thought he could pick off the Livonian cities one by one, much as he picked off our own cities during the Oprichnina!"

Volos said in his true form. "To spread his murder and oppression even there. The problem is, Northern Livonia has been spoken for by the king of Sweden, Southern Livonia by the king of Poland and grand prince of Lithuania. The royal fool's arrogance and reckless ambition will be this country's undoing."

Volos had surprised me with his disapproval of Tsar Ivan; sometimes, as a god, he couldn't be bothered with a mortal tsar. I was glad, though, never having approved of the tsar's war for Livonia. It would only lead to bloodshed. As if we needed any more of that after his Oprichnina.

Now I also wondered if my sister had regained her strength and power, and was once more diseasing Ivan with her darkness. There was no return to the Oprichnina of old, but there were stirrings of unrest, a possibility of war, this time, with Russia's neighbors, which meant the death goddess was not far. And her ash filled the air.

"No, we aren't done fighting," I said to Vasily. *We are never done fighting.* "Just be careful, Vasya," I relented, and he flashed me one of his now rarer careless smiles and caught Marina in his arms until she was giggling.

They started to spar in the mornings, before Vasily's work, at their favorite place by the river where we used to picnic, eventually switching to a real sword.

I continued to teach her my ways also. The magical properties of herbs and roots, the charms and enchantments Mother had taught me, the earth magic Dusha had shown me. While Marina didn't understand animals as well as I did, she had a particular affinity to spirits. And by the following year's autumn, she could make any potion and charm it.

"Pretend Aunt Varvara's tavern is besieged by a vedma," I said to her one night, when the rain beat upon our roof.

"That is too easy, Mama," said Marina. She selected a clove of garlic, several koliuka blossoms, hawkweed, and weeper grass, very close to the charm that had weakened Selica. Marina ground the herbs in her own mortar and pestle.

Vasily threw open the door. "Where are my girls?" he boomed, stomping in, his cloak dripping rain. Marina threw aside the herbs and ran up to Vasily, who swept her up in his arms. "What potions are you cooking up?" He brushed his nose against hers before giving me a wink. But there was a tiredness in him. And his eyes were hard.

"What happened?" I asked him later, as he sat on the bench at our table.

"Bad news from the front. The coalition of Germans, Lithuanians, Poles, and Swedes has killed off a third of the Russian army and captured the Livonian lands for themselves. They will attack Russia now." He dropped his head in his hands. "It is over. War is coming for us, dorogaya. I . . . will not be able to sit by as they tear apart what's left of our country, come for my city and my family. You and Marin."

Vasily, Marya, and our men refused to fight for Tsar Ivan, also believing the war for Livonia to be unnecessary, also tired of the bloodshed. But now that our survival was at stake, they couldn't avoid it. What had started long ago as a senseless war because of one autocrat's greed and ambition was turning into a battle for our lives. And if my sister was back, it was a cause championed by a death goddess who would spread darkness not only to the tsar and our people, but to our neighbors.

I ran a hand through Vasily's hair, trying to be as comforting as I could in my own distress. He grasped my waist and buried his face in my tunic. And all I could do was hold him.

Vasily's prediction came true. By late summer of 1580, the foreign armies fought their way into Russia. Battles broke out across the country. In Pskov, we knew of the bad tidings and could no longer be impervious to them. War would find us. And soon.

By the summer of 1581, an attack on our city became all but inevitable. Disturbing reports had been disseminated of the invaders' desperation to win Pskov. Entire cities had already fallen, and we were in a state of terror. The attack was expected any day.

One evening, as Marina and I were practicing our earth magic in the forest, our fire chasing away the dark and cold, I glimpsed something white materializing in front of the trees. At first, I thought it was the mist. But then I saw the wiry figure, the long braid, and I leapt up. "Dusha!"

Over the years, especially after I had settled in Pskov, Dusha and I had exchanged messages, even sought each other out in the spiritual realms.

"Yaga," she said now, "the ash is everywhere. The Lady of Death is dispersing it throughout all of Russia."

"I know"—for it was in the very air—"she has regained her power and is coming."

Marina, now almost eleven, came around the fire and took my hand.

"Not only that. She is infecting the country with her violence, her war and death."

I went very, very cold at this confirmation of my fears. I tightened my grip on my daughter's hand.

When Selica had escaped into the Land of the Living, I knew she would be back, knew a time would come when we would need to stop her once and for all. This was why Dusha was here. To remind me I needed to find my mother. As a dead god and also Selica's mother, Mokosh was the only god who would know how to kill my sister, for that was what it would take. And Mokosh was the only god who would be willing to tell me. But in order to look for my mother, I would have to descend into the dimensions, the kingdoms, of the Land of the Dead.

"What if I get lost?" I had time to ask. *What if I do not return?*

"Remember what is important to you, and you shall find your way."

I wanted to ask her more, but Dusha had vanished.

Marina and I huddled together as the shadows grew, forming and twisting until I thought I saw a face, a body, the figure of a woman. This time, not Dusha.

The few tired soldiers who had returned home from the front reported seeing a black-haired woman, half shadow, half flesh, stalking the battle-fields when shadows twisted into dawn or twilight. It was said she was young and beautiful, with sad green eyes that stared into their souls, possessing them with a frenzy for battle.

All they could think was, *Blood, blood, blood.* All they could dream about was death. In that moment, they forgot where they had come from, who they were. They forgot their names. All that existed was war, even if it killed them.

My sister would destroy what was left of Russia following Tsar Ivan's Oprichnina by turning us against each other, by spurring our foreign neighbors to fight for our lands, by creating darkness and chaos. She had used the tsar to restart his war for Livonia and now she no longer needed him. For once war was on the mind, it burrowed in; the more of it on Earth, the more death, the more souls descended into Nav, and the firmer Selica's hold on humanity.

I had no doubt my sister and her wars were hastening toward Pskov, toward my family and friends, and I would need to defend them. Dusha was right. I had to face my fears and find my mother, no matter what it cost me.

38

AUGUST 1581

"I DO NOT RECOMMEND it, Yaga. Are you going to listen to me, the Lord of the Dead, or some mortal koldunya from the taiga?" Volos hovered in front of his dwelling, pelts and horns askew, having hurried into his yard at the sight of my bonfire.

"No, Volos, I am listening to myself." I sat on the grass, close to the blazing flames. The heat was a rare indulgence, making this August day feel almost like a real summer. Still, the air smelled of snow, mingling oddly with overripe apricots.

In the yard behind Volos's house, the trees were so thick, the sky could barely be seen. Bands of shimmering white striped the ground as if the sun really shone. But it was not the same yard. The exotic birds were no more; their plumes of canary yellow, emerald green, and azure blue had faded before they had drawn their last breaths. The blossoming flowers had wilted in a Russia now starved and bare. Still, the yard masked the stench of blood, stayed remarkably free of the smoke and dust of warfare that reached even our city.

I had to convince Volos to help me find my mother.

"Do you really intend to sit by while what is left of Russia is being torn apart, her people slaughtered *again*?" I asked the god. "You know as well as I do, as well as anyone in Pskov, that Selica and the foreign armies will be on our doorstep before we know it. And she no longer needs the tsar! She will not stop this time. We must act."

Volos pulled at his bear pelt, straightened his horns. "We can try to lure her—"

"We have already tried that!" I gritted my teeth to control the heat of my anger. All Volos wanted was to sit in Pskov, unnoticed by Perun, who had gone back to his Heavens. "Even if we succeeded, it would only send her back to the Land of the Dead, back to your throne," I said in a softer voice. "She will keep returning, keep regenerating, keep being reborn, stronger, more powerful, like now. No, we need to find a way to kill her . . ." By finding Mother, no matter how dead. And suddenly, it occurred to me: I didn't need Mother to tell me how to kill Selica. That's what Nav's dead kingdoms were for. "We need to put her in a place she can never break out of, a place very far away, a place for dead gods." I gave Volos a significant look.

"If you are referring to the dead kingdoms—" Even his old, lazy eye swiveled to me. "Then you are mad."

I rose. "Tell me it is not possible."

He shook his head, beard swaying. "Whether it is possible or not, Yaga, I cannot help you. If Selica were to be forced into the place you speak of, she would no longer be the Lady of Death, which would force me back to the Land of the Dead. Perun will not allow Nav's throne to be empty for long. No, I cannot help you."

"It is already empty!" I took a step toward Volos. "You will be forced to return there sooner or later, and you know it. It is where you belong."

He crossed his arms over his half-sagging, half-muscular chest. "I belong here."

"Here?" I repeated. "There will be no here, no Pskov, if we do not do this."

"Then I shall—"

"We shall all be dead," I whispered. "You have come to care for me, for Marin, for all of us. Even for this country, as torn up as she is now. You hate what Ivan did to Russia and her people, hate what Selica is doing. You cannot let this happen. We cannot let her win." Gods were lonely creatures, and a strong bond had developed between us over the years. It was a love that a grandfather had for his family, and a daughter for a father she never had. Volos said nothing, and I took another step toward him. "Is it possible to force Selica into the dead kingdoms?"

Volos took a breath, scratched one of his horns. "A god's death is a mysterious business, Yaga. Some end up in the dead kingdoms, like your mother. Others reincarnate or disappear. Theoretically, it is possible. But"—Volos raised a long finger—"you would need to ensure that Selica ended up where you want her."

My heart beat erratically. "But it is possible . . ."

"If you had someone on the other end—"

"My mother," I breathed, unable to control my heart. I might not need Mokosh to tell me how to kill Selica, but I needed her to help me do it, which meant I still had to travel through the dead kingdoms to find her.

"Do you remember what I asked you when Pskov was saved," Volos said at length, "when you had wanted to find your mother then?"

"You asked me if I valued my life."

"And do you?"

My hands were starting to shake. His and Dusha's warnings were what had stopped me from trying to look for Mother after Selica had been weakened, then over the years as I settled into a mortal existence that gave me two new reasons to live—my husband and my daughter. They needed me. I especially could not imagine my little girl growing up without her mother as I had been forced to. After we had started receiving the reports of Ivan reinstigating the war for Livonia and the subsequent foreign military campaigns in Russia, I knew Selica was rising again, knew she would eventually come for us. But it seemed far away, slow in coming, almost unreal. It made me cling to my mortal existence, to Vasily and Marina, to our lives in Pskov. Now, with Selica and the foreign armies on their way, I could no longer hide from it.

"You heard what the foreign armies did to the Padis fortress nearby," I said in a hushed voice that had even the fire ceasing its crackling. "They slaughtered everyone inside. I cannot imagine such a fate for Pskov, for our friends and neighbors. For Vasily. For my darling girl." I swallowed the last against a tight throat. "When I think of what could be, our city overrun, everyone inside killed, I . . . value my life a lot less."

Volos's hands appeared curiously empty without his staff. And his gold eye on me was sad for once. "There are many kingdoms in the Land of the Dead, all cloaked in a very old black magic, in darkness and death," he finally said. "Even if your earth magic is strong enough to get you through to your mother, what if you won't be able to return?"

I put my own hands into my trouser pockets so Volos wouldn't see their shaking. I had judged Ivanushka and Koshey for being afraid to make the hard decisions at the expense of their lives, but every time my life was truly threatened, I became no better than them, as being separated from my daughter would be the death of me. But I would no longer have a daughter or anyone else if I didn't attempt it. Unlike Ivanushka and Koshey, I would not let fear rule me. "It is worth the risk," I said as firmly as I could, "if there is even a slight chance that it will save Marina and Vasily—and the country."

"All right." Volos gave a shake of his head. "I suppose I cannot stop you."

I glanced around the yard, thought I saw a ghost of a bird with a long, dangling tail in the foliage. "If I can find Mokosh and she agrees to help, how do I draw my sister to us? She may be on her way to Pskov, but I doubt she will make it easy for us. And after the last time, she will not be in the same place as Tsar Ivan, nor will I be able to reach her through the spiritual realm. I doubt eleven years with the living has made her any less dead."

"No, she is still of more spiritual than physical matter, not as solid as you and me. She has been dead for too long. And reaching for her through the spiritual realms would not help, as you need her physically present for the ritual." Both of Volos's eyes were hazy with distance. "Though if she were present, she would try to stop you."

I thought about the times I had seen Volos, even Kupalo and Dusha, in the spiritual dimensions, the way they had appeared to me. "What if we forced her spirit to come to us instead? She would be present, but not physically enough to stop us."

Volos's gold eye sharpened. "Like a summoning?"

"Does that exist?" He did not answer, and I pressed, "Well?"

Volos produced a turnip from his pelts. He turned it over in his hand. "I have seen it only once"—his gold eye shifted away—"when it was done to me."

I lowered my hands onto my hips, filling the silence with my waiting.

"Well, what can I tell you?" His sigh was more like a grunt. "Perun could not find me, so he, Kupalo, Morozko, and Mokosh summoned me. It felt as if my spirit was wrenched from my body. No matter how I tried to resist, I was forced to them."

"How did they do it?" There was no way Morozko would tell me, and neither would Kupalo or Perun, since they had refused to answer me all these years.

"How should I know? That is not something they have ever shared with me."

So finding my mother was also the only way to learn how summoning worked.

Volos swept past me and dropped down beside the fire. He shed his horns, thankfully keeping on his pelts. His gold eye shifted to me. "Well? Aren't you coming?"

"You are going to help me?"

"I shall guide you. We shall start near the Nav you know. But the farther and deeper into the kingdoms you go, the more on your own you shall be. Do you understand, Yaga?"

The Land of the Dead, with its river and tree, came into focus slowly. Already, it was hard to breathe. The air was heavier than I remembered.

With a shaking hand, I reached for the next dimension, hesitant, fearful.

I stumbled into a kingdom that was darker, still like the dead, with mountains that stained the land like black ink. I tried to take a breath, choked on shadows. The air hummed with an energy that was as horrific as a nightmare. It cast a darkness over me that had nothing to do with the lack of light. It dragged down my insides, my very soul. And my head spun, my body sore and aching, as if I had really climbed that mountain of glass. But I reached for the next nightmarish layer, and was sucked into a whirling tide pool, the bottom of which was tempest-blue and littered with destroyed ships, skeletons of their former glory, and rusalkas, upyr-like, vampiric.

I opened my mouth to scream, but no sound came. I clawed at my throat before I heard a voice, then sensed a pull, and I was dragged back. That's when I could finally scream. And I did.

I felt cold water on my face, and I was gasping for air. Volos stood over me with a bucket. "I am here!" I lifted a hand that shook. "I am back."

He lowered the bucket. "Which kingdom did you reach?"

But it all blurred. Weakness, heavy and torrential, weighed me down. I was suddenly so light-headed I saw stars. I had thought myself weakened after traveling through the Land of the Living's dimensions. But it was nothing compared to this horror-filled darkness that had me curling into myself. All I could do was lie on my side with my knees pressed tightly to my chest and my eyes closed, intent only on breathing.

How would I find my mother in that nightmare, or even return to it? The mere thought of it made me ill.

"Well?" Volos demanded.

"I need time," I muttered before slowly rising.

"We do not have time."

We did not. But Vasily's work would begin soon, and he and Marina would be practicing their sword fighting by the river, waiting for me. And maybe they and that place, our place, would revive me enough to try again.

39

AS I MADE my way to the Velikaya River, the air was bitter, the people scarce. But walking dispelled the weakness, gave me my strength and will back. Though it did not ease my apprehension; dust filled the acrid-smelling air, turning day into twilight. Like the ash that had settled over the city when I first came face-to-face with my sister.

In the market, I passed by wooden tables laden with the skins of animals, the scales of great fish, jars of honey and jams, ceramic tiles glazed apple green, and, most of all, timber and flax for shipbuilding—the crown jewel of Pskov's trade, though it was not what it used to be.

Instead of smiles, the people wore grim, down-turned expressions.

Across the street, Sanya raised a hand to me from his stall, beckoning me over urgently. As I arrived at his cart, he grabbed my arms. "There is a rumor—and it may be just a rumor—that this dust is being kicked up by hundreds of horses not far from the gates of Pskov. That an army approaches. Where is Vasya?"

My hands shook as I pulled at my fringed shawl. If this were true, then the armies led by the king of Poland were advancing on Pskov. "You should stay in the city," I said to Sanya. "Our walls shall protect us."

He nodded. "We were heading to Varvara's. I was about to look for Vasya—"

"I'll find him," I said, giving Sanya's hand a quick squeeze, and nodding at his sons, Bogdan and Miroslav, who nodded back at me. Their faces were drawn and unsmiling.

I averted my face as several Russian soldiers passed by, inadvertently inhaling a whiff of their sweat. Since the country had been invaded, they had been scattered throughout the major towns. I pulled my shawl closer and attempted to smooth my wild hair. While the townspeople were used to my unconventional appearance, the soldiers would start asking questions.

I quickened my pace through the market, relieved once I was free of Pskov's walls; the armies would come at the city from the other side, and we had a little time before the gates closed. I squinted into the dark smudge of the horizon and shivered.

As the water came into view, so did the boats, bobbing on a river that was greenish, as if taken with sickness. The two figures at the edge instantly caught my eye. They were executing a complicated series of movements with their swords, striking, then pulling back. For a moment, I watched my daughter—her slim figure and bronze hair, looking somehow older than her almost eleven years. My heart contracted. My docha, my dear girl, was growing up. Yet she was too young for war, too young to learn of its losses.

I was loath to interrupt. I did not want to tell my family the news that would change our lives forever.

"Come, Father, do *not* hold back!"

Vasily's carefree laugh wafted to me, the laugh that had first drawn me to him.

The light reflected off my daughter's shashka, abnormally large in her dainty hand. She raised the curved blade before a whirl of movement consumed them both. I caught glimpses of my husband. A lock of bronze-blond hair. One ruddy cheek. His beard, wild and untrimmed. Then the zing and clang of blades. My heart thudded at the merciless way they slashed and thrust. As if that were my only fear.

Vasily met my gaze. While Marina kept practicing, he strode over to where I stood in the wall's shadow and pulled me into his arms. The sleeves of his gray zipun were pulled up to the elbow, and his skin against mine sparked with the usual heat.

He made to pull away, but I held on. "Can we stay like this a bit longer, Vasya?"

His body stiffened, as if he knew the news I carried. But he said only, "All right," and pressed me to him tightly. My body folded into his, feeling his every muscle, his every curve. We had a child and a life that we had shared for many years, yet it did not seem like it, not now that this might be the last time we could hold each other like this.

"There is a rumor they are nearly here," I said, finally.

"I know." He did not move. "Your face said all."

"We must return to the city before the gates close."

Vasily tilted his head back, slightly, enough to look into my eyes. "Everything will be different now, won't it?"

I traced the roughened line of his jaw, up close, his face pale, strained, not bright at all. "Yes, it will," I said. But I would keep them safe. I would go back to those dead kingdoms and find Mother, I would stop Selica and her wars. She would not destroy everything I had built, everything that had taken me centuries to find. To Vasily, I only said, "We must be strong, for each other, and for Marina."

He touched his forehead to mine. "Always, my love." He waved to Marina, and she ran up to us, breathless, exhilarated, unaware her life was about to be upended.

We slipped past the gates, then hurried through the market, Marina's hand in mine. The streets now filled with frazzled conversation and merchants boarding up their stalls. People pressed on all sides of us, so that we had to cling to each other to avoid being separated in the crowd. Marya was waiting for us on the doorstep of our izba.

"The king of Poland's troops have been sighted," she said without preamble, grabbing my hands. "Prince Ivan Shuysky has also arrived, calling on us to swear to the icons that we will die before surrendering the city. All able-bodied citizens have been ordered to the gates to engage the invading armies." She glanced at Vasily. "Will you fight?"

His gaze slid to me. "An invading army is at the gates of Pskov. War has come for us whether we like it or not."

"Yes, it has," I said, thinking of the ash and my sister.

"Of course I will fight," Vasily said. "I will not sit idly by while other men are out there risking their lives to defend our city." He turned to me. "Is *she* here, Yaga?"

"I believe so," I said, avoiding that penetrating gaze.

"What do you have planned? Is it dangerous?"

Marya glanced between us. "I think I shall go make ready." She kissed me on both cheeks. "You aren't coming, are you?"

I shook my head. "There is something I have to do."

Marya nodded. "Then do it. The gods know we will need all the help we can get." She gripped my elbow, whispering, "Worry not, Yaga. I shall take care of Vasya."

Vasily's eyes followed Marya's retreating figure even after she had disappeared. He went into the house, too quickly. Marina and I hurried in, not bothering to close the door behind us.

Inside, Vasily was already placing steel plates over his chest and back. The chain mail connecting the plates clinked and gleamed like diamonds. Zertsalo was Vasily's heaviest armor, meant for his bloodiest battles. I went cold just as he glanced up at me. "You never answered me, Yaga, about what you intend to do."

Marina was watching us carefully, and I let out a long breath. "I am going to attempt to find my mother in the Land of the Dead."

Vasily put strips of armor on his arms and legs, then threw his musket over his shoulder. "And you will confront the death goddess again?" He stood. His sword and shield shone ready at his side. "What if—?" He stopped, tried again. "Can't we see how this goes first? Perhaps we can push the invaders back, and you won't have to—"

"She will not stop, Vasya. This nightmare will not end until I find my mother and force my sister into a place she cannot break out of, from which she can no longer hurt us, a place where she will be dead." I paused, dreading what I was about to tell him. "Marina will need to help me with the ritual."

Vasily gave me an incredulous look.

"Can I not fight with Father?" came Marina's piping voice.

"How very brave of you, sweetheart." Vasily dropped to one knee without answering me. "But what about next time, Marinochka?" My heart beat a little more painfully at the endearment. He gathered her in his arms, her feet lifting off the ground, a delighted grin replacing the somberness. "I am trusting you to look after Mother—"

"Look after me?" I repeated, still unsure what he thought of our daughter helping with the ritual.

But then I heard, "—make sure you help her and do everything she asks."

Vasily set Marina down and straightened. The eyes that gazed back at me had sorrow in them, but not anger. "Even our children must fight, and not always with a sword. Let her help you, Yaga. Just, for the love of God, take care of her and take care of yourself. Come back to me no matter what, do you hear?"

But a feeling, so elusive and yet so clear, pierced me. That something disastrous was about to befall us. Or maybe it already had, for we were out of time. Fate was not an easy mistress to walk away from. She was always there, waiting, biding her time.

"I want you to know something, before I go." Vasily took my face in his hands. Sorrow now bathed his entire face. "You have been the love of my life," he whispered. He caught my mouth in a deep kiss that lasted forever and only an instant—a kiss of regret, yearning, tears. Then, he was out the door, and all I could see was his back.

Marya's braid, too, as she sprinted up to him with the brothers, Sanya, and Mitka. They blended in with the people running for the gates and were gone from sight.

A sob tore through me. Why had that sounded like goodbye? I wiped away the tears and, in my steadiest voice, said, "Come, Marin. We have much work to do."

"Are we going to perform the ritual to vanquish Aunt Selica?" asked Marina.

"Yes, but first I must find my mother." And this time, I would not be afraid. I would travel as far and as deep into the dead kingdoms as necessary. "Let us make haste to Lord Volos's house."

The sky was a puffed-up, battered blue. After grabbing my satchel, Marina and I locked our little izba—the home Vasily and I had built together so lovingly—and plunged into the crowd of people marching toward the gates into the darkness.

40

Volos's yard was dimmer, the dust and smoke seeping through his enchantments like a very thick fog, the smell of war finding us even here.

I knelt in front of Marina on a ground that was bitterly cold. "You must listen to everything Lord Volos says," I told her. "He will guide you through the ritual."

"All right, Mama," she said in her smallest voice.

Volos was already sitting by the fire. "I will take care of her, Yaga— even if you do not return." He wore a beaver headpiece that puffed out like a black cloud above him.

I looked into my daughter's frightened face, the sword dipping at her side, and knew I had to return. I had to stop my sister, had to see my daughter grow into a woman, had to come back to Vasily. Was he already fighting beyond the walls? Or was he still by the icons, praying with the rest of the city? Either way, I would get our lives back.

"Advance through the dead kingdoms layer by layer," Volos was saying. "Take small sips of air, do not think, and, whatever you do, do not let the darkness in."

I gave him a nod before turning back to Marina. I took her chin, forcing her to meet my gaze. "I shall return, I promise," I said, so that I would remember, so that I did not give up.

I was back in that soundless dark, its heavy shadows pressing into me as I pushed into the next dimension, no longer hesitant or fearful, but sure, like Vasily, like our daughter.

The nightmarish energy of this kingdom with its black mountains trickled into me like very cold water. The darkness would not give, emptying me of all sense, all memory, all desire to fight. But then I pictured my daughter and husband, practicing their sword fighting, the exhilaration in their bright faces. I ignored the pain in my body, the horror in my mind, and I was swallowed into that tide pool—no rescuer to be had now.

Though Volos's voice did not come, I felt him near. Marin, too. I imagined her at her earth magic, face intent, hair like the flames. I held on to her as I screamed my way through the heavy water. It darkened into black before hardening and becoming twine-like, then more like very long hair. It wrapped around my body, reminding me of snakes, of Selica's rags in Nav. And suddenly, the hair morphed into real snakes. They hissed and slithered all over me. I tasted my scream. Except for the snakes, there was nothing.

Marin. Vasya. Masha and Varvara. Pskov.

This isn't real. This is not real.

The snakes melted into my skin like lava. Then it really was lava, slick and scalding. I opened my eyes, wide, heard my scream. Forced myself to remember the heat of Vasily's arms, his beard against my skin, the feverish warmth of his touch—and the lava vanished. I had always thought mortality my weakness, but in this nightmare, it was my strength. I loved Marina and Vasily, loved Marya and Varvara and all our friends with a fiercely mortal love, evaporating like light, fleeting, lost at any moment. I pushed through to the next dead kingdom. Then on and on, until, finally, I fell into a familiar land.

It was dusty gray, the ash-filled air fading into an empty, sullen kingdom. In front of me rose that mountain of glass from my nightmares. It glinted transparently, its jagged peaks reaching into an endless sky. I could breathe easier here, but the ash made it hard to see. I thought I glimpsed a figure—a woman. But I wasn't sure, not until I saw her face.

Mother was not the goddess from my girlhood. Her skin was blue, chipping like paint, her hair had lost its color, and the snowdrops in the wreath she wore on her head had browned. Her eyes were as vacant as in that dream with the ravens. And I couldn't think of her in the same way, as the same mother, not after learning what she had done to my sister.

I took a tentative step forward. "Matushka?"

Yaga, Daughter. Her voice was no more than a current of air. *How are you here?*

"My earth magic." I could barely breathe, as much from the fear that she would vanish as from the smell, like the ground beneath my feet had only stopped burning.

Go back. If you stay too long, you may not be able to return at all. Or you may miss days, weeks, years.

I nearly choked on the ash, not having realized there could be a time delay in the dead kingdoms. Before, I had not gone as far. What if I would be too late to help anyone? Still. "I cannot go back, not until we have spoken. I know I have a sister called Selica. She is destroying the Land of the Living, all of Russia and her people. She has brought war and death upon us. It threatens my city," I fumbled for words, "and my family."

I know, Mokosh said.

"Then help me kill her . . . help me put her away forever—into this kingdom."

Mother's eyes, mere shadows in their sockets, seemed to widen.

"Would you be able to pull her into this land during a summoning ritual? I know you have done one before."

Perhaps. Mokosh was quiet. *I shall tell you how to attempt it if you wish it. But you may not survive it.*

The air was knocked out of me. But. "Could it force her here?"

Mokosh inclined her head slightly.

So it was my death in exchange for Selica's. My legs went weak, my hands shook, all in a body that was not actually here. Death—an existence without Marina, without Vasily, without our friends, without life itself. But Selica would be gone, her wars and thirst for blood also, my family and friends safe. "I will do it."

Very well. Was there a sadness in her voice? *You must first understand something. Selica is of Chernobog, you of Belobog. Duality will bring balance to an imbalanced world.*

"Chernobog and Belobog were enemies—as Selica and I were raised to be." *By you.* "How could you have abandoned your own daughter? Why did you sell her into a marriage that was little better than servitude?" *And make her into a killer?*

Mokosh was silent, and I thought of what could have been, had my sister and I not grown into enemies, had she not been forced to become who she was. I suddenly had the most vivid picture of us as girls. Us running through the woods with wild smiles on our faces, our hands clasped, secure in our sisterly bond.

The Universe had willed it so, Mokosh said, shredding what could have been.

I watched her for a moment. "Is that really what you believe?"

It is what I used to believe. Now I know the Universe cannot anticipate everything. Destiny can be taken back. Choices made. Fate changed. It is my fault she has turned into what she is. But I shall set it right. You and Selica were meant to be opposites, like Belobog and Chernobog, like light and darkness. But like those dual beings, you are dependent on one another and can bring balance to the world and to the Universe. Both must exist.

"To send her to this kingdom we must kill her. That is why I may not survive it. I could die also." Still, I no longer thought mortality my weakness. It had led me to a life, to love, to family. And if it saved those I loved, it was well worth the risk. At Mokosh's nod, I said, "I accept this. Now, how do I summon her?"

Since you are summoning her spirit, you shall need an article of significance to anchor her to the ritual. The duality in your blood may be enough. But have a bit of white fabric handy, too, representing her wedding dress, that which ruined her.

"And how do we force her into this land, once she is dead?"

The last time I did a summoning, I banished Volos to Nav with the help of the dual gods. You must do the same. Use the other dualities, the interconnected gods.

Though he had failed to mention his banishment, I recalled Volos telling me of the gods at his summoning. Perun was the sky and Heavens; Volos, Earth and Nav. Kupalo was everything green, life, summer; Morozko, frost, death, winter.

"So the gods of light and dark must be present at the ritual. Or, rather, their spirits. Which means I need to summon them along with Selica."

Correct, with an article of significance to anchor each god to the ritual. Volos's staff for his power, Perun's thunderbolt arrow for his might, Kupalo's wreath of flowers for his drowned sister Kostroma, and Morozko's scythe for his ice and snow.

I could try to obtain Roz's and Kupalo's articles. But I would have to ask Volos for his staff, as well as for the sky god's thunderbolt arrow. No doubt he had one hidden somewhere. "What about your article?" I asked Mother.

Mokosh did not blink. *My medallion, from the ruins of our home.*

I glanced away in shame. "I . . . lost it."

You shall find it again. She stepped toward me. *When you summon me, the ritual shall open a temporary pathway to this land. You must kill Selica in that precise moment.*

It occurred to me then. "If she is the Goddess of Rebirth, how can she die?"

When she is more flesh than spirit, when she is made human—with the blood of humanity, the duality of darkness and light, of corruption and purity. The blood of Ivan the Terrible, a mortal she has corrupted, and . . . the blood of your daughter.

I stared at my mother. "Marina?"

Her light and purity must balance his darkness and corruption.

My heart filled with dread. My daughter's blood would be used for a violent act. And a dangerous one at that.

There is always a price, Yaga, Mokosh said sadly. *The balance in the Universe is upset. Your daughter's purity is one ingredient to righting it.*

I inhaled a breath full of ash. "Was this why Marina was born?"

She was destined to defeat the tsar—and your sister—at your side . . .

To my horror, my mother's voice was fading, even as she instructed me on how to summon the spirit of each god through the burning of their articles, how to perform the blood sacrifices that would give enough substance to Selica's flesh to kill her, and how to summon Mokosh to hurl my sister into this dead land with the help of the dual gods. Then Mother was gone.

I ran after her, as in the dream when my labor pains came. But the land was just as empty. I looked about, expecting the familiar pull to return me to the living. But there was none. I was too far. Volos and Marina would not hear me. No one would. I was buried deep underground in a dead kingdom. I was trapped.

Interlude

THE SUN IS melting, big and bloody, into the froth of sullen clouds. Pskov's alabaster walls are aflame with red light, and outside them, bodies lie unmoving on the trodden, bloodstained grass. Their horses lie beside them, sacrifices left for the Lord of the Dead.

What soldiers still stand are covered in sweat and blood. It does not matter which side they fight for, or which language they speak.

Their words have ceased to sound human, reduced as they are to primal grunts and growls, to desperate shouts, to high-pitched screams more akin to those of wild beasts. Their bodies are caught in the endless slash and thrust of their swords, the aim of their muskets, the forward motion of an ever-drifting battle. Their minds are clouded over, a kaleidoscope of faces belonging to lovers and wives and husbands, mothers and fathers, daughters and sons. But the faces there are fading, becoming indistinct, as if time is blurring them.

One of these soldiers is Vasily Alekseyevich Adashev.

His sword seems to move on its own, as if his hand has been severed from his body. He hears the clang of steel, tastes dust, feels Marya Morevna's blade swish next to him as she runs a soldier through with her shashka. But Vasily's mind is elsewhere. With every strike of his sword, he forces himself to remember a detail of his daughter's face. The freckle in the shape of a shooting star above her right eyebrow, the spark of challenge in her gaze, her infectious toothy smile when he takes her in his arms.

Then Vasily thinks of his wife. The cloud of black hair, never covered, always free, like her. The pale blue of her eyes, clear as the water in their well. Her features, prominent in a face sharp with knowing. And the pictures inked into her skin. He could have spent an entire lifetime deciphering their meaning, her meaning. She is an enigma forever out of his reach. Strong and brave as a warrior, wise as the goddess she is.

His blade goes through flesh. The man in front of him is a foreigner, the supposed enemy, yet he breathes the same air as him. Vasily watches a red droplet trickle out of his lips, then the dark stain that spreads across his gray tunic, the same scarlet color of the horses patterning the tablecloth in his little house with Yaga.

Vasily can only dream of his home now. His heart beats with hatred, with fury, anything but peace. There will be none with this tsar on the throne, with a death goddess bringing darkness to the living. Has Yaga found a way to defeat her?

Suddenly, there is a spurt of blood and someone beside him falls.

He looks, and it is his friend, his Sanya, the man he has fought so many battles with, the man he thought would never die. Vasily does not realize he is screaming. He drops to his knees by his friend, whose eyes are wide, whose mouth is open in the same shock. But Sanya's throat is a gaping hole, slit open, torn through, and there is so much blood. All Vasily can do is hold his hand as his body stills forever.

Vasily searches for his other friends, the ones who had been at his side when the gates were thrown open—Marya, Stepan, Mitka, even Bogdan and Miroslav, Sanya's now fatherless boys. But they are gone. Perhaps he had imagined them. Perhaps he had been alone all this time. All he sees are the foreign soldiers streaming toward him. He takes one last look at his friend and rises—when there is a flash of red in the corner of his eye.

He clutches his shield to his chest and drives his sword into a soldier who is nearly upon him. Vasily does not feel the hot gush of blood on his cheeks. A little face is now peering back at him. The girl's bronze hair sweeps across her shoulders as she runs on.

"Marin!" He takes off his helmet and follows his daughter. What could she be doing here?

The hem of her linen rubakha is dirtied, her bare feet stained with blood. She is smaller, thinner, frailer, like his sister the night she died in his arms.

"Marinochka!" This time, Vasily is calling for his sister.

The jeweled hilt of his sword slides out of his grip. The heavy shield and helmet, too. He threads through corpses until the enemy's tents are before him with their flags and banners.

The girl turns. He recognizes his sister, the golden-orange wisps of hair, the bright sapphire gaze, the bones jutting out of the starved frame. She lifts a hand; whether in greeting or farewell, he cannot tell.

Vasily falls at her feet. "I am sorry," he says, voice breaking. "It should have been me." He tastes the salt of his tears, mingling with the dirt and blood.

A woman in black appears behind his sister, the same one he had seen the night Pskov was saved. Yaga's sister? But no, he cannot remember. She is beautiful, yet there is an unnatural glow to her. Her lips are as red as the blood on his armor, which gleams no more. Her vomit-green gaze is intent on Vasily as she envelops his sister in her arms. When the woman smiles, her teeth are like exposed bones, sharp and grotesque.

Vasily blinks, and it is his daughter and Yaga in his sister and this woman's place.

He opens his mouth, but no words come. He charges forward, but the distance between him and his family grows. He peers at his wife and daughter, but he cannot remember their achingly familiar, lovely faces. They are smudged, barely visible. There is the taste of blood in his mouth, the clang of blades and the shouts of soldiers, the battlefield hard and unforgiving beneath him. He can no longer see his family.

Vasily Alekseyevich Adashev spins on his heel, confused. *Does* he have a family? He thought he did. Now, he is not so sure. He grabs a sword from one of the dead soldiers lying on the field, and he plunges back into the battle.

Selica watches him. This man is the rescuer she had wished for, come alive from her childhood dreams. There is a pang in her heart. For once, it is not envy. She recalls how Yaga had seen into her the night Pskov was saved. Selica wants to hate her sister as before, but she cannot. There is a connection between them, a bond that cannot be broken. And because of this, a part of her had hoped Vasily Adashev could have resisted her, remained faithful as Morozko had never been. Yet he is a man, and how easily they forget.

She is doing Yaga a favor. Look where men have gotten Selica.

Like all women, her sister is better on her own.

41

I HAD CIRCLED THE glass mountain several times now, had tried to push through to another dimension, backward or forward, but it was as if I were trapped in the muck and mire of a swamp. The land around me was an unbroken, colorless sea of smoke and ash.

What if Volos had been right, and I could not return to the living? What if Dusha's warnings became my reality?

Stop it, Yaga, I commanded myself. I recalled my daughter's face and the promise I had made to her. We had to perform the ritual that would put Selica away forever, in this dead kingdom where she belonged. We had to rescue Vasily, Marya, all our friends. We had to save our country and destroy Ivan the Terrible for good.

I gazed out over the land, then at the mountain glimmering above me.

I had dreamed it even before I had known of the dead kingdoms, probably because of Mother. I remembered the first time I had seen it, in a nightmare when I had been imprisoned by Koshey. I had climbed the mountain of glass. After all, some called Nav the Thrice-Tenth Kingdom—only, it was not Nav, but one of its dead kingdoms, unreachable by mortals. But perhaps I could reach the mortal realm by climbing the mountain and jumping down.

Before I could talk myself out of it, I rushed to the mountain. The first glassy rock was slippery under my fingers and unsteady under my feet. Yet I pulled myself onto the next glassy rock, then the next and the next, until I was climbing the mountain. The land beneath me was alarmingly transparent, too far now to change my mind.

After what seemed like hours, I saw the summit up ahead.

But in that moment, my foot slipped.

I screamed. I was dangling precariously over a land that was a very great distance below me. If I fell . . . But I pictured Marina's face when I had promised to return, the hope in her eyes. I held on to the image of my daughter as I tightened my grip on the glassy rock, almost clinging to it with my nails. One last push, and I pulled myself onto the summit. I gasped for air. But there was none. And before this place could strangle me, I broke into a sprint—and I flung myself over the edge.

42

NOVEMBER 1581

I GASPED AWAKE, IMMEDIATELY leaping to my feet.

But I could not stay upright. The world was fraying around me, losing its color, until I felt myself fall. Great arms caught me from behind, I could not tell whose. My insides were liquid, as if I were not all here. But then I saw the green yard and orange fire, breathed in the air, the sky above me a hazy steel blue, not the black of that nightmare.

I spun to see Volos staring down at me, his stillness the only sign of his anxiety. He kept his hands on my shoulders, steadying me. "Thank the gods you have returned," the god said in his bottomless, divine voice. "Marina Vasilyevna and I tried to pull you back, but you were too far for us to reach. Did you find Mokosh?"

"I did." Some clarity returned. "How long have I been gone?"

"You have been lost to us for more than two months," said Volos.

"Two months?" I repeated in horror. It was at least November. I peered at Volos's yard for signs of the invaders, of the city having been breached. But all was before. I turned back to the god, grasping him by his pelts. "What happened? Where is Marina?"

Just then, "Where should I put the plums for the soldiers, Lord Volos?" And there she was. "Mama!" Marina ran to me, and I to her.

We collided into each other, and I pressed her little body to mine so fiercely my ribs ached. "Thank the gods you are all right, Marin." I leaned down to make sure her face was still unmarred, still unhurt. I ran my fingers over her eyes, her nose, her cheeks.

"I am all right, Mama," she said, with a hint of a smile.

I looked at my daughter, *really* looked at her. Like me, she stubbornly eschewed traditional dress, wearing a tunic and trousers and her hair loose. "I can see that, dorogaya moya." Tears pricked my eyes—I had not expected to see Marina again. But a sadness pulled at her gaze, eclipsing the pale of the blue. "What is it?" I asked, tensing.

My daughter said nothing, and Volos spoke. "The battle goes on at the gates."

I stood. "It does?" Relief flooded through me—at least I had not missed it, and maybe, just maybe, I was not too late. But the tension clutched at me. "Where is Vasily? Marya? Sanya and Stepan—?" Volos and Marina exchanged a glance I could not read, and my hands started to shake. I clasped them together. "Tell me now."

"Pskov's walls and towers have withstood the king of Poland's cannon and firebombs," Volos said in a quiet voice. "But he has refused to give up his siege, waiting for the city to crumble or for us to open our gates in surrender. We have refused. So the blockade continues."

Marina came over to me, placing her hands on either side of my face. "Father is . . . not himself." She said this softly, gently, as if I might break. "But he is alive," she added hastily, "and he can come back to himself, I know it, and we can live together as before, all of us, after we perform the ritual to vanquish Aunt Selica—" Marina sniffed, as if she was tired of spinning her pretty tales. Her blue eyes shimmered with tears.

Vasily—not himself? Had I lost him? But no, it could not be. She said he was alive. He *was* alive.

Marina told me how at the end of that first day of fighting, Vasily had not come home for the first time in her life. No one had. The soldiers slept by the gates and along the walls, as though by their proximity, they would prevent the invaders from breaching the city. After a few tense days, she, Varvara, and Volos had gone in search of Vasily, Marya, and the rest of our friends. But when they found them, it was not them, not really. Only Marya had kept a semblance of herself, and even she was changed.

I placed my hands over Marina's. "I must see him," I said.

"I would not recommend it, Yaga," Volos warned. "It would only pain you."

"I care not." I watched the dying light on the grass, the dimming sky. "I shall see if they are back." I looked up at the god. "Where is Marya? Is she all right? And Varvara?"

"She is fine, they are fine." Volos was pacing in the last dregs of light. "But—"

"It is Uncle Sanya," Marina said softly. "He is dead."

There wasn't enough air, as if I were hurled back into that suffocating nightmare belowground. I sank to the grass, stunned and very cold. Poor, poor Agniya . . .

Volos pulled at his pelts, still pacing. "And Bogdan and Mitka are missing."

Oh, gods. Bogdan, a young man in his prime, and Mitka, only now recovering from the horrors he had witnessed all those years ago at Tsar Ivan's fortress. "How is Raisa?" I asked, thinking of Mitka's now wife, pregnant with their fourth child.

"As well as can be." Volos shrugged. "She and the children are at Varvara's."

I nodded numbly. This was the price of war, immeasurable loss, lives upended, families destroyed. Only I could stop it, with a ritual that could bring a different loss: the loss of my life. But I was ready to pay the price, ready to force my sister into the death where she belonged. It was the quickest way to end the blockade and prevent the invaders from starving the city into submission then killing everyone inside. The way to end this war and save those I loved, as well as my city and country. But first I had to see Vasily.

Outside Volos's yard, there was ice on the streets, frost on the windows, a dusting of snow on the roofs. The never-opened browned buds fell from the blighted trees like dead beetles. By the time I reached the gates, twilight had doused the light, and everything was a murky, very dark blue, like the tide pool in that dead kingdom.

Soldiers milled at the gates. I heard the clang of their blades and armor, their whispered conversations, the neigh of their horses; I felt the brush of their shoulders against mine, the influx of energy following battle. I tightened my grip on the wicker basket at my elbow and made sure the blankets under my arm were not dragging.

A soldier barreled into me. It was only when they lifted their helmet and I saw the long braid that I recognized Marya Morevna. She dropped her weapons and drew me into a fierce embrace that was all heat and tears and leather.

"Yaga! My gods!" She looked into my face; hers had lost its certainty, its hardness. It was just lost now. "We thought the worst—"

"I did, too, Masha." I took her face in my hands and kissed both her cheeks, tasting blood and warfare on her. But I didn't care. My friend was in my arms.

"Yaga—" She pulled away. Her forehead creased in concern.

"I know," I said, smoothing her hair. "Marina and Volos have prepared me."

"I'm not sure anything can prepare you." Her eyes were impossibly large. "I am sorry, Yaga. I am so sorry. I tried to watch over him, but then, in the heat of battle, he disappeared. I know not where he went. When he returned, he was different. But then, most of the soldiers are different. This war is different—"

A scream, and Varvara was flying at us with her arms outstretched. The three of us clutched each other in the middle of the street, with the battlefield just past the gates and the soldiers jostling against us, staring, sometimes swearing with shakes of their heads.

"To hell with you!" Varvara shook her fist at a man who had started to complain, loudly, of us taking up the street. "Did you get what you needed, Yaga?" she asked me.

I nodded, clasping her and Marya to me one last time. "I wanted to see him before . . . I have to go away again."

They exchanged a pained glance and gestured to a group of soldiers kneeling before the holy icons by the gates. I grasped their hands, hard, loath to say goodbye, then turned toward the gates. In the candlelight, I glimpsed Stepan's handsome face, and that of Miroslav, appearing lonely without his brother. But their gazes were averted, lost in prayer.

When I found Vasily, he was on his knees facing the ground, as if that was all he wanted to see. I stood frozen, unable to move, as hesitant as with a stranger.

I touched his shoulder, and he raised his head to look up at me.

His hair clung to his skin, slick with sweat and dirt and blood. His gaze was unfocused, haunted, as if he were trapped in a battle he had no intention of leaving. Odd, given how many battles he had seen. But this was no ordinary battle; Selica had diseased the minds of our soldiers. Indeed, the eyes that stared back at me were those of another man. Certainly not my Vasya, full of life and love. This was a man who saw nothing, who knew nothing, who cared for nothing. I did not think he even recognized me.

My heart beat furiously fast. Marya had been right. Nothing could have prepared me for this change in Vasily. I led him away from the praying soldiers. I took him in my arms and pressed my cold forehead to his burning one.

"Come home, Vasenka," I whispered, trying not to weep, sensing him lost to me.

"Home?" He peered at me as though we had ceased to speak the same language.

"Our home." I felt the sting of tears. "Have you forgotten, my love? We live here in Pskov, in a tiny house, where we are happy, so happy. We have a daughter we call Marin. She smiles like you, she *is* you, all you. For gods' sakes! You must remember!"

He looked at me as if I was the one now spinning the pretty tales. His eyes strayed. To the wall, to the discarded flags and banners, unfurling on the ground in flaming reds and yellows, then back to the icons. "Home," he said again. "Yes, I will be home soon."

I tried to get Vasily to eat some of the dried fish and cheese I had brought in my basket. Then I scrubbed the filth and blood off his skin. He could not stop shaking, so I wrapped him in blankets, even slipping into his bedroll to warm him a little, to feel his body against mine. But he was rigid, not really there, like a corpse instead of a living, breathing man. And he did not put his arms around me. Instead, he wrapped them around himself, his eyes open wide to horrors only he saw. My body ached with the loss of him, of our life together. But it also stirred up my rage—at the monster that was my sister.

It was her. She had done it. She had taken him from me. And she would pay.

By the time I left Vasily, it was night, damp and cold and very, very lonely. I could not stop picturing his bloodstained face, those empty eyes, a stranger's eyes, as if all our years together had been wiped away with a flick of my sister's shadowy hand.

I hurried along the deserted streets to Volos's house and found him and Marina in the yard behind his dwelling. I held her to me tightly. Then, pacing the yard, I told them of my travels into Nav's dead kingdoms, of finding my mother, of the summoning ritual. I did not speak to them of the price of Selica's death. But I suspected Volos knew. When I mentioned duality and balance, his eyes narrowed. I would not tell Marina yet, for fear of worrying and distracting her. We had too much ahead of us; there would be time enough later. But I did have to tell my daughter about her role in the ritual.

Destined to defeat the tsar. And your sister.

I sat beside Marina on the grass, felt the dew even through my trousers. "Dorogaya moya." I gathered her hands in mine. "You are the purity necessary for Selica to truly die before she is hurled into the dead kingdom where we will try to entrap her. For this, your blood will be needed . . ."

Marina did not hesitate. "Of course, Mama. I shall do what you ask."

I shook my head at her sadly. "Dorogaya, your blood will have a hand in destroying a life, no matter how dark and corrupt, your purity in exchange for it. Are you certain you are ready for that?"

"Yes." Her little face was as intent as Vasily's. "Whatever will save our city, Aunt Masha, everyone . . ." She swallowed. "Whatever will bring Father back."

I kissed her hands. "You are very brave. He . . ." I glanced away, spoke through a tight throat. "He would be very proud of you, Marin, very proud." Despite the tears welling up again, I whispered for Dyen, for him to come to me, to help me. "We will need to go where the tsar is," I said in a low voice. "His blood is also a necessary component to Selica's death. He must be with his armies—"

Volos shook his head. "He left the city of Staritsa after the Polish king's raiding party reached Rzhev, about fifty kilometers from Staritsa, where the tsar was with his troops—"

"Ivan was that close to Pskov and chose to do nothing?" Understanding dawned. "The tsar fled to his fortress in Aleksandrov, taking his army with him in fear there would not be enough soldiers to protect him."

Volos lifted his bony shoulder. "Ivan has never been a courageous man."

"But to abandon Pskov!" My chest flared in hatred of that cowardly tsar. "To refuse to supply us with basic necessities, much less reinforcements!"

An image of Vasily crashed into me, drenched in blood, hollow from the inside out. And Marya, with that lost look in her eye. The other men and women of Pskov, too. All extraordinarily brave, all giving up their lives for this war, all fighting for a tsar who would never fight for them. But this meant that, to perform the ritual, we would need to travel to Aleksandrov, to Tsar Ivan's fortress of death, the one Mitka had returned from forever changed. This also meant we would need to leave a city under siege.

Dyen bounded up to us. *I hear we are on our way to kill the bitch.*

My eyes widened at his words, so entirely out of character. Marina must have understood, for she laughed, actually laughed, before throwing her arms around his neck.

"Only"—I glanced from one to the other—"I have no idea how to leave the city. The gates are closed. They only open for the soldiers—"

Do you really have such little faith in me? Dyen met my eye.

"The walls are high, Dyen," I said, "even for you."

I am offended. Noch will be, too, once she hears of this.

"We must trust in him, Mama!" Marina insisted, giggling, as she scratched Dyen's belly, a child for the first time since my return.

"What about the articles to summon the gods?" Volos broke in.

"I shall take a bit of my wedding dress and some dried juniper for Selica," I replied. "And she will have left the Lord of Winter to protect the tsar. We will see him on our way to Aleksandrov. I can convince him—"

"To give you his scythe?" Volos snorted. "I wish you much luck with that."

"It seems none of us have faith in each other anymore. Don't worry about Morozko." I gave Volos a pointed look. "Do *you* have something for me?"

"Wait here," he said begrudgingly and disappeared into his dwelling.

"Mama—" Marina sat cross-legged with Dyen's head in her lap. "What is Mokosh's article?"

I remembered Mother's words, that her medallion would be found again. I became aware of a lump in my trouser pocket. I felt it, heart sprinting—could it be?—and pulled out the medallion as if it had lived in my pocket these hundreds of years, returned safe and whole by magic. It was the same tarnished silver and gold as when I had pulled it out of the burning remains of our izba. I showed Mokosh's medallion to Marina and Dyen, told them about the World Tree on its surface and how my mother had never removed it in all our time together.

Once Volos returned, he handed me his staff, which he had broken into parts. Next, the shard-like thunderbolt arrow—I had been right, the wily god had somehow caught at least one the day Pskov was saved. Volos then handed me a flower wreath of the palest yellow tea roses. "For Kupalo," he said. "Any flowers remind him of his sister, and these will do." He hesitated before taking out another wreath and putting it in

Marina's hair like a crown. "And this one is for you, Marina Vasily-evna."

She caught his hand and put it to her cheek.

I gritted my teeth against the swell of emotion. Volos had given me real help when almost no other god would, even with his hatred of Perun and the Land of the Dead. "Thank you, Lord Volos," I told him with real gratitude.

He waved my gratitude away. "Do you have everything you need, Yaga?"

That is when I realized Mother had never told me how to kill Selica. "When Selica is made human," I asked Volos, "how do I kill her?"

"As you would any human. But"—he raised a finger—"it would not hurt to have a strong blade. Selica is a dark force, a dead god, and every bit against her will help. Some say love can not only break any enchant-ment, it can also kill—"

"A blade belonging to Vasily." I shook my head. "Even if I wanted to, I could not get it. He took them all—"

"Not all." Marina did not try to hide her smile. "I may have stolen his battle axe."

Volos grinned. "I admire your spirit, Marina Vasilyevna."

With that, we prepared our possessions, readied Dyen and Noch, and layered on our coats and furs. We bade farewell to Volos and to Pskov before setting out that very night.

The quiet was as deep as the sleep of the dead. Nothing stirred. To my surprise, Dyen jumped over the forty-foot-high wall in one leap, racing past the darkened tents of the king of Poland's camp like a firebird finally let out of captivity. All I could do was press Marina to me tightly, her hair lashing at my cheeks as violently as the dust whirling into my mouth. I was thankful for the fern in my pocket, cloaking us from sight. Otherwise, the sentries would surely have noticed us. As it was, we streaked past them so fast that all we left behind were swirls of ice and snow.

I had looked for Vasily in the darkness, but all I had seen were rows of bedrolls with unfamiliar men, dreaming of battles and blood. Volos and Varvara had promised to visit him in my stead. But I doubted Vasily would notice. I had whispered a prayer to the Lord of Battles, Perun, to keep our soldiers safe, to keep Vasily and all our friends safe, to save our city.

We sped across dense northern forests, the bare trees alongside us blurring, the wide fields dappled in shadows. Dyen went over the drifts of snow, the marshy roads, as if they were barely there at all. It felt a little like soaring through a black and starless sky.

43

16 NOVEMBER 1581

DESPITE DYEN'S SPEED, it took us days to reach Moscow, which was more than 730 kilometers southeast of Pskov by way of treacherously thick and already snow-covered forests.

We traveled through the capital in the early dawn before turning northeast onto the road that led to the city of Aleksandrov, where stood Tsar Ivan's fortress of Aleksandrovskaya Sloboda. There were ruined towers and demolished forts everywhere we looked, likely guard posts from the days of the Oprichnina. Yet it was maddingly quiet and desolate. The air retained that smell of death. Our land had a long memory, and its soil was soaked in blood. I held my daughter to me even more tightly on this stretch of our journey. But I was comforted knowing my faithful companions were with us. I tipped my head back to the lightening sky and whistled to my owl.

Noch descended and flew eye level with us as we ran. *Yes, Ya?*

I had been planning our arrival at Aleksandrovskaya Sloboda. Though my plan still had its deficiencies, it was now time to share it with Marina and my companions so they were prepared. "See if you can scout out the tsar's compound ahead of our arrival," I told Noch. "Where the tsar is and what he is doing." It would be much easier if Ivan were alone, but back at the Kremlin, I had learned this was almost never the case. "And we need to know how to steal into whatever palace he is in unnoticed."

I will do what I can, Ya. Noch hooted. *I cannot wait for this to be over.*

"I know," I said. "You are tired of doing my bidding."

You have no idea how much. And she hurled herself back into the haze.

"Why is she helping us," came Marina's voice, "if she hates it so much?"

Despite the seriousness of the situation, I laughed. "Well, dorogaya, Noch doesn't actually hate it. She has been craving a little attention is all," I said into Marina's ear with a smile, smoothing her windswept hair and kissing the top of her head. "Now, once we find the palace with the tsar, Dyen will create enough of a disturbance to distract the guards and let us slip inside."

Dyen snorted. *I have done this before.*

"Many times," I agreed.

"I am guessing the tsar will not be happy to see you, Mama," said Marina, and I could imagine the intentness of her face. "How will he let you speak to him?"

"No, my clever girl, he will not be happy. But knowing him, he will not be able to resist hearing what I have to say, why I have sought him out now."

And what do you have to say? came my wolf's voice, wry with amusement.

"To Tsar Ivan the Terrible? Plenty."

"But can't we stay invisible with the fern?" Marina asked.

"Not I, dorogaya. I must speak to the tsar to get him to draw blood." Any mouse or rat could easily do that. But. *I want to confront him,* I realized. And I had wanted to do so since first meeting his oprichniki in that northern village. "But you must hold on to your fern branch and keep yourself out of sight. You will be in enough danger as is. Alas, even if we could avoid it, that place of suffering and death will make for a stronger ritual. Now, Marin, when I am with the tsar, you must begin the ritual exactly as we have discussed. Do you understand?"

"Yes, Mama. But what if you are wrong, and the tsar will not listen to you?"

"Worry not, my solnishko." Oh, my little sun. I pressed my lips to her cheek. "I will make sure he listens." And immediately. We were still several hours from Aleksandrov, yet this was close enough for my powers to do their work. So I whispered to the animals without delay: "Find the tsar—and wait for me in the shadows."

I shall also call on the wolves, said Dyen.

"And make sure Noch lets her fellow owls know." I ran my hand along his neck, giving him a fond caress. "If things go horribly wrong," I added in a low voice to Marina, "get out of the palace and wait for Dyen. Animals see through the fern's cloak of invisibility. He will see you, and he will take you away."

Either way, we needed all the help we could get in the confrontation so long in coming—my confrontation with Tsar Ivan the Terrible.

The temperature suddenly plummeted. The wind started to thrash at us, the frost to numb our skin. We were not an hour from Aleksandrov. I peered into the trees, searching for Morozko.

"Do you remember what I told you?" I asked Marina and Dyen.

"Yes, Mama. We must not let the Lord of Winter see how cold we are."

"Never ever admit it." I tightened my grip on Marina and patted Dyen, hoping to give them both a little of my heat—to keep them warm, to keep them alive.

As the minutes wore on, my wolf's pace slackened. I rubbed a dollop of sparrow fat into Marina's hands and Dyen's back. Flurries of snow fell with a frigid touch. They filled the air like ash, drowning the fields in white and veiling the wood in a haze that quickened the heart with foreboding.

"Shhh," I soothed Marina, who was shaking so hard she was beginning to whimper. "It will not be long now, Daughter." I turned my head from east to west and whispered a prayer to Mokosh.

"Oh, lapochka, my sweet, cease!" said a voice. "Mother cannot hear you."

Always theatrical. "We are not cold, Lord Morozko," I said dutifully, even as he refused to show, and I massaged my daughter's arms to hasten the flow of blood there.

"Then why pray to Moist Mother Earth?"

"It is but habit." I showed my hands. "See? No jar of hemp oil to offer her."

"Mothers are hard to shake off, eh?"

"Th-they are." The cold and wind became unbearable and the snow whirled so fiercely that I had to cling to Dyen just to stay on his back.

"Is that why you hold on to your daughter so?"

Dyen's legs buckled under us suddenly. The indigo-blue tops of the trees slipped out of sight, too quickly, and I was blinking up at the shifting white sky. I gasped for air, my head spinning. The wind was knocked out of me. My limbs were splayed out in the mud. The wetness was ravenous as it seeped into my clothing, into my very skin. Marina and Vasily's faces flashed by, as if I would never see them again.

Marina lay a few paces away. I crawled to my daughter, knees numb, heart skipping in distress. *Oh, gods, please let her be all right.* I shook her, rubbed at her arms and legs, said her name over and over until, at last, her eyes fluttered open.

"Surely you are cold now."

What do you think, wretched god? I could hear Marina's strained breaths. "No, L-Lord Morozko, we are warm, so warm. It is no different than the hottest, most sun-filled day of summer." Blackness crept into my vision and my blood grew cold.

The snow stopped whirling, the wind abated, the cold softened. I drew in a breath that didn't hurt. Roz stood on the road. At his side, the scythe glimmered, glass-like.

"Where are you going, Yaga?" he asked, voice thoughtful.

I touched Marina's cheek and, after she had given me a small nod, I walked toward the Lord of Winter. "There is a way to kill Selica, to put her away for good—" He opened his mouth. "You do not need to be there," I rushed to say. "For it to work, though, I need something of yours—" My eyes strayed to his scythe.

Roz did not laugh as I had expected. He ran agitated fingers through his beard.

"I know Selica is your wife," I said, ignoring the icicle-blue gaze that he had shot to me. "But if she continues on her path, Russia and her people will be no more. And you cannot be Lord of Winter without this land. You need it as much as winter and death need summer and life. The balance has been upset, and you are losing control."

Roz took a deep, wistful breath, the symbols on his scalp shimmering into view. "It is true. Nature is not easy to please these days. The temperatures, the rains and snows, the frost and ice—they had all been under my control. But somewhere along the way, she took over. Winter began to bleed into the other seasons. Summer became too cold. Spring and autumn ceased to exist. Now, there is only winter, winter, winter."

"You have tampered with her so much she no longer needs you, and it makes you restless. You once told me how you hated repetition, loneliness, death. You may not be dying, but the land is. The more starved it is, the less worship there is for you."

His eyes drifted from me to my daughter, where they lit with curiosity. "I have heard of this newest child of the gods," he said evasively. "They say the Universe practically willed her into existence."

I tried not to think of Mother's words on Marina's destiny, the ritual to come and my daughter's role in defeating Tsar Ivan the Terrible and the Lady of Death.

A tinkle of a sound, like ice shattering, and Roz was holding out the sharp end of his scythe. He had broken it off, just like that. I took it from him, still disbelieving. It was icy to my touch. Yet it did not melt in my fingers. "What about your scythe?"

"It will grow back." He gestured toward the road. "I will not stop you, Yaga." I was starting to smile when the Lord of Winter added, "Nor will I make it easy."

My smile froze. The cold was back, along with the gusting winds and whirling snows. Morozko had vanished.

44

BY THE TIME we sighted the black domes and wooden roofs of Aleksandrov through the wood, our eyes were raw from the wind, our lips chapped from cold, our bodies shaking. The Lord of Winter had kept his promise. He had not made it easy. Snow and ice had pelted us the entire way, making the rest of our journey slow, wet, and arduous.

I clutched the fern branch in my pocket with a trembling hand, hoping its invisibility would hold. "Easy, Dyen," I whispered.

He slowed. Over the izbas, the green spires of Tsar Ivan's Aleksandrovskaya Sloboda needled the sky. A pale ray of morning light burst through a swell of flinty cloud, the air brisk yet free of snow, of dust and ash. The war was far from here, after all.

I searched the black-fringed skies for Noch and recoiled in horror.

I had glimpsed not my owl, but a raven, then heard its gurgling screech. I had not factored Koshey into our plans, though of course he would be with the tsar. I would worry about him when I had to. For now, I only hoped Noch was safe, that she would find us, and soon. In that moment, she burst from the froth of cloud . . . with three more ravens following close behind. I whispered urgently to any bird willing to listen, any owl, stork, or eagle, to help us, to delay the ravens, to free Noch. Yet nothing happened.

Fear slid over my heart like a cold draft. What if no birds came? It had happened before, birds being more unpredictable than animals. I watched helplessly as the ravens closed in on Noch. Though Marina was sniffing and shaking in my arms, she was also looking up at the sky, her head tilted and body tense. Just as the ravens closed the space between them and Noch, an eagle soared out of the wood. Its brown plumage glimmered golden as it made toward the ravens. Noch spread her wings and dove to us.

The entire place is overrun with ravens, Noch said once she landed on me, her talons sinking into my shoulder. I felt them even through my pelt.

I pulled her to Marina and me, into the warmth of our embrace. "How glad I am that you are all right, dear Noch." I pressed my face to her cold wings.

As am I, she cooed against me. In a very different voice, she said, *Now, listen, Ya. You must approach the compound on the right side of the gates, toward the back. Go past a small church until you come to a large building. That is the Tsar's Palace. He is in a chamber inside with his boyars.* Noch met my gaze. *Koshey Bessmertny is there also.*

"I knew he would be." I was due for a face-to-face with that wretch.

And if he tries to stop you?

"Selica holds his heart. In the end, he is nothing but her servant, doing her bidding, subjugated and enslaved. This rankles Koshey. If I tell him that Selica might be destroyed, he might take the chance to free his heart."

If you say so, Ya. Noch wriggled out of our embrace. *I shall gather the owls.*

Aleksandrovskaya Sloboda *was* a fortress. I considered the moat around it, then the palisade of white stone. The only splash of color was in the green-topped towers, their spires like pine needles that pierced the skin. The narrow windows made my breaths come out in shallow bursts, as if I found myself in that cell, imprisoned by Koshey.

I felt for my daughter. I was not in that cell. Any cell. Not ever again.

Here we go, ladies. Hold on tight, came Dyen's voice.

And we were flying through the air. I squeezed my eyes shut and did not open them until we were past the moat and on the other side of the palisade, though I had half expected Dyen's leg to catch on it, and us to tumble to the snow, or worse.

The first I noticed was the smell. It was the same smell that hung over all of Russia, but stronger, of spilled blood long scrubbed away, of decomposing bodies long buried, of death long past yet still hovering.

Inside, the fortress was as oppressive as it looked. Dead tree branches twisted above. In places, the ground was frozen over; in others, my feet plunged into the marshy land. Odd, given the cold. Like all royal compounds, Aleksandrovskaya Slobodá consisted of many buildings, all with tiny latticed windows, all in claustrophobic white, as if designed for the weak-minded, the suffering, the mad. In short, Tsar Ivan.

There were no corpses, not anymore, yet I did not doubt that if I reached past the Otherworld, I would see the spirits of the dead, stumbling past us, restless and out for blood. But I did see ravens, as well as guards and soldiers, huddling against the cold in the distance. Most were likely in their barracks or at the gates, given the weather. Morozko's enchantments now seemed more like a blessing than a curse.

We walked past a small church before coming to a much larger building of stone and brick. Its tiered tower reminded me of the Kolomenskoye church. Guards milled by the beaten doors at the top of the canopied stairs. I saw that the fortress's gates were at the opposite end of the compound. This had to be the Tsar's Palace.

I tugged on Dyen's mane, and I felt his nod.

We crept around the building, coming to a stop at the corner.

I am assuming this is my time to shine, I heard my wolf's voice in my head.

I gave him a pat in answer. "Make ready, dorogaya," I said in a whisper to Marina, who nodded.

Behind us, a few gray wolves leapt over the wall.

Marina and I each clutched a fern branch, and I tightened my hold on my satchel, the items for the ritual secure inside. Then we slid off Dyen as silently as we could before he streaked forward, toward the entrance of the Tsar's Palace and the guards there.

"What is this?" I heard the men shout. "Where did this damn wolf come from?"

"Are you ready?" I touched Marina's cold cheek.

She unsheathed her sword. "Yes, Mama," she had time to say as Dyen's wolves rushed past us, the guards sprinting from Dyen and the wolves with shaking fists.

As we rounded the corner of the Tsar's Palace, the sun dazzled my eyes with a torrent of white light. The ravens descended on us then, not having seen us before. We nearly collided with a few straggling guards. In surprise, I let go of my fern branch. Flecks of snow landed on my cheek as several lunged at us, the branch's invisibility gone from me. They snarled and swaggered, even as the ravens attacked us with their wings and beaks. I gave a whistle, calling for Noch and her fellow owls.

Their screeches filled my ears, and the feathery, clawing darkness was pushed back, along with the guards.

We rushed up the stairs and through the doors into a darkened vestibule and finally, blessedly, into a hall. I breathed in the rushes strewing the floors.

Dim light spilled from the wrought-iron candelabras, so that at first, I saw only low ceilings and curved walls, like those of the Kremlin's Granovitaya Palata but decorated with curtains. They fluttered like shreds of white cloud, their embroidered flowers glittering with ice. Behind the central pillar, its display of gold plate and goblets, stood the ivory throne from the Kremlin. But it was not the tsar on the throne.

It was Koshey Bessmertny.

45

BONES PROTRUDED FROM his face, his eyes set deep and sunken in his skull. Koshey was more skeleton than man, especially in his rich costume of burgundy cloth and black fur. My flesh crawled in disgust at his extravagance as much as at the physical proof of his poison. He was a spy and a slave to death. He deserved the marks his dark deeds left on him.

Haughty as ever, he lounged on the throne as if it belonged to him.

I noticed the hall's emptiness. Where was the tsar? Where were his boyars? As if in answer, I became aware of men's voices, issuing from under an arch leading to some other chamber within. Koshey's eyes burned into me.

"I see Russia has a new tsar on the throne," I said, channeling that disgust, that rage, at this man whom I used to love and who was now nothing more than my enemy, at the mercy of his fears of mortality and my sister. "I wish I could say treason and treachery become you, but you look like the darkness you serve."

Koshey flashed me a smile. But his gaze was riveted on Marina. She must have dropped her fern branch. But no, she still held on to it. Koshey must be able to see her. I pulled her behind me.

"Your daughter resembles you." A strange emotion flitted across his features—wistfulness, maybe regret. "And where is your gallant Adashev?"

Marina struggled free from my grasp and, swaying a little, walked up to Koshey. "Fighting the invaders at the walls of Pskov. What are you doing?"

I couldn't suppress a smile. "You must forgive my daughter," I said, moving to stand beside her. "She has grown up with the sword. Given how the tsar's soldiers terrorize the North, even our children must learn to defend themselves."

"She takes after both her parents, then." Koshey dragged his eyes back to mine. "You should not be here, Yaga." Surprisingly, his voice was soft.

"And yet I am."

"I will not be able to protect you, not from the tsar, not from—"

"My sister." *Protect me, ha!* Koshey was trying his hand at comedy.

His eyes sharpened, apparently not missing the curl of my lip, the hostility in my posture. "I have heard of your . . . efforts against her in Pskov. If you think—"

"If I told you that you could reclaim your heart," I interrupted him, "would you?"

The gaze he turned to me with was momentarily scattered. "That will never happen." Absently, he pressed one hand to the empty cavity of his chest.

"And yet, if it could . . ."

"She would have to be dead, her power over Nav's throne severed—"

"Would you do it?" I demanded, out of patience with his theorizing.

Koshey recoiled, blinking at me, considering me, then my daughter, now silent at my side. "You have changed, Yaga." He sat back on the throne. "Of course I would."

I stepped toward him. "Then let me pass," I said, with a glance at the chamber behind him from whence issued the men's voices, the murmur of their frenzied conversation, fraught, I was sure, with dissent and controversy. "You could remain with the tsar and rule Russia, as you always wanted, but without Selica forcing you into"—I let my eyes glide over his emaciated figure—"doing what you hate."

Koshey tilted his head. "And what is that?"

"The Kostya I knew loved this country above all. You once protected this land. You fought for it. Now, with Selica spreading her madness, the king of Poland means to seize Pskov and Novgorod. And he will not stop there. City after city will fall. Russia will be no more. Selica will not stop until the entire country is destroyed. That is not what you want. No, Kostya, that is what you hate, what you have always hated, about the princes of the past, the Mongols who followed them, the boyars who competed for the throne when the tsar was a boy. Now it is what you hate about her."

His black eyes were burning up orange, and I could have sworn that, even from where I stood, I saw his hand—the one clutching his ringed leather belt—shake.

"The only reason you serve her is because she has your heart. Because should you turn against her, she would destroy it as she is destroying Russia. And you love your life more. You fear death, have always feared it, so you let her rule you. You are nothing but a coward, a servant, a slave. But if she were dead, and you had your heart—"

Koshey was suddenly on his feet. "What guarantee do I have that you will win?"

"You don't." I took another step, and we were face-to-face. I could almost see the man I had once loved, would have done anything for, the man who had once had such power over me. "I am not asking for your help. Just to let me pass. And if I lose, all you will lose is the chance to reclaim your heart. You can lie about the rest. Charm her into believing you. That is your specialty, after all."

Koshey was silent. Then he brought one thin hand to my cheek. "What will happen to you?" His touch was very, very cold, his skin papery, like the wings of moths.

I blinked up at him, surprised. Then I lifted my hand to his, and I removed it from my face. "Let us pass, Kostya."

He leaned back, not taking his eyes from me. His gaze traced every curve of my face. It paused on my mouth, lingering on my lips as if he had reached out and touched them. "I wish everything were different." *I wish I were different*, he seemed to say. But the words, unsaid, remained so. He swept aside with a flourish and, with one hand, motioned toward the chamber behind the throne, the one with the tsar inside.

I caught Marina's hand in mine. Then we were hurrying past Koshey, into the chapel where Tsar Ivan the Terrible crouched on his knees in the midst of the billowing furs, toppling hats, and severe faces of his boyars, talking furiously and all at once.

46

AT OUR ENTRANCE, the boyars blustered into a stunned silence. The tsar's eyes widened.

I let go of Marina's hand. Though she held the fern branch and was
invisible to others, I could still see a hazy version of her because of the
faint traces of fern on my own fingers.

"She is here!" Ivan rasped. He leapt to his feet and pressed his body to
a chapel wall teeming with frescoed angels and saints in a sea of chipped
gold. His staff was raised in front of his body, as if to shield it from an
imaginary blow. "I can feel her curses! Baba Yaga seeks my death—one
spell, and I shall lie dead upon this floor!"

I went up to the mad old loon, neither confirming nor denying his
ravings. I would gladly welcome the wretched tsar's death. But it was
hastening toward him without any witchery of mine. I suppressed a satisfied smile at the sores on his face, the anguish cutting into his skin, the
rich garments that had lost their luster, the golden robes yellow as piss,
the pearls on his collar and cuffs a poor imitation of the real thing.

"Baba Yaga?" A squat man with a red face and thin beard stepped
forward.

I recognized him from Mitka's tales. This was none other than the tsar's Boriska, otherwise known as Boris Godunov. Along with Malyuta Skuratov, the wily Boriska had managed to escape the tsar's wrath against his oprichniki in 1573, though Malyuta had been killed besieging a Livonian fortress the following year.

"What is the meaning of this?" demanded the newly anointed boyar Godunov. "How did the traitorous vedma get into the palace?"

But I was no longer looking at Boris Godunov. My eyes had landed on a pale face and slight figure, though taller now, a man, not just a boy. It was Ivanushka.

My throat constricted. A part of me wanted to rush to him, to see him as the boy who had vowed to protect me with his toy sword in Moscow, the young man who had started a rebellion against his father's soldiers. I wanted to see Anastasia in him.

Ivanushka took several steps toward me. He opened his mouth, said something. It could have been "Yaga," but I couldn't hear it past the boyars' talk.

After defying his father on the night Pskov was saved, Ivanushka had been more closely guarded than even Ivan. And while father and son had been quiet these years, I had not forgotten Ivanushka's role in Novgorod's massacre, and in many other massacres besides. But the last time I had seen him, he *had* joined our cause. Maybe he was still on our side, his imprisonment turning him even more fiercely against his father. Especially given Ivan had forced two of Ivanushka's wives into convents for failing to produce an heir. Rumor had it, Ivanushka's newest wife was with child, though even so, Ivan had been heard berating his son and his son's wife on many occasions.

Yes, it was definitely possible that Ivanushka was on our side even now. He was watching me with his old look of reverence, as if I could solve all the world's problems with a flick of my pestle.

As Boris Godunov continued his tirade against vedmas, the boyars gave us a wide berth, as though witchcraft caught as quickly as the chuma plague. I used their fear to my advantage. I gave Marina a nod to begin, and her lithe body dissolved into the pack of big men and their tall hats. The boyars did not see her, as she was protected by the fern, but even if they had, they would have paid no attention to a child; their gazes were fixed on the unfolding royal tableau. Marina had crept up to a wooden prayer stand, forgotten in a withdrawn recess of the chapel, and dropped to her knees with the satchel.

Satisfied that she was safe and proceeding with our ritual, I faced the tsar. "I assume you know of Pskov's blockade, Ivan. And instead of helping the surrounded city, you ran. You are a coward, a weak man and an even weaker tsar."

He did not move from the wall, nor did he call his guards. And even if he had, Dyen and his wolves had likely made quick work of them by now. I assumed Koshey was waiting by the throne, listening, picking his side based on what would happen in this room.

"But Father said he sent a third of our army there." The tsarevich glanced between me and the tsar.

I turned to him. "No, my lord tsarevich. The tsar has not sent any kind of aid, whether it be reinforcements or supplies. He lied to you." *As he lies to everyone.*

The tsarevich fell silent, but I thought I saw his jaw clench.

Between the boyars' whispers, stones clinked as Marina tried to kindle the fire.

I turned back to Ivan. "What would your god say? What would your mother of god say, and the saints? What about Grand Prince Monomakh, whom you had idolized so? All you have done is drown Russia and her people in blood."

The tsar dropped his staff. I heard its clang as it hit the stone floor. Ivan covered his face with his hands.

"What would Tsaritsa Anastasia think of you now, I wonder?" I whispered finally, my trump card against him. "I will tell you—she would think you a monster."

"No!" wrung from behind his hands.

"Unlike her, you have never cared for your people. You have starved them, you have tried to kill them, but you have never, ever helped them."

He slid down the wall to the floor.

Marina was still trying to build the fire. But the damp air was stifling her efforts.

"My lord father," came from the tsarevich. His cheeks had turned the loud salmon color of his richly embroidered kaftan, and he had walked over to the cowering tsar with his back straight. "Let me go to Pskov with a small contingent of troops. We would liberate the city from the invaders. We would show our strength, our resilience, our army. We would be victorious. Give me command of the troops. I will do the rest!"

My chest grew warm. In that moment, the tsarevich was once more the prince I had known, Anastasia's son and my Ivanushka. He *was* on our side. And, even if he wasn't, his restless nature craved action.

But the tsar's eyes bore into me. His lips moved in prayer. He clutched at a gilded cross at his chest. Stared up at the colorfully painted brick dome above us.

"Let me go, Father," repeated Ivanushka. "Please."

An acrid smell burned into my nose. Flames were licking at the prayer stand. My shoulders lowered in relief. But a few boyars were now sniffing at the air, turning toward the small fire with bulging eyes. One even opened his mouth. The fern could not cloak anything beyond Marina. She tossed another fern branch into the flames for their own invisibility. The boyars blinked rapidly. They shook their heads, no doubt chastising themselves for imagining things at such a moment, and turned back to the tsarevich. Boyar Godunov had come to stand by him.

"My lord tsar," he said as he executed a bow, "the tsarevich has a point. If he goes to Pskov, the people will see that you support them, that you have not forgotten them—"

"I have *not* forgotten them!" Ivan turned a flushed face quivering with rage at Boyar Godunov. "How can I forget maggots that constantly eat at my brain? That is what the people are! *Your* people, Boyar Godunov, for you come not from the princes that have ruled this country for centuries but from the peasants ruled by them!"

The fire had grown. Marina opened my satchel. She threw a handful of mushrooms into the flames with a sachet of herbs—three leaves of rosemary, three cloves, three erek blossoms, a sprinkling of sage, and a pinch of salt—all tied with a scarlet ribbon, to protect the ritual from interference and prying eyes.

"Of course, my lord tsar." Boyar Godunov bowed. "I am but your humble servant."

The flames were now consuming the prayer stand in a blaze of light. They belched smoke, spat out ash. Slowly, I started to move toward Marina.

To my surprise, the boyar kept going. "Only envision it, my lord tsar. Our young and handsome tsarevich, riding through the villages to battle, and our brawny soldiers, engaging the invaders in Pskov. The city liberated, the enemy vanquished, your heir gloriously victorious—" Boyar Godunov fell silent as the tsar straightened.

"Why my son?" Ivan demanded, having quite forgotten me. "I too am young and handsome. I too can win the people."

"No, you have grown weak with fear, Father." Ivanushka's voice was clear and strong. "And you have grown inert. I have no such qualms. On the contrary, I desire action. Let me go in your stead. Please."

To that, a deranged Ivan lunged at his son with his staff lifted high above his head. I broke into a sprint toward Marina. Among other words, I heard "Usurper!" Ivanushka was finally standing up to his father and unknowingly helping me by deflecting attention from me and the ritual. All I could do was pray for his safety.

"So, you wish to take my place, do you? I knew it! You have been plotting to depose me the entire time. Fool! How dare you seek to commit treason? How dare you defy me?" The tsar was waving his staff about. "He wants power, can you believe it? *My* power, *my* throne, *my* crown. Mine! It is all mine, do you hear, my traitorous son?"

Ivanushka ducked to avoid the staff. "All I want is an army to defeat the king of Poland and bring you glory!"

"Guards!" Ivan snarled to guards that would not hear him, pointing his staff at Ivanushka. "Arrest this treasonous wretch!"

There was a ripple among the boyars, several of whom coughed, adjusted their furs, glanced down. A few hats fell. But not one of those men called for the guards.

"Guards!" Ivan went on ranting. "The tsarevich has committed treason!"

I knelt on the startlingly cold floor. I shut my eyes and started to chant alongside Marina. Then I raised my arms toward the ceiling, to the sky beyond, and my blood heated. The energy inside me met with the fire in a spark of light that was warm and sizzling. Though I should have been focused solely on the ritual, I opened one eye.

The tsar's staff was cutting through the air like a blade.

In horror, I watched Ivanushka duck again. Boyar Godunov dived between father and son, but Ivan elbowed the boyar in the ribs, and he stumbled back.

Gods, please keep Ivanushka safe, I prayed. He would still make a better tsar than Ivan. And he was still Anastasia's son. Though I had not always agreed with his actions, had judged him for following his father, he was doing the right thing now.

The other boyars huddled together. They pressed away from the tsar and tsarevich. Instead of intervening, in fear or calculation, the boyars chose to play the spectators in the match of a lifetime for the throne of Russia.

The iron point of Tsar Ivan's staff flashed over Ivanushka.

My surroundings plunged into gray smoke, and I lost sight of them.

THE SMOKE WAS parting in the chapel. I saw a red-faced Ivan lower his staff.

But in one swift motion, he raised it over his son once more. The cross at his chest leapt into the air with a mad glimmer, like a star about to fall. Ivanushka's feet shifted. He tried to pull himself away. Yet he was trapped beneath his father's furious gaze. Tied to the moment, his eyes were upturned, expectant, waiting.

Then the tsar was bringing down his staff, its iron point striking his son's head, and Ivanushka was falling, tumbling onto the cold stones.

I think the cry that echoed was mine.

Marina chanted on. The air was filling with ash, as on the night Pskov was saved. Ivanushka lay still. Too still. The ash whirled into my eyes, my ears, my nose. It tangled with my tongue. Blood dripped onto the stones. How bright it was! How insistent! Like the juice of too-ripe pomegranates, bursting forth and staining the skin.

There was another cry, guttural, a wild beast shot through the heart.

More blood dripped. This time, the tsar's. He was kneeling by his son's body, his robes darkening, the pearls springing off one by one as he tore at them and scratched at his face, as if he would tear himself apart.

Despite my impulse to run to Ivanushka, to make sure he was all right—he *had* to be all right—I stayed rooted to that cold floor, beside that raging fire, chanting, as Marina moved toward the tsar with the fern in one hand and a vial for his blood in the other.

Out of the satchel I took a scrap of my wedding dress and the dried juniper, and flung them both into the fire. I unsheathed the dagger at my hip, brought it to my fingers. A stab, and blood trickled out, the blood of Mokosh, of Belobog, my light—the opposite of Selica, of Chernobog, her darkness—and I said the words my mother had told me to say to anchor my sister to me, and to summon her spirit. It had been eleven years since we had last seen each other and yet I remembered every detail of her face. I tensed at the prospect of seeing it again just as the flames flared darkly, as if in reminder that I wasn't done.

In the same way, with the same words, I threw into the fire Morozko's scythe, Kupalo's garland, Volos's broken staff, and, finally, Perun's thunderbolt arrow, which sizzled against my skin as I let the fire take it.

The flames consumed the articles in a spark of brightness, readying to summon the spirits of the dual gods.

Marina returned, and we resumed our chant.

A scream clawed at my ears, desperate and trapped. The ash morphed into a tall, whirling shadow of a woman in an ivory gown with long black hair and eyes shaped like mine—my sister.

The louder we chanted, the quicker the other gods appeared in the ash, though also mere shadows. I saw the half-youthful, half-aging body of Volos; the muscular one of Perun. The handsome face of Kupalo, the bearded one of Morozko. The gods were gripping my sister by her arms, twisting them at unnatural angles. Morozko stood at a distance, not helping, not hindering, as he watched his wife with a shocking detachment.

Selica strained against her captors, the hem of her shadowy skirts lifting along with her bare feet.

I pulled the medallion out of my pocket. The metal was cold against my fingers as I held it out to the fire. I hesitated, having only just found the precious article, but released it with the same words, this time to summon my mother.

A few minutes passed. The shadow gods kept holding on to the wrangling Selica in the smoke.

No pathway opened; no Mother appeared.

I swallowed down my panic. I had to move forward with the ritual and hope Mokosh would show. Marina handed me the vial still warm with Ivan's blood—the blood of humanity's darkness and corruption. Tossing the vial into the fire, I took Marina's hand. "Are you sure?" I asked her one final time. My daughter gave me a nod, and I pricked her finger with the tip of my dagger.

Several drops of blood fell into the flames, dyeing them a bright white—the blood of humanity's light and purity, together with Ivan's blood, to make my sister more flesh than spirit, a human, so I could strike her with my blade. The ash swirled like snow. It rose into the gray-blue smoke above the fire.

I grasped Marina by the shoulders, forcing her to look into my face. "Stay back no matter what happens, do you understand?" At her hesitant nod, I turned back to the fire.

I couldn't tell if the shadowy Selica was more flesh than spirit. And there was still no pathway, still no Mokosh, the gods standing unmoving in the smoke. I took up Vasily's battle axe with hands that shook, and I approached the fire. I didn't know if I could kill some part of my sister, even if I couldn't put her away forever into the dead kingdom below-ground, even if I hadn't been able to summon Mokosh. But I had to try.

I swung the axe. Out of nowhere, the smiling would-be image of us as girls crashed into me. I couldn't help it—I was midswing, but I risked a glance at the only sister I had ever known.

There was fear in that beautiful face. Her wide eyes fixed on me—beseechingly? The axe was heavy yet warm and sure, like my beloved. Vasily would not hesitate to kill this woman, an enemy of our country and our people. But if she were his sister . . .

As if on cue, Selica spoke. "Are you really going to kill your own sister?"

While the idea of killing my sister, my blood, soured my stomach, this was the woman who had murdered my dearest friend; took Vasily,

Sanya, and many of our other friends and neighbors; tried to destroy an entire country and people with her wars and violence. Sweat trickled down my face. "Yes," I said.

"Help me," she whispered.

"Why would I do that?"

The gods, even Morozko, looked over at me. Their eyes blazed in anger. I was taking too long. Or maybe it was the flames, their restless flicker and movement.

"You have seen my pain, my loneliness. You have seen what they did to me." She glared at the gods, at Morozko. "I am alone. I need my sister. I need you, Yaga."

I *had* seen her pain and loneliness, the night Pskov was saved, when I had glimpsed flashbacks of her life, the prisons that had held her. But there was still that cruel glint in her eye, and her lip curved in a sneer despite her words. "You do not need anyone," I said. "You may want the light—" It was her weakness, after all, the reason she wanted the Land of the Living, the same reason Volos wanted it. To be alive, to be among the living, is what dead gods craved. "But you can never have it. You've made your choices. And you've chosen to murder and destroy, to bring darkness."

"No, Yaga." Her eyes glinted, as if there were tears there. "I simply chose to embrace my destiny. It was the only way to alter my fate, to survive. First in freeing myself from my husband by enticing him to live all year long. Then in freeing myself from Nav by drinking in the human souls. You see? I had no choice."

"We all have a choice," I said, thinking of myself and Vasily and our daughter, of our friends, even of Ivanushka, all fighting through the pain. "I am sorry for you," I went on, meaning it. "I am sorry how our mother treated you, how she abandoned you for me, left you in those prisons, forced you into an unhappy marriage. I wish she hadn't. I wish . . ." That image of us flashed back at me. "I wish we could have been real sisters."

A gust of wind blew at me suddenly and chaotically. I was very aware of my daughter behind me, her life at stake and many others' besides. Selica would continue to disease the land and its people. And she had taken too much already. I grasped the axe, this time, not hesitatating as I swung the blade at my sister.

The axe lodged in her chest, but the bodice of her gown remained ivory. I now saw she had no flesh, no bone, no muscle. She was still more dead than alive.

Selica's body wavered. One arm struggled free from Kupalo's grip, the other from Perun's cloudlike binding. Were the screams coming from the gods or the tsar, crying over a motionless Ivanushka?

I pulled back from the fire, shielding Marina, as Selica stumbled toward me, dipping and swaying, a horrific sight with that axe in her chest and her wild hair flying.

I expected her to be full of blame and rage. But her eyes were soft, the green in them muted, like mossy stones left too long in the sun where they belonged not. "I also wish we could have been sisters," she said, to my surprise. She contemplated me. "I thought I hated you, Yaga, but I—" Her gaze focused behind me, then hardened, becoming the putrid green from my nightmares. "What have you done?"

Her body grew substantive, until she was as solid and real as my daughter and me. Her skin had lost its glow; there was an angry influx of blood to her cheeks, the veins underneath her flesh. She was alive. Really alive.

I turned to see a slash appear in the empty space behind me, as if someone was tearing at the fabric between the Lands of the Living and the Dead. As if Volos were doing it as before. But it wasn't Volos. And the tear was widening into a deep hole. A blade emerged from the darkness, then a bluish hand, and finally Mokosh herself, leaning out with her colorless hair lashing at her face. She had opened the passageway after all.

Selica doubled with a shriek, her body folding over the blade in her chest.

Blood devoured her bodice and skirts, coloring the ivory scarlet. As the blood dripped down, it blackened, turning thick and oily. Behind her, the gods stood immobile in the smoke and ash, the flames becoming hotter and more dazzling than ever.

"I cannot go back there," she whispered, even as the wind whipped at us. Her eyes on me were mossy green, large and frightened.

I had time to lunge out of the way as Mother reached for Selica and grasped her by the axe handle sticking out of her chest. There was a piercing scream as my sister tried to pull away, but it was no use. She was being dragged toward the passageway and the darkness beyond.

Pain blossomed in my chest, in the spot where Vasily's axe clung to my sister. I felt a wetness there, saw the red stain. Dazed, gasping for air, I forced myself to stand, to see this through. But Mokosh was losing her grip on the axe, and Selica was staggering away, out of our mother's reach. I looked desperately at the fire, at the gods above it in the smoke. Weren't they supposed to help Mokosh?

To Nav with them. Breathing through the pain, I dived for my sister.

Her face had gone very white, but her eyes blazed that putrid green. "Once war is on men's minds, it festers within, claiming them. He is gone, never to return to you as he was," she said, her voice barely there, yet grating, like metal on metal.

I wanted to cover my ears, to scream for eternity. And I did scream. But with the last of my strength, I also grabbed for Vasily's axe and pulled on the handle. We were face-to-face now, both straining, each pulling and pushing and resisting, holding strong.

"And even if you drag me into that darkness"—a drop of blood the color of the blackest ravens trickled from Selica's lips—"I can come back, I can—"

"You will not," I gasped, "for you will be in a dead kingdom, dead and forgotten."

There was a flash of panic in Selica's face. "I never thought . . . to die—"

But I tightened my hold on the axe handle, and I swung her in front of the passageway, drawing Vasily's blade out of her chest just as she stumbled back with a gush of black blood. One step, two—and Mokosh was reaching for Selica. That is when the other gods—Volos, Perun, Kupalo, even Morozko—appeared at the passageway.

The gods seized my sister and dragged her to Mokosh. Mother's arms wrapped around Selica in an embrace. I heard Selica cursing and screaming, but all I could do was meet my mother's gaze one last time before she and my sister disappeared into the passageway in a burst of dying wind.

I staggered to Marina and pulled her face to mine. "You must be strong, Daughter, you must survive." Her eyes got very blue, filling with tears, but I could barely register where I was. My head was splintering, my body on fire. "Forsake this place—" I drew in an agonizing sip of air, even as a tear trickled down her cheek. "Dyen and Noch will take you to Little Hen." I took out of my pocket a sprinkling of poppy seeds and dropped them into Marina's palm. "For strength beyond your years." I had time to touch my daughter's cheek. Then the fire burst into a white flame and the pain within me boiled over, scorching my insides and hurling me into the void.

Interlude

KONSTANTIN, KNOWN AS Koshey Bessmertny, stands on the spit of land under the Throne of Nav. A part of him wants to go back to the Tsar's Palace, to the chapel with Yaga.

As a man who can transform into a bird, he was able to peer past the invisibility cloaking the ritual. Though it was blurred, as if happening in some other land, Konstantin saw the flames, the gods, *her*, his mistress, the Lady of Death. Then the passageway with Mokosh. He wanted to help Yaga, but his fear had kept him rooted.

It matters not, Konstantin tells himself now. Selica is dead.

He is free to reclaim his heart, just as Yaga said he would be.

The Throne of Nav stands empty, though there is a rumor Volos is back.

But the reluctant Lord of the Dead isn't here. Only the bog hag, playing in the swamp behind him. Konstantin hears Kikimora's prattle, her whistles and catcalls, snatches of the songs she hums while she twirls in the decaying, fetid waters. He tries to shut out the noise. The iron chest sits beneath the throne. Selica has not moved it since placing his heart inside. For hundreds of years, it has remained unopened and untouched.

Konstantin kneels before the chest, touches the cold iron.

But his mind flashes back to Yaga lying on the floor of that chapel, with her red, red blood spilling from her chest, *his* daughter weeping over her. Should he return? But why would he? Yaga has made it clear she does not desire his help, or anything to do with him. She isn't his enemy, not like before. But she isn't his friend, either.

"You have been itching to open that chest for what feels like hours," Kikimora taunts him from her swamp. "You may as well do it—or keep an old lady company. Not many men stop by, you know, not unless they are dead. Heh! Heh! Heh!"

Konstantin keeps his eyes on the chest with his heart. Seeing Kikimora is a bad omen. Stronger men than he, even gods, have gone mad after a glance. "Leave me be, hag," he says.

A giggle, half-submerged in water, then nothing, nothing but a beat, slow and rhythmic. His heart.

It *is* time. He is here. Selica is gone, and with her, his servitude. Konstantin knows he cannot put his heart back into his chest, or he will die. But he can take his heart in its iron chest from this land and bury it where no one can ever find it, along with his fears and the last vestiges of his humanity. Then he will forget about Konstantin, and he will live his forever—as he was always meant to, as the deathless Koshey Bessmertny.

THE FIRST TO return was the face of my daughter. I saw her mouth open. But I heard nothing of what she said. I simply stared and marveled, not quite believing that I was seeing her again, that I was actually alive. I grasped her hand and brought it to my lips. By some invisible force, some magic, sound returned.

Marina called me Mamochka in a soft, tender voice.

"I am sorry to have scared you, Marin." My tongue was heavy. I tasted blood, inhaled the memory of burning flames. "I meant to tell you—"

She wrapped her arms around me. "I thought I had lost you, Mama."

"You will not lose me," I repeated Vasily's words to me from long ago. I looked into her pale face. "Do you hear me?"

She nodded, slowly, then helped me to sit upright.

I gazed at the site of the ritual. It was now reduced to charred wood and ash. The passageway and the gods were gone. "I . . . do not remember what happened."

Marina followed my gaze. "The wind stopped and the passageway sealed. Then the other gods vanished into the flames before they went out."

Vasily's axe lay in the remains of the fire. Its handle had disintegrated. The blade was smeared charcoal black. My sister's blood.

I never thought . . . to die, she had whispered in disbelief, in fear. But she had—at least, she had gotten as close to death as was possible for a god. I studied my hands. I knew it had been necessary, knew my sister would have destroyed the rest of the country with her thirst for mortal souls, for blood, for death. But I wished it could have been otherwise.

My daughter seemed to hear my thoughts. "Is Aunt Selica gone now?"

"Yes, dorogaya," for she was, the tsar and the country freed from her. War would cease and mortal lives would be saved. But it would take time for Russia and her people to recover, and there would be a cost.

Once war is on men's minds, Selica had said, *it festers within, claiming them.*

I swallowed, recalling Vasily's blank stare, those eyes holding no recognition. How I wished to see him again as he had been! *He is gone, never to return to you as he was.* But I would happily take him, however he was, as long as he returned. The wet spot on my tunic clung to my skin. The blood there had darkened, crusted over. It would heal. I would live. So would Marina and countless others. And hopefully so would Vasily.

There was a murmuring close by, interrupted every few seconds by a wailing. We were still in the chapel of the Tsar's Palace. Because of the invisibility barrier, I had momentarily forgotten. My heart thudded too loudly in that hushed space. "Where is Ivanushka?" It was far too quiet, a graveyard ready to receive one of its own.

Marina hesitated. Then she gestured to the boyars, huddled before an icon of the Christian god's holy son. He floated haloed in his robes of bloody scarlet, pointing and judging. I did not like the hopeless severity in his face nor Marina's guarded, halting look. Her hand tightened on my arm, the other holding a fern branch before us, and we carefully, quietly made our way forward. I held my breath, only vaguely aware of the brush of the boyars' fur coats against me, the floor beneath my feet, as we stopped in the middle of the huddled group.

The gasp died in my throat. I covered my face with my hands.

Tsar Ivan was cradling a pallid, closed-eyed Ivanushka in a pool of blood. When he was not wailing pitifully, Ivan held a silk cloth to Ivanushka's head. And he whispered, his words no longer prayers but slippery confessions. "I have killed my son." His tears mingled with the blood running down his face. "What have I done?"

The boyars pressed together, their hats clutched in shaking fists, murmuring with the same frenzy as their shifting eyes. Brisk, alert, expectant. "Where is the doctor?" Boyar Godunov inquired, craning his small head, ever the consummate politician.

Tsar Ivan did not seem to hear. "Forgive me, my son," he whispered, pushing the hair from Ivanushka's bloodied forehead. "Forgive your miserable father."

Suddenly, the tsarevich raised his head. There was a collective gasp. My vision blackened at the edges. But I kept a steady gaze on him, hardly daring to breathe.

"I . . ." Ivanushka blinked. "I have always been loyal to Mother Russia, my lord father and tsar," he said in a soft, barely there voice. "All I have done has been for her." His eyes strayed to me, as if he could see me. "I am sorry I could not do more." His eyes strayed back to Ivan. He grasped his father's bloodstained hand and shakily brought it to his lips. Then the tsarevich of Russia lay back and said no more.

49

19 NOVEMBER 1581

ALMOST THREE DAYS later, three hours before the sun rose in a surge of new light, Ivanushka drew his last breath. They say he did not make a sound, much less a movement. He did not even open his eyes, not since the chapel where he had said his last words and fallen asleep.

I was not at the tsarevich's bedside when he died. I had wanted to go to him, but I had looked into my daughter's small, frightened face, and hesitated. I had put her in enough danger, had almost left her as motherless and alone in the world as I had been. I could not leave her now, especially since, according to Noch, the tsarevich was never alone. A flurry of doctors, guards, and boyars surrounded him morning and night, as he lay like a figure cut from marble, the ones slumbering in onion-domed cathedrals all over Russia. But I knew that even if I were to go to him, I could not save him. I had thought the price of the ritual would be my death. But it had been the death of the tsarevich of Russia.

I had broken my promise to Anastasia in not being able to protect her son from his father, in not being able to protect Ivanushka from himself. But he had chosen his path without me long ago, though he had tried to redeem himself in the end, too late becoming the prince he could have been for his country. I prayed my dear friend Anastasia forgave me, wherever she was.

Marina and I did not stay for the tsarevich's procession back to Moscow.

Rumor reached us that Ivanushka's poor widowed wife had lost their child, and that Tsar Ivan had walked at his son's side the entire journey to the capital. He buried our tsarevich in the Kremlin's golden-domed Cathedral of the Archangel, where Russia's princes and saints slept.

By then, Marina and I were already on the northern road to Pskov with Dyen and Noch—to see if Vasily was still in Pskov, and if he was himself. All we knew was the restlessness of travel, the long-suffering peasants in need of healing and their simple wooden villages, the countryside white and vast around us.

When we arrived in Pskov, we learned the foreign armies had moved on, the battle with them. The city had withstood the king of Poland's blockade. But it wasn't the lovely white-walled city of before. It was bare and gutted. Its walls were blackened and did not shine as they used to. We walked its too-silent streets, dazed and disbelieving this was the same city, our city. Its churches did not toll; neither were there many people, and almost no men, just a few women and children, blank and starved from the last few months.

Marina and I decided to stop by our izba first. But just as we were approaching the door, I turned to my daughter. "Why don't we go to Varvara's instead?" From the lock, intact, and the blackened windows, I knew Vasily wasn't there.

Come, Marin, I will race you, Dyen leapt ahead, and Marina, the child she still was, raced after him.

I was glad for his distracting her, for my legs had given out. I slid to the cold ground and leaned against the door from which Vasily had walked out for the last time, never to return. Even if he were alive, he wasn't in Pskov. My sister's cruel taunt returned to torment me.

He is gone.

I felt feathers against my face as Noch snuggled into me.

"What am I to do?" I covered my face with my hands, and for the first time since that chapel, I wept.

Hope dies last, Ya, Noch said, when I had been able to tear myself from that door, from our house, the one that had given us so many happy years. *He may return yet. And look around you.* My owl spread her wings. *Everything is new, everything will be different now.*

I took a breath, still tasting my tears. The sun shone coldly. Yet it shone. For the first time in many years, the sky was the luminous blue of the rarest sapphires; not a froth of cloud, not a speck of dust or ash marred it. Though it was winter again, the air smelled of something fresh, something old, something distinctly Russian. The wars were ending. Our country and her people had survived. I hoped Marina and I would also.

When I finally made it to Varvara's tavern, she put her arms around me without a word.

And she took me and Marina in without questions, though there were already women staying with her, including Agniya, still grieving the loss of Sanya, and Raisa and her now four children. They were loath to go back to their homes, if they had any left. Stepan, thankfully, had returned and rejoined Yelena, her father, and their eight children in their house in the city. But Stepan had been the fortunate one, as many of Pskov's soldiers were dead, wounded, or simply gone, having drifted with the battle away from Pskov on the heels of the foreign armies.

Vasily was not the only soldier missing. Marya, Fedya, and Gorya had not returned, and neither had Mitka or the brothers Bogdan and Miroslav. Whether they lived or not, no one knew.

"Will you stay?" Varvara asked me one night, glancing over at a pale Marina, who was half-heartedly playing with some of the other children by the fire.

"For now," I said. I still hoped Vasily would return like a few men had in the weeks since our arrival in Pskov. I also hoped Selica was wrong, and our men would recover from her wars and her darkness.

Weeks started to turn into months before I even dared to think of leaving Pskov. Marina had become withdrawn and much too pale, a shadow of her old self. I would frequently catch her stealing outside the city, to the strip of land by the river where she and Vasily used to practice their sword fighting. She would sit on the snow-covered ground and look out at the horizon, as if her father might appear there on the water.

I had to take her away from this place, now filled with nothing but ghosts and lingering memories. We would find Little Hen and return to my glade. Maybe the fresh air and uncomplicated quiet of the woodland would revive our spirits. After all, those woods had always been my refuge, a place that had waited for me no matter what twists and turns life took. If I were destined for widowhood, well, there was no better way for me to embrace my inner Baba Yaga than to take up my secluded abode deep in the forest with its air of mystery, skulls, and chicken legs.

Still, I hesitated. Still, I waited for Vasily.

It was not until one spring morning, as we were gathering in the kitchen to savor the quiet of the tavern at this time of day, that the door unexpectedly burst open, and in strode Marya and Gorya, though not Fedya. They rushed to us with open arms, tears streaking down their cheeks, home at last. They were not as lost as the last time I had seen them, nor were they as carefree as before Selica's wars.

When Marya met my questioning gaze, she shook her head once and pressed her lips together. "I have not seen Vasya since Pskov, Yaga," she said. "Gorya and I went looking for him as soon as the foreign armies had retreated, but . . . I am sorry."

I had prepared myself for this, had known that with each passing day, it was less and less likely Vasily would return. But no matter how I had prepared myself, it was a loss that crashed into me all over again. We found out later that Sanya's boys, Mitka, and a few of the other men from the Skomorokhi Knights were also lost to us.

That was when Marina and I made our preparations, said goodbye to our friends and neighbors, and, leaving directions to my glade with Marya and Varvara, departed Pskov with my companions to seek out Little Hen in the northern woods where I had left her.

I had also told Vasily about my glade. If he was alive, he would know where to look for us. Of this I was sure.

A little color returned to my daughter's cheeks as she beheld Little Hen.

"Your house on chicken legs!" Her eyes lit up for the first time in what seemed like months. Without hesitating, she ran up to my hut and stroked her legs.

The window shutters popped open, as if Little Hen had blinked her eyes from a long slumber. She nestled against Marina, hopping a little.

"It is nice to meet you, too, Little Hen." Marina giggled and patted the hut's chicken legs. "We shall be great friends."

I smiled, greeting Little Hen warmly just as Dyen ran up to us.

What a reunion! my wolf howled in pleasure.

See, Ya? Noch flapped her wings at me from Little Hen's roof. *Hope dies last.*

"Yes, it does." I nodded, slowly, watching Marina, Little Hen, my companions. My family.

By the time we turned south, toward Moscow and our woods, the fortress of Aleksandrovskaya Sloboda had been shut down, and a broken Tsar Ivan had fallen into a deep depression, withdrawing from the world. I envisioned him as he had been in that chapel, with his tormented soul and ruined body. For he had lost not only the strength of a death goddess, he had lost his heir and tsarevich, an entire dynasty. Everyone knew the simpleminded Fyodor would not be able to rule a vast, wild country like Russia, would be ruled by others too easily. *By someone like Koshey*, I thought with a shiver, remembering his dark deeds and where they had led us.

The people, shaking their heads, said all the tsar did now was compile lists of names—of the women and men he had murdered. *Serves him right*, I thought. Life was a more fitting punishment for a weak, penitent tsar in fear of divine retribution. But at least his tyrannical Oprichnina king-dom was dead and gone, along with his bloodthirsty oprichniki guards; his senseless wars were dwindling to nothing, his reign of terror and op-pression over our country and her people was at an end.

It was as if nothing had changed since I had last lived in my woodland more than twenty years before.

The age-old trees were just as tall and silent, the greenery as tangled and wild as ever. Little Hen stood on her chicken legs surrounded by the skulls of dead animals. And behind her was the passageway to the Land of the Dead, there whenever I needed it, with the Water of Life flowing through its river and Lord Volos on his throne a ritual away—with the earth magic that Mokosh and Dusha had taught me. Dyen once more showed with the flush of day, and Noch with its waning. The mortals began to seek me out again, under cover of darkness, not wanting to be found in the hut of the iron-nosed Baba Yaga and her worrisome obsession with bones and blood.

But I would look at my daughter, my companions, Little Hen, and realize everything *had* changed. It no longer mattered whether people spread their tales about me or how I lived. I knew who I was, a daughter of the Earth Goddess Mokosh, a sister, a vedma, a healer, a wife, and a mother. I was a half goddess, half mortal.

I was Baba Yaga, and she was me.

The sun shone, and the land was more vibrant than ever, awakening with new life. Vasily had never really left. He was in our daughter, in our family, in our home. Like us, he was alive, gloriously and wonderfully alive. That was what mattered.

Interlude

SUMMER 1582

DEEP IN THE forest, in the glade with the chicken-legged hut, Yaga sits among red poppies that stain the grass like drops of blood. She is aware of the orange-eyed raven perching on one of the skulls but does not acknowledge it. She is watching her daughter practice her sword fighting.

Marina Vasilyevna has grown over the winter. Her hair has darkened, the bronze turning an almost reddish-brown, and her eyes have lightened to a blue so faint as to be almost white.

The sky is a rich azure blue. Not a cloud is in sight. And the sun is at its most radiant, its rays bright and warm. Those years of snows, of perpetual winters, seem a long-forgotten nightmare. So what if frost still decorates the windows in the mornings?

The sword in Marina's hand flashes a blinding white. It soars into the air as the girl spins, leaps, extends her arm . . . The blade falls to the ground, its point piercing the spot where no grass grows, being trampled by too many footsteps and too many fires.

"Marin?" Yaga stands. What in Nav could have happened to the girl to scare her so? She shields her eyes. Blood drips from her daughter's hand.

Marina Vasilyevna hardly notices. She is looking at the man standing behind her mother. He wears a faded soldier's uniform, though he is older than she remembers him. His face is weathered and sunburnt, his hair more golden than bronze, as though he has been without shelter for a long time. And his beard grows wild with streaks of gray.

"What is it?" Yaga asks, annoyed. How dramatic can one child be?

Marina's mouth is open, her eyes so wide they reflect the brilliant green of the world, the shadow of the man.

Yaga draws in a sharp breath. She cannot bring herself to see the man she once loved and believed to have lost, the man she still loves. She turns.

He drops his helmet, his shield, his sword. Then, he says one word—"Home." His voice is low, scratchy, as if he has not used it in a while. And it is not so sure and so careless as it had been. But it is that of her husband, her Vasily.

Their eyes meet, and Yaga thinks that his, while not quite the same as when they had first met, are almost as they had been before Selica's wars. She thinks he is himself.

"You cannot know how long it took me to get here," says Vasily Alekseyevich Adashev. What he does not tell Yaga is before he set out for her, he was trapped in the madness of war, drifting with the dark tide of it as its battles expanded to other parts of Russia and beyond her lands, too. "One day, the dust and ash in the air whirled so terribly we thought the world was ending. A red light pierced the clouds, and I fell back. I dreamed of a hazel-eyed woman with two horses, one white, one black. When I awoke, I was myself."

Tears spring to Yaga's eyes. The ritual *had* brought Vasily back to himself.

"I remembered you, only very slowly." Vasily glances at Marina Vasilyevna. "I dreamed of our daughter, too, our Marin."

In this moment, Yaga does not believe that her daughter is alive and well, that her husband is standing beside her, whole and himself, that the sun is shining in a sky that isn't filled with dust and ash and darkness. Her heart is beating fast. The logical part of her says, *Wait a minute*. It seems too good to be true. Yet the look Vasily gives her! It is so intent yet so tentative, so like her old Vasya, that her heart beats a little faster. She sees the pain he has suffered, the despair he has lived through, the strain of war that has left its mark.

A smile breaks through his grim expression. "Did I not tell you a long time ago that you will not lose me, Yaga?"

No, it is him. All him. Closing the sliver of space between them, she pulls his face toward hers, and she kisses him fiercely.

The heat from her lips rushes into his body. He feels more himself than ever, like the man he used to be. He gives Yaga one last kiss and envelops his daughter in his arms, then his wife again. The three of them stare at each other in wonder. They laugh through their tears. For the first time in a long time, they are home, all of them.

They do not pay attention to the raven on the skull, the tilt of its head. There is something sad and lonely in the movement. Something distinctly human. The smiles in front of this humanlike bird are so bright and so full that it hurts to look at them.

As the raven takes flight, only his shadow accompanies him, gliding over the ancient trees and vast prairies, the hastening rivers and endless marshes, the wild and haunting expanse that is the Russian land.

Author's Note

Ever since I was a little girl in Moscow, Russia, particularly when I misbehaved, my mother would tell me stories about the Slavic witch Baba Yaga. In these stories, Baba Yaga was always portrayed as a fearsome and villainous old woman, a hag who stole children from their beds and flew them in her mortar to her mysterious chicken-legged hut deep in the woods.

As I got older and moved to the United States, I kept thinking about Baba Yaga's often elusive character: a benefactor and a villain, a mother and an old maid, a witch and a woman. I wondered if there wasn't another story about her and her origins. Maybe she wasn't as evil or as old and ugly as she was made out to be. Maybe I had to find out.

After I read Andreas Johns's *Baba Yaga: The Ambiguous Mother and Witch of the Russian Folktale*, I learned that the Baba Yaga we know is an invention of the fairy tales written and disseminated in the nineteenth century—mostly by men. Some believe that before Christianity arrived in Russia, Baba Yaga had been a fertility and earth goddess worshipped by Slavic pagans. She may even have been a version of or a descendent of the deity Mokosh herself.

That's when I knew I had to write a feminist tale about a powerful yet vulnerable woman reduced to a witch by the men of her time. And I would call her simply Yaga.

I subverted the more traditional elements of the Baba Yaga myth while keeping her powerful sense of self, her very sharp and critical tongue coupled with an attitude that sends men scurrying, her witchiness and her affinity for animals, as well as her connection to night and day, which appear in my story as her mysterious companions, Noch and Dyen. I imagined the fertility and earth goddess Mokosh was Yaga's mother. And that Yaga, as in some fairy tales, had a sometimes friend, sometimes enemy in the folktale antihero and villain Koshey Bessmertny.

I also subverted some of the other folktale characters—Koshey the Deathless has some humanity in him, being in many ways a tragic character instead of a black-and-white villain, while Marya Morevna would never let men rule her as they tend to do in the fairy tales.

Other spirits and creatures populate the story, all based on the ancestral and nature spirits that ancient Slavs once worshipped—with my own unique spin and interpretation. I took the idea of the Otherworld, a place where these spirits are said to dwell, and combined it with the old Slavic and shamanistic belief that the Earth is a multidimensional space with many dimensions or planes, where I imagined these beings would live. And I imagined the Land of the Dead would have its own dimensions or planes, where both the mortal and immortal dead would dwell. It is important to note that ancient Slavs did not believe the dead went to Heaven or Hell but to one Underworld, sometimes referred to as Nav.

The World Tree, most commonly an oak, is an integral element of Slavic mythology. Siberian and European shamans—and my Yaga and her magic, while simplified and fictionalized, is rooted in these shamanistic practices—believe there are three levels of worlds: Heaven, Earth, and the Underworld, all connected by the World Tree. In my story, the three lands—the Heavens, the Land of the Living, and the Land of the Dead (or Nav)—are inspired by these concepts and beliefs.

The lore of Slavic pagan gods is more complicated. Unlike the Greek and ancient Near East traditions, Slavic pagan mythology originates in scant sources, consisting primarily in short chronicle entries, sermons, and instructions, all dating from the Christian era and therefore hostile to pre-Christian belief. The best-known deities were those in the pantheon of idols on the hills of Kiev erected by Vladimir the Great in the 980s. Most relevant here are Perun, Dazhbog, Mokosh, Simargl, and Stribog, an ancestor of Morozko (in my story, his father). Scholars have formed an idea of what these gods and their stories may have been like through a comparative study of the world's mythologies. Other deities emerged, some mentioned by name in the records, including Kupalo and Kostroma, Svarog and Svarovitch, and Volos. But these deities and many others that have since emerged from scholarly study are cloaked in shadow; we don't know much about them, and what we do know is often contradictory.

The mythological world around Yaga is therefore loosely based on these stories. Two excellent sources that I relied on heavily were *Slavic Sorcery: Shamanic Journey of Initiation* by Kenneth Johnson, and *Russian Folk Belief* by Linda J. Ivanits. For Yaga's knowledge of herbs and spells, I relied on *The Bathhouse at Midnight: An Historical Survey of Magic and Divination in Russia* by W.F. Ryan.

The time of Ivan the Terrible was a cataclysmic one for Russia, ultimately weakening her with an aggressive realpolitik system of governance that resulted in depleted economic resources and a depleted army, a dynastic line facing extinction, an impoverished people, and the loss of at least sixty thousand lives, as well as the destruction of numerous cities, towns, and villages. While in some ways a progressive leader, Ivan was tortured by his motherless and loveless childhood, during which the ancient boyar families competed for power over his minority. Unfortunately, this made Ivan into a paranoid, ruthless, and violent ruler.

His behavior did not completely manifest itself until his beloved first wife, Anastasia Romanovna, died under mysterious circumstances. It is now widely believed that Anastasia was indeed poisoned. After her death, Ivan fell into grief, followed quickly by denial. Eventually, he came up with the Oprichnina kingdom, carved out of the Russian territory for his own personal use, as an instrument to consolidate his autocratic power over both the boyars and his people, and he carried out the murder and massacre not only of thousands of people but entire cities. Two resources that I relied on heavily were Cambridge's *Medieval Russia 980-1584* by Janet Martin, and *Ivan the Terrible* by Robert Payne and Nikita Romanoff, a descendant of the imperial family.

I tried to be as faithful as I could to Ivan's character, his personality and childhood and delusions of sainthood, his marriage to Anastasia, his subsequent delirium and descent into madness, and his transition to the tyrannical Ivan the Terrible. While the mechanics of the Oprichnina were simplified for the purpose of the story, I tried to be as historically accurate as possible in portraying the oprichniki, the fortress of Aleksandrovskaya Sloboda, and the oppression and violence that Ivan and his Oprichnina wreaked on Russia.

The instances of violence, specifically in the city of Novgorod, are based on real historical events, as are the scenes in Pskov. Pskov's governor, Prince Yuri Tokmakov, helped save the city. He instructed the people to submit to the tsar by welcoming him with bread, salt, and tables of meats. But the city's ultimate savior was a holy man named Nikolai Salos, known as Mikula. The scene between him and the tsar was inspired by a real conversation.

Russia's wars for the then country of Livonia were once again simplified for the sake of the story, but all are based on real events. Ivan instigated these wars hoping to acquire his neighbor's geographically strategic lands, not caring how many lives or cities would be lost in the process. Pskov was under siege for months. The city did not capitulate mostly because of the bravery of its men and women, as well as that of Prince Ivan Shuysky, who refused to submit to the demands of the foreign armies.

Like the other Russian cities attacked by the foreigners, Ivan made no effort to help Pskov. His son and heir, Tsarevich Ivan Ivanovich, was critical of these decisions. Even so, there is disagreement about what happened on 16 November 1581 (and disagreement about what day in November 1581 this happened), when Ivan fatally wounded his son. Some believe it was the result of Ivan criticizing the tsarevich's wife; others believe that it was about the tsar's policies regarding the war for Livonia.

What we do know is Ivan was so incensed that he hit his son on the head with his staff or scepter, leading to the tsarevich's death a few days later. I adopted the view that the disagreement stemmed from the father and son's differing views on the Livonian conflict and the defense of Pskov. Some of the scene with the ritual is taken from the record, including Boris Godunov's attempted intervention and Ivan's grief at what he had done.

There is no evidence that the tsarevich actively rebelled against his father; he took part in the tsar's campaigns during the Oprichnina. But there is evidence that the tsarevich was capable of mercy and intent on defending his country. I used these traits as a basis for Ivanushka and imagined (and hoped) he believed in a Russia that deserved better than his father. And the Russian people did fight against the tsar and his oprichniki. I hope a group like the Skomorokhi Knights existed, and that they gave the people hope in such a time of darkness.

Vasily Alekseyevich Adashev is a fictional character, but one that embodies the tireless Russian spirit—brave and reckless, warm and passionate, and incredibly patriotic, someone who would give his life for his motherland, even in fighting autocracy and oppression from within. It is because of men like Vasily that the Oprichnina fell in 1572 and that the country was saved from invasion in 1581.

While I tried to be faithful to the historical figures and events, as well as to the specific years, months, and even days that these historical events took place, some have been compressed, lengthened, or slightly altered due to a scant or elusive historical record, or for the purpose of storytelling.

There are a few key instances, including the fires before Anastasia's death. The first fire, which had started on 17 July 1560, likely did not reach the Kremlin (and Anastasia may already have been at the Kolomenskoye royal estate by that time). The second fire happened two days later, not several weeks later. Another point of departure was Sylvester's and Aleksey Adashev's deaths, which were several months after Anastasia's death, not immediately after. Lastly, it is worth mentioning that Aleksey Adashev was sent to Livonia in May 1560 before being put under house arrest in what is now modern-day Estonia, not the Russian countryside. There is no evidence of a love affair between him and Anastasia; rather, Aleksey was against Anastasia's family, which contributed to his disfavor at court.

My aim was to be true to the details of sixteenth-century Russia, its customs, clothing, and foods, which were relatively scarce in the historical record. A unique primary source was *The "Domostroi": Rules for Russian Households in the Time of Ivan the Terrible*, edited and translated by Carolyn Johnston Pouncy, but believed to have been originally written by the tsar's onetime advisor, the priest Sylvester.

The same goes for the places where these events took place. Moscow, Pskov, and Novgorod looked very different in the sixteenth century. As did the Moscow Kremlin. Most of the scenes described there are based on what those rooms *could* have looked like but are ultimately fictionalized because most of the palaces at the Kremlin and at Kolomenskoye from Ivan the Terrible's time did not survive.

An exception is the fortress of Aleksandrovskaya Sloboda in the city of Aleksandrov. Nearly all the structures from Ivan's time can be viewed in this fabulous fairy tale–like museum, including rooms modeled after the chambers that Ivan would have lived in.

I did my best in describing Russia as I know her through the lens of a Russian-born American citizen and as I learned about her history through my research. Any errors, either in the settings or the historical figures and events, are entirely my own.

Glossary

The following is a glossary of the places and key figures, some historical and some mythological, at the center of *The Witch and the Tsar*. The information here is from the key sources that I relied on in researching and writing the book. You can find these sources in my author's note.

A quick note on Russian names: a Russian person has three names, including the first name, the patronymic (derived from the father's first name), and the family (last) name. In formal settings, especially in olden times and sometimes even today, the first name and the patronymic were/are used together. In informal settings, only the first name is used. Frequently, a diminutive (or nickname) is preferred. I have tried to be very clear when I use a diminutive of a name.

An even quicker note on my transliteration of Russian words: I have tried to use English words and spellings that are true to the Russian language. Wherever possible, and if it did not interfere with authenticity, I chose the spelling most easily digestible for the non-Russian reader.

GLOSSARY

Real People

Aleksey Fyodorovich Adashev—a boyar's son and former advisor to Tsar Ivan; specifically, his batozhnik (or wielder of the baton, i.e., security), his chief advisor on foreign affairs, and a founding member of the Chosen Council—a small group of advisors who ruled Russia in the name of the tsar. Aleksey lost Ivan's favor by spring 1560.

Anastasia Romanovna Zakharyina-Yurieva (also Nastenka)—the tsaritsa and first wife of Tsar Ivan IV, as well as the daughter of Roman Zakharin, a boyar from the noble family later known as the House of Romanov. During the year 1559–1560, Anastasia developed a mysterious illness that doctors couldn't diagnose for six months.

Boris Godunov (also Boriska)—one of Tsar Ivan's oprichniki guards and husband to the daughter of fellow oprichnik Malyuta Skuratov. Godunov became a boyar; then Fyodor Ivanovich's brother-in-law, councillor, and regent; then the first non–Rurik Dynasty tsar of Russia.

Fyodor Ivanovich—younger son of Tsar Ivan and Anastasia, who became Tsar Fyodor I after Ivan's death

Ivan Ivanovich (also Ivanushka)—Tsar Ivan and Anastasia's heir and tsarevich. While Ivan Ivanovich held some promise, was seen to disagree with Ivan on certain policy decisions, and showed mercy where his father did not, he still accompanied Ivan on his expeditions of terror and massacres throughout Russia, including the ones to Novgorod and Pskov.

Ivan Vasilyevich (also Ivan IV, Ivashka, Ivan Grozny, and Ivan the Terrible)— grand prince and tsar of Russia from the ancient Rurik Dynasty, Anastasia's husband, and father of Ivanushka and Fyodor. Ivan was the first tsar of the newly established Tsardom of Russia. From the beginning, he was an auto-cratic ruler. Following Anastasia's death, Ivan also founded the Oprichnina, his own personal kingdom within Russia, through which he committed various acts of terror and murder, oppressing the Russian people and killing off much of his court, administration, army, and population. He also started many foreign wars with Russia's neighbors, including the war for the then country of Livonia depicted in the story.

Malyuta Skuratov—a favorite of Tsar Ivan and head of his oprichniki guards. Malyuta was famously known as the tsar's hangman, for whom no act of terror or murder was too much.

Metropolitan Makarii—the leader of the Russian Orthodox Church and former advisor to Tsar Ivan. Some have suggested Makarii had his eye on Anastasia as a wife for Ivan and arranged the match. He also crowned Ivan as the grand prince and first tsar, lending divinity, continuity, and absolutism to the role of emperor of a country seen as the new Orthodox Byzantium.

Mikula (also Holy Fool, and Nikolai Salos)—a yurodivy, or holy man, living in Pskov and famous throughout the region at the time of Tsar Ivan's expedition there

Sylvester—a priest and the former chief advisor to Tsar Ivan, as well as a founding member of the Chosen Council. Sylvester was also widely believed to be the author of *The "Domostroi": Rules for Russian Households in the Time of Ivan the Terrible*. Sylvester lost the tsar's favor by the end of 1559 and went to live at the Kirillov Monastery in the North.

Yuri Danilovich—the prince of Moscow and grand prince of Vladimir in the early fourteenth century. He was opposed by his cousin Dmitri of Tver, who persuaded the then occupier of the Russian lands, the Golden Horde, that Yuri appropriated a large portion of the tribute due to the Horde. Yuri was summoned to the Horde for a trial but was killed on the road by Dmitri, who was then caught by the Horde and executed.

Fairy-Tale and Mythological Figures

Belobog (also Lord of Light)—a name meaning *white god*; the god of light and day

Chernobog (also Lord of Darkness)—a name meaning *black god*; the god of shadows and night

Dazhbog (also Lord of the Sun)—the solar god, son of the god Svarog and brother of the god Svarovitch, and ruler of Heaven along with his brother, his father, and the god Perun. Dazhbog was included by Vladimir the Great in his pantheon of idols on the hills of Kiev.

Dodola (also Dodo, Lady of the Rain)—sometimes the goddess of the rain and Perun's wife

Kikimora—a female house spirit, sometimes married to her male counterpart the domovoy; other times, a spirit of the swamp and married to the leshy

Koshey Bessmertny (also Konstantin Buyanovich, and Kostya)—a folktale antihero, sometimes villain, sometimes dragon. He is known for separating his soul, his mortality, from his body and hiding it under an oak tree on the island of Buyan. Most notably, he appears in Aleksandr Afanasyev's fairy tales *Koshey the Deathless* and *Marya Morevna*. Koshey is sometimes a companion or partner of Baba Yaga.

Kostroma—a goddess of fertility and spring and in some versions of mythology and in my story, sister of the god Kupalo

Kupalo (also Lord of Vegetation)—a vegetation god and in some versions of mythology and in my story, brother of the goddess Kostroma. Kupalo has the same root as the word *kupati*, which means *to bathe*, and is the spirit of water, as well as the god of plants and herbs.

Marya Morevna (also Masha)—a folktale character, a princess, a queen, and a warrior, seen in Aleksandr Afanasyev's fairy tale *Marya Morevna*. She is best known for imprisoning Koshey in her closet and telling her disobedient husband Prince Ivan not to look there in her absence.

Mokosh—the Earth Mother and Goddess, Moist Mother Earth, the goddess of fertility, protector of women's work and destiny, and personification of a woman's growth from maiden to mother to old woman, from life to death.

Mokosh was the only female goddess included by Vladimir the Great in his pantheon of idols on the hills of Kiev. In my story, she is also the mother of Yaga.

Morozko (also Lord of Winter, and Roz)—a folktale character seen in Aleksandr Afanasyev's fairy tale *Jack Frost*. Morozko is likely a descendent of Stribog, the god of wind, storm, and dissension, maybe even of cold and frost as well. Stribog was included by Vladimir the Great in his pantheon of idols on the hills of Kiev. In the story, Stribog is also Morozko's father.

Perun (also Supreme God, Lord of the Heavens and Battles, and the Thunderer)—lord of the universe and most important of the sky gods, being the god of thunder, storms, and rains, as well as of warriors. Perun was the chief deity of Vladimir the Great's pagan pantheon of idols on the hills of Kiev.

Selica (also Lady of Death, Lady of Rebirth, Marzanna, Marena, Kyselica, and many others)—goddess of the death and rebirth of nature, the death of winter and the rebirth of spring personified as the goddess Kostroma

Simargl—a winged dog and divine guardian of seed and new shoots, possibly an ancestor of the firebird. In my story, he is also the guardian of young goddesses. Simargl was included by Vladimir the Great in his pantheon of idols on the hills of Kiev.

Sivka-Burka—a folktale character from the fairy tale *Sivka-Burka*. In my story, Sivka-Burka is Koshey's immortal and speedy horse.

Svarog (also Lord of the Sky)—the sky god, father of the gods Dazhbog and Svarovitch, and ruler of Heaven along with his sons and the god Perun

Svarovitch—god of fire, brother of the god Dazhbog and son of the god Svarog, and ruler of Heaven along with his brother, his father, and the god Perun

Volos (also Lord of the Dead)—god of the Underworld, as well as the god of cattle and other beasts, divination and magic, wealth and the arts. He is also associated with hangings and the hanged. He is the god Perun's antagonist and enemy and sometimes his friend. In my story, Volos disguises himself as Mikula the Holy Fool in order to remain in the Land of the Living.

Yaga (also Baba Yaga the Bony Leg, Yaga Mokoshevna, Yagusya, and Yagusynka)—a witch from the folktales of Aleksandr Afanasyev and Aleksandr Pushkin, among others. Baba Yaga is known for her elusive character, being both a benefactor and a villain, a mother and an old maid, a witch and a woman. She is portrayed as a fearsome and villainous old woman, a hag who steals children from their beds and flies them in her mortar to her mysterious chicken-legged hut deep in the woods. Now we know "Baba Yaga" is an invention of the fairy tales written and disseminated in the nineteenth century—mostly by men. Some believe that before Christianity arrived in Russia, Baba Yaga had been a fertility and earth goddess worshipped by Slavic pagans. In my story, Yaga is not the villainous old hag of the folktales, though she retains some of her elusive character, attitude, and witchiness. She is the daughter of the fertility and earth goddess Mokosh.

Places

Aleksandrovskaya Sloboda—a fortress, a palace complex, and the capital of Tsar Ivan's separate Oprichnina kingdom, located in the city of Aleksandrov, approximately 122 kilometers (or seventy-six miles) northeast of Moscow. Ivan converted this former royal hunting lodge into a full court (indeed, Sloboda means *a large village*), including the Tsar's Palace; chapels and churches; offices, residences, and barracks; guesthouses and dormitories; and prisons, warehouses, and storehouses.

Buyan—a mysterious island first mentioned in medieval Russian books and poems, particularly in the spiritual verse *Dove Book* (though by a different name), then incorporated into Slavic incantations and even folklore. It was popularized by Russian poet Aleksandr Pushkin in the *Tale of Tsar Saltan*, and by Ivan Bilibin in his illustration *Buyan Island*. In some stories, Koshey Bessmertny keeps his soul, his mortality, hidden on this island under an oak tree. In my story, Buyan is Koshey's island and home.

Heavens—the name used for the upper world. In Slavic mythology, particularly in Siberian and European shamanism, there are three levels of worlds: Heaven, Earth, and the Underworld. The World Tree connects these worlds, with its highest branches passing through the upper world where, in mythology, there dwells a bird; in my story, it is the gods who dwell there. It is important to note that ancient Slavs did not believe the dead went to Heaven or Hell but to one Underworld, sometimes referred to as Nav.

Kolomenskoye—a royal estate approximately eleven kilometers (or seven miles) southeast of the city center of Moscow, where a wooden palace once stood, frequented by Tsar Ivan and his family. Ivan sent the ill Tsaritsa Anastasia there hoping she would benefit from the quieter life outside the busy and, at the time, burning capital.

Kremlin—a fortress surrounding most medieval Russian cities. The Kremlin in Moscow is the largest and therefore the centerpiece of the capital. While its walls have existed for a long time, it wasn't until the 1450s and the reign of Ivan's father, Vasily III, that the Kremlin we know today took shape. This included new brick walls and an ensemble of palaces, cathedrals, and churches.

Land of the Dead (also Nav, and the Thrice-Tenth Kingdom)—the name used for the lower world, or the Underworld, sometimes referred to as Nav. In Slavic mythology, particularly in Siberian and European shamanism, there are three levels of worlds: Heaven, Earth, and the Underworld. The World Tree connects these worlds, its roots lying in the lower world, from where the god Volos rules over the dead. It is important to note that ancient Slavs did not believe the dead went to Heaven or Hell but to one Underworld, sometimes referred to as Nav. The Thrice-Tenth Kingdom is a magical land in folklore located "beyond thrice nine lands," or beyond our world. It is mentioned in Aleksandr Afanasyev's fairy tales like *The Maiden Tsar*, and was a place where maidens went to be found by the hero after many trials. In my story, it is part of the Underworld.

Land of the Living—the name used for the middle world of Earth. In Slavic mythology, particularly in Siberian and European shamanism, there are three levels of worlds: Heaven, Earth, and the Underworld. The World Tree connects these worlds, with its trunk passing through the middle world where we live.

Moscow—the capital of Russia and the center of the Russian Orthodox Church during Tsar Ivan's reign and now. Moscow was where the tsar and his family were based, along with other elite families, boyars, and nobles, as well as political, administrative, and religious officials. It was also one of the major commercial hubs in the country.

Novgorod—a city approximately 575 kilometers (or 357 miles) from Moscow on the Volkhov River. Its name means *new city*, but it is actually one of Russia's most ancient cities, existing even before Moscow itself. For hundreds of years it was an independent principality ruling over vast northern lands. It therefore acquired vast wealth and reputation, even among the European kingdoms, as it traded with many of them. It was conquered by Ivan III in the fifteenth century, but retained its independent and individualistic mindset, which grated on rulers like Tsar Ivan.

Oprichnina—from the word *oprich*, meaning *separate*; a kingdom that Tsar Ivan carved out of the Russian territory, reserved for his own personal use and over which he ruled directly and absolutely. The Oprichnina had its own capital of Aleksandrovskaya Sloboda, its own army, its own boyars and nobles and officials, and its own territories with its own estates, towns, and even whole provinces. Oprichnik (pl. oprichniki), meaning *separated ones*, were officials, servants, guards, and soldiers of Tsar Ivan's Oprichnina kingdom.

Otherworld—a realm where the ancestral and nature spirits first worshipped by ancient Slavs dwell. It is unclear exactly where this world is. Sometimes, it is part of our own world; other times, in a realm just beyond it, close to the realm of the gods. I connected the idea of the Otherworld to the old Slavic and Shamanistic belief that the Earth is a multidimensional space with many dimensions or planes, where I imagined these beings would live.

Pskov—a city approximately 730 kilometers (or 453 miles) northwest of Moscow on the Velikaya River, located about twenty kilometers (twelve miles) east of the Estonian border. Like Novgorod, Pskov is one of Russia's most ancient cities. It was previously the capital of an independent republic where the people elected their rulers until it was annexed by Muscovy in 1510. Pskov continued to be a major commercial hub in Russia, partially due to its free, enterprising, and westernized nature, and partially to its direct access to the Gulf of Finland and the Baltic by way of Lake Chud.

Rus'—refers to what became known as the medieval Russian state, after a Varangian (Norse) prince of the Rurik Dynasty called Vladimir (or Volodimer) Sviatoslavich landed there in the year 980 from Scandinavia. He became Vladimir the Great and is the ruler who brought Orthodox Christianity to the Russian lands. Before that, these lands were established by Scandinavian traders and warriors led by Vladimir's ancestor Rurik, who founded the dynasty that survived until the death of Tsar Ivan's second son, Fyodor I. Tsar Ivan unified the lands previously known as Rus' in 1547, establishing the Tsardom of Russia.

Ryazan—a city approximately two hundred kilometers (or 124 miles) southeast of Moscow on the Oka River. Ryazan was one of ancient Rus' most damaged cities following the military onslaught of the invading Mongol armies under Batu Khan in 1237–1240, which established the rule of the Golden Horde over the Russian lands. In my story, it is there that Koshey Bessmertny, then the mortal Konstantin, fights for his city and, ultimately, his life.

Zemshchina—meaning *the dominion*, or the Russian territory outside the Oprichnina kingdom, ruled by the boyars in conjunction with Tsar Ivan. While the boyars were allowed to make the final decisions, Ivan still reserved the right to decide on military matters and affairs of state.

Acknowledgments

So many generously gave their time and support to me on this wild, un-predictable, *unbelievable* journey to the publication of *The Witch and the Tsar.*

Thank you first and foremost to my rock-star dream agent, Jennifer Weltz, for taking a chance on me and my Yaga. Your deep knowledge, always-sound advice, and unwavering belief in me are pure magic. Thank you for saying yes to me that day and making my dreams of a career in publishing come true.

To my editor, Jessica Wade, who knew my vision for this novel even before I knew it myself. I wouldn't be surprised if you had Yaga whispering her life story in your ear. You are an absolute dream of an editor, from taking my writing and storytelling to levels I had never thought possible to knowing exactly what to do with my complicated little tale. Thank you for making me a published author. I can't wait to write more books with you.

To the brilliant team at Penguin Random House, especially Claire Zion, Ivan Held, Christine Ball, Jeanne-Marie Hudson, Craig Burke, Mi-randa Hill, Janine Barlow, Jessica Plummer, Alexis Nixon, Daniela Ried-lova, Yazmine Hassan, and everyone else who brought *The Witch and the Tsar* to life. And to David Curtis, for an incomparable cover that gorgeously depicts a strong female warrior, goddess, and witch, with a fairy-tale theme inspired by my favorite artist, Ivan Bilibin.

To my critique partner and best friend, Gabriella Saab, for always being there for me—in writing, in publishing, and in life. You were the first to truly love this book and got me through querying, submission, and everything since. Your wisdom and talent as a writer inspire and guide me every single day. And your good humor makes this wild ride the best time. I am grateful beyond words for your friendship and love.

To my beta readers and friends, Paulette Kennedy, Rose de Guzman, and Rebecca Mildren, for being the first in the industry to read this book and take it to where it needed to be to succeed. I'll always be grateful for your much needed and honest feedback, your support, and for making Yaga the feisty, lovable witch she is. To the other writers who read this book and provided advice, especially Amanda McCrina, Cristin Williams, Kassiella Kingsley, and Rebecca Siegel. And to Marina Scott and Anika Scott for helping me on this publication journey.

To Sydney Young and Janna Noelle and the rest of the #HFChitChat community, for your passion for historical fiction and your belief in me. It is what kept me going through the darker days.

To the authors on Twitter and Instagram who have shown such wonderful enthusiasm for this book.

To freelance editors Sarah Terez Rosenblum and Kaitlyn Johnson, for teaching me fiction writing when I was just a burned-out lawyer with a distant dream of becoming an author. Thank you for the invaluable guidance.

To my professors at Northwestern Law School and Pepperdine University, especially Laurie Goodman, Paul Contino, Maire Mullins, and Candice Ortbals, for believing in me as a writer when I didn't believe it myself and for insisting I should follow my passion. Thanks to you, I am finally where I should be.

To my teacher Dr. Ray Bird, for truly inspiring me. Your class changed my life. Without you, I would never have developed this lifelong obsession with literature, or the desire to one day write a book.

ACKNOWLEDGMENTS

To my beloved sister, Katerina Salnikova, who dreamed with me from the very beginning. Our stories, our worlds and characters, are what made me the storyteller I am today. Thank you for believing in me, for reading my words (even those nightmarish first drafts), and for being the first reader of what was then simply *Yaga*.

To my parents, Tatiana and Alexander, for filling our house with books, movies, and music; for never failing to believe in me and support me without question; for bringing me to America and giving me this wonderful life. And to my mom, who has been so generously helping with childcare, giving me that precious time to write.

To my grandmothers and grandfathers, for being the reason I became a writer. Ever since Dedushka Vanya read to me the immortal words of Pushkin and Lermontov, I was lost, addicted, couldn't get enough of stories. Dedushka Seva told me to stop wasting my time and follow my dreams. And Babushka Irina waited with me for my dreams to come true—thank you for making it all happen for me up there. One year from the day you were gone, I got to announce the news that *The Witch and the Tsar* would be published.

To the rest of my family, to Uncle Volodya and Aunt Natasha; to my in-laws, Maureen, George, Stephanie, and John—for the unconditional support and for always being there for me.

To my best friend, Megan Nelson, for believing in me even before I told you I wanted to write books; for reading the first novel I ever wrote and being (too) kind about it; for the support, book talk, and love.

To my husband, Sean Gilmore, to whom this book is dedicated, for being the first person to realistically take a chance on my writing. I would still be practicing law if not for you, my love. Thank you for encouraging and supporting me in every way possible, for talking stories and characters with me, and for reading every word. You are my inspiration and my motivation. I love you.

To my daughter, Nina, for being the best baby I could ever have dreamed up. I am so honored to be your mom and hope to make you proud of me, always.

ACKNOWLEDGMENTS

To everyone who has ever supported me, to my mentors and teachers and friends, and to the writing and reading communities that have touched my life in such a meaningful way.

And last but certainly not least, my deepest gratitude to you, dear reader. I hope you love reading Yaga's story as much as I loved writing it.